THE DINOSAUR CONSPIRACY

MATTHEW COLEMAN

*Freda,
God's Blessings
Matthew D Coleman*

authorHOUSE®

AuthorHouse™
1663 Liberty Drive
Bloomington, IN 47403
www.authorhouse.com
Phone: 1-800-839-8640

© 2013 Matthew Coleman. All rights reserved.

No part of this book may be reproduced, stored in a retrieval system, or transmitted by any means without the written permission of the author.

Published by AuthorHouse 1/11/2013

ISBN: 978-1-4817-0684-1 (sc)
ISBN: 978-1-4817-0686-5 (hc)
ISBN: 978-1-4817-0685-8 (e)

Library of Congress Control Number: 2013900544

Any people depicted in stock imagery provided by Thinkstock are models, and such images are being used for illustrative purposes only.
Certain stock imagery © Thinkstock.

This book is printed on acid-free paper.

Because of the dynamic nature of the Internet, any web addresses or links contained in this book may have changed since publication and may no longer be valid. The views expressed in this work are solely those of the author and do not necessarily reflect the views of the publisher, and the publisher hereby disclaims any responsibility for them.

The wind banged against the car as snow was driven down at a forty-five degree angle. Mike gripped the steering wheel, aiming it alongside the white solid line and fighting with the wheel to stay to the right of the dotted yellow. The snow hypnotized as it flew towards the car. He remembered the Star Wars movies as the spaceships jumped into hyperspace. Blinding. Real.

Mike sneaked his eyes to the speedometer. Thirty miles per hour. The eyes moved to the left to catch a glimpse of the gas. Half a tank.

Mike lifted his eyes to gaze upon the road as he felt a headache coming on. He expected it. The snow, wind, and the amount of concentration he was exerting was beginning to take its toll. If it wasn't for the adrenaline, exhaustion would have overcome the body by now.

A flash in the rear view mirror caught his attention. "No", he whispered out loud sensing his own fear in his voice.

The truck inched closer. Mike desperately wanted to push the Camry faster. Having lived in the rugged Wyoming winters had taught him to take it easy. Impatience heightened the cause of accidents.

Mike shifted his body to gain a more comfortable position. With a six foot four frame, that was near impossible in a compact. A glimpse at the mirror sent a shiver up that frame. The truck was gaining. Mike guessed that it had four-wheel drive and the driver was also used to treacherous conditions.

With the secret that Mike had he knew that the Organization would send only their best.

Mike decided to push the Toyota to thirty-five. The wind seemed to push harder against the car like a giant hand taking cheap shots to the passenger side of the car. The knuckles were turning whiter.

The bounce of lights in the rear view alerted Mike that the truck was gaining. For the first time in over two hours real fear came over Mike. He was still fifteen minutes from the safety of the city lights.

Should he push it to forty?

The howling of the wind screamed its anger at a man daring to push the limits of the storm. Mike pushed down on the gas pedal; a determination replaced the fear as a hue of light barely seen arched in the horizon.

"I'm only minutes away. I can make it," Mike said with a mixture of hope and uncertainty.

The glare in the rear view became constant. Mike strived to ignore it while focusing on the lines. Focus on the lines.

The light disappeared only to be replaced with a new noise. Mike recognized a diesel engine, even above the driving wind. The truck came alongside. His imagination created images. But he chose to focus on the lines. The lines became a comfort. A necessary distraction.

The Organization wanted his research. The same research that had taken Mike away from his friends, family, and teaching for the last three years and also took him around the world. What he discovered, what he learned he knew would change the world. It changed him. Everything he thought about the world, beliefs, his values, changed. So convinced was he in this, that he was willing to risk his life, to protect this research.

Why else would he be driving over a hundred miles in a blizzard in the middle of the night?

The howling wind and relative silence in the car allowed him to reflect on the last three years. He knew he had hurt people, especially his daughter Cathy. He hoped and prayed that she would one day understand.

To protect her and his research there was his best friend. He could be trusted with information. Mike thought, I have trusted the man with my life.

Twenty more miles.

As if sensing an unspoken urgency, the wind seemed to pick up power. The gust fist-slammed into the Camry with boxer-like punches. Mike felt his arms becoming sore by trying to maintain a straight direction and manhandling the vehicle.

Focus.

Despite the freezing temperatures outside Mike felt sweat. The adrenaline pumping keeping Mike alert.

Fight or flight? Mike thought about it. "I am doing both." Fighting for the truth. Fighting for what is right? Flight? It was definetly survival.

Nothing more that the survival instinct kicking up from the depths of man's ancestoral being. The animal instinct in every human bursting like a pentup geyser.

Mike glanced up at the rear view mirror. "What are they doing? They can't be going that fast on purpose. Can they?" Mike decided to chance it and picked up the speed knowing this road like the back of his hand. He drove it often as he taught classes in Casper as well as the University of Wyoming. He hoped that finally, after all these years, this knowledge would serve him well.

Fifteen more miles.

A desperation settled in the bones. "Don't panic. Stay cool," he thought to himself. "I am almost there." But with desperation also comes reflection. He thought of what Cathy had to go through the last three years. He knew it was his fault for their relationship to have weakened, to be become broken. There was no excuse given today's vast array of technology to communicate from emails to video calls. He didn't write or call. The research, and her, needed to be protected. Now, without any reason, he was rushing to her. Now he realized he should have included her but the father's instinct of protection was strong. So strong that it clouded out common sense.

He knew that sending all his research to his friend was right. It would be protected and he would honor Mike's request. But, just in case, he desperately wanted to deliver the research to Cathy. He hoped. For the first time in his life he allowed his work to interfere with family and friends. But this work was bigger than all of them. Cathy will learn that quickly.

Ten more miles.

The headlights became a permament fixture in the rearview mirror. The lights seemed to be growing by the minute, sending a rectangular glare right across Mike's face. Loosening his right hand he adjusted the mirror. The wind sending a blow into the side of the car. In milliseconds the hand gripped the steering wheel, regaining control that momentarily lost. Mike knew who trailed behind him. A group, that works alongside dictators and businesses, to protect their own interests and their own version of the truth. Mike learned a hard truth about a year ago; it is difficult to tell the good guys from the bad guys. And it made protecting the truth difficult.

He duplicated all his research and sent it to another group. A group committed to truth seeking and protecting.

The lights were close. Mike knew that the brights were on high beam on purpose. The drive was a nightmare for concentration. The hypnotic snow, pounding wind, late hour, and the vehicle hunting him down. Mike knew he had to do something and fast if he was going to survive through the night.

Grabbing his cell phone and tightening his left hand grip on the wheel, Mike used his right hand to text Cathy. She was a nightowl. Maybe not this late but Mike was hopeful. He also texted the group he sent his research to. Finally, he dialed 911. He hoped the operator was savvy enough to figure how to trace the phone to his location. Having done all that he needed to do there was only one thing left to do.

Go faster.

Five more miles.

Mike imagined the headlights were also working out of desperation as they not only picked up speed but also closed the gap. Now, the cab was blindly bright.

Focus. White line. Yellow dotted line. Stay in the lines.

Mike would have began swerving except the visibility was so bad that he wasn't sure if there would be a car coming in the other direction.

This didn't bother the vehicle behind him. Suddenly it aligned next to him. The blinding light was gone only to be replaced with a black Yukon on his left side. Mike dared a glance to his left. Windows were shaded so discerning any person was impossible.

Focus. White line. Yellow dotted line. Stay in the lines.

Mike thought a massive gust of wind hit. It sent him to the shoulder of the road. A vibration rattled through the Camry and Mike struggled to keep the vehicle on the road.

That was no wind.

He then knew what slammed into him. The survival instinct reached a new high, adrenaline was rushing and a determined and more focus Mike took stock of his situation.

Three more miles.

Mike thought he could see city lights ahead but right at this present moment the lights seemed a thousand miles away.

The two vehicles were now bashing against each other and the wind. Mike's shoulders ached as he spent the last three hours battling nature.

The adrenaline helped as it coursed throughout his body. Mike was fired up and ready for battle.

"They will not win," he yelled determinedly in the car.

Both vehicles recklessly bashed against each other. Mike took a peek to his left side. This time the window was down and an Asian man was smiling at him. The moment seemed surreal. Mike didn't hear the blast of the gun over the wind but he felt the impact.

A fiery hot flash flared throughout Mike's left shoulder. The moment the shoulder got hit Mike's strength to control the vehicle also left him. Passenger side tires rumbled down the vibrate strip and Mike was soon no longer on the road. A mile marker bent over but not without first leaving its mark on the front grill.

Mike no longer faced the direction he was going on the highway. But somehow he continued moving, anyplace better than waiting for the yahoos in the Yukon.

Wyoming is famous for its drifts. After going fifty yards the Camry hit one of those drifts and was halfway buried.

Trapped.

He had one last chance of survival. He turned off his lights and vehicle. The Yukon would have to turn around and try to locate Mike. He knew the wind and blowing snow would cover enough of the tire tracks in a short amount of time. Yukon would be just as blind and facing the same conditions as he was.

So he waited. First five minutes. Then another five more.

Mike felt the temperature drop exponientially in the next five minutes. He didn't feel the wind directly but he was feeling the cold the wind brought. With shooting pains throughout his body he reached into the back seat to grab one of the winter blankets he packed. He had heard of enough stories of tourists and new residents to the state who had gotten themselves trapped in a blizzard. So confident were they in their driving skills that they didn't pack essential supplies; extra food, blankets, coats, and winter gear, a cell phone. Cell phone! Mike reached into the passenger seat for his phone. "Time to call 911 again."

"911. How can I help you?"

"I have been shot and I was run off the highway. Please send someone."

"Where are you at sir?"

Good question thought Mike. "I'm not sure. I am about one to two miles away from Casper on Highway 43. I am on the right side of the highway. Please hurry."

Mike was sure of the silence on the other end of the line. "Okay sir, I am trying to find someone to go out there but the conditions are extremely difficult for all emergency crews and vehicles. The highway was closed three hours ago. Did you not get that information?"

"Great," thought Mike, "No crews and no traffic." "I did but I had an emergency bigger than the blizzard." Bigger than the blizzard? She must think I am an idiot," Mike thought.

The operator getting more difficult to hear as the blizzard wrecked havoc on communications Mike surmised. He flipped closed the cell phone and waited some more. He guessed he had only a few minutes. With the cold and wind mixing it up outside and the heater off it would not take long for the heat to escape and be replaced with subzero temeratures.

He looked around the vehicle and noticed that snow creeped in. Good. Snow can provide insulation from the temperatures. As time passed so too the worry of his pursuers. The new fright became a realization as he looked down and saw blood continuing to flow from his shirt.

There was no way he was getting to a doctor anytime soon. Mike tried to apply pressure but after a few minutes it didn't matter. Flashes of light began to dance behind the eyes interspersed with black spells. Mike felt his breathing become heavier. Labored. Slower. Time had crawled to a stop inside the Camry.

After fifteen minutes Mike felt his life slipping away. He imagined that nobody would come and find him for days, maybe weeks with the snow covering his vehicle. He focused his thoughts into prayers.

A prayer for his daughter Cathy; that she would first forgive him and that she would understand. That she will seek out the truth in her life. For his friend, his dearest in the world, that he would have courage. A smile crept over Mike's face, a final prayer, that his research will change the world.

As his lips turned blue and with eyes closing Mike Jurkovich eased into the arms of death.

Four days later the wind shifted the snow and highway crews recognized a vehicle about seventy-five yards off the road.

Sgt. Sampont brushed aside the snow and peeked inside. The scene nothing less than disturbing. A man, frozen to death, with blood frozen on his right hand. The eyes were shut giving him a content look. Brushing aside the rest of the snow on the windshield there didn't seem to be anything out of place except the broken glass from the driver's window. After many years of seeing drunk hunters shoot at vehicles it was easy for Sgt. Sampont to recognize how the glass ended up inside the vehicle.

He was also pretty sure where the bullet landed.

Examining the vehicle he spotted a box on the passenger seat with a name on it.

John Bush.

Sampont's first reaction was that the frozen man was John. "Nothing is at it seems," he thought. Was the man delivering it? Stealing it?

Sampont trounced back through the knee high snow to his patrol car. He radioed in what he saw and made a request for a tow truck. Going to his trunk he pulled out a survival shovel.

The crisp hit his lungs. Having grown up in Wyoming he thanked God for the weather. It made a person tough. So many times he had seen people move to the high plains and live out the western dream. It only took the first winter to send them packing somewhere else. Sampont was thankful for the lack of wind. The first time in three days without it and the sky radiated a sharp, light blue.

As Sampont set to digging out the driver's side he kept glancing back to his car and the highway. Trained to always be alert, See the unusual, Sampont hoped that this was the only weird thing to happen today.

During the next twenty minutes he made good progress. On a glance to the patrol car he thought he saw something unusual. A Yukon, black, kept driving by. There was an exit ramp two miles down the road. Once in awhile, during an accident, some people would drive by multiple times to catch glimpses of the morbid scenes of car crashes. But this wasn't a morbid scene, at least from the highway.

Sampont decided to be more alert for this. "Could be nothing," he thought.

In another ten minutes the door was ready to be opened. He pulled on the handle. Locked. Again, nothing is ever easy. Sampont pulled out his camera to take a picture of the window before he punched his stick in and break out the rest of the glass. As he prepared the camera he glanced back to the highway.

A black Yukon drove by again. With the camera ready he pointed to the highway and snapped. The Yukon picked up speed and headed north.

By this time the tow truck and another highway patrol showed up. A minute later the ambulance parked on the highway.

"Hopefully the boys back at the lab should be able to pull out the license number on that Yukon," Mike hoped.

After the man was loaded into the ambulance Sampont had to decide about the box.

The Wyoming wind picked up after the crews had left the crash sight. The Wyoming day had returned to normal.

CASPER, WYOMING

The wind whistled from the north making the plane descent rocky at best. John Bush hated plane rides, especially turbulent ones. When the wheels screeched to a slowing pace at Casper International Airport John left out a breath of relief. He made it a purpose of sitting near the front to exit the plane quickly.

Claustrophobia is a terrible weakness. It left him paralyzed during football games when under a pile of defensive lineman. When the captain finished his spiel of temperatures, local times, and exiting procedures John reached for his buckle. Freedom waited within seconds.

Two days ago a phone call roused him from his sleep and drew him to Casper. Mike Jurkovich was a dear friend and colleague in the field of archeology and history. It was because of Mike that John became interested in Native American artifacts, history, and culture. The call from Mike's daughter informed him that Mike passed away. Shot and left for dead along the highway.

John departed the plane and quickly navigated through the airport to the rental car area. This trip was the worse; first Mike's death, a turbulent plane ride, then a rental car which means that he didn't know what to receive. At least the fiery red head clerk at the rental counter was cute. Not a bad way to enter into Casper. John left the airport and tried to find the Accord that would match his keys. The January driving wind didn't help much.

Crossing through west Casper brought back memories. Last time John visited was ten years ago to see Mike's daughter Cathy graduate from high school. John watched her grow up and helped inspire her towards a degree in education and history. She currently worked on her masters at the University of Wyoming in biology and another degree in paleontology.

John realized that he had missed Casper; a town that learned to adapt with the times. Springing up as an army post along the Platte River it soon became a vital spot of trade. In the dangerous high mountain plains an area needed protection from trail thieves and weather and warring tribes. Casper grew from an outpost to the economic hub of Wyoming. Oil and coal turned Casper into a place of prosperity. Oil refineries and storage containers marked progress. Along with progress came the people which brought about more businesses, schools, and parks. It became a place that families were happy to live in, all the benefits of a city without the problems of one.

Then came the crash.

As the oil prices dropped so did the population. Thousands left to find a new place of prosperity leaving behind a shell of town. As John drove through Casper to meander to downtown he could see progress of revitalization. Casper prepared to reshape itself. He marveled at the perseverance of one town. Some metropolises couldn't make such a claim. They depended on one type of industry and when it died, so too the town.

John wandered the one ways of downtown to Mike's office building. When Mike wasn't teaching he was researching and writing. In recent years Mike isolated himself more and more. John's last contact with Mike was over a year agoin the form of a letter. John tried thru email, phone calls, and even Christmas letters. Nothing. Not until the phone call of Mike's death when John was surprised to hear from Mike's daughter, Cathy.

As John parked the car and entered the Wilcox building a sense of finality hit. It was eerie to enter the elevator and rise up to the fifth floor. Emerging from the elevator was emerging from a steel trap. Claustrophobia. The office, three doors on the left, did not scream special. John, surprised to find the door unlocked, and even more surprised to see Cathy sitting on the floor, surrounded by books, piles of papers, and chairs once occupied by her father.

"Good afternoon Mr. Wallace."

John taken aback by the beauty of Cathy, had grown into a sophisticated woman. Her face was lined perfectly by her shoulder length blond hair. Wearing a t-shirt that advertised AC/DC and jeans defined her as being well-toned, even as she sat cross-legged on the floor amid stacks of papers and folders.

"How are you holding up?"

Cathy gave a half nod of dancing around the subject. "As good as can be expected." A content smile crossed her face. "I bet you wonder why I am here." She lowered her head, gaining some inner strength and looked back up. "My father had grown more mysterious in the last year, actually last three years. It seems that the mystery expands to you Mr. Wallace. He left you something." She pointed to a box on a chair, thick, and with his name across the side.

"What's this?" Surprised John stepped across the piles and grabbed the mysterious box. It had weight to it as John weighed it in both hands. Wondering at the mystery and the answers contained inside.

Cathy leaned forward. "My dad was working on something. Something big. It caused him to isolate himself. The last time I talked to him all he mentioned was you, that you would understand. Towards the end he had paranoia, delusions. He mentioned that he had a secret, one that would change the world." Cathy paused. "Crazy huh? But, he believed it enough to put what he believed was true together." She pointed to the box. "And supposedly you can figure it out."

Suddenly the box felt heavier. John stared at the square he was holding, hoping the answers would come through the dark brown coloring magically. "Did he mention anything else?" John was confused about this interaction. This wasn't a normal conversation to have on the heels of someone's death. John sensed the urgency in Cathy as well as the curiosity.

"No. But to be honest with you, I sure would like to know what is in that box as well. Is there a chance of that happening?"

John looked up and saw Cathy with a teenage devious look. Wry. Curious. John knew this was a woman who got what she wanted. "Well, Ms. Jurkovich. Since I have no idea what is in here I would have to say, let me think about it. Second, I would want to honor your father's wishes. And third," John gave his own wry smile, "I am used to getting what I want as well."

"Then Mr. Wallace. I will wait, not patiently but I will wait."

BEIJING, CHINA

Xi Chan was pleased. The apartment building was surrounded by snipers with every alley and street guarded. Even the sewers were guarded. The plan was perfect. The rebels were as good as dead.

Inside were twenty-five rebels in a range of ages. Xi had been monitoring this group for the last four months. Noticing that they met in private, in different places, and at various times. But they had a pattern. Confusing. Almost genius. But there was a pattern.

Xi figured that they had the city divided into five sections. They would meet in the third section twice in a row. He also figured that they met every week. Morning.Noon.Night. The days of the week rotated. The system was complex. Xi had to admire the communication that must have gone out to make the arrangements and send out changes. A couple of times the groups would change the pattern and Xi had to start over again figuring out the system. Now Xi was on the verge of success.

Xi was trained to root out the rebels. For years he studied their doxology. What made them tick? None of it made sense. Everything the rebels believed in was against common sense, yet the rebels grew in size. They were becoming like locust. Schools, government agencies, and even seats of power were being occupied. Among the billions of people in China the rebels were of insignificant size. Only in the thousands, but that was seven years ago. Now the numbers were in the millions.

Growing.

It was time for the signal. The adrenaline was flowing and the heart pounding. Xi checked in with his checkpoints. All was in order. Xi closed his eyes to savor the moment. Taking a deep breath he ushered the command. Through his earpiece he could hear the footsteps of the commandos. The yelling of commands. Then the screams. The sweet screams. Xi opened his eyes and saw the flashes of gun fire through the windows. Shadows raced across. Blood splattered on the walls. It was chaos orchestrated by Xi. A symphony of a massacre.

Xi moved towards the apartment building. It would be satisfying to see the rebels dead. He moved across the street and stared up at the apartment building. The carnage would set most people into frenzy. The sight of the blood. Dismembered bodies. Lifeless eyes. He was looking forward to the sight.

As Xi entered the building he could hear the gunshots from the floors above. The shouts echoed from floor to floor. Xi entered the elevator and enjoyed the anticipation of the expected sight. Six more floors to go. Five. Four. Three. Two. One. The sight was beautiful.

Blood ran across the floor. The eyes stared up into nothing reflecting the end of life. The bodies danced the contorted death. Men. Women. Children. They wanted to be together. They received their wish. The rebels broke the law. They rose up against the country and the government. They deserved to die.

In China Christians had no place except for the grave and Xi gave them them their just rewards.

It had been a wonderful day.

DALLAS, TEXAS

Carl Bennet was a stoutly man. Despite his physical appearance of looking twenty pounds overweight Carl was probably the fittest man on campus. A former professional football player and weightlifting coach turned pastor; he had a taste of what the world had to offer. Money. Influence. Materials. Women. But a collision with a tree, a forgiving wife, and a God fearing friend pointed Carl to his true calling and a new life. As he strode across the campus plaza of Western Bible Seminary he pondered the letter that brought him back to his seminary.

Two days ago an old professor of his sent a letter. Professor Albert Larson, an expert in biblical history and creation science was asking for Carl to come back to Western. Carl was used to phone calls and invites for speaking engagements. Rarely did he hear from former professors and even more rare for him to come before the Twelve.

The Twelve were the top professors of the college, leaders in the Christian movement, experts in the field of Christianity; biblical ethnography, end times, demonic and angelic forces, creationism, and biblical politics. Together the Twelve worked towards understanding the Bible in all its truthfulness. They were also advocates and warriors who defended the faith on television, talk shows, through books, and speaking engagments. To be summoned to see the Twelve together was a special event.

Carl walked across the campus with its manicured lawns and well thought out walkways. Brick buildings housed everything from offices, dorms, and classrooms. The only moment Carl took to savor the serenity of the campus was to watch a chipmunk scurrying across the walkway with a treasure full of food as evidenced with the bulging cheeks.

The college of theological studies loomed just ahead. On the top floor were the professors who equipped the future pastors and Christian leaders of the future. The Twelve. These were men who shaped modern Christianity.

Carl faced two-hundred fifty pound defensive backs without fear, but this meeting made him nervous. Carl entered the front doors of the twenty story structure and headed towards the elevators. The golden doors opened and Carl pushed button twenty. As the elevator raised so did the nerves. Prayer. Carl needed prayer. "Lord grant me peace and contentment."

The doors opened into a massive room. White furniture was spread across the room. Ottomans, two sofas, and it looked like four loveseats were arranged in a square leaving plenty of room for comfort. An aroma mixture of coffee and tea hung in the air. Two chandeliers hung from the room giving an airy feel. Seated upon the furniture were the Twelve.

Professor Larson, a wiry man with a snow-white hair, approached Carl extending out his hand and sharing a contagious smile. "Hello Mr. Bennett. We have been looking forward to meeting with you."

CASPER, WYOMING

John opened the box and looked through the contents. As he flipped through the pages to get a look he noticed maps, diagrams, and hand scribbled journal entries. John looked over the front page and couldn't believe what he was reading.

> Dear John,
> If you are reading this letter then the worse has happened. My findings have been discovered and have fallen into the wrong hands. It is imperative that you protect the contents of this package.
> For many years I have worked on this research and even I couldn't believe what I have discovered. The contents of this package will erase current human thinking and destroy many aspects of the scientific community. Because of this, I paid the price. As a fellow scientist, and friend, I have passed this information to you. Your integrity, loyalty to the advancement of science, and high morale character are beyond question. It is because of this that I have given you this information.
> I am truly sorry for passing on this responsibility and burden. Believe me when I mention this John, what you hold in your hands will change the course of human history. Be careful with who you share it with. Use discretion and caution.
> Many will want this information and will want to destroy it. Already many powerful agencies and organizations are seeking out these contents. Do not delay! Follow through and it will explain what it is you are looking for.

God's speed to you my old friend. My final prayer was for you and this journey. Be strong.

Your colleague and friend,
Mike

John sat stunned. Mike's last thoughts on this planet were for him and the information in his hands. Looking down at his hands he noticed they were trembling. Was it fear? Nerves? Excitement? Whatever it was it took Cathy shaking him to call him out of his daze.

"What did it say? What's going on? You look like you have seen a ghost."

"In a way I have. Cathy, what was your father working on? Do you know?"

Cathy shook her head. "Not really. I just know that it consumed him. There would be times that he would be locked up in this office for days. That was not like him."

John knew she was right. Mike was a family man. He liked being in the open spaces of his yard and with his loved ones. He hated to be on business trips and at the office. Whatever was in this box was important enough to change Mike's habits and priorities.

"Cathy. Did your dad do any traveling? Go overseas or anything?"

Cathy stared back with a quizzical look. "Well. There were times when he was out of touch for a few days. He wouldn't tell anybody why he was not returning calls or where he was. I guess it would be ok to say he was out of town. Why?"

John stared down at the paper. He could feel the weight of responsibility of each and every word.

"I think I made up my mind on sharing the box. How do you feel about a little homework?"

BEIJING, CHINA

Xi stood before Commander We Mine Kim a legend in the Chinese military. Kim was the most successful man in Chinese history when it came to covert operations. He masterminded the missile delivery to the Iranians, controlled political races in America, operated guerilla attacks in Central America, Africa, and areas of Asia. There wasn't much in the world that Kim didn't dabble his hands in. Xi knew that he was standing in front of one the most powerful men in the world.

"Xi. Do you know why you are here?"

"No sir."

Kim took a puff of his Cuban cigar. "It seems that an American scientist has discovered something unusual." Another puff of the cigar.

Xi stood patiently amid the weighted silence. Xi knew he was being sized up. Didn't know for what but he knew.

Puff. "This discovery has the potential to change the world and our way of living. It can be quite devastating." A long puff. "This discovery must be stopped at all costs."

Xi let a smile creep upon his face. "I will eliminate the scientist."

"It is not the scientist that must be stopped. That has already been taken care of. It is the information that must be destroyed." A long drawn out puff followed.

Xi stood at full attention. The muscles drew tight and the heart quickened. This is what Xi looked forward to; the hunt and the kill.

"The research information is currently with the scientist's friend. That is the last information I have. Your job is to find the research. Destroy it and whoever has looked at it. If this information gets out it will change the course of history and world thinking."

Xi kept his composure but the questions were itching to get out. He knew he had to choose his words carefully as they might be his last. "Sir, Can I be so bold as to ask a question?"

Xi was answered with a puff a smoke. "You want to know why this information needs to be destroyed if it has the potential to change history. Is that correct?" Kim looked with hardened eyes knowing already what Xi was going to say.

"Yes sir, if I can be so bold as to ask?" Xi worked to maintain his confidence while asking questions. This struggle of presenting a charade in front of Kim was become tiresome for Xi for Kim was difficult to read.

Kim ground his cigar into his ashtray. Twisting and pushing down in a methodical manner. Clasping his hands he looked upon Xi. "I am not a person who believes in God. I believe in the power of me. I created who I am. I gather the resources. I strike fear into people and I control those I need to control. Because of these things I have determined the course of human history and destiny. For those I choose to influence and for myself. I did not look upon some make believe fairy-tale to create my fate. I control my fate." Kim took a deep breath and laid his beefy hands on the table. "But, let me ask you this Xi. What if there was evidence? Hard core, unquestionable evidence that God existed. Do you know what that means? Do you know the repercussions?" Kim clasped his hands together and leaned back maintaining a steady stare at Xi.

Xi shook his head. "No sir. Like you I too create my own fate. I continue to do so. I have seen too much death, inflicted too much suffering to believe in a God. I am not the first assassin, nor will I be the last. I am curious why a man of immense power like you would go to great lengths for such dribble?"

Kim allowed himself a chuckle. His broad chest heaved with each laugh as he pushed himself away from his desk and folded his hands behind his head. "Don't you see Xi, if there is a God, then we would be bad guys. I have gained my power by destroying hope in people. If there was a God then people like you and me would lose control over people for they would place their hope and confidence in something we can't control. Also, we would have to be held accountable. Do you want to be held accountable Xi?" A smile came upon Kim's face. "I didn't think so."

DALLAS, TEXAS

Carl took the complimentary glass of water and sat in one of the plush white chairs. He noticed that the glass was shaking and decided it would be best to set it on a table. Even the table seemed too nice for a possible water ring so Carl decided to hold the glass as steady as possible with both hands. At least it occupied them and looked better than fidgeting.

He scanned the room and noticed twelve men. They ranged in ages from the mid-forties to the seventies. Give or take. Carl recognized some of the faces from the back of book flap covers and television. These men guided the modern church of America. Men of true conviction and a heart for God. Even looking upon these powerful men Carl sensed humbleness within each face. In each pair of eyes was an inner strength. The room had a warmth that reminded Carl of home. Safe. Secure.

Carl noticed the glass wasn't shaking.

"Mr. Bennett. Do you know everybody in the room?" Carl noticed the man was Kelsey Brahm; an outspoken man on protecting marriage and the family. Recently he was criticized sharply on national television for denouncing the homosexual movement and how it undermines the family. Kelsey mentioned that he did like homosexuals, only that their beliefs and actions are destroying family values and how it hurts children in many ways. He gave evidence upon evidence of the suicide rates, mental health breakdowns, identity crisis that arises. He may have been better speaking to the moon. The host of the show was rude. Interupting Brahm constantly and by the end of the show attacked viciously with name calling. Brahm never lost his composure. Carl remembered feeling sorry for Brahm. Brahm's face was loving and sincere. There was sadness lacing his face as he seemed to scan the crowd.

Yet here he was; benevolent, considerate, and caring. Hardly the menace to society as described by a newscaster.

"No sir. I mean, I know some of these men but not all. I'm sorry." Carl felt stupid for the last part but nerves were kicking in again.

"No need for apologies. It is our honor to have you with us. I am Kelsey Brahm."

"I am Dr. Rodney Guide."

"And I am Dr. Julius Simpson."

Each man introduced himself. No talk of honors or awards or accolades. Just names.

"You are probably wondering why you are here. To be honest we are wondering the same thing ourselves."

Carl felt a sting. "I'm not worthy enough for these guys", he thought to himself.

"That came out badly. You are here because of your high integrity and commitment to the Lord. Your reputation for staying strong in adversity is well known and admired. What I mean is, well, a strange set of circumstances has brought you to us and we need your help."

Carl was in a sea of mixed emotions. He was receiving the highest compliments from the men he most admire but there seemed a "but" statement coming. "I am afraid I don't understand sir."

"Let me start from the beginning." Kelsey took a long drink of water. Closed his eyes and seemed in prayer. He opened his eyes and looked with an incredible sadness upon Carl. There was so much concern in the man's eyes that Carl became afraid. The look was comparable to the policeman who stopped by his house when he was fifteen years old to tell the family that Carl's dad died in a car accident. A drunk driver. Carl became cold.

"Three years ago a scientist began an amazing discovery. This discovery was so big it could not be released publicly. In fact, nations have agreed to keep this secret a secret. The scientist was so set on releasing the truth that he threatened to tell his findings in anyway possible. This upset many nations to the point that they sent covert agents after him to silence him. For many months he was successful in hiding and staying a step ahead. The scientist knew that the end was coming so he hid his findings, his research, and his secret. Eventually an agent came upon this scientist and killed him. An agent that works for a nasty group. A group called Force."

Kelsey took a deep breath and continued, "But not until he left a series of clues for someone to follow to uncover this secret. The scientist took three years to manipulate the clues and waited. He waited until everything was just right then allowed himself to be killed to protect this discovery. That's right Carl; this discovery is worth dying for."

Carl was silent. Not that he wanted to be. He had many questions but to know that a discovery was worth a life. He juggled through the files of his mind to think of a secret that would be worth a man's life. Empty.

"I know what you are thinking, what secret would be so great? I too thought that. I mean there is the secret to the Bermuda Triangle. The secret of Area 51. Bigfoot. The Pyramids. The world is full of unanswered secrets and mysteries. But this one is the biggest one of all."

Carl noticed a smile come upon Kelsey's face. Carl looked around the room and every man was smiling. Twelve men, powerful and influential, were smiling like little boys at Christmas time.

"What discovery could this be?"

Kelsey leaned forward. "What if there was a discovery that proves God exists beyond a shadow of a doubt? What if there was physical evidence that leaves no question in any person's mind. Would that be worth something?"

Spinning. That was now the state of mind that Carl was in. The room. His mind. His emotions. All spinning. Was it Noah's Ark? Ark of the Covenant? Carl knew that many discoveries have been made that have proved the Bible. In 2004 an ossuary was discovered that belonged to James, the brother of Jesus. The Dead Sea Scrolls contained the book of Isaiah. In 2007 an excavation was underway of Mary Magdalene's hometown.

But none of these findings cost a person his life.

"I guess I don't understand sir. There have been many findings. Important ones."

Kelsey jumped in, "You are thinking of things? Scrolls. Walls. Boxes. Right? But what if the discovery was alive?"

Now Carl felt sick. A living thing that testifies to the Bible? All the prophets are dead. It has been over two thousand years.

"Still confused? So were we until we got the first clue from the scientist and learned what it leads to."

CASPER, WYOMING

Cathy and John went through the packet of documents. They couldn't believe what they were reading. Mike had traveled throughout the world and gathered evidence on an amazing discovery. But the evidence before them was unbelievable. Mike was gathering evidence that would shock the scientific community. Sheet after sheet described dinosaurs, the age of dinosaurs. There were photographs and drawings and maps. John even came across napkins with handwritten notes. He imagined Mike at some restaurant, who knows where, jotting down a thought. It was surreal to hold a piece of Mike's thoughts.

"What do you think of all this?" Cathy said. She was thumbing through the leafs again. Some she had seen two or three times already.

"I'm not sure. Many things your dad stated here seem real enough. The places are real; Ankor Wat, Dinosaur Monument, Arizona, Peru. It would be easy to verify these documents, your dad's theory. What do you think?"

Cathy stared at the packet and the mess of papers. She pursed her lips and shook her head. Mixed thoughts were running through her head. No scientist in his right mind would put out this kind of a theory. "I don't know. Throughout history other scientist put out theories that seemed odd or weird at the time. Copernicus. Galileo. Newton. But this? This is pretty much out there."

John had to agree.

John knew Mike to be a conservative scientist. More on the desk type of research. Mike reiterated already proved theories. It wasn't his style to be groundbreaking and controversial. This theory was the antithesis of Mike's style. One thing couldn't be argued with, Mike, if anything, was thorough. If Mike put it into writing he had done his homework and thus was where he gained respect in the scientific community.

John and Cathy were thinking the same thing. To put this theory into scientific journals could devastate Mike's reputation. Or, if the theory was right, put Mike as one of the most famous scientist in history.

"There are two things we could do", John said through a long exhaled breath, " we can ignore this. Let life continue as always. No harm done. Your father's name stays respectable. Or, we can follow through on this."

"You mean?"

"We can pack our bags and take a trip."

SALT LAKE CITY

Carl stared upon the lake. The bare mountains that surrounded the deep blue lake shared a contrast only nature could provide. Carl couldn't believe he was here. He had spent the last forty-eight hours studying the documents and articles that the committee gave him. According to the evidence a scientist named Mike spent the last three years investigating a rumor and Mike traveled around the world to seeking undeniable proof.

It seems he found the proof.

Then Mike mysteriously died.

The evidence Mike gathered was copied and sent to two places; to his daughter in Casper and to Dallas. Because of this the two parties were to meet and work together and verify the evidence. Carl represented the Twelve.

Carl walked down the concourse to the baggage claim. Dodging business people, families, and custodians helped distract Carl amid his thoughts. It didn't take long for Carl to recognize his name. Holding it was an attractive woman with a middle-aged name. Carl cocked his head to the side as he sized up this odd couple. The two people before him did not match his preconceived thoughts. Then again, how many times does that actually happen thought Carl.

"Carl Bennet? I am Cathy Jurkovich. It is a pleasure to meet you."

SAN FRANCISCO, CALIFORNIA

Xi made it through customs. He knew he would. A smart assassin never carried his weapons with him. Instead, he had connections throughout the world that provided the necessary supplies.

And Chinatown would be the place of those connections.

Xi always made sure to keep people owing him. Bringing a brother out of debt, eliminating a barrier to building a business, getting a daughter through college; Xi worked these connections together to ultimately his own benefit. Today, it would be Lu Ming's turn to payback Xi.

Xi made his way through the congested traffic and parked two blocks from Lu's shop. Lu specialized in providing restaurant supplies and food to Chinatown. Behind the scenes Lu had connections to weapons of all shapes and sizes. Xi would also need supplies for hiking and survival.

Lu's face went white when Xi entered the shop.

"Good morning Lu. It seems that you have done well since our last meeting. I am glad that you have made the most of your given resources."

"Yes. I have worked hard. Sacrificed much."

Xi gave a smile. Lu knew to be leary when Xi smiled. " Lu. I am sorry that I could not be here for a social visit. Unfortunately I am here on business. It seems that I in need of your special gifts."

Xi noticed the fear in Lu through the shifting in his eyes, shuffling of the feet, the nervous wiping of the counter. "I am no longer in that business."

Xi began walking around the shop. He knew Lu was lying. Most of the people lied to Xi. The game begins.

"Lu. Lu. You know the agreement. I gave you money. A chance for success. I did my part. It is time for you to do your part. Surely you know business deals."

"I have a daughter. A wife. If I get caught I will go back to China. There is nothing for me in China."

"Lu. If you don't pay back there is nothing for you here." The ice in the voice reminded Lu of the raid. At five years old Lu watched his father and mother get shot through the back of the head. The other adults were also shot. The teenagers in the group were tortured; the girls were raped while the boys were castrated. The younger children watched all this. Then the captain of the group walked in. His stare bore into each child and when it was Lu's turn he never knew true fear until that moment. "You have witnessed what it means to be a Christian. It doesn't. Christianity is a lie. Your parents were fools and you see what happens to fools. You now belong to me. You belong to China."

Lu was then raised to appreciate China. Government sponsored children homes raised the orphans that the state created. Future military officers, government workers, and city officials came from these homes. Lu was trained to be a military officer. Military history was drilled into him every day as was small arms training. Physical conditioning and hand to hand combat strengthened Lu's skills.

Lu had missions in Vietnam, South America, Europe, and Russia. When he finally had a mission to America Lu saw his opportunity to escape China's system. He learned to hack the computer system gain access to monies to survive and researched places in which he could blend in the easiest. The only thing he couldn't do was create a new identity and understand the American system.

Then he met Xi. Xi created a new history for Lu. According to the databanks for America Lu was born and raised in San Francisco, graduated from Heights High School, went to Northern California Community College, and opened up his own shop.

Xi mentioned that someday Lu would have to pay back. Lu accepted this as the American way. A business dealing.

As Lu grew accostumed to his new life and neighbors he began to hear the talk. Many people in Chinatown knew of Xi. Many surprising and mysterious disappearances happened. Though no one spoke of them everyone knew why. Someone chose to not pay back Xi.

And here was Xi before Lu. Ready for his payback. Lu knew what would happen if he didn't follow through. For years he received messages to collect weapons and ammo. But Lu had fallen in love with his new life and new country. He loved his neighborhood, wife, and kids.

It was all at stake at this very moment.

"Lu. Can I please go get my weapons now."

Lu turned and went into the back room. Behind the janitor's closet was a latch. The latch opened another door that led to a hidden room. In that room was shelves of guns and knives. Pistols, shotguns, uzis, and machine guns. Machetes, hunting knives, and even swords.

Lu had prepared for this event. There was a pistol that was always loaded. Lu was relying on the military training from his days in China. Lu would simply take the pistol and quickly turn and kill Xi. He would become the hero of Chinatown. An evil would be eradicated. Lu grabbed the pistol and turned. Staring him in the face was Xi.

Before Lu could pull the trigger he felt the pain in his stomach. His wrist was snapped and broken.

"All you had to do was open the door. Thanks for the cache Lu."

ARCHES NATIONAL PARK - UTAH

John hated to hike. The idea of dirt, sweat, and sometimes water in his boots freaked him out. Already Carl, Cathy, and John trudged through small streams, sandy dunes, and scaled boulders.

Arches National Park was a rolling high plain that had limited vegetation and at times limited oxygen. The wind cut over the desolation and reminded the visitor of how powerful it was as a force of nature. Testimonies of its power were clearly evidenced by the rock formations that gave the park its name.

Splayed across the park were rock formations that played tricks with the mind. Twisting and arching pieces of nature. John was reminded of how his nephews would play with Play-doh. They would roll out a piece of Play-doh into long pieces then would twist those pieces and create bridges, snakes, and ropes.

Arches National Park must have been God's Play-doh fun area.

For right now though John was trying to keep up with Carl and Cathy. They were heading for Kachina Bridge. A natural bridge of rock that is over two hundred feet high and also spans over two hundred feet. It didn't' take long to identify it over the rolling plain.

Within twenty minutes the trio arrived. For Carl and John this was their first visit to Arches so Cathy let them have their moment to gawk over this structure. It still sent chills up and down her spine to think of the power that created all this. The wind cutting through the rock as well as the water. She was taught that water gouged the softer rock underneath and that the wind polished.

The feeling was still an awesome one to behold.

"So are you two ready to play hide and seek?" Carl asked. His voice echoed under the massive arch above them.

"I guess so. What are we looking for again?" Cathy knew but she needed to hear clarification. It seemed so odd to be seeking out evidence that her father had already found. But a true scientist needed to reaffirm the proof before them and clarify it.

It was the least she could do for her father.

"Petroglyphs. Let's just find some petroglyphs around the bridge area." Carl was getting excited by now. Actual evidence that proves God's word is true and here in the United States. Could it be real? Most sought out evidence in the Middle East, Israel, even parts of Europe. But the middle of the western United States? It seemed like the worst kind of joke to be played.

"Here. I found some," John called to the others. Cathy and Carl bounded over boulders and jumped the stream to reach John. There, on the smooth pink surface were some petroglyphs.

For almost thirty minutes Cathy and John stared and squinted at the ancient art before them. There were some mutterings exchanged and the on-going scientific conversation that left Carl feeling left out. Still, he knew he was here on a purpose.

"There, is that it? It seems to match. What do you think John?"

Carl and John looked over Cathy's shoulder as followed her pointed finger. The petroglyph showed an animal of extreme size. The other petroglyphs clearly showed the other animals of the area, antelope, buffalo and deer. This particular piece of art showed an animal of enormous size. Several hunters surrounded this animal. John air traced the animal and was mumbling to himself.

"This is impossible. It can't be real."

"What is this John? It's not a mammoth, there is no tusk and look at the size of that tail. The neck is long like a giraffe's but with a tail of a kangaroo. I don't know of any animal that looks like this."

"It looks like a sauropod. They were over a hundred feet long. Some even more so. They were herbivores which meant only plant eaters. Sauropods are actually a type of dinosaur. You probably know a couple of them by their names; brontosaurus, brachiosaurus, diplodocus. These were the big boys of the day. Some scientist believe that they were the largest land animals to ever exist. Sauropods are easy to recognize because of their long tails, and huge bodies. They are also recognized by their thick, tree-like legs with blunt feet. The feet had five toes but only three would have claws or nails for digging and traction." Cathy couldn't help but show off her knowledge. Being the only female she felt she had to show some sort of advantage. She also wanted to prove that she belonged to this mismatched group.

Carl stood straight up. "Are you telling me that this is a dinosaur?" He couldn't even believe the words were coming out of his mouth.

"But that is impossible. Dinosaurs died out, were extinct, long before humans came into the picture." Cathy said. "This has to be a fake."

Carl began digging into his pack. A binder was opened and John and Cathy recognized the notes being from Mike. "According to your dad's notes, the petroglyphs have not been tampered with. Every day the rangers check for vandalism or changes to the petroglyphs. It seems your dad believed in this picture."

John was sick on the inside. It didn't take long to understand the implications of this discovery. What if man and dinosaur lived together? It was mind numbing.

"Ok. Let's say that this picture is real. It is only one. There should be other pieces of evidence to back up this ultimate theory my dad has proposed. I mean come on, dinosaurs with man. That's impossible. Isn't it?"

Carl was looking through the binder again. "If your dad could be trusted, and right now the evidence shows he can, there are dinosaur tracks in southeast Utah. In fact, millions of them around Moab, Utah. In Copper Ridge, Utah there are therapod tracks. Here in Arches at Bishop's Bell are petroglyphs of other large creatures similar to dinosaurs. Whoa, if your father is correct, here is a picture of a petroglyph from the Sioux Indians. According to your father it is labeled a pterosaur. Similar drawings have been found throughout the American South-West." Carl closed his binder. "It seems that we are sitting in a spot where the deer and the dinosaurs played."

ANCIENT UTAH

The great beasts lumbered through the valley. Each step seemingly shaking the ground. Each roar rippling through the air. The ground became dustier with each beast. Just this morning a rain came to dampen the ground. But with so many beasts treading through the moisture was soon gone.

Stanzi loved the spring. This year brought even more excitement. It would be his first time hunting the great beast. There was fear in his belly but anticipation overplayed the fear. Hidden among the boulders he waited with his uncles Yochuch, Toomay, and Britich. His dad took a different vantage point. His dad, Muko, was the leader of their hunting group and for the tribe. Muko has had more kills with the great beast than any other person in the tribe. Standing a good head taller than any other man in the village Muko was an intimidating figure. Across his body were scars from enemies, both man and animal. Across his chest was the knife mark from a neighboring tribe. Down his arm was a scar from a great beast hunt. Stanzi remembered dragging his father back to camp so that his mom could heal him. Muko was indeed a great hunter and leader. For this he was richly rewarded and respected by all the Anasazi tribe's people.

The Anasazi people hunted the great beast for many generations. Stories have been handed down from father to child of the great hunts and how family and community worked together to bring down just one beast. Stanzi himself had seen the pictures on the twisted and arching rocks of how the hunters of his forefathers hunted the many animals of this area. Deer. Beaver. Quail. Beast. Each animal provided the community with what it needed to survive. The deer and beaver provided pelts for clothing and shelter. Quail provided the bones for sewing and feathers for writing and drawing. Each animal also provided the most valuable resource, meat. No animal was better at this than the beast.

Each beast can feed a family unit for many moon cycles. Much like their native cousins in the plains states with their buffalo, each part of the beast is used. There is no waste. And with each family unit having a hunting group, there is no fear of hunger.

Stanzi waited.

He knew what his role was. To distract the big beast until the uncles attacked from the sides and from on top. As the beast reared up Stanzi would throw the spear into the belly of the beast, the softest part. The uncles would also drive their spears into the neck area while trying to avoid the beast's head whipping back and forth.

Stanzi did not fear the beast. What he feared is that he would fail his family. Or that he would hurt one of his uncles. Or worse, accidentally kill them. Stanzi felt the weapon in his hands. It was crafted by both him and his father. A long shaft made of pine with a rock piece at the end. Arrowhead making was a necessary skill among the men in the tribe. It was the difference between life and death.

Soon. It would be very soon.

The baying and the roars were coming closer. Within the tribe were men who separated the beast from the herd and sent the isolated ones down canyons or man-made funnels. It was within these confines that Stanzi and his family would attack. An isolated sound echoed among the canyon walls alerting the hunters that the prey was on the way. The earth seemed to crash and sway below Stanzi's feet.

Sweat began to trickle down Stanzi's back. His legs began to twitch with anticipation. He watched his dad and saw his hand raise slowly up. The time was finally coming.

The hand dropped.

From out of nowhere came Stanzi's uncles. Yochuch jumped onto the back. With a spear grasped in both hands the spear was thrust into the neck. The beast reared up.

Stanzi, without thinking, rushed out with his spear. Toomay and Britich were stabbing the sides. Stanzi drew back his spear. With all of his strength and eyes locked on his target he let loose the spear. With a thud the spear landed in its mark. The beast released a sound of so much pain that it terrified Stanzi. For a brief moment sadness settled into Stanzi's being. But as the beast continued to shake, rear up, and try to attack his uncles the feeling left.

The beast reared up to a great height and Stanzi could see the terror in the beast's eyes. There was also fear. Confusion. With another spear

Stanzi thrust it next to the first spear. As the beast came down it drove the spear deeper into the gut till only a foot of the spear was showing.

The beast let out one last mournful bellow. The uncles recognized the beast was finally dying and leaped off. It's been known that a beast would find a second strength and attack its attackers. Not today. The eyes began rolling back. Blood covered the thick skin. Shakes began to settle into the beast. Stanzi watched as the beast crumpled to two legs. Finally, it rolled over. The belly rose and fell. Each time it become slower and slower. Then stopped.

After a few minutes of waiting to ensure that the beast was dead, both men and women came to begin the process of preparing the beast for food and supplies. All around Stanzi he could hear bellows from other beasts as other families hunted their prey.

There were many sounds of dying beasts.

As Stanzi was gathering up his tools for gutting and preparing the beast a thought crossed his mind, could these great beasts be around forever? Are the tribes hunting too many? Are we taking them for granted?

Foolish thoughts. These beasts are like the buffalo of the plains. They roam in packs. They are as numerous as the stars in the sky.

The great creator could never take such an important animal from us Stanzi thought.

And with these comforting thoughts Stanzi took his tools to help his mother and sisters with the preparing of the wonderful and plentiful beast.

DALLAS, TEXAS

As the Twelve were gathering for their daily prayer meeting the phone rang. Dr. Randy Johnson being the closest answered.

"Do not hang up. I am aware of who you are and of your exploring group. Understand that I will do anything I have to to ensure that they fail. My means and resources are unlimited. My connections are many. I am not to be trifled with. Pull back your group if you want them to live. Is that understood?"

Dr. Johnson just stood there. The Twelve prayed everyday for Carl, Cathy and John's safety. But safety never included this. Satan is really attacking thought Dr. Johnson.

"I said, is that understood? You either pull back the group or they will be hurt." The hatred and venom could be felt through the phone.

"I understand. I need to pray about it." Dr. Johnson strained to keep his calm. Every fiber. Every nerve in his body wanted to react to the threats. Who are you? Why the hatred?

"Pray? Pray? There is no need for prayer here. It is a life and death situation you fool. What could you possibly be needing prayer for in this situation? This is a choice situation, not a prayer situation." Laughter accompanied.

Dr. Johnson released a heavy sigh. "Every situation, every choice, every decision requires prayer. This one especially." He could hear the laughter on the other side of the phone.

"Your choice. Their lives. Think about it." With that the phone line ended.

Dr. Johnson placed the phone back on its stand. He could feel the weight of the eyes on him from the others.

"Randy. Are you all right?"

"Gentlemen. Our prayer focus has shifted."

ARCHES NATIONAL PARK- UTAH

John just stared at the petroglyphs. Never in his life could he imagine that dinosaurs and man lived together. Yet here was proof that possibly a Native American tribe not only lived with the dinosaurs but hunted them as well.

"I don't understand. All the science in the world points out that dinosaurs lived millions of years ago and that they died out millions of years before man. How is this possible?" asked Cathy.

Carl was perplexed as well. As a Christian he knew that God created everything in six days. Yet, he still believed the viewpoint of science. He didn't consider it a faith issue but more of a common sense issue.

"Well, the Bible states that animals were created on the fifth day and that man was created on the sixth. Everything was created in six days. Since dinosaurs are animals, then I guess they were created on day five."

"That's absurd," stated John. "The carbon dating. The fossils. All the evidence points to the scientific viewpoint."

Carl gave wry smile. "Well, in the past science was wrong on things. It was wrong on the world being flat. It was wrong about the earth being the center of the universe. Could it be possible that science is wrong about this?"

John and Cathy just stared, dumbfounded over the possibility. Everything they thought about dinosaurs and timelines were being washed away in a sea of doubt.

"Cathy. Your father may have come across the strongest and most controversial evidence in modern science. If what he found is true, and can be verified, this will in turn…"

"devastate many in the scientific community," finished John.

Carl just stared with confusion at Cathy and John. Here they were, literally, sitting on a great scientific discovery and these two scientists were not elated. Carl was estatic to find proof that creation happened in six days. He wanted so badly to call the Twelve and share his news but a gut feeling told him to not do it around John and Cathy.

"Look. There is more to discover around here from your father's notes. There are also more places to visit. The scientific process needs to be applied. Obviously Mike wanted us to go on this journey to verify the evidence. That may explain why he didn't publish."

Cathy hung her head low. "It just feels like I didn't know my father at all. Why would he keep this from me? Why?"

Carl felt his heart breaking for Cathy. It is not easy to stumble upon a great secret of a parent. He knew though that Mike was an intelligent man. There was a reason for not telling Cathy. As Carl rummaged through his thoughts he sensed a greater reason for not telling Cathy. Safety.

Could his death and keeping his findings silent be tied together? Why would he send out his evidence to two different entities? Was the timing deliberate? Meaning that Mike sensed something was going to happen and he had to protect the evidence. Carl began to have that gut sense again.

This was going to require a great amount of prayer.

The three began to explore other parts of the park. They found numerous fossilized dinosaur tracks and many more petroglyphs. John concluded that the tracks and the petroglyphs were probably never been tested to see if they were at about the same time in history. Cathy concluded that the petroglyphs from the first site are similar in drawing style to the other sites. It was safe to conclude that the drawings are from the same tribes.

That night back in the hotel room Carl scoured through Mike's documents. At least it looked to the outsider that Carl was studying. Carl was praying over the documents. The weight of today's discovery was upon him and he began to see the full implications. Would the world even listen and care? Dinosaurs with people? Even he had a hard time accepting the statement. For so long and in so many ways he heard that dinosaurs ruled the world long before man. He also knew, in the back of his mind, that it couldn't be so. And yet he still had a leaning towards the scientific viewpoint. Inside Carl was constant conflict of accepting something he knows he should have accepted on faith yet it still took solid evidence to accept. Yet he still didn't accept fully. Not yet.

He felt like he needed to internalize the information and settle it firmly into his being. Much like accepting gravity, or the speed of light, or even that a simple chair will be strong enough to support when you sit upon it.

It was all about faith and Carl was struggling with facts and guilt.

This was going to be a long night.

Cathy just sat in bed staring at the flickering images of the television. She had no idea that some contestant had just won hundred thousand dollars and was jumping around the screen. She didn't notice the hugs that were given by the host and the beautiful assistant to the winner. The loud authoratative voice of the announcer may as well been muted since he wasn't being listended to anyway in room 216.

Instead her thoughts and feelings were on her father. A wrestling match of ideas, preconceived notions, and simple assumptions were dukeing it out in her head. Each thought making as much sense as the other while at the same time seeming so ridiculous. She knew the integrity of her father and his reputation in the scientific community. She knew how he would painstakingly examine each artifact for accuracy despite the tedious nature. Many times growing up she would wonder if a shard of pottery was more important than her. But then he would come home. The science hat was off and he was just dad. It was his passion and devotion to his studies that drew her into his world. She wanted to know what drove her dad and hoped it would drive her to know him even better. As an adult she loved working side by side with her father.

That was up till three years ago.

Now beside her on the bed were those three years of work. She was closed out on this part of her father's life. She felt betrayed and unworthy. Only after he was gone was she allowed to enter into this part of his life.

Why?

There was one constant thought that kept nagging behind all the other thoughts; the answer lies in following the evidence.

As soon as that thought popped up many more questions would come and a cloud of confusion would form in her head. It took effort to reach for that thought again and hang onto it.

Cathy accepted the fact that tonight she would not sleep very well.

It seemed quirky but John removed his shoes. The pacing back and forth was sure to leave a well worn path in the carpet and he didn't want to have anything else on his room bill. Already he indulged in two Diet

Cokes and a Snickers bar from the room's refridgerator and snack bar. He placed his hands upon the desktop and stared into the mirror.

He too was wrestling with his thoughts. Every fiber in his body said that Carl was wrong. Mike was wrong. How could decades of modern science be wrong? He knew of peers in other universities that were laid off from their teaching positions for promoting or teaching a theory that differed from evolution. Now, John was facing the same dilemma. There was proof. At least there was subtle proof that could not be ignored any longer. He knew what the road ahead looked like if he continued to collect the evidence.

How many other scientists chose to ignore the evidence and remain ignorant just to keep a paycheck?

John didn't recognize the face in the mirror. He thought he was a moral man. He thought he would do the right thing when confronted. He thought science was the answer. But the sucker punch of today John was left reeling and battered.

John bowed his head and took a deep breath. The pinched nerve in his upper back began to act up. It always did with stress. As he lifted his head and raised his arms to stretch John hit something on the desk and knocked it to the floor.

A Bible.

The pain was ignored as John began a staring contest with the object on the ground. The orange book just sat there. John wasn't sure on how to react to such a strange object. He bent down and picked it up. The book was shaking and John knew it was his hand. Standing up John began the pacing while staring at the book.

All his adult life religion was for the weak minded. Church was for those who needed friends and a social life, had nothing better to do. Religion slowed down the scientific progress and thus discoveries that actually improved human life. From stem cell research to cloning to controlling the world's population, religion hindered human progress. But the question from Carl raged inside John's head, "What if science is wrong?"

John sat on the edge of the bed and flipped through the pages. He didn't know what he expected. Just kept flipping. Thumbing. He looked up at the ceiling and back down at the Bible. He stopped at the book of John. Relenting to the fact that sleep was out of the question, and that he was tired of scouring through Mike's papers, he decided to read the Bible.

"In the beginning was the Word, and the Word was with God, and the Word was God. He was with God in the beginning."

RENO, NEVADA

Xi took in the casino towers and the morning sun. The mountains that surrounded this tiny city glowed under the sun's radiance. To the west snow clung to the peaks while in the valley the temps rose to uncomfortableness. The streets began to come alive with delivery trucks, police vehicles, construction noises, and the humming of cars speeding away from traffic signals.

Xi breathed in the air from the hotel balconey. Last night he felt great accomplishment. Down the street from his casino he found a wonderful restaurant for steak which is his favorite meal. He even gambled some of Lu's money that he helped himself to and came out ahead at the tables. And found two beautiful women.

Then there was the phone call. Xi let out a small chuckle. He could feel the fear on the other line. Religious people had such weak hearts and resolve. He figured that the Twelve would immediantely pull the trio away from their expedition and his job would be finished.

Pity.

He was looking forward to the hunt; searching out the prey, seeing the fear in their eyes while he took their life from them. Instead he sent out the warning as instructed by Commander Kim.

Oh well. A job is a job.

Xi let the sun hit his skin and he enjoyed the warmth that bathed over him.

"My pretties. You should come and take in this view. See the sun rise above the mountains." Xi was speaking sarcastically.

Last night's accomplishments also included two deaths of college student Rayanne and her waitress friend Stacy. Xi would make the deaths look like a murder-suicide. All traces of him being there would be erased. Kim would take care of the computer side of things. No credit cards. No survelliance cameras. Xi would go through and erase all fingerprints and possible DNA traces.

Then it was time to begin the hunt.

Today was going to be a good day.

FOUR CORNERS - USA

Cathy was gulping down the bitter coffee as if it was a necessary evil. John stared outside with a constant quizical look. And Carl glanced at each person in the place. Each person possibly living within a lie. A lie so masterfully crafted that it permeates every aspect of every society on earth.

The waitress arrived with the three orders; a Denver omelet, eggs and hashbrowns, and Cathy wanted cereal and fruit. Unable to handle the burdensome weight silence Carl spoke. "I don't know about you two but yesterday was a pretty heavy day. I was unable to sleep and the questions keep flowing through my mind. In fact, the questions came faster and faster. By the time I try to analyze one, ten more would have popped up. I have never felt so confused in my life."

Cathy was glad for Carl speaking up. She too wanted to unload the burden but fear and possible embarassement held her. "I'm with you Carl. I tossed and turned pondering question after question and of course there were no answers. Well, no answers that seemed to satisfy me at least." She cupped the coffee with her hands as if it was a lifesaving device. She could at least touch, feel the roundness of the cup and feel the heat of the dark liquid inside. It was real.

The two locked their eyes on John and without looking up from his omelet he could feel them. Staring at the omelet, "Mike has sent us on a journey that we were not expecting. But we are on it now. There are more places to go and hopefully some of the questions we have can be answered." Then looking up he stared at Carl. "I have began to consider all possibilities." With that he held up the orange Bible.

Carl felt a million weights coming off the shoulders. Many of the questions that he had dealt with was how John and Cathy would view the evidence. Would it be an honest consideration? Is it possible that nonbelievers can view such evidence and see God? Those answers were staring at him. The eyes may have dark circles around them, appear to be bloodshot, and look worn out and tired, but they were searching eyes.

Carl couldn't help but smile.

"The way I see it is that we have evidence that needs verifying. Mike has left us many locations where he deemed the evidence to be the strongest. I say we follow the yellow brick road and keep our minds open to the possibilities." With that John returned to his omelet.

The exchange between Carl and John was not lost on Cathy. Over the Frosted Flakes she noticed the smile on Carl's face. More questions began to burrow into her mind. Did her dad become some religious nut? His reputation as a scientist would be over if this was the case. She herself condemned Christian scientists. They were unable to have open minds to the evidence. Everything had to have an agenda. Prove God. If what the three of them are on is some chase to collect evidence to prove God she needed to get out and fast. Her name was being recognized in educational circles. To gain a professorship at a prestigious university was becoming a reality. To be associated with this wild goose chase would devastate her career.

She was curious as to what her dad was doing for the last three years of his life. The scientist in her was also curious as to where the evidence would lead. Finishing her cereal she decided to go along. In respect for her father she decided to focus on having an open mind.

The evidence yesterday was pretty convincing.

Finishing his omelet John reached into his briefcase. "I think the next logical place to go is Cambodia. Ankor Wat to be exact."

Carl looked up. He had never been outside of the country before. There was a deep fear of being in other countries. Watching the news he saw riots and wars. The countries' names would not matter to him. All he knew was that it was somewhere else. All those bad events happened somewhere else. And now he may be going to that somewhere else.

Carl's fear of the unknown was coming to fruition. His safety net being ripped out from underneath him. He could feel the fear picking at his skin.

The only comfort that seemed to blanket him was that he was on this journey because of God. God wouldn't send him to anyplace just to be hurt. Or would he? His ways are not my ways thought Carl to himself. But the thought was not comforting.

Cathy leaned onto her elbows. "Ankor Wat?" She searched her mind for a recollection of her being there. Did her father take her to Cambodia as a child? She knew the answer was no but desperation clinged. "I'm packed and ready to go."

"I'm as ready as I am going to be. What about you Carl?"

"I'll grab my stuff. Have I told you two that I have never been outside of the country before?"

DALLAS, TEXAS

Looking at over campus gave Dr. Kelsey Brahm joy. The Dallas skyline was seen on the horizon and the city spread out before him. A prideful man would stand and fantasize seeing the expanse before them.

From his top floor office he could see students scurrying from building to building, socializing on the administration lawn, or lazily walking across campus from playing basketball or from studying at the library. The energy that was created by a university intrigued Kelsey. The youthfulness brought hope.

Right now Kelsey could use all the hope and energy he could muster.

The phone call yesterday brought dread among the Twelve. Fear crept among every man. Second guessing began to happen among some of the members. Kelsey was afraid of splintering. It was at these times that doubt would find a home in Kelsey. This doubt would make him second guess decisions and hinder his leadership. This was not the time to have hindrances.

Doubt. Fear. Worry. Untrusting.

The very reasons sin entered into the world in the first place. The phone call was like the serpent. It sowed the seed of doubt and mistrust and human nature made the seed grow.

Dr. Julius Simpson said to bring the three home right away. Who are we to make a judgement call on their safety? They have the right to know what is happening and the danger they are in. Kelsey had never heard the angry tone used by Julius. Kelsey had known Julius for close to twenty years. The man last night was a stranger.

Dr. Rodney Guide said that we as a group have prayed about this and that we put it into God's hands. He will protect them. He will put the hedge around them. The most important weapon we have is group prayer. We cannot second guess God's will.

Albert Larson mentioned sending a delegate or even some sort of bodyguard to protect the trio.

The one concensus thought was that something had to be done.

And on and on it went. The bantering back and forth. The arguments. Each man had justification on his position. Each man made a strong and common sense argument. Heated words were exchanged and hands raised in intimidation. But no one relented

Pride.

Another reason sin entered the world.

As Kelsey looked at over the campus the excitement of the unknown that came with seeing the students now came with fear. Three people's lives are at stake. It was the Twelve who organized this expedition. What is their responsibility? Do they even have responsibility? Did we not put everything into God's hands? What does that mean really?

He turned away from the window and crossed the office floor. He decided to do something he hasn't done in a long time. It was a habit he had gotten away from in the last couple of years. Business and professional responsibilities had taken over. Family obligations had also chipped away at his time.

He locked the door, went to the middle of the floor, knelt down and prayed.

For the next two hours Kelsey, a pillar of the Christian faith and role model for Christians everywhere, submitted his sins and doubts to his creator as a broken and sinful man. Only God would have have seen a sobbing man. At times Kelsey yelled at God then asked for forgiveness. The cycle of emotions were prayed through. At the end, Kelsey felt exhausted, drained. Tears ran but of joy. It was good to be with God. It took minutes for Kelsey to find the strength to stand and when he did it was just long enough to fall into the couch. How could prayer physically debilitate? A joy surrounded Kelsey as he realized what he had to do. He knew how to lead the Twelve now.

BEIJING, CHINA

The morning briefing arrived along with the steaming cup of green tea. Kim demanded that the reports be on his desk when he arrived every morning. Most people had a morning ritual that they went through to help them wake up. For Kim it was reviewing the reports from the day before, glance throught the events that happened while he was sleeping, and enjoy his green tea set at the temperature of one hundred ten degrees.

Being in charge of the covert operations for China's military, Kim thought of the important and necessary people under him. But nobody was as important in the world as Soshi Lus at six in the morning. She was the one who prepared his green tea and ensured that the reports were on his desk every morning. Her calming demeanor and influence had saved many officers' careers and they knew it. The word among China's officers was that Soshi was the most powerful person in the military since she controlled Kim.

When Kim heard this rumor the first time anger and raged boiled inside him. Now, it was a joke. Shoshi could care less about having power or influence over military men. She understood her unique position. Her job helped secure her family's safety. They were fed and treated better than most Chinese people. Her younger siblings never had to work in factories but were able to attend school and receive an education. Soshi would never jeapordize a family member's opportunity and Kim knew that.

Scanning the reports most of the news and information was updates of events already going on. The civil war in Somalia still raged with no victor or end in sight. Kim thought there was an opportunity that China could benefit from this skirmish. But how and why gnawed at him. To have China gain a foothold on the African continent would give easier access to the Middle East and Europe for trade routes and military bases. There were untold resources in Africa and China should have access.

Cuba's leader is dying. "I can't believe the old man hasn't keeled over yet," mumbled Kim. This was a wonderful opportunity for China to sit in the backyard of the United States. For the enemies of the US Cuba was prime real estate. The Cuban Missle Crisis proved that. But Russia over extended its presence and thus put Cuba under the microscope. If China could somehow plant a team in Cuba to begin setting up covert operations then access to the US would be easier. "I'll work on this one for the next few days."

The next report made Kim's blood cold. He had a personal vendetta against Christian organizations. When Kim was a child two missionaries came to his village. They were loving and caring and took a real interest in everyone in the village. Kim remembered hanging with the young man and soaking in every word that was mentioned about Jesus and God.

Kim's parents and sisters invited the couple over for a dinner one night. It was a celebration dinner as everyone except Kim had accepted Christ as their savior. Kim remembered the feast; roast duck, fresh vegetables, rice milk. Tears of joy ran all night long and stories were shared.

Two months later the couple left to return to the states.

A month after that the Chinese military visited the village.

The captain gathered the townpeople together. Kim was hiding in the forest on the edge of the village. Kim had never seen soldiers close up. They looked strong, determined, and they showed no fear. As the captain spoke to the townspeople Kim remembered that he had a strong and confident voice. The kind of voice that made you listen to him. It begged to be heard.

The captain made a speech that made a Chinese citizen proud to be Chinese. Kim felt great joy in his country just listening to the man. As the captain continued he stated that outsiders are poisoning our people with thoughts and beliefs that undermine China and threatens to divide the nation.

At this many of the villagers clung tighter to their children or their spouse's hands. Some of the men showed distaste in the faces. The captain continued that these outsiders come and preach about a religion that contradicts what makes China great.

As Kim scanned the crowd he saw a new kind of fear creep across some of the faces. As a boy Kim could see the difference but had not understood it. He searched the crowd for his family.

The captain stated that to keep China clean and powerful that these outsiders must be reported and that anyone who follows these beliefs must also be reported. It was the patriotic duty of every Chinese person to keep China strong.

It didn't take long for villager to turn on villager. Neighbors pointed out neighbors for having the outsiders over for dinner. So and so was baptized. This family hosted a Bible study. From among the crowd soldiers rounded up the believers and Kim saw his mom and dad huddled away.

Confusion and fear paralyzed Kim. He wanted to rescue his parents. He wanted to be with them but he was planted in place by fear. The scene before him was playing out before him like a movie screen and all he could do was watch.

Each person was questioned by a soldier. Did you have the missionaries at your house? Were you baptized? What do you believe in?

Those that answered in the positive were rounded up and moved to the other side of town.

The soldiers allowed the rest of the villagers to follow them. The captain said that it sadden him to do this particular duty. It was disheartening to punish fellow countrymen. For the good of the country sometimes sacrifices had to be made and these people needed to be made examples so that others will not fall into deception.

With that an eruption of gunfire happened. The noise was deafening but still could not drown out the screams and the agony. Blood erupted from every man, woman, and child. The smell of gunpowder soon spread over the village. Within seconds it was the smell of blood.

Within a minute's time a quarter of the village population was mowed down. Among them were Kim's parents and sisters.

The weight of the silence hung over the village. Friends, neighbors, and family members now lay in a twisted bloody mass.

The captain spoke again. This time the soft but strong voice was gone. It was replaced with an icy harshness. My fellow countrymen. Do not let your fate be like theirs." Without even looking at the bodies he swung his arm, like a door, for the villagers to see. "Report these outsiders. It is your duty, as Chinese, to keep China strong. To keep it from foreign filth. Do not become weak and feeble minded. It is your duty and it is the law."

With that he walked through the crowd and climbed back into his military vehicle. The rest of the soldiers followed and climbed into trucks and transports. Soon the rumblings and smell of diesel were gone.

All that remained of their presence were the dead.

Kim went to a military academy as a child and was owned by the state. He learned to blame the missionaries for the deaths of his family. They came in and left. Behind them was death, destruction, and heartache. As Kim grew he was recognized by the state for his military mind. It didn't take long for the grooming process to begin for a service of military duty.

Kim moved through the ranks quickly. His reputation for having an iron fist spread throughout the ranks as well as his devotion towards the soldiers. Every soldier knew that if you did your job, Commander Kim would protect you as much as possible. You didn't do your job, well, you may as well write your death sentence. Throughout the years soldiers have turned up missing and never to be found.

Kim stared at the report. Fury was rising in him as a lifetime of revenge, hatred, and blame swirled. Kim's secret mission, not even his superiors knew about, was to stamp out Christianity in China. He gathered his best officers, the ones most devoted to Kim and to China, and they were to hunt down these missionaries.

With both hands placed upon his desk and failure looming up at him questions were bombarding his brain.

Kim looked at the report again. The first sentence said it all: "China has the fastest growing Christian conversions of any country in the world."

Time for a new game plan thought Kim.

HONOLULU, HAWAII

Carl could handle traveling overseas if it stayed like this. The trio had a three day layover in Hawaii before moving onto Cambodia. Carl decided to take advantage of the opportunity to sightsee and relax. Now with the sun easing its way into the water Carl decided that he now found his favorite place on earth.

As he layed on the beach he contemplated the findings in Utah. In his eyes, and also Cathy and John's, there was proof of man with dinosaurs. What confused Carl was surely they were not the first ones to discover this. But what if they were? They had just left the evidence without reporting to proper authorities. Wasn't there some scientific protocol for announcing findings?

He pulled out his laptop and began to search around. After a lengthy thirty minutes he found something. It seems that many professors and scientists are aware of the strange petroglyphs. It has even been reported in scientific journals.

Why hasn't it been made public thought Carl?

He continued the search. Across the southwest there were many petroglyphs that showed similar markings and from different tribes. Tribes from New Mexico to California and from Wyoming to Texas showed similar petroglyphs.

Carl leaned back into his white plastic recliner. There is concrete evidence of dinosaurs with man. Drawings from many tribes, many different people, from the same time period show the same thing. Carl was no lawyer but it seems the evidence was strong in providing a case.

There were many questions he needed to ask Cathy and John. They were the scientists. He was the religious nut. Carl had to laugh. It seems like the nut is the one doing the cracking this time.

Carl flipped the laptop down and enjoyed the orange orb sinking into the blue waters. The breeze off the ocean blowing the right amount of paradise over him.

One of Carl's favorite songs popped into his head and lasted until he could see the sun no more.

My God is an awesome God. He comes from heaven above. He rules with power and love. My God is an awesome God.

John studied his notes with those of Mike's. Among the scattered notes was a Bible that John picked up in the airport at San Francisco. Already in the Bible were passages highlighted, underlined, with notes and questions in the margins. For a book that was purchased only two days ago it had the wear and tear of many years.

Mike's notes mentions over and over again the evidence of dinosaurs among humans. It was this evidence that kept disturbing John.

What gnawed at John was the fact that he didn't know this piece of information was out there. He did his research and kept up with the latest journals. Had even published numerous times and received the attention due him.

But somehow. Someway. This information was hidden. It caused John to question his entire career. What else was hidden from him? What else was covered up?

Was Carl right in that there was a God? That maybe, just maybe the earth is young and that it did only take six days?

Laying on the bed was that Bible from San Francisco. It was just a book. It had some good morals to teach to people and some inspiring stories John thought. John highlighted the stories on the plane that he remembered from Sunday school; Jonah and the whale, Noah's Ark, the Jesus stories.

Now it seemed to beckon him, like it wanted to show more. Give more. As John sat in the hotel room's office chair he felt geniunely afraid. A gut feeling that if he opened that book his life, his world, would change forever.

And he fought it. The thought of a life change made his stomach churn. But the curiosity flowed through every fiber of his being. What is it that the book wants to tell me thought John.

He got up and paced around the room. The hum of the fan was the only sound in the room. Every other step had John glancing at the book on the bed. It was getting late but John was at a war. His mind and heart were battling it out. Common sense and curiosity were waging back and forth.

It was just a book.

John found himself sweating. He also picked up an old habit from his days in college. He had long ago dropped it until this point. He glanced down to find himself chewing his nails. The idea of being revolted didn't encourage him to stop.

Back and forth. Back and forth.

Like a child on the end of the dock wondering if the water is cold or not, the best way to find out is to just jump in. John sat on the bed and grabbed the Bible. He found himself shaking and tears coming down his face.

"What is happening to me," he thought.

Both hands were wrapped around the brown covered book. Memories of his childhood rushed from the recesses of his mind. Grandpa singing Amazing Grace out of tune but with all the love he had in his heart. Grandma cooking elaborate meals for the potlucks and dissapointed if she had to take food home. Mom spending Saturday nights preparing for the Sunday school lesson the next day. John remembered ripping out stories from books, organizing the materials for the art project, and sharpening pencils. Saturday mornings dad would be out there on the John Deere lawnmower ensuring a perfectly cut lawn for the worshippers on Sunday. John liked Sundays as it was the only day his dad dressed up. When service was over John would head to the church's kitchen and grab his dad a cup of coffee. Black. No cream. He would carefully walk it back to his dad who would already be in conversation with other men from the church.

What happened to me?

John sat there and held this plain looking book in his hands and felt immense guilt. Trembling he opened the book. He was at the book of Luke and came across one of Jesus' parables. As John read he felt the guilt of not recognizing God before. John recognized that he was rebelling. There was also relief.

For through the story of the Prodigal Son John bowed his head and accepted Jesus. The tears a moment ago of guilt became tears of joy. Alone in a hotel room, far away from any loved ones and friends, John felt more connected than he did in any other time in his life.

For the rest of the night John continued to read and continued to cry the tears of joy.

SALT LAKE CITY

It didn't take long for Xi to realize that he had already missed the trio. He wasn't upset or angry. He just accepted this as part of the hunt. Staring down on the Mormon Temple in downtown Salt Lake he let a smile cross his face.

The world considered him crazy and dangerous. Insane. The idea of killing people for the joy of it made most of the world repulsed.

Xi knew better.

Most of the world was weak. Each country and groups of people had their religion. The Middle East had Muslim and Islam. The United States were Christians. The European continent were Catholics. The far East had Hinduism and Buddism. It was through these religions that people justified wars and judging others. It was through people's faith that they condemned and justified their actions of cruelty. Xi knew that the only way people were able to do these actions was as a mob. By themselves a person would denounce their faith to save their own skin.

Xi knew that he controlled his own fate. When he killed he was rewarded. When he executed cruelty it was for a purpose. And when he acted he was alone.

Xi wondered who were the hypocrites in the world? Who were the weak ones? Who radiated more fear into people, monsters who hid among the people or organized religions?

He was surprising himself in that he never considered himself on the philosophic side. He was a weapon. He was paid to do jobs and he did with great effectiveness.

Seeing the light bounce off the white temple made Xi wonder what ugliness was hidden inside. He saw the temple like people; clean on the outside, dirty, lying, manipulating on the inside.

Xi closed the hotel curtain and went to bed. The thoughts quickly went away and Xi enjoyed a restful night of sleep. Tomorrow was going to be an exciting day.

CAMBODIA- 1198 A.D.

King Jayavarman stood upon the grand balcony and took in the glorious site. Four years ago he gathered his engineers and archectects to build a great temple monastery. The land was leveled out, the resources were sought after and brought in, and the hundreds of workers were gathered. Now, the great temple that would be the focal point of the monastery was nearing completion.

After the death of his wife, Princess Jayarajadevi, religion took on a greater importance in his life. His beliefs were always strong and the values guided his leadership but he wanted something monumental. The monument was before him.

It stood as a finger pointing to the sky. Even the sun was blocked out by this great edifice. Yayavarman had seen many things in his life so it took much to take his breath away.

This time it did.

A great shadow was cast upon the farmlands and jungle of vines and trees. Jayavarman hoped that his shadow would also be cast; through generations of people and that his legacy would be great and powerful. It was one of the reasons for this fantastic endeavor.

Even though it was early in the morning the sounds of metal hitting rock, workers grunting, and animals baying could already be heard. These sounds were melodious to Jayavarman. Each rock and person is a testament to his religious belief. At this moment King Jayavarman felt powerful, strong, and mighty yet humble as the teachings of Budha would state.

The moment soon passed as a new sound carried over the jungle. The sounds of metal and workers came to an abrupt stop. Silence soon followed as hundreds waited in anticipation. Each person knew what the sound was. Even the king recognized the powerful sound.

Each second that passed weighed heavy in the air. A hammer could be heard that broke the silence. A few more began to bang at rock when the roar came through again. This time workers were standing, agitated, and scared. The roar seemed closer.

Jayavarman scanned the jungle looking for moving trees, listening for footsteps, anything that would indicate a position. Nothing in the jungle seemed out of place, yet the jungle was a mystery unto itself. Jayavarman was determined to conquer the jungle with roads connecting his kingdom. He truly wanted to serve the people and connecting the towns seemed logical. But the jungle held her secrets. Once in awhile a secret would slip out. This was such a time.

Soldiers quickly gathered and awaited orders. These men were trained to deal with the beast. It took a special man to go after a monster with only a spear. But teamwork, experience, and training had saved many lives. The soldiers waited with anticipation.

"There. There it is. It is in that direction." A lookout pointed and yelled to the soldiers below.

Immediately the soldiers disappeared into the jungle of vines. The beast was close now. Workers dropped their hammers and tools to move to the far side of the construction site.

A growl echoed through the air and sent chills through Jayavarman. The beast was close. Very close. The snapping of trees could be heard distinctly now. Fear rose among the workers. Still, the blanket of jungle hid the beast.

Jayavarman knew the beast was going to make it to the construction site. The question was how much damage the beast was going to inflict. He prayed to Budha that the soldiers would kill the beast before any damage could be done.

Jayavarman stared again at the great finger pointing to the sky. Would it survive the beast attack?

A great crashing of trees and leaping out into the open was the beast. Jayvarman admired the great size and power of the beast. It commanded respect and fear. Jayvarman wanted those qualities for himself. He knew that some people did not respect him. Some people only did things because of his position. But to command respect as one enters a room or group of people, Jayvarman could only imagine what that would be like.

The beast scanned the new environment around him. Its rounded head swept back and forth. The tail, a length of seven soldiers, snapped back and forth. Expanding in and out was the huge stomach. Jayavarman was shocked to see the beast resemble his boy's cat. Like a cat, the beast methodically analyzed the new situation it was in. It seemed to determine what the next best move was going to be.

A screeching yell escaped its great mouth as spears came flying from the jungle. The soldiers had arrived. Jayavarman and the workers gazed upon the dance now before them. The beast swung its body around to gain a visual on its attackers. Before it could get its bearings two soldiers leaped from the trees onto the beast's back. With two hands each soldier rammed a large spear, eight foot long, into the back of the beast's neck.

The beast roared and reared upon its hind legs. Jayavarman had seen elephants stand on hind legs. That was pale in comparison to the display currently shown. The two soldiers fell off. With a step back from the beast, as it gained balance, its foot stepped on one of the soldiers instantly crushing the man's rib cage. Spears flew with great velocity towards the belly of the beast. The roars of pain and fury swallowed all other sounds. Unable to remain on its hind legs for any length of time the beast crashed back to standing on four legs. The ground vibrated and caused some workers to stumble and fall over. Jayvarman had to grab the railing as his palace felt the vibration.

The giant finger in the sky swayed causing the shadow to shift back and forth.

As the beast landed the spears in the belly rammed even further. The screeching caused those closest to it to cup their ears. Workers began to pray as the sound was unlike any they had heard before. But it would be the last great sound of the beast.

Blood flowed from its great belly and towards the great pinnacle. Jayvarman watched with great amazement as the spears continued to fly towards the beast making it look like a great porcupine. The beast tried to fight back. After a few moments it began to sway like a drunkard. The soldiers now came from the protection of the forest to look the beast eye to eye. With one last final effort the beast attacked two soldiers who were standing close together. In a flash each man was crushed.

Seconds later the beast's breath was staggering. Gasping with hard rapid breaths. The workers became brave and cautiously made their way towards the beast. For most of them this was the closest they had even been to a great beast.

The beast had fallen to its side. More spears dug themselves deeper into the flesh. Blood poured from the nose and mouth. Shallow breaths exited.

Jayavarman had come down from his balcony and stood with the workers and soldiers and gazed upon the mighty beast. It took twenty well trained soldiers to bring down one beast. Three had lost their lives.

Jayvarman respected the animal before him. So much strength. So much power.

It was for these reasons that he loved this animal above all others. While others feared it, he respected. While others fleed, he stayed to watch. Now, here he was looking down upon the beast, dying, struggling.

Jayavarman walked around the beast. Its belly was taller than Jayavarman. Its length was longer than ten grown men. The legs were as thick as the trees of the forest.

When Jayavarman completed his circle the beast was dead.

The sounds of the jungle returned. Birds chirped. Insects buzzed. Jayavarman ordered the workers back to work. Not with a commanding voice but a voice of respect. He knew he was like them. A man. A man lucky enough to have the position of king. He knew a time would come when he too would pass away like this beast.

Surely a beast as powerful as this would leave a lasting legacy. Its kind would survive all other animals. He stared at the great spire. He hoped that he would also leave a lasting and powerful legacy. One that would last many generations.

SIEM REAP, CAMBODIA – ANGKOR ARCHAELOGICAL PARK

Cathy had heard of Angkor. It was composed of towering spires, temples, palaces, libraries, and monasteries. She tried to compare it to other structures from other similar civilizations such as the Mayas and the Incas. Nothing could prepare her for what she saw at Ankgor.

The emerald colored ruins that were the courtyard. The Bayon Face with its flat nose and green algae colored eyebrows overlooked the courtyard. Carved into a stone ws a woman dressed as a dancer holding snakes in each hand.

Cathy knew that Angkor Thom was the last and most enduring capital city of the Khmer Empire and that King Jayavarman began the construction of Angkor. Many kings and rulers added onto the site as they ruled. Today, the buildings are considered in ruins. Cathy was heartened by the fact that restoration of these sites were underway. With the recent history of the Cambodian people they needed a source of pride. Angkor was that source, a shining example of the powerful history of the Cambodian people.

As Carl, John, and Cathy exited their taxi they spotted the Terrace of Elephants. Cathy explained to the other two that from this terrace King Jayavarman would stand to view the returning victorious armies. While amazement was etched into each face it didn't take long for the three to remember why they were there.

John pulled out a map of the park. From where they were standing they needed to head due north to Ta Prohm. According to Mike's notes they needed to search for a huge stone entrance. The notes didn't say why but only that Mike had heard that there was something of interest there. Given the size of the park the three began the trek.

While Carl was used to physical activity nothing could prepare him for the humidity and the heat. Much as he tried to keep his t-shirt from sticking to him he found that it was a losing battle. Sweat dripped off of each face and evidence of underarm pools showed on each persons well. The air was humming with the sounds of the insects and bugs that populated the area. Carl's fear of being overseas was taking root. His gut was telling him to encourage the others to get in and out as soon as possible. He had heard of the leftover rebels from the nineteen seventies. Men and women who still believed in genocide. Once in awhile a high profile kidnappign would happen to remind the people of Cambodia that they were still around and to be taken seriously.

John enjoyed the walk between the two shimmering pools. The dirt walkway split the greenest grass that he had ever seen. Between two trees he spotted a platform. He imagined it to be used by ancient monks or priests. He took in the oblong faces with frowns forever etched. Each face was different from the others. One such face had a three tiered hair piece. John guessed he was royalty.

Since last night John felt lighter in his step. A newness of the world worked itself into John's being. He still wasn't sure what to expect but he had already noticed small changes. He couldn't wait until the proper time to talk to Carl. He had many questions and the fire to learn was burning strong. He was hoping for tonight. Anticipation was replacing caffeine as the method of staying alert and awake.

The three were within ten meters of To Prohm. The temple was staggering. Already, just after mid-day, the shadow cast a long. Many other tourist huddled in that great shadow and took in the relief from the heat. It wasn't until the Carl, John, and Cathy got closer that they truly appreciated what Mike had to say about the huge stone entrance. Huge was an understatement.

From twenty meters out Xi watched the three. He found the humidity comforting as it reminded him of his hometown in China. Gazing upon the three's faces it was easy to see that they were out of their element. Sweat. Constant drinking of water. Daydreaming. All signs of weakness.

It didn't take Xi long to figure out where the three were headed after Utah. By playing the fourth member of their exploration group he was able to find out about airlines, destinations, and arrivals. The always courteous check in people would rather help a person out than have open and direct confrontation. It was on this that Xi depended on.

Weakness.

It was easy to get the reservations for a flight from Salt Lake City to

San Francisco and from there directly to Cambodia. Everyone who comes to Cambodia, whether they intend it or not, stops in to view Angkor. It truly was a wonderful sight.

Even Xi had to admire the handiwork of the place. He respected the kings who built temples to themselves. The pharoh's of Egypt had the right idea. Build your burying place big, build it strong, and build it with slaves. Talk about adding insult to injury.

Now, Xi watched the three meander up to Ta Prohm. They had the look of tourist; t-shirts, cameras, and out of fashion sun glasses. Unlike the tourist these three headed away from the shade and beelined it towards the massive stone entrance on the west side of the temple.

Xi decided to wait. Be patient. Let's see what the three will do. The time for attack will come soon enough. Depending on long the three stick around the shadows and the jungle will provide enough protection to stay hidden. It will him to attack and hide quickly.

Yes, Xi decided, patience will do nicely now. The time will come soon enough.

DALLAS, TEXAS

It has been a difficult forty eight hours for Dr. Curtis Trough. The twelve have never been so split as they were when Dr. Randy Johnson received the phone call. In his mind it was quite obvious, let the three know about the danger they are in and pull them back. The decision was made, pray for the three and God will protect them.

Added onto the stress was the homefront. His teenage daughter was pregant and his marriage was flailing. His reputation as both a national speaker on fatherhood and family were in peril. He knew that his seat among the twelve would be lost. His book deals would be voided. Dr. Trough despised the fact that he would have to become a regular church pastor. The thought of preparing weekly sermons and attending potlucks made him queasy.

He enjoyed the life that he made for himself. He truly believed that he was saved but along the way of gaining more on his education, writing books, and becoming a Christian celebrity hindered his main focus.

He knew his daughter's pregancy was his fault. For many years he threatened all members of is family if they didn't act perfect, say the right things, or look like the model family. There were many nights of crying and yelling as the stress of being perfect took its toll.

In public the deception looked real enough. Hand in hand Curtis and his wife Kathleen would stride across the stage, smiling and waving to the thousands in the crowd. Walking behind them would be his oldest daughter; Emily, the one currently pregnant, their son Jonathan, and their youngest Sharon. Each smile was a mask of verbal abuse, deep emotional scars, and indescribable hurts.

Curtis knew that his house of cards was falling apart. A sense of hopelesness attacked him and no amount of education or experience was going to get him out of this mess that he created.

He knew what was coming down the road. The tabloids and magazines would splash his and Emily's picture across their covers. News networks would call asking for interviews. Sooner or later, through no fault of anybody, somebody would slip on the abuse and the cycle would start again.

Curtis thought about how to make things right with his family. Spending time with each child, getting to know who they were, their interest. It saddened him to not know any of his child's likes and dislikes. He couldn't remember the last time he spent time with Jonathan. The boy was becoming a man and Curtis was missing it.

Time was something that one could never get back.

Curtis prided himself on being a team player but he did not agree with the twelve. For once in his life he decided to do what he considered the right thing. He knew he had to start somewhere. Through his connections with the FBI Curtis managed to get ahold of former Green Beret named David Ford. David was specifically trained in assasination techniques as well as protection services.

Perfect thought Curtis.

After a lunch meeting David agreed to the terms set forth by Curtis. Yesterday David flew off to Cambodia. Curtis hoped that David would arrive in time.

Curtis knew his time was short with the Twelve. Going behind their back wasn't going to cause him to lose any sleep. Curtis just hoped that others would see that his intentions were right, that he did care about others and not just about himself.

Folding his hands behind his head Curtis focused on the media backlash that he was going to soon be facing.

The phone rang and caller ID let him know it was from home. Later he thought. I have more important things to do.

Kathleen heard Curtis' phone ring seven times. She was used to him not answering his phone. Still, the call was important. She was just notified that Johnathan was just booked into the local jail for the possession and distrubution of meth. As she hung up the phone she stared down at the stack of papers in front of her. It seemed that there was no way to reconcile with Curtis. No way to reach him anymore. Grabbing the pen she signed her name on the divorce papers.

SIEM RIEP CAMBODIA – ANGKOR ARCHEALOGICAL PARK

John examined the roundels that surrounded that were on the pilasters surrounding the west entrance. There were the common animals of the area; monkeys, water buffaloes, roosters, pigs and snakes. One in particular kept John's attention. On the south side of the west entrance, about six feet high was a strange roundel. It was peculiar in that it did not represent any animals that were common to the area. John examined each roundel again just to test a hypothesis. Each roundel show real animals, no mythological creatures, no dragons which is common for this part of the world, but real animals. John went back to the strange, out of place roundel.

"Carl. Cathy. I think I have something over here." Carl and Cathy were studying other parts of Angkor Thom. Upon hearing John's voice both came rushing over. "What do you think of this?"

Cathy sqinted to where John was pointing. Inside the roundel was an animal that had four legs. It had a tail swooping down to its feet. The head had anelongated face. While all the roundels had faceless features it was strange to see this one because it already seemed foreign.

"What is it," asked Carl. He too was squinting and twisting his head from side to side hoping that these movements would somehow improve the roundel's picture.

"I guessing, only guessing, that what we are looking at is a stegosaurus." John could hardly believe that the words escaped his own mouth.

The stegosaurus was the size of a school bus. Plates stood up on end on its back to protect itself from its meat eating predators. At the tail's end stood razor sharp spikes called thagomizers. This was the animal's main offensive weapon. The tail would swing with such velocity that many predators would leave with bloody legs and limping. Only the most hungry would stick around and fight for a meal.

"Wait just a minute. That is a pretty big assumption. How did you come to that conclusion?" Cathy said these things while staring at the roundel. Her guess was also of a stegosaurus but it seemed so ridiculous that she dismissed the idea. To hear it come another person's mouth shocked her.

"Listen. I know it sounds absurd. Trust me when I say that I can't believe it myself. But look at the tail. I thought at first it was one of those giant ancient pigs. Scientist have shown over and over again that those pigs had the short tails that present day pigs have. Then there is the horse-shaped head. Its unusual shape isn't one of any animal that I know of in today's world. I know that these drawings are not to scale but if this roundel was made at the same time as the others, then how come we can identify all the others but not this one? It seems that despite what we want to think, we have another piece that shows evidence of a dinosaur."

"That's impossible. This temple was built eight hundred years ago. You are telling me that dinosaurs were around in as little as eight hundred years ago." There was an uncontrollable shakiness to Cathy's voice. The realization of human and dinosaurs coexisting sent Cathy's emotions into a tailspin.

"Actually, I would say less than that." Carl interjected. "Who is to say when the dinosaurs actually died out around here? This part of the world was largely undocumented and uncharted till the last two hundred years."

"Stop right there cowboy. If you are telling me that dinosaurs existed up till two hundred years ago you are officially crazy and I know of places for people like you."

"That's not exactly what I am saying." Carl knew he better choose his words carefully. To misspeak would take more time and effort to clarify what he intended to say. "What I am saying is that they could have lasted anytime from the last two hundred years to the last eight hundred years. Anytime during that time span they could have disappeared for any number of reasons."

"Are you hearing yourselves? You are saying that dinosaurs existed with people. That within the last thousand years of human history that dinosaurs existed with people. This is absurd. Do you think anyone is going to take you seriously?"

"Someone took your father seriously. Enough to have him send his findings to two different groups of people." John turned away and stared into nothing. "I'm beginning to think that your father's death was no accident. I believe that someone else knew about your father's findings and understood its implications."

Despite the humidity and heat Cathy turned cold. For the second time someone stated what she thought but wasn't brave enough to state it. Now, within a time span of a couple of minutes, two unthinkable thoughts were spouted and she couldn't think of anything to say.

"Hear me out," John continued. "What if someone got ahold of this information that didn't agree with that information? All three of us can think of organizations, groups, and businesses that would be devasted by these pieces of evidence. Billions of dollars and thousands of jobs worldwide depend on holding to the fact that dinosaurs existed millions of years before man came upon the earth. The entire world culture believes that statement to be true. But what if it isn't?"

The words hung there.

"Are you saying that we, the entire world, are living a lie?"

John pondered her words. How long had he been living a lie? Up until yesterday he had lived a lie for the last forty-five years. "That is exactly what I am saying."

A zing sent pieces of rock up into the air. A pop sound followed. It took only a second for them to realize that they were being shot at. Like mice being exposed to light the three scattered into different directions.

Xi couldn't believe he missed. He knew that he would only get one of the group so he aimed for the tall white man. There was no particular reason why only that he seemed the smartest. By taking out the brains he would be able to slow down the expedition.

The shot though missed its target.

What should have been a lethal shot turned out to be a foghorn. It gave a warning and reinforced the theory that they were being followed and their lives were in danger.

Xi cursed under his breath and packed up the assassin rifle. The time for killing would have to wait until a different time and a different place.

Within minutes Xi was walking the broad walkways around Angkor. Looking like a tourist Xi exited the park and headed toward the airport. From there he would know of the trio's next destination.

David turned from looking at the Terrace of Elephants toward the popping sound. The hunt was on. He figured that the assassin would try to blend into the crowd. While it would make things difficult it would not be impossible.

Things were becoming more interesting.

BEIJING, CHINA

Kim hated to attend parties. There was so much overcoating that it made him sick. All the mover and shakers were trying to outdo each other and trying to prove themselves. It disgusted him.

Kim learned long ago to come to these get togethers. A military is closely tied to its business partners. Business meant networking whether it was golf courses, island get aways, or parties. It was through this networking that Kim was able to get the latest in nano technology to be able to use for survelliance from the Chin-Yo Corporation. By letting the owner of China telecommunications win a few rounds of gold Kim was able to tap into every server in the world.

He also knew that business ran both ways. Kim had to guarantee that these corporations, meaning the head honchos, received their just monetary rewards. So far Kim was able to convince his superiors that these necessary purchases strengthened China's capability to defend itself and also be to aggressive if necessary.

Kim attended tonight's party sponsored by business executive Tu Long. Long made a fortune on developing ways of purifying water. Third world countries as well as international powerhouses sought his technology and patents. There was even talk that Long was finding ways of using water in weapons. If this was to happen, the country that controlled that would dominate the seas and oceans.

Kim kept Long's name high on the mental list.

But Kim was not here for Long. He was seeking a different individual. China was beginning to break and fracture under the influence of foreign ideas. Capitalism, women's rights, and religion were invading China and weakening her. What truly angered Kim was that it was being allowed by China's leaders. Kim was seeking a Benjamin Bortho, the American ambassador.

Kim had dealings with Bortho before. It was always business dealings or politics. Tonight Kim wanted to know Bortho on the social side, to make him more open and hopefully gain a foothold to more information for the future.

Kim spotted the American. Dressed in a tuxedo Bortho's white hair and blue eyes matched the suit with the cumberbund. As a former basketball player it was easy to spot the former forward amongst the other dignitaries and business people. Kim knew the man was polite and geniune. He also knew the man was steely strong. Many people thought they could manipulate the man based off of how he presented himself and found themselves completely surprised by the heavy hand of Bortho.

Kim made it his duty to study every ally and foe. He was also positive that Bortho had undergone the same process with Kim.

Kim worked his way through the crowd. He told several women that they looked lovely tonight. Given and received several handshakes as well as a few pats on the back. One young man even wanted his picture taken with Kim. After twisting and turning his way to Bortho he finally caught up to the man. The timing was perfect.

Bortho was just finishing a conversation with a gentleman when Kim happened to walk into the man's place.

"Good evening Ambassdor Bortho. Do you remember me? I am Commander We Mine Kim. Most people call me Kim." Kim knew that the ambassador would remember him. Kim wanted to come across as humble, patient.

"Ah yes. Commander Kim. How are you this fine evening?"

"Quite well. Thank you. I see that you are doing good?" Kim stated it as a question to help keep conversation going.

"Yes. Things are going well on my end. I was thinking to myself the other day that I wanted to meet up with you. It seems that we run into each other with business but never in a casual meeting."

The man is reading my mind thought Kim.

"Between you and me. I hate parties. I only attend these things for the networking aspect and because the job requires it." Bortho continued, "But I have been wanting to talk to you about some ideas on joint ventures between the Chinese military and the American military. Our two countries have been striving closer together in recent years. It seems in the last few that acceleration has increased to lightenng speed."

"I couldn't agree more." Kim fought hard to say this without it coming across as venomous. Keep it positive, flowing he thought.

"It is wonderful to see China becoming more open to ideas. I never thought I would see this happen in my lifetime."

"Nor mine," Kim was speaking the truth. He never thought he would see his beloved country falter and weaken itself to appease to other countries.

"I would love to meet with you sometime to discuss some opportunities if you have the time." With that Bortho handed Kim a card.

Kim knew through intelligence how to get connected with anybody. Politely and with thankfulness Kim took the business card. "I will make the time. Can I contact you in the next couple of days Ambassador Bortho?"

"Absolutely. Enjoy the rest of the evening. I can't wait till this is over." With that the ambassdor shook hands with Kim and moved onto another conversation.

Kim stood there with a card in one hand and red wine in the other. Kim finished his glass of wine and walked over to the serving table to set the glass down. Tonight's mission was a success. Kim eyed the exit and knew that he no longer had to be at the party. Hanging onto the card Kim began the dance again of weaving through the crowd, shaking hands, congratulating women, and patting backs.

Once outside Kim inhaled the cool fresh air. It was refreshing compared to the stale air of inside. Kim climbed into the backseat of black car and ordered his driver to take him home.

Laying his head back and closing his eyes he thought back to his childhood of running and playing on a playground. The sun warmed his face and encouraged youthful activity. Every child was enjoying each other's company. Chasing and running after each other. Kim longed for another day in his life where he could be carefree and loosen the shackles of responsibility.

Someone had to defend China.

Kim let out a long breath and opened his eyes. He was within a block of his home. Get plenty of sleep tonight he thought. Tomorrow is another day to wage the battle.

SIEM REIP, CAMBODIA

The table overlooked the city and jungle. It wasn't hard to miss the jungle since it surrounded the city. Around the table Carl, Cathy, and John were just finishing their meals. Each knew that they had to regroup, gain on a foothold on what happened today, and decide the next step.

The shooting left them more confused than scared. Even Carl, whose fear of being overseas, wasn't sure how to interpret today's events. They knew that what they were uncovering was disastrous to many entities. But was it worth killing over?

What they didn't know was if they were the targets of today's shooting. Each wanted to accept the fact that that it was random. Deep in the recesses of their minds they wouldn't bet money on that fact.

Clearing away the plates, which meant piling them up in the middle of the hotel room's desk, the three gathered together their notes.

Carl didn't hesitate about getting down to business. "I believe that there is clear evidence that Mike was right, there were dinosaurs roaming around at the same time as humans. We may not know the exact time period, yet, but we have at least a range. In historical terms that is pretty good."

John felt obligated to jump in, "We have two different sites stating the same thing. Based off of this I feel confident that the rest of Mike's documentation will say the same thing. But..."

Cathy knew what John was thinking, "what about the possibility of someone coming after us."

John nodded. "I have been debating about this and the same thought keeps popping up in my mind. We need to split up."

Carl and Cathy stared in shock. So far each member had contributed significant information.

"Here is what I am thinking. By splitting up we can first protect ourselves and able to get information faster," John stated. He had a sheepish look, hoping that the other two would buy into his theory.

Carl mulled over John's proposal. "I agree. It may be dangerous to separate but even more to stay together. With us separated we throw a curve ball to whoever may have shot at us. Plus we buy ourselves some time."

Being her usual self Cathy was more skeptical. "What about strength in numbers? Birds of a feather flock together?" It was clear to John and Carl that fear had emerged itself into Cathy.

"We can stay in contact with each other by satellite phones. We also have email accounts. Plus if we can promise each other to contact at set times we can hold each other accountable and provide encouragement." Carl was trying to lift Cathy's spirits by staying positive. He hoped it was working.

John leaned forward and Cathy couldn't help but look into the puppy dog eyes. "I know you are scared. I am too. But something big is happening here. Something tells me that time is short and we need to obtain all the information we can. I don't want your father's work, and death, to go in vain."

Cathy looked away. Embarassement. Fear. Confusion. She knew deep down that John was right. Still, facts were a miserable way to comfort a person. "Fair enough. How do we split up?"

Xi paced up and down the airport terminals. He had expected the trio to come rushing into the airport and leave Cambodia right away. Four hours later there was no sign of them. Xi now considered the fact that the trio went into hiding. Maybe they had a different escape route; boat, private plane, seaplane. Or maybe they just retreated back to their hotel room, wherever that may be.

Xi weighed his options. This would be considered a failure. Not good. It's not that Commander Kim handled failure well, in fact, he handled it quite well. The person was punished until they learned the meaning of failure.

Xi had heard the stories. A thousand pricks of hot steel throughout your body was one of Kim's favorites. Kim also enjoyed the classics such as Chinese water torture. The physical pain Xi could handle. It was the mental tortures that he feared the most. The idea of losing one's sanity, perhaps never to claim it back again made Xi want to go AWOL right away.

No he thought. The hunt is only beginning. They will need to go through here eventually. A boat is too slow. Sea planes have limited range.

With this comforting thought he rested in one of the reclining chairs for those visitors with long layovers. Patience will always be rewarded he thought.

David pretended to study the arrival and departure signs. He followed Xi here from Angkor Archaeological Park. David noticed that Xi was the only person running around with a carrying case. While Xi was running around like many of the other people, he lacked the fear in the eyes that everyone else had. To the untrained eye Xi looked like part of the crowd, but to David's eyes Xi stuck out like an elephant amongst poodles. David knew that Xi was waiting for the trio.

David was given strict directions; don't let the trio know who you are and why you are there. Find their potential assassin and protect them. David had full confidence he had found the assassin. He glanced over at the chairs again. There he sat, the assassin, resting and waiting.

I can wait too thought David. I can wait too.

SEIM REIP, CAMBODIA

It was getting late but Carl believed that they were close to finishing up the loose ends. It was already decided to let John go to the next piece of evidence. He had the background and knowledge to interpret it. Plus the fact he did the last two helped his case.

Carl was to interview a scientist on these findings. He was to bring the evidence forward and listen to what scholar had to say. John and Cathy both wanted the evidence to be verified before they moved forward too much farther.

The debate came when Cathy was also supposed to go to another scholar. Carl admired her grit when she explained, then argued, then was on the verge of fighting with John that she was a field person. She let him know that her entire career was digging in the dirt and seeking out the lost relics and bones. John's soothing, controlled voice only made Cathy more agitated.

John, Carl could tell, was not used to dealing with strong women. At one point during the conversation Carl let a smile come across his face. He knew from the get go that John would not win this argument but it was fun to watch him go through the pressure cooker that was Cathy. John used facts. He explained with common sense. But Carl knew that a passioned woman didn't care about those things. And a strong passionate woman will fight to the death.

Finally John relented. The battle was over and Cathy won.

John decided that he would go to Australia. With so many unique creatures and an unusual history he could see that Mike would have them going there next. Cathy was going to a site in China. According to Mike's notes the idea of fossilization was also being challenged. This intrigued Cathy and she wanted to be the one to investigate. Carl was heading to Peru.

Carl sensed that each person was relieved that decisions were made and a plan in place. As John and Cathy exited his room to go to their own rooms Carl felt a great sense of friendship being built between them. Just as Carl's door was about to shut the door stopped and swung back open. Carl was surprised to see John enter back into the room. Carl assumed that John forgot something.

"Carl. Do you have a few minutes?"

Carl, through his training and experience as a pastor, could read turmoil on faces. "Absolutely. What can I do for you?"

John took a seat across the table from Carl. He explained the Bible back in Utah and then how he bought one in San Francisco. He stated how the evidence was convicting him and challenging every bit of learning that he had gained. Carl saw tears dropping from John's face as John continued to stare at the table and talk. Finally John got to the time when he accepted Jesus Christ as his savior.

Carl couldn't hold back his happiness. It was his turn for tears of joy.

John was hoping for this kind of reaction. He was nervous about talking to Carl about this but he knew he had to. Someone had to know and Carl was the logical one.

Throughout the night Carl walked John discussed their faith. Many times John struggled with the fact that God punishes but Carl explained that God is just and cannot let sin and wrong actions go unheeded. John had to hear in many different explanations that bad things happen to Christians as well. He thought since he became a Christian that life would be easier, God would take care of him, things would be alright. Carl explained that God doesn't operate that way. God does bring peace within a storm. That as a Christian our perspective on events changes. We begin to see things God's way. We learn patience and humbleness. This is a part of living out God's will for us.

As the sun etched upwards over the jungle Carl and John realized that their discussion would have to come to an end. Today they would depart ways. Carl promised John that as they communicated on their progress of seeking out evidence that he would also pray and check on John's spiritual walk as well.

Carl stood up and went over to John. Placing his hand on John's soldier he prayed, " My father in heaven. How wonderful you are. You are the beginning and the end. It was you who brought us together in this place and on this journey. You brought us together for a reason and I want to thank you. I thank you for my brother John. I pray that you strengthen him in his new faith. Guard him and put a hedge around him. I also pray that you provide me with the discipline to be his discipler. Give me the patience, knowledge, and wisdom to mentor John but also the love to have him as a friend. As we depart today I pray you protect all three of us. Allow what we are doing as a way of worshipping you and bring you praise. Bless our journey. Through your son Jesus Christ we pray, amen."

As both men looked up tears filled their eyes. The alarm clock reminded them that it was time to get ready for their day.

As John left to go to his room Carl thanked God again for this journey. Even if they found no evidence whatsoever John had become a believer in Christ. A host of angels celebrated in heaven and another soul was saved from the depths of hell.

Carl sent up another prayer of thanksgiving but now prayed for Cathy.

DALLAS, TEXAS

At two in the morning one could search the refridgerator full of food and still not find anything to eat. Not that Troy Reiner was that hungry. He munched on some of the macademian nut cookies his twelve year old daughter made and washed it down with some milk. His stomach had the munchies but nothing looked appealing.

The evening news announced the shooting in Cambodia at Angkor. The announcement turned Troy's stomach inside out and he had to leave the meeting with the Twelve to go throw up. He knew that the shooting was aimed at Carl, John, and Cathy. He also knew that the Twelve had the power to stop it and chose to keep silent. The fact that as a group they decided to let the expedition go forward with warning the three was weighing upon him. He was one in favor of not informing the trio.

Who would possibly care about three people seeking out archaeological sites? Who would even know what their motives or purposes would be? It was under this assumption that Troy made his decision. One that he knows regret.

Now that the shooting was real and lives are at stake Troy's conscience was eating him alive.

Added into this confusion was the sudden resignation of Curtis from the Twelve. All he stated was that he needed to for personal reasons, mostly family. Troy knew Curtis for close to twelve years now and everything seemed to be alright. Troy and his wife sought Curtis when they themselves were having marital problems. That was four years ago.

Now Troy couldn't imagine being married to anyone else. The happiness and love that he shared with his wife Deborah was unlike he could imagine. He saw the improvement in his children's behavior. He found himself being more giving and less selfish. He used Curtis' techniques when he was counseling couples at his congregation.

To have Curtis leave was quite a blow. He was the one that invited

Troy into the group as well as mentored him. There were many times when the families got together and had barbeques and visits to the lake. Granted that was a couple of years ago. Recently Curtis and his family traveled around the United States and Canada. Troy chalked it up as preaching and teaching.

It was going to be Curtis that Troy was going to confide in about the trio and the situation they were in. If Curtis was leaving for family reasons it seemed unfair to burden him more with my guilty conscience thought Troy.

Again he checked the refridgerator, hoping that something would look appetizing. Again. Nothing.

Troy marched back upstairs knowing that tossing and turning would be ahead. Deborah isn't going to be too happy about this.

At the doorway the streetlamp light shone through a window and illuminated Deborah's face. So peaceful. So content.

More guilt hit Troy. Why didn't I do it before? Hurrying back downstairs he dropped to his knees. Deborah always reminded Troy of his blessings. How that God saved his marriage and is in control of all things. Doubt was entering Troy but now, now Troy was going to hand it over to God.

With a bow of his head Troy prayed. A prayer went up for Curtis and his family. A prayer went up for Carl, Cathy, and John. Another went up for the assassin. The Bible tells us to pray for our enemies. Prayer after prayer was said. Troy was shaking. Swaying. He felt the burdens being lifted. Calmness descended upon him. When he was done he was surprised to find himself sweating but smiling. He wrestled with his burdens. The man in him wanted to handle things on his own. But the real man in him knew better.

Troy gave out a low chuckle. How many times in his life did he doubt God? Then how many more times did God deliver. Not only deliver but in a fashion that was better.

Troy washed his face in the bathroom sink and went back upstairs. He climbed into bed and immediantly felt peace come upon him.

ANCIENT CHINA

The two beasts eyed each other. Across the clearing each knew what had to be done. The velociraptor opened its mouth. Razor sharp teeth lined the inside and its three razor claws seemed eager to strike. It began to circle closer to its soon to be prey. But it had to be careful. The prey was much bigger and was armed.

The protoceratops was confused. It was following the herd when a strange scent caught its attention. Following its nose rather than the safety of the herd it soon found itself here. Confronted with a meat eater that looked desperately hungry. It gave a bellow to call to the others, all the time keeping its eye on the now moving meat eater. When no bellow was returned the protoceratops lowered its head. This would be a fight to the death. A snort filled the brief silence.

Crounching down on its honches the velociraptor looked for its best opportunity to leap. With no other raptors around to compete for food, the raptor thought this was a dream come true. When the protoceratops lowered its head the raptor knew it was almost time. As the snort ended the raptor attacked.

The protoceratops had never seen such speed before. He knew exactly where the attack would happen. Neck. With that he turned and lowered his head again.

The raptor bounced off the bony protection that covered the neck of the protoceratops. Rolling back among the dirt the raptor gained its composure and returned to the fighting stance once more.

The protoceratops knew that it had won a battle but not the war. Until this meat eater was dead or dying the war was not done.

Both beast began to circle each other. Each knew the other's role. One was always going to be the defender. Using its brute strength and size in combat. The other always the aggressor. Its jumping ability and razor teeth and claws made it an offensive weapon.

At once, as though mentally each decided it was time, the attack came. Protoceratops spread its two front legs and pulled back its head. It was hoping to head butt its attacker then look to stomp on the desperate beast.

Raptor learned not to attack the neck area. Too well protected. Instead it looked for the other soft spot, the belly. The raptor jumped on the top of the plant eater and dug in its middle claw, a three inch sickle meant for digging in for running or tearing off pieces of meat.

A howl escaped the protoceratops. With the raptor on its back the battle raged.

Trees were breaking. Clouds of sand anddust rose above the tree line. Screeches and howls carried over the forest. Birds flew into the air and smaller animals scurried away towards safety.

Blood escaped both animals as each fought for its survival. Then a noise unlike anything experienced in history filled the jungle. All animals gave a silence as they strained their minds to understand this new phenomenon. Was it beneficial? Harmful? Whatever it was it was coming and coming fast. Every animals waited. Anticipated.

All but two. The raptor and the protoceratops kept fighting. Looking for an advantage over the other. In close quarters, their bellows, their growls, their snorts were the only sounds to be heard.

Skies darkened as clouds moved in and blocked the sun. In an instant day became night. The dust around the two combatants increased as the wind swept throught the jungle carrying the mysterious noise.

Snarling. Attacking, Each beast looked to its strengths.

The noise hit the jungle. Trees were ripped from the ground. Animals ran only to be caught up and swept away. Even the birds of the air couldn't escape the wave that hit them. A wall of water, as long as the tree line of the jungle barreled over the landscape. The wave hit the ground with such force a ground moved and shook the nearby mountains.

Sediment pushed up and a dirt wave was pushed ahead of the water wall. The wave of dirt covered everything in its path, instantly burying anything and everything. The wall of water rushing behind, pounding, pressurizing the ground below it. Swirling around in its torrents were animal carcasses, trees, and rocks.

The two combantants, without seeing the greater threat around them were buried. The wave of dirt hit with such force and speed each beasts' lungs filled with dirt and sand.Death was immediate for each beast.

Forever they remain together, locked in eternal combat position.

Lima, Peru

The plane banked alongside the Andes Mountains. The towering peaks was able to block the sun, clouds, and the whipping winds that come off the South American desert. Carl was able to take in the view of Lima. The capital city would just be waking up as the plane would be landing.

Carl had an appointment to meet with Dr. Juan Santiago. Dr. Santiago was a leading expert in paleontology, the study of prehistoric life. Carl checked the database on Dr. Santiago. Carl couldn't help but be impressed. A graduate of Harvard, first in his class, author of twenty-five books, and guest lecturer to universities around the world. Carl knew that he better prepared when dealing with the good doctor.

Carl gathered his stuff together as the plance descended at Jorge Chavez International. Within minutes Carl would be in his rental car and heading into the city. Going from one compacted seat to another. Carl was surprised to see how he has been adapting to traveling overseas.

"Thank you for flying American Airlines. We hope you enjoy your visit to Lima."

In twenty minutes Carl was heading towards his destination. He wished he had a chance to check out the sites; the Museo Larco which houses one of the largest collections of pre-Columbian art, the Plaza de Armas in the heart of old Lima, and the Museo de la Nacion the largest museum in Lima. He knew that he would never again have an opportunity to visit such worldly places or see such sites.

Carl was surprised on how quickly the traffic moved. It didn't take long for him to see the white alabaster walls of the buildings. Now this is unusual thought Carl, I found a parking spot. Pulling the black sedan in front of the administration building Carl gathered his briefcase and walked across the parking lot.

Here goes nothing he thought.

Down the hallway Carl saw pictures of Peruvian history in art. Incan relics sat stoic in glass cases. Further down the deans of the past lined the walls. Each man had the black suit and white shirt with a face that said, "I mean business." At the end of the hallway was Dr. Juan Santiago's office. Before entering Carl noticed a sign hanging right beside his door. It was big enough that one couldn't miss it when entering. Carl gave a chuckle as he read the sign. It seemed so appropriate for a time such as this.

ONLY TRUTH SEEKERS ARE WELCOMED

"Right on time Mr. Bennet. I have been looking forward to meeting with you. You phone call was intriguing. Come, you must be tired from your trip. Have a seat. Do you need some water?" and with that Dr. Santiago disappeared.

Carl took this moment to look around the office. He expected a professor of paleotology to have artifacts in their office but not Dr. Santiago. The office was void of any Incan or pre-Colonial artifacts. There were pictures of Juan's family, a wife with flowing black hair and deep brown eyes, and three children. Carl guessed the oldest to be a ten year old boy, a seven year old girl, and a four year old girl. Just as Carl was getting ready to take in the view from behind the desk Dr. Santiago reappeared with two bottle of water.

Giving a laugh that disarmed the embarassement that Carl was feeling at this moment Juan said, "I too cannot fight the urge to check out offices. A person's office is a reflection of that person. What is in the office defines to others what their personality is. Also, what is not in a person's can be of equal importance."

Carl stood in shock as if the man was reading his mind.

Juan continued, "Most people are surprise that I don't have dusy artifacts in the office, taking up space. It's not that I don't appreciate them. I do! They past fascinates me. Keeps me awake at nights. But, I also believe that the past belongs to all people. I am in the business of understanding cultures. Cultures are made up of people. They are the ones who define it, live it, and pass it on down to others. All the artifacts I have collected I have given to museums for display around the world. It must be shared to be appreciated."

Carl was liking this man by the minute. Standing about six five Juan Santiago was wiry and lean. At first it seemed unnatural to see a grown man so skinny. Carl expected uncoordination but Juan moved with such fluidity and grace that Carl now thought the man was an athlete. Staring at more pictures he saw Dr. Santiago on bikes. Judging from a couple of them the man liked to compete in bike races.

"Now Mr. Bennet. What can I do for you?"

"Please, call me Carl."

"Very well Carl."

Carl went into explained to Dr. Santiago the last few days. As he finished the events at Angkor Dr. Santiago leaned back in his chair and touched his fingers together.

"Dr. Santiago."

"Please, call me Juan," Juan said with a smile.

Returning the smile Carl asked, "My friends and I are confused. Is it possible that man and dinosaur could have existed? Is there proof out there that the two interacted with each other? It seems so ridiculous but I, myself, cannot deny what I saw in Utah and Cambodia. But it doesn't make sense to me."

Juan must have been holding his breath during Carl's questioning. A long breath was let out and he leaned forward on his desk. "Carl. Your friends and you have stumbled on the greatest coverups in scientific history."

Carl sat back in his chair. "What are you talking about Juan? I mean no disrespect but I am not seeking out a conspiracy here. I just want information. Some answers to my questions."

"Carl. What did my sign say out there? Huh? Truth seekers are welcomed. You are here to seek the truth. But understand this, the truth can be a hard pill to swallow and an even harder thing to live with sometimes." Juan lowered his head and his voice dropped as if mill stone was just draped across his neck.

"Carl," Juan looked up, "this journey that you are on is a powerful one. Each day you need to decide if it is worth it to you personally. You will be attacked physically and emotionally. People will want to tear you down, ruin your reputation, and discredit you."

It was only then that Carl understood that he wasn't just looking at a professor but a veteran of many battles. A warrior fighting to get the truth out to people. Despite the jovial attitude of the professor Carl could see emotional scars appear in Juan's eyes.

Juan's eyes gained focus and then bore into Carl. "I will answer your question. But once you have this information you will be held responsible to it. Many people will use whatever means necessary to stop this information from getting out. Are you ready for the consequences of seeking and knowing the truth?"

Carl met the hardened gaze of Juan, "I am."

SYDNEY, AUSTRALIA

The landing bounced and manhandled John from his sleep. John didn't mind flying over the ocean but one did get tired of seeing blue; blue sky, blue water, even the wing of the airplane was blue. After the thirteen hour flight John had decided that blue was his least favorite color.

After collecting his baggage and going through the motions of getting his rental car John was delighted to stroll outside to find his car. Sydney was one of those few cities in the world that no matter where you are in the city you could feel the ocean air and breeze. It was refreshing compared to the canned air on the airplane.

John scanned the numbers looking for slot thirty-nine. He knew he was getting close; 36, 37, 38. "You have to be kidding me," John said sarcastically. Sitting in slot thirty-nine was the mini van he requested.

Blue.

All John could do was laugh and shake his head. He was beginning to learn that God had a wonderful sense of humor.

Throwing his luggage into the back of the van and adjusting his mirrors John set off for University of Sydney. He was looking forward to seeing an old friend of his who specialized in mathematics and construction. It was an odd combination but the man was used as an advisor on the construction of the skyscrapers in Dubai, Thailand, and Chicago. His speciality was knowing how to maximize space while designing a building.

John's curiousity needed answers and Michael Wilks was the man with the answers. At least John hoped.

John loved Sydney. Every other year John would vacation down in Australia. The people were friendly, the city clean, and the weather perfect. John decided long ago that if he should ever retire he was coming here. He already had a condo along the beach that had a circular view of the ocean and the city.

Ten more years to go he thought to himself.

For now he was thinking of current situation. A few days ago he was attending a friend's funeral. Since that time he met a total stranger, became friends with his dead friend's daughter, traveled to Utah and Cambodia, saw evidence that contradicted current modern thinking, and became a believer in Christ. Now, he was in Sydney calling upon a friend who he had just visited four months ago.

All this was financed by a group that John had never heard of or have seen. He was beginning to also understand that God does work in mysterious ways.

Within minutes John was manuevering the minivan around the university. College students sunbathed on the green lawns, huddled in groups to chat and laugh, most were strolling around with their backpacks and cells phones glued to their ears. It amazed John how universities around the world are set up the same way and the students act the same. If John didn't just have the thirteen hour flight to remind him that he was in Australia he would have sworn he was back at the University of Wyoming. Sure the buildings may look different but the atmosphere was the same.

John wanted to stretch his legs so parked off campus and began the trek across maninured lawns and well kept sidewalks. The salty ocean smell filled the air. John took his time to enjoy this walk. It was nice to stretch out the legs and be refreshed by the youthful energy that surrounds every college campus. Within twenty minutes John was knocking on Michael Wilks' door even though it was already open and John could spot Michael among the piles of books and folders.

The giant of a man gracefully stepped over the piles and caught John in a bear hug. The slaps on John's back nearly took his breath away. Mike was one of the biggest men that John had ever seen. As well as the strongest.

Mike grew up in the oil fields of Wyoming. The harsh winters was enough to make anyone tough. At fourteen Mike's dad passed away from an oil rig accident. Taking on the chores of his father included gathering firewood and hunting deer and elk. In the summertime Mike worked construction and news of his strength spread. A teenage boy was able to lift and carry more materials than any of the men at the work site. Mike would have stayed in that life had it not been for a football coach at Mike's high school.

The coach encouraged Mike to work hard in school, that he was college material, and that by going to college Mike would be helping out his mother and sisters more. By Mike's junior year university scouts were regular visitors at the house. Halfway through his junior year he was lined up for the University of Colorado to play defensive lineman. For Mike's first two years he lived up to the hype of being a potential NFL player. But a torn ACL and the unexpected death of his mother changed the plans for the future in an instant.

Mike always stated that he had no regrets. He was just happy with the opportunity as he stated to people who ask the what might have questions. Mike still keeps in contact with that old coach of his. John had the priviledge of meeting that coach and he found himself inspired just talking to the man.

As John settled on the coach in Mike's office he sipped the coffee handed to him.

Minutes passed as the two exchanged small talk and some laughs. John knew that time was of the essence.

"Mike. I would love to be able to stay and do the social visit…"

"John. Your call sounded urgent. I understand. What can I do to help?"

As big as the man was physically his heart was even bigger. John had never met a more compassionate man than Mike. "As I stated in my call I am with a group and we stumbled across some interesting things. I must also admit to you. A few days ago I became a Christian."

A smile flashed across Mike's face, "Welcome to the good side my brother! I have been one for the last ten years. It's about time you joined the winning side. You know that I have been praying for you for ten years. Ten years!"

John laughed but was stunned. Collecting his thoughts again he looked at his notes, "When I was reading the Bible I noticed the story of Noah and his ark. On my recent adventures I came across evidence, and this is going to sound strange, that dinosaurs may have lived at the same tiem as humans. I am very confused here. If the Bible is true, that there really was a flood, that dinosaurs and man existed at the same time, then how is that possible? How could the ark hold all those animals?"

Mike leaned back in his chair. Then leaned forward again. "My friend. That is one of the greatest questions out there. Fortunately there is an answer. But I cannot tell you, I have to show you. Ready for a drive?"

GOBI DESERT, CHINA

Talk about being out of place. Cathy felt like a square peg in a round hole; she was sitting on the crowded bus surrounded by farmers, chickens, and cages holding a variety of other animals. It was so much the being packed like sardine effect that was getting to Cathy, it was the smells and lack of air. The first hour was bearable. The second was becoming intolerable.

Still, she wanted to be in a crowd to protect herself. Since Cambodia she thought of ways to protect herself and being among people seemed the logical way. If she took a car she could be ran off the road and no one would know where she was. As uncomfortable as this was, it was still better than being dead.

After another twenty minutes the bus reached its destination of the Gobi Desert. The Gobi is the fifth largest desert in the world but located in the most populated country. The Himalayas block the rain clouds from coming to the rain shadow desert. The Altai Mountains and the Tibetan Plateau surround the desert. The Gobi is most famous for two things; it was an important aspect of the Mongol Empire. The desert stretches for about a thousand miles east to west and about five hundred miles north to south. The Mongols ruled the desert and used it against its enemies. Starvation and lack of resources caused many enemies to perish or to be tortured. The second aspect of the desert is the amount of fossil finds. It was here that the first dinosaur eggs were found. It was also here that one of the most famous discoveries was found that shook the scientific world. It was for this reason that Cathy was here.

Cathy contacted an old student of her father's, Yun Long. He came to the university as an exchange student. According to her father Yun had a knack for finding the impossible. Mike told stories of how Yun would wiggle himself into holes and caverns because his gut told him that something was there. Within a couple of hours shovels, picks, and sweepers were brought in to exavate the new site discovered by Yun. He was gaining a reputation in academia circles as the expert on fossils.

With his uncanny ability to find fossils, and his vast knowledge of the Gobi Desert it was a no brainer for Cathy. Yun was her guy.

Cathy stared at the village before her. Despite its small size she wondered how she was going to find Yun. Surely everyone here would know who he was. A shrieking sound came from behind her and rushing at her was a man with a chicken in each hand. Behind him another man was throwing eggs, pelting the first. Both men screeched at each other in Mandarin Chinese. The first man decided that enough was enough and he turned, it was easy to see what his intentions were. He was going to punch the second man with the chicken in his hand. As he swung the second man ducked and punched the first man in the stomach. Both the man and the chickens let out squawks. The man dropped the chickens and ran off.

Cathy stood there taking in the spectacle.

The man continued to throw eggs at the other man until he ran out of eggs, even though the man was clearly past throwing distance. He finished his screaming in Chinese, brushd himself off and looked at the strange woman before him. He scanned the area around him and saw near strangeled chicken on the ground. Picking them up the man finished the job by breaking their necks. Putting both chickens into his left hand he extended out his right.

"You must be Cathy. I am Yun Long." He looked around the area as is if he was scanning for any foreign ears to this conversation. "You will have to forgive some of these people. They sometimes tend to be a little backwards. But overall they are good people." Yun then raised his voice a few octaves, "except when people are trying to steal chickens."

Cathy found it ironic that Yun would say this in English when she knew all the people spoke Chinese. She interpretted the act as Yun just showing off. She admitted to herself that kind of enjoyed that extra attention, even as strange as it was.

Cathy found herself staring at Yun. He was an attractive man. Standing just under six feet he sported the traditional ponytail of ancient China. With his shirt off Cathy couldn't help but admire the fact that Yun worked out. Now in the sun with Yun sweating, Cathy found herself like a junior high girl at the dance.

"You are probably hungry from the trip. Come, we will go to my place and get something to eat. I'm sure you also have many questions for me. I too have questions for you. But first let me say my condolences on the passing of your father. He was a good teacher and even better man. He will be greatly missed."

Cathy couldn't help herself; she enjoyed being in Yun's company. He was sincere, attractive, humorous, and intelligent.

"Thank you. It's been such a whirlwind the last few days; although it has been nice to have the distraction." Cathy stared right at Yun, "I will take you up on that meal though. I am pretty hungry."

When Yun gave a crooked smile Cathy returned the gesture. This is going to be an interesting trip thought Cathy. Interesting indeed.

Cathy walked with Yun down the street to his home. The outside looked just the others in the village with a slight difference, the size. The villagers lived in the domed shaped huts with a hole on top to let out the smoke. Sometimes a home will house up to a family of six or seven. Cathy could only imagine what he sleeping arrangements would be like. Yun's home was domed but was the size of four of five other domes put together. Cathy could only figure out that Yun wanted to fit in with the locals but wanted to have the space of an American.

When Cathy entered the domed home she had to remember to breathe. She expected a bachelor pad. Then considering location she expected dust, flies, and bugs. Instead she saw before her a tranquil setting. The place was meticously neat. On the walls were draped blankets that the local women gave Yun. A table was set up in the middle of the giant room complete with a centerpiece of dinosaur skull.

"Conversation piece for when I have guests," said Yun. Cathy could spot the kitchen off to the left of her. Again, great care was taken for neatness and appearance. Traditional cooking ware was present along with the spices. A computer hummed on a desk on the opposite side of the kitchen. Cathy could see the flying toasters on the screen.

After a moment of silence of taking in this odd mixture of modern with the ancient, Cathy could hear a humming sound. Straining to decipher what the sound could be Yun answered, seeming to sense what Cathy was thinking. "I have a generator that is solar powered. It is how I get the power to run this place. We are after all on the desert." He went over to his computer and moved the desk over. Opening up the wall Cathy could see black panels lined up next to each other. "This is where the energy gets stored. This allows me to run this place on those rare cloudy and rainy days. Come, let me show you."

With that he led Cathy to the back of the hut to another door. Behind the hut laid ten solar panels. Each panel blinding to the eye as they reflected the sun's rays as well as absorbed its power. Cathy couldn't help but be impressed.

Yun is also industrious and creative thought Cathy.

Coming back inside Yun began to fix something to eat. Cathy strolled around and took in more of the surroundings. It amazed her that just outside these walls was the world's fifth largest desert, people living an ancient lifestyle, and possibly answers to burning questions. But now, Cathy felt more comfortable and at east than she had for days. She could feel the stress leave her body and her spirits lifted.

Within minutes Yun brought to the table a bowl of steaming rice with roasted vegetables mixed in. A glass of wine was brought out. The smell of the rice and vegetables reminded Cathy that she had not had a home cooked meal in days. Taking her first bite she had decided that she had never tasted rice like this. It melted right in her mouth. Each grain soaking up the flavors of the vegetables. The sip of wine only enhancing the food's flavor.

After finishing three bowls Cathy decided that was enough. She could have kept eating. She had never had anything so unique and delicious in her life. Anyway, she wanted to talk to Yun. She had to keep reminding herself that she was here on business. To find answers. She felt comfortable enough to think that Yun would have several answers for her.

Yun leaned into the chair opposite of Cathy. She was an attractive woman. The recent tan added a glow to Cathy. Yun could sense a calmness radiating from Cathy. It has been a long time since Yun had been around an attractive woman. The local, younger women irritated him. All they could see was his big house. Every father of an eligible bride in town has bribed Yun into marrying their daughter. Each was a bigger turnoff than the one before. So for the last two years Yun has lived the life of a hermit bachelor.

It gave him time to do his main passion, exploring the Gobi Desert. He knew he was respected around the world for his expertise on locating fossils and exploring the desert. Universities and organizations contacted him via internet for a guide and expertise.

Now, John was in his own house but felt like a stranger. The person around him made him want to be unselfish. This woman demanded his attention and he was glad to give it.

Yun turned to Cathy, "I gathered from your email that you want to see the site of the famous fossil fight." Yun popped a handful of nuts into his mouth.

Cathy lowered her head. "My father said that the fossil fight debunks the idea of long term fossilization. If this is the case, then the idea of millions of years that many scientists use for explaining eras is also not true."

Cathy could see Yun contemplating what she had said. As she stared into Yun's eyes she could see the gears turning in his mind.

"Your father is right. The finding of the fossil fight has been largely kept out of the public eye because it contradicts what many people have learned in school."

Cathy knew what he was talking about. Millions of people around the world learned that fossilization was a slow, tedious process. An animal would fall into a tar pit, mud, or quicksand. The animal would descend into the natural trap and die. The carcass was buried from layer upon layer of sediments and preserving the body. The carcass would erode leaving the bones. These bones would slowly become fossilized.

Yun continued, "The fossil fight debunks that myth. Have you seen the fossil fight for yourself?"

"No I haven't. I have only seen pictures."

Yun let out a laugh. "My dear, I do apologize for I mean no disrespect. The pictures do not do it justice. It is a rare find. A find that should turn the scientific world upon its ear."

Cathy could see that Yun was becoming excited and more animated. Cathy didn't think it was possible but his passion and energy made him even more attractive.

"Cathy, let me describe it to you. Two dinosaurs are facing each other. One is a raptor the other is a protoceratops. The raptor attacks the protoceratops. The two fight. Out of nowhere a sandstorm hits burying the two." He takes a breath and continues, "Here is where it gets weird. The two animals never sensed the storm. Animal instinct is well documented when it comes to sensing natural forces such as storms, tornadoes, hurricanes, and even earthquakes. These two animals never sense an incoming storm? The two fought through the storm even while they were being buried? It doesn't make sense.

This means that the burial was fas;.so fast that the two dinosaurs died instantly and were buried. The find shows the raptor grabbing the protoceratops head shield. Its sickle claw is lodged deep into the body cavity. The protoceratops is biting down on the raptor's right arm. This was a fight to the death. What happened was that both died in the midst of the battle.

Do you understand what this means?"

Cathy let the information sink in. "If I understand you right, whatever buried them was so quick that animal instinct could not even react to it."

Yun gave a nod. "So far you got it."

"Then the burial was so intense that it buried the animals in action."

"Bingo. Whatever buried them was cataclysmic."

Cathy pondered that. "What could have done that? Volcanoes don't send sand. Earthquakes don't shift that kind of sand."

Yun jumped in with a devilish smile, "What about a flood."

BEIJING, CHINA

Xi had followed Cathy. Out of the three she seemed the most vulnerable; plus, by taking out the woman first it would make the men irrational and funner to deal with. He had to admit to himself that three of them getting on separate planes in Cambodia surprised him. He was still trying to figure out the rational behind it.

Oh well. He didn't care. His job was not to figure people out unless it was to analyze their weaknesses and strengths. So far these three people had more weaknesses than strengths. First they ran away from the crowd after the shooting, then they split themselves up into different parts of the world, then the woman goes off into the desert by herself. Too easy.

Xi sat only two seats behind her on the bus ride. Through the strange aromas he could smell her sweet scent. The entire time he watched the back of her head. As she turned to look at the window he gazed upon the right side of her face. Beautiful. Just the thought of seeing her in his mind's eye gave Xi a sneerful smile.

He watched as the woman left with the crazy man with the chickens. He saw them enter the big hut at the end of the village. Village? Xi had to laugh; more like a the end of the world. Xi felt a slight amount of pity for the woman. She was going to die at the end of the earth, away from family and friends, in a place where no one will know her or care that she is dead.

Xi quickly dismissed the feeling.

She would die like many others. Xi would conquer her body. This will destroy her mind and her heart. From there he will torture her. He will gain energy and more enthusiasm as her fear rises. Then he will watch the life in the eyes give way to panic and then to death. Watching death settle in a person's eyes gave Xi an undescribable rush. It was power. It was conquering. It was commanding respect.

Xi wanted it all.

The door closed on the large hut. Xi could only imagine what it was like and what was going on in the hut. No matter. Tonight he will strike. Tonight he will conquer. Tonight he will command.

A lustful look crept over Xi's demeanor. Tonight is mine for the taking.

DALLAS, TEXAS

The Twelve gathered together minus one. News programs from around the country were going crazy over the news of Curtis Trough. First there was his son being thrown into jail. News clip after news clip showed the blond haired boy with facial piercings being unloaded from the back of the police car and escorted into the station.

Then half an hour ago it was leaked that Curtis and his wife of twenty years were going to divorce. Images of the divorce papers splashed across screens with Curtis' name highlighted whiter than the rest of the document.

Then, mere seconds ago the whammy of all whammies, the oldest daughter is pregnant. Church basher after church basher sat on the screen stating their case of church leaders being hypocrites, being only after people's money, and the idea of religion is archaic, and out of date with today's modern world.

Defenders of the church were few on the TV screens. Defenders of Curtis was even less.

Rumors of extramaritel affairs filled the airwaves as well as the ticker tape that news programs have. Rumors of Emily having an abortion came next.

The Twelve had heard enough. The TV went out and silence weighed heavy in the room. Each man was thinking the same thing; what do we do from here, what will Curtis share with the world, and most importantly, what can we do to help the family out? Guilt and shame fell upon each man. Inside each man thought what they could have done to help, to reach out to Curtis, his wife, his children.

Silence continued.

Outside the sun shone and the sky was a brilliant blue. Inside the oxygen seemed to be sucked out and replaced with worry and confusion.

The five minutes from the time the TV was turned off until Dr. Julius Simpson spoke seemed like eternity. "Gentlemen we are at a crisis. But, you and I know that our God is in control of all things; he is in control in Australia, in China, and in Peru. He is also in control of Curtis and his family. I know that doubts, anger, and confusion are springing up in our minds and hearts. But! And this is a huge 'but', I believe that God will be glorified through this. I believe that Curtis and his family will survive this and stay intact. Why? Because our God is all powerful. He controls everything. All things are to his good.

Will we find Curtis' replacement? In time, yes. Through diligent prayer and listening for God we will find his replacement."

Murmurings of agreement filled the room. Nods.

"My friends, my heart aches. I agree with Julius. During our morning prayer meetins have we prayed for us? Have we prayed for our families? Have we been open and honest with each other?" Dr. Rodney Guide stood up and stood alongside his friend Julius. Tears came to Rodney's eyes. "I must admit that I have not been transparent with you. I have held back prayer requests for my family and for myself. I have been needing accountability and prayer for a long time. It is my fault. I believe that we were focused on the wrong things." Rodney gained his composure. By this time the man was wracked with emotion. Julius wrapped his huge arms around his friend, his brother in faith.

Rodney gained strength from the compassionate man next to him. "Do we need to pray for the trio? Absolutely. Those three are the most courageous of us all. They went without blinking. They are following God's plan without a thought of hesitation. Carl overcame his fear of traveling to obey God. Who are we? We sit in this 'ivory tower', goin through the motions of prayer. Have we been transparent? If I haven't been. If Curtis wasn't. Then I am certain that there is more. Let's be honest now. How many of you have been honest and transparent?"

Every man's head was down. No hand had to be raised as guilt was written upon each face. Then a hand inched slowly up like an earthworm poking through the ground. Another came up, shaking. A hand started up but came back down, covering his face and hiding the tears. Soon men were crying. Leaning upon each other.

Then, as if an unspoken word was spoken, each man dropped to his knees. A circle was formed and each man rested his hands on the man beside him. Prayers were offered up for Curtis and each of his family members. Prayers went up for each man and his wife in the group. Every child and grandchild was lifted up to God. Carl. Cathy. John. Each was lifted up with praise and thanked for being dutiful to obeying God. At times a man would fall upon his face but the circle was never broken. The men beside him would place their hands on his back.

Minute after minute the men prayed. Doubt, fears, and sins were spoken from each man and given to God. Prayers of encouragement were said after each confession. When Dr. Thomas Regan stated his addiction to internet pornography, all the men got up and circled the man and rested their hands upon him. Prayers of healing, strength, encouragement were given.

All morning the mighty prayer group was a prayer group. Each man felt that they have looked upon the face of God. Four hours later the men were changed. A new commitment was given to be open and to hold each other accountable. Each man dedicated themselves to holding two other men accountable.

Each man at the end felt a burden was lifted. A joyous beginning was happening and a new hope and purpose radiated from the Twelve. The only disappointment was that it had to end. As each man left the elevator to enter the world a renewed strength flowed through their veins.

Troy wondered if this is what the original disciples felt when Jesus empowered them with the Holy Spirit.

HONG KONG, CHINA

The hustle and noise was enough for Kim. He had come down with Ambassador Benjamin Bortho. Since Hong Kong became a part of China in 1999 it became an important naval and shipping port for the country. China's ability to export and import goods both by air and sea increased and improved. And since 1999 China has taken all the credit of Hong Kong's success as its own.

Ambassador Bortho showed Kim the city. Bortho was amazed that Kim had never visited Hong Kong. Kim, through many attempts, tried to convey to the American that he never cared if he visited.

But Kim needed to visit with Bortho. He needed information. For Kim the information was important enough to leave the mainland and play buddy-buddy.

Borto suggested that they take in dinner before departing back to Beijing. After an all day marathon of visiting naval ships, banks, and financial institutions Kim and his stomach agreed.

The restaurant sat at the top of the tower. Down below the coast line could be seen. Hong Kong's coastline is one of the most developed in the world. At night the buildings demonstrate a light show; blues, pinks, reds, purples, flash and dance from building to building.

None of this distracted Kim.

"Ambassador. I have been wanting to meet with you a long time. For many years China has let western influence in; capitalism, sports, and entertainment. We have also been getting more lenient towards other types of influences." Kim was getting a feel for the ambassador. Is he being defensive? Open minded? When the ambassador chewed his last morsel and sat back, eyes attentative, Kim interpreted this as a good sign. "Your country has been sending over people to teach our people. They could be teachers, doctors, or just volunteers. I have often wondered why? We are a powerful country. We are industialized. We are modern. Why has your country felt the need for this?" Kim was hoping the ambassador would say he didn't know really. That it was a sign of that more open relationship. Kim was hoping the ambassador would take the bait.

"That is a great question Commander. No offense, but many people in your country, as interpreted by the people in my country, are still not receiving adequate care, a quality education, or are starving. They are not trying to overrun a country or influence it towards their ideals and values. They do not want to change the culture. They want to save people's lives." Wiping his mouth with a napkin he continued, "I have talked to many of these people. The last thing they want to do is change the culture. They love their visits to China, interacting with the people, and have the lifetime experiences. I think most of the time the people from America are more influeced and change more than the people in China." A soft chuckle followed along with a drink of water.

"I appreciate that as a country your people care about my people. But, do some of these people come in with honest intentions? Do they come in as one thing but do another while they are here?" Kim didn't want to come right out and say what he meant. He knew it would scare the ambassador and the brick wall would be up. No he decided, let the ambassador figure it out for himself.

"Well, I am sure that some people do come in that way. Drug trafficking is a problem around the world. Human trafficking is also a growing problem. You and I know that since 9/11 the United States is more cautious towards people coming in and out of the country. That we have caught up with other countries. People coming in as one thing with the intentions of doing something else. So yes, I am sure some of our people come in with dishonest motives. I believe that is where the two countries need to work together to agree to law and punishment."

Kim didn't show it but frustration was sitting in. This man was a great politician. Able to answer and dodge the questions at the same time.

"What about those who come in and teach ideals that are against the law in our country? Those that teach a philosophy that contradicts China's belief system?"

Bortho took a breath and put his fingers together. He knew that this was a touchy subject between the two countries and he also knew that Kim was a powerful man in Chinese circles. As an ambassador this is where the rubber meets the road. You pave the road to make progress but try to avoid the speed bumps and obstacles that are in the way. Here was a chance to make progress, to build that road but word choice, tone, demeanor would be absolutely necessary to the next few sentences he would speak.

"I am going to make the leap that you are talking about missionaries?" When Bortho received the nod from Kim he continued. "I know that this is sensitive subject. I know that across your country people are converting to Christianity at a record pace. According to the data we have China is the fastest growing Christian nation in the world." Bortho could see the crimson rise in the Commander's face. Borto knew he needed to be cautious but honest. "I agree that many of these people come in as teachers and doctors and volunteers. I also know that they come in on their own free will. They are not sponsored by the United States. Do we care what happens to them as American citizens? Absolutely. We want them to be treated with dignity and respect. But, they have made their choice and with choices come consequences."

This seemed to appease Kim to a certain degree. The crimson settled back into the body and the rigid structure of the man relaxed. A smile even appeared.

"I am glad to hear you say that Ambassador. I believe also that choices have consequences. You make a good choice you receive good consequences. You make bad choices, there will be bad consequences."

Bortho nodded in agreement while sipping his water. In the political world words meant nothing. They were twisted, manipulated, and misinterpreted. He knew that this was going on right now.

"I want to thank you Ambassador for a wonderful day. I will have to excuse myself now. I do have business dealings in Hong Kong to deal with tomorrow and I do not want to be, how do you say, groggy tomorrow. Thank you again." With that Kim stood. Bortho stood and shook Kim's hand.

As Kim exited the restaurant Bortho remained at the table and revisted the conversation. Kim was up to something and it had to deal with missionaries. Bortho paid the bill and went to his car. As the driver weaved through Hong Kong traffic to deliver Bortho to the airport Bortho decided to brush up on his knowledge of Americans traveling in China. He also decided to find out the missionary organizations in America and put out a warning.

Bortho sensed a storm coming and it may involve latching down the hatches and securing the storm doors.

LIMA, PERU

Juan went over to a bookshelf and pulled out a few books and folders. A few loose papers floated down to the floor. Juan waltzed back to his desk and spread out the books, each folder was laid so not a one was sitting on top of the other.

"Carl. Have you ever read the *Origin of Species* by Charles Darwin?" Carl had to admit that he did not. "It is interesting to me that many people oppose Darwin without having ever read the very thing they are opposing. But this," Juan held up the book, "is the reason for the division between science and Christianity. It is the cornerstone of the greatest lie science has ever promoted."

Carl sat there shocked. He let the words sink in. Science is promoting a lie. "What do you mean that science is promoting a lie?"

Juan swept his hands over the folders and books on his desk then gave a grand sweep over his office. "Scientists around the world have so bought into this lie that millions, maybe billions, of dollars are funneled into it. Professors and scientists lose their jobs if they even consider anything but evolution in the classroom or workplace. And yet, evidence after evidence points out that evolution cannot exist. It doesn't work. Even common sense says that evolution doesn't work."

Now Carl straightened up. "I am not a scientist so help me out a little." Carl felt a little embarassed but he wanted to know. How is this going to tie into my findings at Utah and Cambodia?

"Ok. There are certain laws in science. These laws are hard and fast. Cannot be broken. Laws that are universal. They have gone through the scientific process of starting out as a hyphothesis."

"You mean like a guess. That you hope something will happen."

"That's right. Then you test that hyphothesis. You record your findings. You test several times in different situations to arrive at a theory. You then test that theory over and over again. It gets reviewed by multiple scientists so errors are found. If the theory fails, then the process starts all over. This is the checks and balances of science. And understand, this is a highly political process. Scientist like to bash each other down. It means money for their own programs, universities, and their own research. Most times, it is not a gentlemen's game. It can be vicious and cruel. Even to the point of destroying careers."

Carl had no idea that this kind of world existed. He had always thought that scientists worked together. Strived for truth and order in the world.

Juan continued, "If a theory survives through the rigomorole of being torn apart, it became a law; for example the law of gravity and the three laws of motion by Newton. It seems cutthroat but the process works. It weeds out lies and has accountability. But the issue becomes this, what happens when a theory remains a theory but is treated like a law?"

Carl had to think about that. "I am not sure. I would think that intelligent people, especially people whose job is to promote truth and higher thinking would not allow such a thing to happen. But, if I understand you right, there is a theory that is being defended, with great costs to individuals, that has not been thoroughly tested to be true."

Juan gave a smile. "You are right on. There are thousands of scientists in the world, knowingly defending a theory that they know is not true. They know it is only a theory. But, to examine other theories, some with more credible evidence, is detrimental to their careers."

"So they continue with the lie out of sheer comfort and because it is safe."

"Absolutely. They are afraid. Think about it. Would you be willing to sacrifice your income, your reputation, your future, your family's security on a theory?"

Carl was beginning to understand the stakes involved.

"Also, as a university, there is no gain financially to rock the boat. By promoting the lie, by reinforcing it, they earn grants and endowments. Is it worth it financially?"

Carl was dumbfounded. Surely Juan was exaggerating. "Aren't you being a little paranoid with this?"

As if on cue Juan opened a folder. "Here is case after case of professors and scientists who challenged the lie. People who came up with a hypothesis, not a theory, but a hypothesis mind you that challenged the current way of thinking. These people were fired from their positions, denied tenure, unable to be published, and unable to find another job. They were blackballed." Then as if to drive home the point Juan pulled out a sheet of paper and pushed it across the desk.

Carl picked up the paper. On it was the logo of Stanford University. The letter stated that Juan was an incompentent professor and scientist. His personal views were interfering with progressive thinking and scientific ideals. Line after line discredited Juan as a lunatic, a fraud, a radical.

"Can you imagine if people like Newton, Galileo, and Einstein were alive in today's climate of academia? They would be outcasts. The idea of developing new ideas, challenging the current world thinking is over," Juan stated matter of factly. "If a scientist does not reinforce the idea of evolution, the idea of that living things are changing and evolving, that all these things are the products of long periods of time, then that scientists is not considered credible. No matter what the evidence states."

Carl didn't know what to say. All his life he had grown up thinking, knowing, that science was the great arena for free thinking. That it was the arena for challenging ideals to seek out truth. Now he heard that the world was being fed a lie and those that challenged the lie were embarassed and discredited. He felt helpless. He felt a stirring that he should do something but what. All those other people, people with credentials and experience tried and looked what happen to them.

"But let me tell you something. The lie is falling apart. More and more scientists are speaking up. The truth, the evidence is becoming too overwhelming for the lie. Like all lies, it will eventually fall apart, unravel if you will. This cornerstone," Juan held up Darwin's book again, "is so full of errors. It is being taken apart piece by piece. If it is the Bible of the biological world, then like the Bible it is being examined with great scrutiny. And it is failing." With a look of hope in Juan's eyes he leaned back in his chair.

Carl tried to imagine Juan's world. A world with an oppressive lie. A world of hypocritical activities so obvious yet so hidden at the same time. For Carl it seemed that everything he learned about science was crumbling apart in him. Every aspect of science was in question; astronomy, chemistry, biology, physics, geology, and geography. He imagined his high school science teachers. He imagined that they probably weren't even aware of the lie they were teaching. Textbook after textbook reiterated the lie. It was safe. It wasn't controversial. And students across the country soaked it up like a sponge. They didn't challenge it. Why should they? To earn a failing grade. To be embarassed in front of their peers. To not be able to play Friday night football or participate in other school activities. And why should a teacher challenge it? They had families to take care of and they were just following the rules. The state said to teach it. It was part of the standards to be learned. And the almighty textbook said so so it must be true.

Carl looked up at Juan. Here was a man who went to war. He fought the battle and he lost. He had to leave a prestigious university and find work elsewhere. Carl could see the hurt in Juan's eyes now. A man that was rising through the scientific ranks only to be knocked down on one hypothesis.

Juan looked at Carl and could see the confusion building in his head. "I could sit here and tell you all this stuff. Someone could say I have a chip on my shoulder based off of my experience," Juan pointed to the sheet of paper in Carl's hands. "But, what if I could show you the evidence? What if I could present to you the facts? What if I pulled back the veil on the lie and expose it to you? What would you say then?"

Carl looked up. Last time he answered a question like this from Juan he became overwhelmed. But he knew he had to move forward. God had brought him this far and God would give him the strength to keep moving forward. Fear was rising but words spoke to him from out of nowhere, "The truth shall set you free."

"I can handle that," Carl spoke slowly and deliberately.

"Good. How do you feel about boat rides?"

SYDNEY, AUSTRALIA

John was surprised to find himself at an abandoned railyard. Rail cars sat upon tracks that led to nowhere. Weeds and grasses grew around the steel and wood while skittering of mice could be heard from unseen places. John was used to seeing ghost towns in Wyoming. This was different. This contained modern pieces of in modern times.

He once went through the Airplane Boneyard in Arizona. Acres and acres of World War Two planes sat next to each other collecting dust and debris that come in with the wind. To see so many pieces of machinery sitting there chilled. John believed the chill came from knowing that these planes had a purpose. They were meant to fly, to go into battle. It was what they were built for. To see them sitting here with no purpose, no future, seemed to John was a waste.

This railyard had the same kind of feeling.

John followed Michael until they were in the middle of the railyard. A curious place to understand an ark though John. He imagined they would be heading towards the ocean and examining a tanker or some other cargo ship. John was looking forward to a trip like that. He would have enjoyed the salty air and warm breeze. To stare upon the blue ocean and cloudless sky would have brought a calmness over John.

Instead, here he was in the middle of nowhere staring at empty railroad cars.

Mike asked John, "Do you know how big the ark was? The one mentioned in the Bible? Do you know how big it was?"

John had to admit that he didn't. He began to imagine that it must have been huge. All he could remember from Sunday School was that Noah had two of every animal and that it rained for forty days and nights. Then Noah sent out a dove and gave proof that there was land. When Noah landed there was the first rainbow. Sadly, that was all that John could remember.

"The ark was 450 feet long, 75 feet wide and 45 feet high. The roof was within eighteen inches of the top. On the side of the ark was a door. Noah was told by God to make sure there were lower, middle, and upper decks. Now think about that for a second, 450 feet long. That is longer than a National Football League field by a hundred and fifty feet. That is one long boat! Especially considering time period, technology available, and the fact that most people who believe in the ark, believe that this may have been the first boat built. Then think that this monstrosity is over three stories high and seven stories wide. This thing was huge no matter how you measure it and what you compare it too."

John tried to fathom the ship in his mind. He knew he had to first erase the idea of the tugboat looking image from his mind. The one that is shown in children's books and nursery decorations. He had to imagine an aircraft carrier type of vessel, made of wood, and wide. Even with all his concentration on imagining such a vessel it still didn't seem possible, real.

"Now with the nitty-gritty, mate. How did all those animals fit on one boat? Well, now that is where Christians lose a lot of people. Most Christians don't know how to answer that question. Their blanket answer is faith. While that is true we actually have data that can back up a honest answer. First, let's remember what God told Noah."

John was surprised to see Mike reach into his back pocket and produce a Bible. Mike flipped a couple of pages and pointed with his finger, "Here in Genesis chapter six, you are to bring into the ark two of all living creatures, male and female, to keep them alive with you. Two of every kind of bird, of every kind of animal, and of every kind of creature that moves along the ground… You are to take every kind of food that is to be eaten and store it away as food for you and for them." Mike flipped a page over and continued to read, "Here in verse three of chapter seven, to keep their various kinds alive on the earth. Did you catch that?"

John was stumped. Again he tried to imagine every beast of the world gathered together and fitting on one boat. It seemed impossible. Improbable.

Mike smiled and acknowledged John's confusion. "Let's start with the basics. God said two of every kind to keep their various kinds alive. Now, most people imagine that God took two poodles, two German Shepherds, two labradors. Noticed that I only listed dogs. This doesn't include all the different kinds of cats, horses, bugs, or birds."

John didn't even think about that. There were dogs and then there were the types of dogs. The number of animals staggered the mind.

"But notice, God said kinds. This is important. God didn't put all those different kinds of dogs on the ark. He only put on two dogs. Two cats. Two horses and so on."

Wait a minute," John couldn't hold it in any longer. Are you telling me that one pair of dogs produced all the other kinds of dogs? One pair of dogs produced saint bernards, that produced poodles, that produced cocker spaniels. You are kidding, right?"

The confidence that Mike exhibited made John's question seem childish. "Here is where evolution and creation bang heads. I want you to imagine the following. Imagine a line of trees. Imagine a line across the bottom of the trees." Mike drew the following on the ground. Below the line he wrote out morphology. He labeled the line as creation and then on the side he wrote time with arrows pointing up and down. "This is how creation sees the world. From one kind, pair, or animals all the others have come about. From one pair of dogs you get the coyote, wolf, fox, jackal, and the border collie. Each tree represents that pair of animal for all the different kinds. This belief is called baraminology." Mike stood up to examine his handiwork.

He stepped over and began to draw another picture. This time it was a single tree with many branches. Then there were branches off of the main branches. "This is evolution. Every kind of animal, including man, came from one thing. The bottom branches on this tree would be your simple cell life forms. As you move up the tree the more advanced the life form. So says evolution."

John studied the two drawings. So far he was understanding what Mike was saying. He also had to admire the drawings that Mike drew.

"I never knew you to be such a Picasso."

"You should see me with stick people," laughed Mike.

John had to laugh. "I can't even draw that."

Mike gave his old friend a pat on the back. "Thank goodness we have day jobs to live off of."

With the joking John visualized in his mind's eye what Mike was saying. He had heard of people breeding dogs to get a particular kind of dog. To gain the better qualities of the two dogs to get better dogs. Horse trainers sought out the best male and female horses to breed the fastest horses for races.

Mike continued his argument without missing a step, "Now remember, God sent these animals. Here is where the biology settles in. Remember in high school biology about character traits? Remember that you had to figure out what the possibilities would be if one parent had brown eyes and one had blue eyes what the child would have?"

John did remember. He remembered drawing a square and then dividing the square into four smaller ones. Then he had to label the squares with the possibilties.

"Imagine if the pair of animals contained all the character traits needed to spawn these various kinds. What if one dog had in them the characteristics for long hair, small size, long tails, big ears, and short legs. Then the other dog had the exact opposites. Each litter of dogs is about, let's say six to eight dogs. How quickly would you have all the different kind of dogs? Then imagine that man begins to sort the dogs to produce the type of dogs they want to get the desired results. Ah yes, early man learned to breed and combine types as well."

John thought this made sense. Man produced seedless grapes, clone dogs, donkeys, and sheep. Why couldn't God do the same?

"Then think about this, these animals were picked by God. You don't think they may have been pretty special animals?"

"Ok. You make a convincing argument on numbers so far. But the sheer amount of animals is still huge. I include the extinct animals as well such as the dodo and European bear. Then the big one, dinosaurs. How did they fit in the ark given their size? If God created all things in six days, that would include dinosaurs. If two of every kind went on the ark, that too would include dinosaurs. How did they all fit?"

Mike laughed. John felt almost hurt like the target of a brunt tasteless joke.

"Mate, that is why I brought you here."

GOBI DESERT

Cathy had to admit to herself, she had a crush on Yun. The man was intelligent, good-looking, and full of many talents. Not only did he build his own house, provide power to that house considering he lived in the middle of nowhere, but here she sat in the passenger seat of a helicopter that Yun piloted. He certainly seemed like a good catch.

Yun stayed about two hundred feet above the ground. It allowed him to save his fuel and allowed him to scour the countryside. From where they were at sand dunes grew from out of the ground. Some these were enormous, up to five hundred feet high. Cathy could sense a harsh beauty to this desert.

"Over there." Yun pointed to the ground. Cathy couldn't see any difference in the landscape until the copter hovered within a couple hundred yards. Huts formed a square perimeter about half the size of a football field. Holes dotted interior and Cathy could see the workers digging and scraping at the dirt. Those same workers covered their eyes as the copter landed.

Once the dust settled they continued as Cathy and Yun exited the cabin. Cathy shivered, surprised by the lack of heat. As if reading her thoughts Yun spoke, "Gobi is a shadow desert. The Himalayas block most of the moisture from getting here. Because of that we don't get rain and hence the desert. We do however get the colder temperatures. It is not uncommon to see frost across vast areas of the desert during most months of the year."

Yun crossed over the barriers protecting the dig site. Everyone smiled warmly for Yun. He greeted each worker by name and either patted their backs or shook their hands. It seems he didn't mind getting dirty. He even asked a couple of them about their families. As they spoke Yun seemed broken hearted to hear of a father dying, another with a mother diagnosed with clinical depression, and rejoiced when he heard that another was an aunt for the first time. Each worker had immediate respect for Yun and it seemed it was reciprocated.

Can this man do no wrong thought Cathy.

After making the rounds Yun led Cathy to a hut on the far side of the dig. Based off of Yun's living quarters Cathy wasn't sure what to expect inside. To her surprise it was exactly what she expected. Stuffy. Hot. Downright uncomfortable. Cathy felt at home.

In the back corner stood a wooden shelving unit. Yun pulled out a wooden box and put it on the table in the middle of the room.

"Here are photos of the fossil fight." With that he opened the box and pushed it over to Cathy. Inside were two thick folders; one labeled photos, the other titled journal. "Are these…"

"The original notes from the paleotologists that found and dug the fossil fight," Yun finished.

Cathy fingered the pages before her. Photo after photo showed an amazing sight; a raptor clutching a protoceratop's head and a limb of the raptor in the top's mouth. A claw embedded into the top's head. A person laid next to the scene giving a size comparison. The protoceratop the size of a two cars.

"Do you see why this is significant? This is proof that fossilization is a quick process. This wasn't caused by some collapsing sand dune, or freak sandstorm, or even quicksand. Let's take the sand dune theory. There is no water in a sand dune. Fossilization needs some of the minerals and nutrients from water to fossilize. This would be true of a sandstorm as well. Plus, the animals would have tried to escape a sandstorm. If quicksand the animals would have tried to escape rather than try to fight each other. The only answer is a flood so sudden, so mighty that nothing could escape."

Cathy remembered the tsunami's that hit a few years ago. Witness accounts put the wave at two stories high and moving rapidly. To this day many bodies and debris have yet to be recovered. But even this disaster was witnessed by people before it hit and many people survived because of the people yelling out to others.

"Now if this was the only quick evidence we had I would have to consider it abnormal and not even consider it." Then with a gleam in his eye Yun continued, "but there are others. In a sandy flood situation we have fish who have been buried so quickly that they didn't even have time to finish what they were swallowing. Here is another kick in the pants;

we have an Ichthyosaur buried so fast that she couldn't even finish giving birth."

Yun had a childlike excitement surrounding him. Great, thought Cathy, another magnetic draw to this man.

Yun and Cathy stepped outside. Cathy relished the fresh air compared to the staleness inside the hut. She tried to imagine that everything around her covered in water. Around here were dinosaurs and other large creatures.

"It's hard to imagine isn't it?"

Yun understood. He looked around too. "It certainly is. It certainly is."

NEW YORK, NEW YORK

"In the news today fallen evangelist Dr. Curtis Trough has more family problems. If you remember we were the first to cover his shocking story of his son's arrest for methaphetamine. Today his problems seem to be piling higher as Scott Tripp is reporting for us from Dallas, Texas. Scott."

"Thanks Dan. Dr. Trough's family problems seem to be getting worse rather than better. Today, his wife of twenty years filed divorce papers."

Camera zooms to the front of a Roman white alabaster building. A manicured lawn contrasts the ornate building with people milling around the benches and the staircase that ascends into the oak doors.

"Kathleen Trough, wife of famous evangelist Dr. Curtis Trough, filed divorce papers. The Trough's have been married for twenty years. Court documents report that the reasons were irreconcilable differences. This comes on the heels of the couple's son, Jonathon Trough's arrest for the making and distributing of methaphetamine. Attempts have been made to Dr. Trough but no response yet."

Camera focuses back on Scott Tripp. Blond hair, blue eyes, a cameraman's dream in terms of being photogenic. Scott stares at the camera with the look of concern and worry. A look that tells the television audience that he understands and is concerned as well.

A voice from nowhere calls to Scott. It is Dan Cleese, the anchor back at the station. "Scott, is there any comment on what the family is doing to deal with this situation?" It is a prepared question. Reporters in the field send the anchors the questions. Producers hate street reporters being caught off guard. It makes the reporters look unprofessional and unprepared. When that happens the station loses viewers. Plus every producer knows that the anchors are paid to read, not to think.

"As I mentioned Dan no comment from the family yet. Sources have stated that Emily, their oldest daughter, attended a Planned Parenthood site on the east side of the family. We are not sure why but we will keep you informed if we find anything out. Back to you Dan."

Scott's face disappears. Dan's face fills the screen with a gun in the upper right corner of the screen. "On the west side gang members...."

Meanwhile the cameraman turns off his camera and Scott begins wrapping the cord around his arm.

"This is turning into a bigger story than I thought," Scott said to the cameraman.

With that microphone and camera were put into the van. Scott went into the passenger seat. A bigger story indeed he thought.

GOBI DESERT

Xi stared at the perimeter of huts. Shooting sick dogs, that's how this easy this will be he thought. Putting down his scope he began to figure out distance and wind. He was told to take out the targets quietly and disappear. Shame. He was looking forward to the personal touch. Of course he knew that he could come up with the excuse that the conditions weren't right for sniping. This would allow him to be up close and personal.

As the sun began to hide behind the mountains Xi looked for ways to isolate the target. She hung close beside the man from the village. Xi began to consider the fact that both may have to be eliminated.

Another step closer to justifying the sniper rifle. A sniper rifle, no matter how good the shooter, is good for one shot before people scurry and hide. Soon defenses go up and that is when the sniper hides away, disappears. Becomes a ghost.

Much to his disappointment the girl and man retreat to separate huts for the night. This left the woman in a hut with other women. The disappointment soon turned into an idea. Xi saw an opportunity to strike more fear. Women were such easy targets and easily scared. Anything that had to do with their bodies sent unimaginable terror through a woman.

A room full will both be fun and challenging.

He made the decision to scrap the rifle and head into the camp. Stealth and patience would be the rule tonight. Xi took his rifle apart and hid it among some bushes. He planned on retreiving it later tonight.

For now, Xi began to inch his way towards the camp. Doned all in black, complete with black facial paint, Xi enjoyed the challenge of remaining silent. During his training he was instructed by a teacher that knew the ways of the ninja. Xi remembered the beatings he took when he made a slight sound on the floor. At one point he had a broken nose, a ripped ear, a swollen eye, and a few broken toes. And still he had to complete the task of moving across a floor without a sound. Each failure made it harder and harder to complete. Each failure resulted in a beating.

After several weeks Xi completed the task. He had never known such accomplishment. Nor did he ever experience so much constant pain.

As his training continued so did his hatred to those who hurt him. Revenge became a motivator. As his training ended a plan formulated in his mind of how to strike back at those who beat him.

He used the training that given to him and moved with stealth into their sleeping quarters. Xi decided to become a modern ninja, one that used guns, bombs, and survelliance techonology. One by one Xi sliced their throats then used a silencer. Each man had a pillow over their head with a single shot into the side of the head.

Twelve people in all. At that moment Xi became hooked on killing.

Before leaving the facility Xi planted bombs throughout. He didn't want another one like himself. He didn't want competition. Worse, he didn't want someone to be constantly hunting him down.

So he destroyed the place.

From a rocky point Xi watched the place. He heard the screams of the remaining trainers. He watched people running around that were on fire. He saw he supreme teacher scream in agony, tearing at his clothes, patting his head to put out flames. In the end the old man crumpled to the ground. Burning.

There was no remorse. No ill feelings. No guilt. What Xi felt was power. He destroyed an entire compound of warriors. By himself. He knew he had become a killing machine. He had found his purpose.

Xi skirted the outskirts of the camp. He could hear conversations going on. There were people laughing in one of the huts. In another he could smell something being cooked. There was only one hut Xi concerned himself about, the one directly across from him. From where he sat he could see a light on. Shadows moving indicated activity going on. How many were in there he didn't know. Yet. It didn't matter to him.

He bounced from hut to hut. Hiding behind each one. Each time he glanced around to ensure he wasn't being seen. Each time he silent as the night.

Xi maneuvered within two huts. He could hear voices from the target's hut. He took the time to identify each voice so he could get a better guess at the number of people in the hut.

Four distinct voices. Judging from the size of the hut he was confident that that was all there was in there; especially when one throws in suitcases, tools, and beds. Xi bounced to the next hut. Still clear.

He bounced to the next hut and introduced to a mountain of a man. Without a word Xi's world went black.

BEIJING, CHINA

Kim felt like it was his birthday. He had received from the U.S. Embassy a listing of all the Americans serving in China. Teachers. Doctors. Volunteers. Along with that came biographies on each person.

There was the birthday, hometown, marital status, addresss, and even blood type. What Kim particulary focused on the second column of each biography, religious preference.

Some claimed no preference. Kim wasn't interested in these people. He took his green highlighter and X'd out these people.

The ones that stated Baptist, Christian, Methodist, and others that he wanted to see. The yellow highlighter lit up these people.

Then the second most important piece of information he wanted to see, where were these people serving. He wanted to see where the foreign filth were at and send a strong message to all outsiders.

Kim wanted to keep China clean, strong, and unified under government. But he had heard the rumors that many nations were flirting with the idea of changing governments and heading towards democracy.

People were meant to be tamed. Controlled. Like well trained dogs in a circus people will do whatever you ask of them as long as you give them a treat. Kim saw this in America. More and more Americans were becoming dependent on the government. It wouldn't be long before America would be like them. The other nations that were speeding towards democracy.

But it would be awhile. In the meantime America still maintained its status as the banner holder, the role model for democracy and capitalism. Their influence and disease had to be stopped.

For Kim, he could stop that disease in his own country. He would be the cure for the disease.

What amazed Kim was the amount of people from America that were in his country. They reached all corners, were in every major city and town, and were at every university. It wasn't just individuals that were here but groups such families and school classes. There were thousands and thousands of people.

This was going to be more difficult than previously thought.

Kim needed a plan to exterminate these people. Or at least a way to drive them out of the country.

How does one rid a pesky rodent? Kim sat back and finished his drink and stared at the ceiling.

The buzzer told him that his receptionist needed to see him. Kim didn't mind the interruption. Su Lee epitimozed the Chinese attractive woman; being in her late twenties and a former Olympic gymnast, she competed in the Atlanta games where they lost to the American team. Su Lee could handle pressure.

Kim buzzed her back letting her know that she can come in. Dressed in a gray dress suit, Su exhibited every aspect of confidence. Her hair pulled back into a bun. Even after a decade of serious competition Su retained a competitive body. The dress suit emphasized her curves.

Something deliberate no doubt thought Kim.

"I am sorry to interrupt. There's a message from the defense department." Su's voice purred.

Kim imagined hearing that voice all day long. Su was the closest thing to an angel he could imagine. If there were truly angels and a God, she would be the evidence of that. "Do you know what the message is Su?"

"Yes sir. They were wondering two things; first, why were you talking to Ambassador Bortho? Second, why did you request information from the American embassy?"

Rage began to boil inside him. He operated under the radar and strived to not draw attention to himself. A casual conversation and then a favor. He knew Chinese policy. Any time someone talks to a diplomat that conversation must be filed with the defense department. They would then record you as you restate what was said during that conversation.

The process is designed to keep people from talking to diplomats. It started with American President Nixon. When he visited China he would talk to the soldier in the army or to a person on the street. Some of these people said things that Nixon brought back to the United States and shared with key members of his cabinet. This began the West's involvement in human rights.

"Su, I will call them back. Thank you." Su bowed her head, turned, and walked out the office. Usually Kim enjoyed watching her walk out but today he just continued to stare at the ceiling.

He didn't want the defense department to know of his plan. They would order him to stop and not to pursue it any further. He would lose his resources for taking any action whatsoever. The defense department was working hard, like every other organization in the country, to keep the West happy. It was a business mentality. The West was the customer and America was the number one buyer. They were allowed a few concessions as long as they kept buying goods. If they stopped buying, China would fall apart financially and chaos would reign over the land. Starvation would settle into the cities causing riots and violence.

Kim could not believe how his country has become so dependent on a foreign one. He believed China to be independent, with enough resources to survive. But, comfort and goods has become the newest standard.

So now he had to answer to the defense department. A roadblock that he had to get through. He knew he couldn't lie about the meeting. There were enough witnesses at both locations to verify he met with the ambassador.

Well, might as well get this over with. He picked up the phone and called.

"This is Chin Lang's office."

"This is Commander Kim. I had a message to call him."

"Certainly Commander Kim. I will put you through directly."

Within moments Chin's voice came over the line. "Kim, I heard that we need to talk. A little birdie told me that you had a couple of meetings with the American ambassador."

"Yes sir." Kim hated taking the servant role. He worked his whole life to be the one in charge. He didn't want to be inferior because he thought of it as weakness. And Chin knew that Kim felt this way and used it against him every time.

"Why don't you come over later on today and let us discuss those meetings. Will one work for you?"

Kim knew it wasn't a choice question. Chin wanted him at one, regardless of what else Kim had going on.

"I will be there by one."

"Thank you Kim. I will see you then." And with that the line went dead.

Kim hung the phone up. He buzzed Su to let her know of today's appointment so she could make the necesarry changes. Then Kim's mind began to race. Staring at him from the desk was the stack of names. Clear evidence of action taken from the meetings with the ambassador.

One o' clock was three and half hours away. Kim figured in driving time and that left only a little over two hours to get his alibi straight.

Paranoia began to set in and Kim knew it. It was the great tool of the military. He used it often enough on others that he could recognize when it was being used on him. It didn't change the fact that it sent fear into his heart and mind. Kim knew that thinking clearly was going to be a challenge.

Time was wasting. Kim pulled out a piece of paper and went over all the details of the meeting seeing if there were ways to dance around what the conversations were about.

He also didn't know if the U.S. Embassy talked to the defense department.

Paranoia.

What did the ambassador say to them? If he didn't say anything who did? Who else was at the party that would have seen us together then report it in?

Kim scribbled a few more notes on the paper.

Paranoia.

The plane ride to Hong Kong. Stupid. That was too obvious. Too careless. The pilot would have to log in the ride, the passengers. There was also the black box to record conversations. Would the department go that far?

More notes.

Paranoia.

Kim could feel the sweat beading on his forehead. His eyes began to lose focus.

More notes.

He struggled to control his thoughts. Get them in order. The thoughts instead turned to the techniques used by the department to gain information.

More notes.

Paranoia.

A buzzing sound stopped Kim in his tracks. He was surprised by how much he was sweating. His clothes stuck to him.

"Commander, your ride is waiting for you downstairs."

Kim looked at the clock. It was time to go. "Thank you Su." He breathed in deeply regaining his composure. Reaching down he grabbed his notes. He glanced at them one more time to help ready his mind. Instead, terror seized him.

There were no notes. Scribbles upon scribbles covered the page. He quickly threw them into the trash and headed out the door. He ignored the greetings from people.

Seeing his black sedan waiting for him he entered the car. In less than half an hour he would be meeting with Chin.

This is not going to be good he thought.

Su went into Kim's office like she always did when he left. She would empty the trash can, wipe off the water marks from his drink class from the table, and align the chairs as he liked them. He wanted people to know that when they entered his office he was the man in charge. Su bent down to get the garbage when she noticed pieces of paper with scribbles on them. She knew that Kim would be gone for probably the rest of the day. Department meetings always lasted awhile.

She pulled out the papers and had to take a step back. They weren't just scribbles. They were drawings. Page after page showed detail drawings. The first page showed a village that was on fire. People were running around, some on fire. Military personnel were shooting at people.

Another drawing showed people on their knees in a line. Behind the line was a man with a pistol and it was pointed at the back of their heads.

Another showed a young child on his knees, crying and reaching out with his hand. Fear was in his eyes.

The last page disturbed Su more than the others. It wasn't a drawing at all but words. Words repeated over and over again, in various sizes and in a multitude of ways. Words written in block letters, cloud formation, and like snakes.

When she competed in the Atlanta games she ran into an American gymnast. The girl told Su about Jesus Christ. Over the two weeks they became good friends and they correspond back and forth even today. Su accepted Jesus and returned back home to China. Over the last decade her parents, siblings, close friends, and cousins have all accepted Jesus.

Looking at the paper sent chills through Su.

DEATH TO ALL CHRISTIANS THE PLAN BEGINS

GALAPAGOS ISLANDS- 1835

Charles Darwin followed the iguana around the beach. He had never seen anything like this before. The iguana was two and half feet long and scampered over the rocks and and was rushing towards the sea. Charles had never heard of an animal that was so adept at living off of both the sea and the freshwater.

He was revolted by the creature as well as fascinated by it. The iguana was able to hide itself among the porous black rocks. But the creature was extremely clumsy. It amazed him how this creature could survive from its enemies being so clumsy. Its tail size was over the length of its entire body and seemed to be getting in the way of the animal's movements.

Charles dropped down to his hands and knees to gain a better perspective of the animal.

From the distance Charles could hear the calls and noises of the other animals that were unique to these islands; the blue footed booby, the waved albatros, the strum sound of the hummingbirds, and Charles' favorite the tortoiese. Just the other day Charles climbed on the back of one and rode it like a horse. The animal moved slowly across the beach. While the ride didn't cover much area it allowed Charles to scan the scenery without interruption.

The iguana was close to where the water reached the beach. Charles could see the animal sniff the air and then scamper a little more. Sniff. Scamper. Sniff. Scamper.

Then a wave washed over the iguana. Charles jumped to his feet and ran to where the wave kidnapped the iguana. From where Charles stood he couldn't believe his luck. He could still observe the creature.

And what he saw amazed him.

The clumsy animal on land transformed into a graceful dancer in water. The tail that hindered the beast on land became a propellant in the sea. The animal shot towards the algae in the sea and ate. Then it would shoot back up to the surface, gain a breath, and shoot back down again. Then the creature would shoot back and forth. The tail guiding and propelling the creature.

After a short amount of time the creature shot itself from the sea back onto the land. It went to the black rocks to warm itself. Water dripping off of its black skin.

Charles sat on the beach and watched the creature. The creature unaware of its impact on the young scientist did exactly as designed; swim, eat, and sun itself.

Back in time, somewhere, the creature came to look like this. How did it happen? When did it happen?

Charles had to know the answer. There had to be an answer.

GALAPAGOS ISLANDS

Carl had never slept on a boat before. He was surprised by how comfortable he slept and when he awoke he had never woke to the view that greeted him now.

The sea surrounded the yacht. Juan 'borrowed the boat from a friend. Carl watched the sun emerge from the water. The yellow orb bounced its rays over the waves. The reflection of heat and light stirred Carl. The ocean reflected a turquoise blue. From where the yacht sat Carl stared at the ocean floor. He knew how deceiving the view was. The floor looked as though it was only a few feet down when in reality at least a hundred. Schools of fish criss-crossed above the floor and Carl even saw a sea tortoise shoot across at an amazing speed.

As he crossed to the other side his eyes focused on the mountain tops jutting into the sky. A mist sat halfway up the mountain allowing the top to glow from the rising sun. Below the mist the island had a mystical look. Carl was surprised by not seeing a tropical forest. Instead the island looked more like a rocky outpost stuck in the middle of the ocean.

Juan didn't tell Carl where they were going and Carl still didn't have a clue as to where they were at.

"Good morning my friend. Did you sleep well?" Juan stood at the top of the ladder that led to the captain's deck. In his left hand a steaming cup of coffee. Holding up the coffee, "There is coffee below deck for you. If you haven't had South American coffee before you are in for a treat."

"Thank you and good morning to you as well." Carl gave a warm morning wave and went below deck. Sure enough he could smell the coffee. Just the aroma stirred a person. Pouring himself a cup he looked forward to what he called the wake up juice. Taking a sip he found himself spitting it out. On the wall in front of him a splatter of coffee and spit. Here he was on a million dollar yacht and Carl spits out South American coffee. Classy he thought.

Behind him laughter erupted. Juan watched the whole incident happen. "I never get tired of watching that." Juan came into the room with a towel in hand already wiping the mess from the wall. "If you aren't used to it the coffee has some kick to it. You can fru-fru it up with some creamer in the fridge over there."

Carl, feeling as though his man card had been revoked reached in and grabbed the vanilla caramel creamer. He wondered what else Juan had in store for him today.

Coming back up on the deck Juan pointed to the island outcrop. "That my friend are the Galapagos Islands. Ring a bell for you?"

Carl searched his mind. "They sound familiar but…"

Juan gazed upon the island. Carl couldn't read his face; a mixture of awe, fear, and curiousity. "That my friend is the birthplace of evolution. It was here that Charles Darwin collected and studied specimens to write his book *The Origin of Species*. It is going to be the place we will search out for the next couple of days."

Carl began looking at the island the same way as Juan. Curiosity began to grow in him as well. What would he see? What would he think about when he found something? Will it stir his imagination?

Carl thought of Darwin like many Christians thought of him, an enemy, a type of anit-Christ, a supplanter of truth. Carl gazed upon the island. For such a little piece of real-estate it contained a history of controversy. In the next couple of days he be able to walk in the shoes of Darwin, gaze upon the species that caused him to question nature, and to examine his own doctrine.

"Lord grant me strength.

The feelings toward the island changed for Carl. It no longer looked mysterious or surreal. It now looked dark and forboding. A challenge that needed to be conquered.

SYDNEY, AUSTRALIA

John looked at the railroad cars. "This is going to help me understand the ark?"

"Yes and no. It is going to help you understand the amount of space in the ark."

John was interested in how this conversation progressed. He hoped that Carl and Cathy were having better success in attaining information.

"First mate, you have to erase what you think you already know. The Sunday school version, not real. It's cute but not accurate by any sort of means. Now, look at all these railroad cars. How many do you think there are?"

John looked around. There were quite a few. "I don't know about a hundred. Give or take."

"There are two hundred cars. Imagine all those cars passing you by while you are waiting behind safety bar. That would be a long wait wouldn't it?"

John did hate those waits. He often wondered though what cargo sat inside those cars. As a child he wondered where they were coming from and where they were going. He thought the engineer had the best job in the world because the world seemed to stop for him. The lights would flash and the rumble of the cars would speed on by.

Mike continued, "Two hundred cars. That many cars can haul a lot of stuff at the same time. Wouldn't you agree mate?"

"Yes. I would imagine so."

"Okay, the ark had a million and half cubic feet of volume. This is equivalent to roughly, oh, five hundred and twenty-two railroad cars. Now here comes the fun stuff"

"Over a million and half square feet? You are kidding right?"

"Sorry mate. God's dimensions. Not mine. But here's what's cool.

Let's see how many animals can fit on these here railroad cars. Each car can hold 240 sheep."

"Sheep? Why sheep?"

"That, mate, is a great question. Only eleven percent of the world's land animals are larger than a sheep. That's it. Eighty-nine percent of the land animals are the size of a sheep or smaller. So if each railroad car can hold two hundred forty sheep, and you had over five hundred railroad cars…"

"That's a lot of sheep."

"That's only sixteen thousand animals that would need to be on the ark. That would only take up half of the space on the ark. That leaves room for food, supplies, and water. So let me take you back. In Sunday school you had the picture that had the giraffes, elephants, and all these other big animals. In reality, most of the animals were quite small. Here is something else mate. Most of the animals weren't even full grown yet."

"What?"

"Think about it. What was the purpose of the animals being on the ark in the first place?"

"To save them?"

"To repopulate. Each animal represented the Adam and Eve of its kind. Like humans, we all came from the same two. It doesn't matter if we are black, white, brown. It doesn't matter. Same with those animals. The animals probably weren't full grown yet, therefore, less space taken up. Why would God send old, mature animals onto the ark when he could send young animals that could, well, breed more often." Then with a chuckle, "I bet the animals were all teenagers."

Mike's theory made sense.

"Ok, so the animals fit. How could possibly seven people take care of all those animals?"

Mike laughed out loud. "I get a kick out of that question. People around the world use that as a crutch to destroy the story. They will ignore all animal behavior to try to justify their idea which is that the ark story is false. Ever heard of hibernation?"

"You think the animals slept the whole time?"

"Why is that so hard to believe? We see animals sleep throughout an entire winter. Their bodies are prepared for the long sleep. And remember…"

It was John's turn to interrupt, "The animals were sent by God."

"Exactly. The animals came ready to sleep. Ready to sleep away the voyage. So then let me ask you this, why couldn't all the animals hibernate during the voyage?"

Anything seemed feasible at this point.

"But, considering the seven people on the boat would be bored if they didn't have anything to do, I'm sure God kept some of the critters awake. God enjoys the hard work of his people."

"What about the dinosaurs? You haven't answered that question?" John thought he had finally stumped Mike.

"Mate, most of the dinosaurs were only the size of a small horse. You are thinking of the big ones, the ones weighing in at eighty tons and being forty feet high. But some of those buggers were only the size of chickens. Remember, most land animals are the size of sheep or smaller. Dinosaurs included."

John scanned the abandoned rail yard again. "That is incredible."

"It surely was mate. It surely was."

GOBI DESERT

Cathy didn't hear the first woman, or the second one, but she did hear the third woman scream, a blood curdling scream. Cathy shot to an upright position. She could hear noises, a struggle was happening but she didn't know where.

She felt a push on her right side and she pushed back. Two vice grip hands grabbed her shoulders and threw her from the bed. She landed on another bed. She felt the bed. Sticky. Warm. Blood. The bump under the sheets didn't move. Cathy could only guess what happened. On her hands and knees she tried to orientate herself on where she was in the hut.

If she screamed she could alert the rest of the camp that there was trouble. On the other hand, it would alert the intruder as well and she might be dead before help arrived.

Somehow the place was pitch dark.

Cathy continued to feel around when a pair of legs backed into her and fell. Another body followed the first. She heard grunting, panting, a choking sound. Cahty didn't know what to do. One of the legs came up and kicked her right in the mouth. A dizziness overcame her.

More disorientation.

Then her mouth warmed as blood began to pour out of her mouth as well as down her throat. She could feel with her tongue a couple of broken teeth. Her lip was swelling at a rapid pace.

Cathy could hear the struggle. A sudden grunt let her know that there was a man in the hut. Cathy forgot about her mouth and continued to feel around. Her head ran into a corner causing a sharp pain.

Cathy could only dream of what she would look like in the morning.

If she made it to morning.

There was another pair of hands was feeling around and one touched hers. Terror shot all around her. The other hand was shaking and Cathy could tell it was a woman's. Cathy was afraid to speak. She didn't want to alert the man on where she was.

Another scream erupted from the hut.

Cathy's stomach knotted and caused her to freeze.

A laughing sound could be heard and then footsteps.

"My pretties, why are you down here?"

Her hair was yanked but she refused to give this maniac the pleasure of her screaming. She tried to fight back but she was sitting on her knees. The man's hand was a vice. The other woman though let out a scream. She thrashed around.

"Would either one of you know where I can find a Cathy?"

Cathy froze. He's looking for me?

"So you must be Cathy. I've been following you for a long time."

By stopping her struggle she alerted the intruder. A new kind of fear swept over her.

"I was watching you this whole time. Night vision goggles." Cathy heard a tapping sound. She still couldn't see a thing. "I will make this quick. This little expedition that you and your friends are on, well, it seems that someone doesn't like it. I was hired stop you. I decided to go with ladies first."

Cathy was yanked to her feet by her hair. "It is too bad you can't look into my eyes. But I can see into yours." A laugh followed. "Are you ready to show me your fear."

From above a light shot through the darkness. Then a couple more. The intruder looked up and yelled. The night vision goggles caught the light causing the man to let go of Cathy and stumble in the dark. A thump in the middle of the hut let Cathy know that someone else just entered the hut.

Streams of light were waving around. Lights were searching for the intruder but a crashing sound alerted everyone he had just left via the front door. Cathy heard shouts and saw people running by the door. Apparently the man went left when he left the hut.

A pair of hands grabbed Cathy by the shoulders. She fought and twisted and turned but the hands held tight.

Then a voice pierced the fear, "Cathy. Cathy. It's me Yun. It's alright. It's going to be alright. He's gone. He's gone."

She opened her eyes and a beam of light highlighted his face. Tears continued to run down her face but this time they weren't from fear but for relief. She buried her head into his chest and sobbed.

His arms wrapped around her and pulled her closer. Sob after sob raked her body.

Yells continued on the outside. Flashlights continued to slice the darkness.

As Cathy and Yun made their way outside Cathy noticed the other women. Eyes were full of confusion, terror, and shame. Some were holding onto each other. Two sat on the ground, just staring into nowhere. Others just watched the confusion around them. Men running around trying to find the intruder.

But he was gone.

As quickly as he showed up he had also disappeared.

Someone nearby began brewing some coffee and had started a fire. Some of the women began to migrate over to the warmth and the light. Cathy felt herself drawn to the comfort of the fire.

Yun continued to hold her tight. She let him. His arms, heartbeat, smell comforted better than any fire.

As her mind slowed down she began to recall the night's events. "Yun?"

He released her a little, just enough to look down into her eyes, "Yes?"

"I need to talk to you about tonight. The man spoke to me. I need something to write down what he said before I forget." Not that she would forget but she had always found writing a comfortable tool.

Yun raced into another hut and brought out a pad of paper and a pencil. She sat on a log and began to do through the events. She wrote down the man's words and the fear washed over her again.

"Yun, I need to get to a reliable phone and now. My friends are in big trouble." She looked down at the words and saw 'This little expedition you and your friends are on.'

Xi disappeared into the sand hole that he made before the attack. He had learned early in his career to always have a place to hide. It didn't matter whether he had accomplished the job of not. About fifty yards from the camp was a sand dune. In reality it was just a covering. On the back side of the dune was a hole. The hole was a tunnel that wound down about ten feet and entered a chamber. The chamber held two days of food, was bid enough for Xi to stretch out in, and gave shelter from the heat and cold of outside.

It also gave a place for Xi to think without being pressured from Commander Kim. Xi had to evaluate tonight's events.

The plan seemed simple enough. Cover the windows and lock the door on the inside. Create darkness so that only he could see with his night vision goggles. Then create chaos by killing one or two women. In the middle of the chaos kill Cathy so that it looked random since others were also dead.

But Xi got sloppy.

He forgot about the hole in the roof.

Xi rubbed his eyes as they continued to sting from the blinding light. Purple dots danced in front of Xi's eyes. It would go away, he hoped.

He stretched out in the cavern. He would wait a day until the energy level died down. Then at night he would leave the cavern and head back to Beijing. He knew where the others were at. He was also confident that the woman would alert her friends.

It would make things more difficult but not impossible.

Leaning his head back he closed his eyes.

Thinking about the woman's eyes, the terror that was in them, the control that he had over her gave Xi some solace.

Within moments he was asleep.

DALLAS, TEXAS

Newsreporters, vans, and satellite dishes became the new fixtures on campus. In the last few days it was not uncommon for students and staff to be stopped and questioned on the current scandal of Dr. Curtis Trough.

"He always seemed like a nice guy. I feel bad for his wife and kids."

"A person has to practice what they preach. I'm thinking of changing schools to be honest."

"No matter how good a person does raising their kids there are sometimes bad apples."

"Kids will make their own choices no matter what a parent does."

"All his wife wants is the money. Why else would she divorce him?"

The Eleven now had the TV removed from their meeting room. Since the prayer vigil each man had fulfilled their responsibility of holding two more accountable. The atmosphere in the room was jovial, lighthearted, encouraging. There was still a mountain to be climbed in terms of dealing with the clean up of the scandal, but every man knew it was going to happen in God's time and in God's way.

Dr. Randy Johnson stood among his brothers in the faith and called for the meeting to start. "My brothers, it is so good to see you this morning. As you know things have been a little hectic around campus the last few days."

Sighs and chuckles were heard around the room at the slight sarcastic remark.

"But this is an opportune time for the church. Our fellow brother and his family are hurting. They are in emotional, spiritual, and physical pain. There are going to be scars that last a lifetime on each member of that family. Each person in that family feels alone and isolated. They have no one to talk to. No on to confide in. In fact, they trust nobody."

Randy let the words hang in the air before he continued, "We have committed ourselves to each other and while that is good it is not enough. Remember, when we came together we committed ourselves to everyone, through good times and bad, not just when it was convenient and easy."

Heads hung low around the room. A few nodded in agreement.

"We need to commit ourselves to the Trough family. Our families need to join us in this commitment. We must not judge or discredit them. Instead, we will love on them, serve them, and most of all honor them. If we are the church, then we need to act like it by doing it. They have needs. We need to serve those needs. When they turn us away, we love even more. My brothers, I believe that God will bless this endeavor because he promised in his Word that he would. Will you join me in this?"

Each man raised his head. Hope. Joy. Love. Every man had these qualities shown upon their faces. They stood up and circled, clasping their arms on top of each other's shoulders.

One by one they went around, offering up prayers for Curtis, Kathleen, Emily, Johnathon, and Sharon. Prayers went up asking for guidance on what the Eleven could do to serve them.

When it was over they felt the Holy Spirit fill the place. They knew there would be a battle but they were strengthened.

INDIA - 330 BC

Alexander scanned the surrounding area. Dense forest loomed until the horizon line. He had heard the locals talk about a monstrous beast, one so huge, so monstrous that even when talking about he beast the locals began talking in whispers.

Fear was not in Alexander's being.

He had conquered most of the world. His own name struck fear in man. His status was becoming legendary.

There was nothing to be feared when you are Alexander, leader of the mighty Greek army.

But Alexander had respect for those things, or creatures, that could also strike fear. He wanted to see for himself this mighty and terrible beast. His guides, a couple of hunters from the village guided him to here. They were too afraid to proceed any futher but were willing to give directions.

On the rock ledge Alexander could view the great forest. The sun was on its downside. A slight shade was protruding from the far reaching mountains.

Off to the right, about two hundred yards out birds shot from the trees into the air. Alexander scanned the area to see what the disturbance was. At first there was nothing.

A mighty roar, more like a screech mixed with a roar, trumpeted over the forest.

It was a sound unlike any Alexander had ever heard. To his great amazement he found himself taking a step back when he heard the noise.

He thought to himself, "I never take a step back for I am Alexander."

Alexander noticed the river, bending and weaving its way through the dense foliage. It was wide enough so that the trees could not hide it, provide you were looking for it. An expert tracker could notice cuts in the forest and recognize those cuts as trails or rivers. Alexander was an experienced tracker, who had seen terrains of all kinds. He recognized the river.

The beast was moving towards it.

Alexander heard the trees bend, the stomping on the ground, the snapping of branches and logs. Whatever it was it was big. Alexander already had in his mind images of what it would look like.

The beast broke into the open. Nothing in this world could prepare a man for such a site. Especially a man like Alexander who had seen most of the known world and many of its animals. It stood on two legs, with two arms that seemed insignificant to the rest of the body. The head was bigger than two chariots. And in that head were pointed teeth made for one purpose. The claws on this beast could cleanly rip a man in two.

It bent down for a drink. Alexander saw the tail of the beast. As long as a tree trunk but only thicker. Alexander could tell the tail was for balance.

On the opposite bank strode another beast, four legged and round. Alexander recognized the beast from previous travels.

In an instant the first beast leaped over the river and sank the razor teeth into the other. A howl escaped the doom animal. One of feet of the first extended its claws and Alexander could hear the flesh being torn into.

In mere seconds the beast had died.

Alexander could hear the flesh being ripped off. He could hear the bones cracking, breaking between the mighty teeth. After the beast had had its fill it disappeared again into the forest. The carcass laid next to the bank. Creatures of the dead came to feast on the new meal.

Alexander had never seen such power and aggressiveness in an animal before. He looked down and saw his hands shaking.

Fear.

For once in his life a thing had sent chills into Alexander. He had seen something that could send heart-stopping terror into people.

Alexander now believed the locals. Their tales of monstrous beasts roaming the countryside and destroying animals.

He believed their stories of dragons for he had just seen one. He heard its cry, had seen it kill and eat.

GALAPAGOS ISLANDS

Carl had to crane his neck to see the top of dormant volcano. It was hard to see with the mist and clouds rolling by the mountain. Carl could still hear the crashing of the waves and smell from the ocean. He imagined that no matter where he was on the island that that would be the case. But, he had to keep reminding himself that he was here on business, to seek the truth.

Juan followed closely behind. He had traveled these island multiple times; always in search for understanding. Lately it seemed as though the islands were mocking him. Daring him to challenge the mysteries they held.

A buzzing sound startled him back to the preset.

Carl sat and stared at the tiny bird. It seemed so insignificant, so ordinary, but it was this bird that Darwin used in concocting his ideas on evolutionary change. Darwin was amazed at the finches, mockingbirds, and the marine iguana when he visited the islands in 1835. He wondered why the islands themselves had different kinds of mockingbirds and finches and also why those some birds would be different from the mainland. According to Darwin, they evolved in order to adapt to their environments.

Carl had to laugh. It was a good thing Darwin never went to Australia, that would have surely played tricks on his mind. Talk about unique animals to a certain place.

For about ten minutes Juan and Carl studied the bird, waiting anxiously for it to do something unique.

But it just flew, collected nectar, and buzzed.

Carl thought this was crazy but he decided to keep an open mind. The bird was no different than other birds. He got up and hiked some more around the island. In a couple of hours Juan and Carl reached to other shoreline. Carl had never seen the blue-footed boobie and had to laugh at their sky-blue feet. It reminded him of the cartoon show the Smurfs where the little creatures were all sky blue in color.

Sweeping down the coastline flew the albatross. These two birds were unique to the islands. But again, Carl had to fight the fact that there birds were not unique in the sense that he had seen birds fly, swoop, land, and eat before. He thought of the kangaroos and koala bears. Animals unique only to the land of Australia. He remembered John talking about the antelope in Wyoming. They were thick like flies and yet they had an uncanny sense of staying only in Wyoming state lines. The mighty buffalo roamed the plains of Montana and Wyoming. Carl began to think that most places in the world had unique animals for a given region. Leopards. Elephants. Polar bears.

Carl and Juan walked along the shoreline discussing Carl's ideas.

"I'm beginning to think that Darwin was off his rocker Juan."

"Stop right there my friend. First, no matter what your view of Darwin is, it must be understood that he was an intelligent man. He was curious about the world around him. In fact, I admire that he put forth the amount of energy and resources he did to understand the world."

"But," Carl said with a questioning tone.

"But, he was human." Juan watched Carl stop in his tracks. He knew that of all the answers Carl was expecting to hear this was last on the list. "He followed the process of scientific method. He formed a hypothesis based off of the evidence he saw. In fact, based off of his sampling, it actually makes sense."

"But," Carl said again, waiting for the scientific punchline.

"His sampling was bad. He based all of animal kingdom on these islands. Darwin does mention a couple of other examples but all his findings are based on these islands. How can one man, with all of the animals in the world, make a claim as big as his, and have it accepted by so many? That is the most puzzling question of all." Juan paused to take a breath, collect his thoughts. "Darwin's theory, in time will come to be known as Darwin's folly. Had Darwin made his hyposthesis on just these islands he still would have been known as a genius. But, to have it blanket the entire world, pure nonsense."

Carl couldn't resist the temptation to ask more questions. He needed to know the truth, "What do you mean by the sampling being bad?"

Juan looked up and scanned the ocean. It was clear to Carl the man was befuddled by what was going on in academia. Carl was looking at a casualty of war, a man who sought the truth and paid some high consequences. "First, the marine iguana; an animal that eats and survives in two environments, land and sea. There are many examples of other animals that do this around the world. There is the steelhead of the Pacific Northwest in America. The platypus in Australia, talk about the contradiction to evolution. That animal can't make up its mind what it wants to be. Is is mammal? Then why does it lay eggs? If it lays eggs it must be a bird of some kind? No, it has fur and no wings. Then, it must be an amphibian. No, again fur, warm blooded. You want to use narrow sampling to base scientific altering knowledge on, then why do scientists ignore the platypus? Then how about those bears?"

Carl could tell Juan was getting fired up. The snowball effect of getting information out of Juan just needed a push and Carl got a sense that having Juan stop now was going to be impossible. Juan's frustration, his past experiences came flowing out of him in fact after fact. Emotions were raw as he brought up example after example of how evolution does not work.

Pandas have teeth for meat but eats bamboo.

Living fossils such as alligators, snakes, and ferns and trees have been found that scientists believed were extinct such as the ginkgo tree.

Bears in general have carnivore features but most are vegetarian.

Bats eat fruit, nectar, insects, and small animals, and blood. But their teeth are not built for these types of food.

Example after example. Plants and animals from around the world. Juan kept going. Finally after twenty minutes he stopped. Just stopped.

Juan gazed up at the sky and closed his eyes. Carl wasn't sure what he was doing. Was he praying? Calming down? Letting the sun bathe him?

When Juan turned back to meet Carl's gaze Carl could see he was crying. "Carl, do you know how frustrating it is to tell people the truth, show them evidence after evidence of something, only to be ridiculed and taken as a fool?"

Carl didn't mean for it to happen. It was a natural reflex. "My friend, everyday I go through that process. Try telling people about Jesus."

SYDNEY, AUSTRALIA

John and Mike drove back to Mike's office. The sun was setting bathing the city in oranges and yellows. With the heat dropping people began to stream out of their homes and walk the sidewalks and play in the parks.

John and Mike continued to talk about the ark and the flood. It amazed John to think of the devastation of the flood. Something so widespread and yet so fast. It was hard to fathom.

But as Mike pointed out to him, "Do you know how much the human brain weighs? Go ahead, take a guess."

"I don't know. About five pounds?"

"Three. Three pounds. Do you know how much of our brain we use to think with?"

John knew when he was being set up but he played along anyway. "I heard somewhere ten percent."

"That's right. Ten percent of something that only weighs three pounds. Now, let me ask you this. Do you think something that is only three pounds can understand the vastness of the universe? Do you think that something we only use ten percent of can figure out all the complexities of the world around us? That mate takes more faith than any Christian I know."

The wound through the spaghetti of streets to return to the university. John enjoyed being back among a college setting. Since he left Laramie he had been hiking in the desert, climbed around ruins in a tropical forest, and studied a rail yard. A college setting was home. It felt comfortable.

As John and Mike made their way to Mike's office they noticed a man sitting in a chair just outside the door. It wasn't unusual for both men to have students waiting for them. What made this unusual was that this man was dressed in a suit with a crew cut. The man clearly played football and even sitting down he was intimidating.

As John and Mike approached the man rose. John's first instinct was to run. But the thought seemed foolish. There was no doubt that this man, despite his size, could probably run down most people and overtake them.

"Mr. John Bush," the man extended his hand. As John took it he was surprised by the strength and size. John glanced down and couldn't see his hand it was enveloped.

"I am." He was shocked to be at Mike's office, in Australia, on the other side of the world and receive an office visit. "What can I do for you?"

"Do you know a Cathy Jurkovich?"

A hesitation in John's voice already gave the answer away.

"We need to talk. Your life maybe in danger."

Mike had coffee brewing and sat in his chair behind the desk. John and the stranger sat next to each other. It was clear the man was uncomfortable with the seating arrangements. John imagined that the man would have preferred to be in Mike's chair as he probably liked being in charge and therefore in a position of authority.

"My name is David. I was sent to protect the three of you by the Twelve."

John had to let that sink in. He still wasn't over the shock of being in a shooting gallery in Angkor. He chalked it up as a random event. Wrong place at the wrong time. Now the fact was settling in that maybe it wasn't so random.

"A couple of weeks ago a man contacted me. He mentioned that the three of you; a Cathy, Carl, and John, you, were seeking out information that may be considered dangerous. As my boss said, 'A liability to others' investments.' So I followed you. I was on the plane with you from Hawaii to Cambodia. I was at the park when the shooting happened."

"Then why didn't you stop it?" John couldn't help himself. The thought of being someone's target practice didn't sit well.

"Calm down Mr. Bush. I did manage to see what the man looked like that shot at you. I have an identification on him. But, you three threw a curve ball on me and on your shooter. You all split up. Don't get me wrong, I understand why, but obviously I can't be in three places at once."

The gurgling sound alerted everyone that the coffee was ready. Mike, being the good host, got up and grabbed three cups and prepared the coffee. Mike and John were surprised when David asked for cream. The man was a man's man and he wanted to soften up his coffee? John liked the fact that he had at least one up on the man for masculinity.

"Thank you." Taking a sip David continued. "I have other people assigned to protect your friends. It seems the threat is real. Cathy, who just recently returned from the Gobi Desert was involved in an attack. She was in a hut with eleven other women. Three of the women were murdered. Cathy was going to be the fourth except our operative arrived to chase off the enemy."

John's heart was in knots. He was relieved to know that Cathy was alright. He couldn't imagine the fear she must have felt of having the murderer that close. He then thought of the other women, brutally slain. Who would do such a thing?

"We are transporting her to Alaska where she will be hiding out for awhile or until we can find out who is behind all this."

"What about Carl? Is he okay?"

"He is fine. Our operative is arriving in Peru today. It was a little trickier getting a person down there. It will be even trickier following him." David's voice trailed off. He took a sip of coffee. More like buying time to collect his thoughts. "I need to know what you three are doing. Whatever it is is big enough to catch the attention of some powerful people."

John felt as though he was in some sort of action film. He was out finding evidence, artifacts to better benefit the world. Along the way there were bad guys trying to stop him and his friends from finding these key pieces. They were willing to kill to stop the find. Only problem was that this was no film, this was real life and John was scared. Just sitting in the chair John could feel his heart racing in his chest. Air was becoming a precious commodity.

He had been through this before. Closing his eyes he began slow, deep breaths. Within a couple of minutes he could feel precious oxygen in his lungs. His heart stopped pounding against his rib cage.

"Asthma?" David asked. "It's a real pain in the backside. Kept me out of the FBI."

John had to laugh at the comment. The man was human after all.

John took a sip of coffee and began to relate the last week's events to David. Mike also paid attention, listening for key details, concerned about his friend and his safety.

When John finished David sat back in his chair. The look on his face showed disbelief and wonder. "Let me get this straight. You have found evidence, actual evidence, that humans and dinosaurs existed at the same time? You also believe that you have evidence that dinosaurs were around less than five hundred years ago? Am I hearing you right?"

John expected this reaction. He couldn't really believe it himself. "Ironically, I believe it now with the shooting happening than I did before."

"What?" Mike choked on his coffee.

"Well, let's think about it. If it wasn't true, why would someone try to kill us or would want us killed? If there is evidence out there that states this, then there must be something at stake if we are correct. Someone out there has a lot to lose if we are right. That person would need to eliminate the possibility of losing everything by eliminating the cause. That would be my friends and I."

"I would have to agree with that." David was aware that the special forces were experts in this. Snipers were used to eliminate people that had information that was detrimental to security. Even international businesses used spies to discredit people who had information on them concerning illegal dealings.

"Then the question is, who would have the most to lose if you are right?" Mike regained his composure after cleaning up the coffee mess on his desk.

"That is a great question." John took a deep breath and let it out. Holding up his hand he began raising fingers for each entity he named off, "Universities. Scientific instutions. Lawyers. Some countries. Some big businesses. Authors and researchers. Scientific organizations."

David interrupted, "Countries? What countries would be interested in something like this? It seems so…so…so insignificant? No offense."

"None taken. But you are right. On the surface it seems insignificant. In reality it is huge. If what we are finding out is true, then it presents a problem to ideologies around the world. It could break down certain belief systems in the world."

"That could create chaos in some countries," finished Mike.

"Exactly," said John. "Exactly."

David, obviously confused, was trying to connect the points. "You are telling me, that a belief in dinosaurs existing alongside man would create havoc in places around the world? How?" He sat back in his chair with a little smugness thrown in. He didn't expect an answer to such a question. It didn't seem that there was one.

As if on cue Mike popped in, "Well, to believe in this theory means that evolution does not exist. If evolution doesn't exist then many scientific entities would be out of business along with millions, if not billions of dollars. Also, if evolution does not exist, then one has to accept the fact that the opposing theory, in this case intelligent design, is the answer." Bowing his head to collect his thoughts and weighing the implications he was saying Mike continued, "To accept intelligent design is to say that there is the possibility that God exists. If we continue with that logic, if God exists, then everything associated with God also exists."

John was bubbling with joy. Mike was tying the loose ends together. He was calculating the implications. John looked over at David and was surprised to see him hanging on every word. He too was weighing every word.

"Lastly, if God exists, then man becomes accountable." Mike looked up, sorrow filled his eyes. "And man does not want to be accountable."

The words stung. David looked as if he had just cut down a tree and it rolled over on top of him. He looked crushed. Defeated. The idea of God existing. The idea that there is physical evidence seemed overwhelming.

"You know. I have studied the ark. It seemed interesting, but it never occurred to me that there were implications."

David looked at John. Wonderment and curiousity filled him. "What do I need to know?"

John didn't know what to say. "Well, I'm new to this whole Christian thing. Just a couple of days ago I became a believer myself." With that John shared his story. David soaked up the words like water to a sponge.

Mike filled in scripture to reinforce what John was saying.

David dropped to his knees. With tears in his eyes he accepted Jesus Christ as his Lord and Savior. Mike had a hand on David's right shoulder, John on the left.

John couldn't believe what was going on. But he was enjoying it.

DALLAS, TEXAS

Troy stood next to his blue Ford pickup. Across the street were newsvans and reporters. They were camped out in front Curtis' home. Packed under his arm was some brownies that his wife had made. It wasn't much. What does a person bring in a situation like this for comfort? There was no card designated for 'Life Going Down the Tubes and Taking Family With You' or 'Life is Public Spectacle' on the market.

Troy contemplated what he was going to say and how he was going to say it. The last time the did that exercise was when he was getting ready to propose to his wife. He remembered the nerves and the fear of rejection. Funny how those same feelings were welling up in him now.

Thump. Thump. Thump.

Troy looked up to see a news helicopter flying overheard. Troy imagined the copter's camera showing the conglamaration of vehicles and people.

Down the street protesters held up signs saying that Curtis was a hypocrite. Money grabber. A liar.

Others held up signs showing support stating forgiveness and compassion.

Police maintained a stately vigil to ensure that no one would start anything stupid.

Troy scanned the house. It was evident that someone had thrown something at the house. Evidence of fruit and eggs were on the windows and decorated the colonial white house.

He wondered what atmosphere was on the inside. He thought through the feelings; scared, alone, desperate. Or was it forgiving? A time of healing despite what the world was doing on the other side of the door?

He couldn't begin to imagine.

Gearing up all his confidence he walked through the throng of reporters. He tried to act casually, not wanting to draw attention to himself or to Curtis' family. He was praying that he would get through unnoticed.

His prayer was answered. The crowd of reporters and camera people gave no second look to Troy. To them he was one of them. Who would be stupid enough to go to the front door of this house?

Troy had to watch his step of cables and equipment, but he snaked his way through the maze. About ten yards ahead of him was the front door. A curving sidewalk cut its way through the front lawn. Flower beds lined the front of the house while two eight foot lamps stood sentry by the front door. Many times he walked this path. Before it was inviting, safe. Now, the path seemed uncertain.

Doubts rose in his mind. Would anyone even want to answer the door? Would they want anyone to come in? Who was he to the family? A nobody.

"Grant me strength Lord. Your will be done."

With that he left the mass of reporters. He ventured alone up the sidewalk. About two thirds of the way he heard a reporter yell something. Without looking behind him he felt the weight of cameras upon his back. Sweat beaded down his back and forehead. He felt the glass container of brownies shaking in his hand.

The doubts fought furiously for his mind. Troy fought them away and kept his eyes on the door. He felt his stomach twisting inside of him. If he felt this way just walking up a sidewalk and having done nothing wrong what must Curtis be feeling?

Troy raised his hand to know when the door opened.

"Hello Mr. Reiner."

"Hello Emily. I thought I would stop by and drop off these brownies." Troy held out with both hands the brownies. He wasn't sure if it was the length of time, the nervousenss, or the weight of cameras on him but the small tray was getting heavy.

"I was wondering if I could come in. I've been praying for you all and…and"

This was a bad idea. I looking like I'm snooping. Just turn and walk away. Walk away.

"Let him in," a voice from somewhere in the house said. Troy recognized that it was Curtis'.

Emily widened the door. With a nod of his head Troy entered. As soon as he cleared the entryway the door shut. Troy began to think that maybe outside with the reporters was safer. It definetely felt cozier than the house.

Thump. Thump. Thump.

Troy could hear the helicopter flying overhead.

He looked around and noticed that things were different; pictures missing from the mantle, the couch sat uneven. On closer inspection the couch had a rip across all three cushions. There were holes in the walls about the size of softballs.

Troy continued to follow Emily into the kitchen. Sitting at the kitchen counter was Curtis. Emily departed the scene without so much as a word or glance at her dad. The silence weighed the room with uncertaintaty. Curtis was scanning a magazine and drinking his coffee.

Thump. Thump. Thump.

Troy stared at the body before him; it was hard to imagine that this shell of a man was once dynamic, charismatic, could control thousands in a stadium, and lift your emotions. Now, the man obviously hasn't shaved in days. The stress and isolation from the world has also thinned him creating a walking skeleton. Troy was guessing on when Curtis ate last. Curtis' eyes were hollow looking and bloodshot and his hair danced in different directions.

Curtis had always taken great pride in his appearance. What irony thought Troy. Shed the exterior and what is left. Troy felt for the first time that he was seeing the real Curtis. The man was alone, devasted, and dirty.

Thump. Thump. Thump.

Troy could see how the barrage from the world can push a man into isolation. Everyday, all day, for the last few days the world was prying to get into this house. Now Troy wanted out.

"Good morning Troy." Curtis didn't look up from his magazine. The sound seemed deafening and out of place, like it didn't belong.

"Good morning Curtis." Curtis laughed at the word good.

"Good? If being alive is good then I'm good. Other than that, I'm not good." Curtis laid down his magazine and stared at Troy with those hollowed, bloodshot eyes. Troy wanted to look away, feeling embarassed by the man but the man was a stranger in appearance. For Troy it was difficult to comprehend that the voice of the man he knew didn't match the appearance of the man he knew. "Why are you here?"

Troy thought about this question many times and still didn't have an answer. He motioned with is right arm if he could sit down and Curtis gave the cursory nod.

"I don't know. I don't know why I am here to be honest with you." Troy searched for the right words to say. "The other day we prayed. We prayed for each member of your family and for you." Troy was gaining a little more confidence, more control.

Thump. Thump. Thump.

"Listen, I don't need your pity or your good works. Okay? I just need time."

Troy looked at his former mentor straight in the eyes, "You are wrong. What you need is someone to love you. To hold you accountable. And to guide you." Troy felt the resolve in his own voice. He prayed that Curtis felt the power of his words also. "It is time you listen to me. You and your family are sitting here, isolating yourselves from the world. The thing is the world isn't isolating you. They are using you to attack family, church, and God."

"Don't tell me about my family or how I am feeling. You have no idea what is going on around here." Curtis was getting up out of his seat with such intensity of anger that for a moment Troy was afraid of the man. But he remembered what the man looked like moments ago; broken, destroyed, hallowed out.

"You are right. I don't know. But this I know, you are not alone. There are people who still love you and your family. They care about you and you are pushing them away. They can help if you will let them in."

Curtis looked at Troy again. Troy could tell that Curtis was trying to keep the ruse up of being the tough guy but the eyes changed. A glimmer of hope softened the look.

Thump. Thump. Thump.

"Listen. Would I be here if I didn't care about you? I can only imagine what you and your family are going through. But you are not alone and this too will pass. There are people who can help you."

Curis sat back down. Weak. Tired. Defeated.

Curtis looked up at Troy. Troy guessed it took a great deal of strength to raise that head. "So, Troy, you want to help? How? What could you possibly do in a situation like this to fix it?"

Troy looked at his mentor. He felt his eyes pooling up as he cared so deeply about this man. "It's not what I can do but God."

At that, the man before Troy lost what remaing strength he had. Tears flowed. Curtis had finally accepted defeat. Troy let his emotions show as well. He got up from his seat and placed his hands on the man's shoulders. Curtis seemed so fragile physically to the touch. Troy closed his eyes and he prayed.

"My father in heaven I pray for your children; Curtis, Kathleen, Emily, Johnathan, and Sharon. I pray that a peace will blanket this house and that understanding will be granted. I pray that your will be done Lord...."

Looking around the corner of the kitchen was Sharon. She watched as her father bowed his head. She saw the tears streaming down and the sobs shaking his body. To watch her once powerful father look so weak made her cower down more. But she couldn't steal her eyes away from the scene before her. She knew something was happening but she didn't know what. Something powerful and surreal was happening. Sharon wasn't sure if she should be watching and taking in this moment.

Then she watched the man place his hands on her father and her father let him. She had always known her father to resist personal touch. For several minutes she watched and listened.

After several minutes of searching her brain she remembered who the man was with her father. He would come with his family and have meals together. They had a daughter that was her age, eight. She enjoyed their company and looked forward to being with them.

But that was long ago. A tear slid down her face as she thought that that was the last time she had a friend. She remembered running around the yard. Swinging on the swings and hurrying up the stairs into her room to play tea party.

Then she also remembered that both families would gather outside and around the table. The man standing over her father now would pray before the meal. She believed that that was the last time she had prayed before a meal.

Those days are long gone. Now, at least, the house reflects what she had been feeling for the last couple of years. Alone. Isolated.

The man finished his prayer. Sharon slid quietly back from the corner and went back to her room. She had to chew over in her mind what she had just seen.

On her way up to her room she could hear the music blaring from her brother's room. As she passed Emily's room she saw a shadow pass under the doorway. Ahead of her was her parent's bedroom. Only her mom was in there now. Soft music played out from behind the door. aHer room was after Emily's.

She went inside and laid on the bed. She closed her eyes and tried to remember the last time the family was together, happy and having fun. When was the last time they enjoyed each other's company and hung out? When it was just them? That they didn't need other people around to help them have fun. She searched her memories. When she opened her eyes she couldn't make out the room. It was hard to focus.

There were no memories. She couldn't remember those times. As she sat up she saw herself in the mirror. Both eyes wanted to cry but something in her said no. So the tears sat.

So Sharon sat in her room.

Alone.

ANCHORAGE, ALASKA

The lights of the city bounced off the snow flakes. Light seemed to dance and twirl in the night sky. Sipping her cup of coffee Cathy felt her nerves simmering down to a normal rhythm.

The escape from China was a blur. Clutching her robe closer to her body she remebered the three women being killed in the hut. The killer's hand was on her throat. His voice was vile, full of hatred and lust. Yun ushered Cathy from the village and back into the helicopter. She was wisked to Beijing and boarded a plane. She had no idea where the plane was headed as this wasn't a commercial flight. Yun must have connections was how Cathy justified it. On the ten hour flight she had time to collect her composure but questions lingered that desperately needed answers.

It wasn't until the plane touched down and Cathy read the outside of the airport that she realized she was in Anchorage. As she watched the people unload the overhead bins it dawned on her that she didn't have to. She had no clothes, no toileteries, no carry on. For that matter she had no baggage.

Yun arranged for a rental car and found a hotel in downtown Anchorage. With a warm shower and room service that was a bacon cheeseburger with curly fries, Cathy felt awake and alert again. It was good to have American food again. She didn't realize how much she missed it until the juices of the burger ran down her chin.

It was all she could remember. The plane ride was a daze as the camp's events consumed her. She took a sip of coffee. Who was that man? Why me? What was he after? What about Carl and John? Yun said that he was going to work on contacting them and letting them know.

Where would she be without Yun? Her thoughts turned on him and found herself enjoying it. In such a short amount of time she found herself wanting to be with him more and more. She hoped that he was having the same feelings that she was.

He was caring and kind. Yun jumped into that hut and was willing to get hurt, or worse, to save her. He was willing to travel with her from China to Alaska and made sure she had a room to stay in and had something to eat. Along with contacting Carl and John he was also getting clothes for her to wear; at least a pair to go out and do the shopping herself. It's been awhile since she had a boyfriend but she heard enough stories to know that men don't know how to shop for women's clothes.

As she sipped on her coffee she tried to put together the last week's events as well. With all the drama and excitement she hadn't the time to think about her father's passing. She realized that she missed him and he was not coming back. An anger rose in her as a thought materialized that the same man who tried to kill her may have killed her father.

She strode over to round glass table in the corner of the room. Using the standard hotel note pad and pen she jotted down as much information as possible from her father's notes. Along with no clothes and toileteries she left all her notes back in China as well. Feverishly she jotted down information as one piece led to another, then to another. She felt herself in a zone.

A knock on the door snapped her out. She went over and looked through the peephole. Yun. She opened the door and Yun held up two bags. "It's not much but hey, tomorrow you can go crazy and get some clothes."

Cathy realized she was only in a bathrobe. Feeling embarassed she cinched her robe a little tighter. "Thank you. For everything."

Cathy realized that Yun turned red around the cheeks and that he was still standing in the hallway. "Come in. Please."

"What have you been working on?" Cathy strode ahead of Yun to gather up her notes that had fallen on the floor. "Well, everything got left back in China, including my father's notes. I'm trying to remember as much as I could."

Yun looked at her dubiously, "You still want to pursue this?"

Cathy stared at the floor but there was no mistaking the steel in her voice, "My dad died because of this information. Someone tried to kill me because it too. In his letter he mentioned that it could change current human thinking. Already I am having to deal with what I have learned.I cannot let his death be in vain." She turned her head and looked at Yun, "If you have information that would better mankind would you keep it a secret?"

Yun raised his head to the ceiling, unable to match her gaze, "No I guess not. You do understand that those people probably won't give up. It may not take them long to figure out where you or your friends are."

"I know. Speaking of, did you…"

"I did. Carl and John are glad that first you are ok. I think you are all crazy. They want to continue on as well."

Cathy smiled. It was good to know that you aren't alone. "Yun, how difficult would it be to arrange different types of transportation, like Sno-cats?"

Through a sheepish grin, "Why do you ask?"

"I remember in my father's notes about a discovery in Alaska in the early eighties. I wanted to check out the museum and then the site if possible. Since you have a knack for arranging transportation within a moment's notice, a day in advance should be more than ample."

"I'll see what I can do. Meanwhile, how about I order some room service and have some banana splits. I have never had one but I hear they are awesome."

"Sounds good to me. They have doubles you know."

"That sounds even better."

HAUTE MARNE, FRANCE
FEBRUARY 9, 1856

Jaques hated his job. He would have rather picked grapes at his uncle's vineyard than this; digging holes in the underground for the railroads. Day in and day out he busted his back, bled, and ached just so someone else could get rich.

It was monotonous work. Jaque would trek over to the meeting place where all the workers would gather. Then a makeshift transport car would haul workers into the tunnel. Once all the workers were in the tunnel the activity begins. The new shift of workers would begin hauling the blasted dirt and rock from the previous shift. If the shift before was running late dust would still be hanging in the air and it never seemed to want to leave. The new shift would use the picks and shovels to break down rock, shovel the dirt, and prepare holes for the dynamite.

Jaques knew the conditions were dangerous. Everyday he showed up he expected to go home with a missing arm or leg or come out being carried in pieces. Jaques heard of cave-ins where the workers were buried alive. The thought made him shudder. Sometimes fights would break out among the men and the picks and shovels went from tools to weapons. He saw a man impale a pick into another's thigh. Surprisingly, the other man was able to still get in a couple of swings with his shovel upside the other's head.

Yes, the conditions down here were dangerous and unpredictable.

Jaques saw the row of lights that led down to the end of the tunnel. Their goal today was to add another twenty feet to the tunnel. He couldn't believe the bosses. They make these demands but have no idea what the work is. All they care about is making money for themselves.

Soon he thought to himself. I will be in the open making wine.

Screams could be heard farther down the tunnel. Everyone on the traspaort car raised their heads and looked into the faint light. Even the light couldn't penetrate this much darkness. More screams came. Chills went up Jaques' back. These were screams and yells of terror.

Everybody was entranced with the new distraction that the transport car continued down the tunnel, towards the screams. Eyes searched the cavern to see what the commotion was.

Men began running up the tunnel and pass the transport car. Jaques saw their faces; pale, terror, afraid. He looked back down the tunnel. Still the transport car trundled forward.

The screams increased. Intermittently a man would be able to run pass the transport car having the same look as the others.

Finally the car stopped. Curiousity overruled common sense as each man stared into the tunnel. Jaques had to know what was going on. He also needed to know if anybody needed help. He knew many of the men, knew their families. They lived in his neighborhood and church.

Jaques walked along the tunnel wall. His hands felt the rock behind him while he kept his helmet light focused on the path ahead of him. He felt sweat beading up on his back, neck, and forehead. His clothes were sticking him to him. He was beginning his shift but if one measured the amount of sweat and heavy breathing that Jaques was doing at this moment one would have thought it was the end of one.

Screams increased while once in awhile a man would run pass him. Each man looked the same; sheer fright written into each face, eyes popping wide open, hands reaching in front of them grasping for hope and safety. As Jaques got closer he began to see men with wounds. One man, Pierre, sat against the wall murmuring the Lord's Prayer while staring at his hands. Only when Jaques looked closer did he notice that Pierre had no hands only bloody stumps where hands should have been. Shock was settling over Pierre as well as terror.

A sound echoed throughout tunnel that froze Jaques' blood. It was as if a thousand cats cried a mournful cry at the same time. Jaques had to cover his ears. The sound pierced through his body making it shake and tremble.

Still Jaques pressed on. Curiousity was tugging him forward. Every ounce of his brain was telling him to turn around, that death was at the next step but that part of the brain that desires to know, that cries for knowledge was thumping hard in his head. It was the same part that was curious at the Garden of Eden. That part that desired to know what God knew and all consequences be set aside.

That was the part driving him forward.

A sudden wind knocked him back two steps. The suddenness was as unexpected as the next wave of wind that hit Jaques. The warmth of the tunnel took some of the chill out.

Until that dreadful sound echoed again. Jaques was close. The sound wanted to make his ears pop from the pressure.

Jaques began to see dead bodies on the ground. Eyes staring at an eternity of fear.

"Turn around. Turn around. Turn around," thought Jaques to himself. "This is stupid. Stupid."

Jaques stopped, frozen before the site before him. Through the haze he could see the end of the tunnel was moving. It was alive. Jaques could feel the flapping of the wind. He cupped his hands over the helmet light just enough to see but not to draw attention to himself.

Jaques hid behind a rock. He then realized he was sharing the rock with Peter, only Peter was missing a right leg and his midsection was opened up. Jaques ignored the corpse and focused on the moving wall.

Some of the men were fighting off the wall. Their weapons seemed insufficient to a moving wall.

It was until some of the men's helmet lights shined on the wall that Jaques could make out what was before him.

A bat, with the wing span twice the size of an average man, was staring at the men coming at it with pick axes and shovels. It was as black as the tunnel with skin that looked oily. Thick. The neck was long and the mouth contained sharp teeth. Eyes bulged yellow like the halogen lamps that line the streets.

Jaques turned himself around. He found himself gasping for breath. Reconciling the thoughts that were flashing in his head. The emotions were mixed; should he run and save his own life or join these brave men and destroy this creature. Pierre with missing hands. Peter beside him. At Jaques' feet was a handle from a shovel. The blade was missing and the end was pointed. Spear.

Jaques grabbed the new weapon. Don't think. React. Thinking would say save your own skin and get out of here. With both hands grasping the new weapon Jaques twisted from behind the rock and joined the army of construction workers.

Up close Jaques could feel the hot breath of the creature. A wing brushed Jaques sending him tumbling back. Regaining his senses he saw an opening for attack.

Rushing forward he held the spear at his waist. As he got closer he prayed that he would not be seen by the creature. Even the creature, Jaques hoped, could not see through the dust.

He pulled his hands back and drove the spear into the creature's belly. Jaques let a war cry that his Norman ancestors would have been proud of.

The creature let out a scream. Its wings flapped back leaving itself unprotected. Other men rushed forward sending pick-axes into its belly.

The creature let out another scream. The men became braver.

Jaques pulled out his spear and thrust it again and again. Blood covered Jaques but the adrenaline and thoughts of his construction brothers made him into a savage warrior.

A sound erupted from the creature that made Jaques and the others step back from their offensive onslaught. The group gathered in a line, helmet lights focused on the dying creature before them.

Weapons were pointed forward. Every muscle was set for attack, but the focus was watching a creature never before seen dying before them.

The creature swayed back and forth. Then it collapsed.

A cloud of dust erupted from the new corpse.

Through the haze men smelled the blood. They could taste the hallow victory as their eyes focused on the bodies of their comrades.

"I'll go get some help if you want to help those that are wounded," someone said.

Jaques went back to Pierre and checked his pulse and chest. He was alive. Deciding that only his hands were injured Jaques carried him back to the entrance for medical care. The blinding light and crowds waiting outside stunned him momentarily.

Medical crews were waiting outside anticipating that there would be injured and fatalities.

Two days later Jaques sat with the seven men who had fought off the creature. In the office of Luke Chaplain, the owner of the railroad company, the men were treated to a wonderful lunch roasted duck, fresh vegetables and fruits, baked potatoes, and wonderful apples pies.

Jaques never considered himself a somebody. He was just existing and made it through life one day at a time. In the last two days he was greeted with smiles, handshakes and pats on the back. Wives came up and gave him kisses of gratitude for saving husbands.

Now here he was having lunch with a rich man, in a rich man's office.

Jaques made it a point to savor every second of this moment, every morsel of food, and every sip of the wine.

Luke entered his spacious office with another man and placed themselves at the end of the table. Jaques found it easy to identify Luke from the stories that he had heard. He was a small man with delicate features. It was easy to see that he had earned his money the old fashion way, inheritance. But, somehow, he had always had the respect of the workers. Luke strived for safer working conditions and that the men were given fair wages.

"Gentlemen, I want to thank you for your acts of heroism. Your actions saved many lives, and well, you saved me a lot of money." People laughed out of kindness and fear they would lose their jobs if they didn't. "This person here is Paul Luxom, a naturalist and scientist. He heard of your battle with the creature and wanted to check out the creature himself. I believe that he has something to tell you gentlemen." With that Luke stepped to the side and let Paul step forward.

Paul Luxom was about as close to ordinary that Jaques had ever seen. Everything about the man was bland. Even the voice was enough to put one to sleep. Jaques would normally had fallen asleep when a man was like this was talking if it wasn't for what the man had to say, "Gentlemen, what I am about to tell you is confidential. Mr. Chaplain will discuss with you afterwards what that will mean to you. What you saw in that tunnel was a pterodactylus anas, a pterodactyl."

"Excuse me sir. Am I hearing you right?"

It was clear by Paul's face that he didn't expect a bunch of lowly tunnel workers to understand what he meant.

"Are you telling us that we fought a dinosaur?"

"Well, um, yes." Paul was befuddled which humored the group, Luke included. "Yes you did. We had assumed that this creature had died out years ago…"

"But clearly you were wrong!" Jaques didn't know the man but enjoyed the comment as did the others.

"Um, yes. The scientific community was quite surprised by the find."

"You were surprised. We were the ones that woke him up."

Paul could tell that he was going to have a hard sell with the group. Jaques enjoyed the fact that Luke was also laughing, comfortable with being with his men.

"The Scientific Institute of France would like for you to not mention what you have discovered in the tunnel."

A moment of stunned silence.

"You are kidding me right? That creature killed good men in that tunnel."

The casual atmosphere was replaced with anger and shock.

"I carried a man out that had lost his hands. He will never be able to hold his daughter again." Jacques had to join the conversation, anger rising from his core.

"Gentlemen," Luke said and instantly the crowd bowed to his authority. "I have talked Paul about this already. I am not happy about keeping it a secret either. I mean, it's not that hard to keep it a secret anyway. His reasoning, I mean the reasoning of the Scientific Institute of France, is that since it is such a rare discovery he, I mean they, need time to analyze and study it. That to me makes sense. Wouldn't you agree?"

Jaques had to agree to that point. Luke had a way of presenting arguments. It was said that he could sell ice to the people of Norway he was so good at persuassion.

"Also, each time we bring up the creature, those families who lost loved ones, and the men injured in the tunnel, will be reminded of that terrible day."

Again, another great point from Luke.

"Finally, I agree to offer you all a financial bonus if you agree to keep this thing quiet."

Jaques was wondering what they were arguing about anyway at this point.

Each man agreed to not mention what they saw. A check was given to each man, personally signed by Luke along with a contract that if they mentioned the occurrence then monies would be paid back. To ensure that pay back was not possible the payment was extremely generous.

Four months later Jaques sipped his first home made wine. The open country, clean air, and casualness suited him just fine. The payment from Luke, along with what he had been saving was enough to buy into his uncle's winery. Each day begins with rising with the sun and enjoying its warmth rather than escaping its warmth by going underground. Each night ended with a taste of the home brew rather than falling asleep exhausted from back breaking labor.

A comfortable greeted him each night along with the stars above. In town he fell asleep with drunks in the streets and polluted air from the trains.

Jaques began to believe that prayers are truly answered.

He was living one out now.

LIMA, PERU

Carl and Juan reviewed the notes that they had collected back at Juan's office at Inca National University. The boat ride back was invigorating for Carl as the salty air and the feel of the ocean wakened his senses.

Carl felt confident that his fear of traveling overseas was over.

Carl looked up from his notes, "Juan, how is it that Darwin was able to get traction on his theories? I mean, he wasn't challenged on any counts when he developed all this. Why?"

Juan met Carl's gaze. "That is easy to answer my friend. First, Darwin happened to live in the most powerful country in the world at the time, the British Empire. This may not sound like much but in terms of national pride, flaunting one's power in all arenas, and establishing that British scientists were the most advanced of all, it matters big. Second, it was the Industrial Revolution. Businesses wanted, basically needed, a theory to justify their monopolies. The idea of survival of the fittest reinforced the idea of taking over the little guys and becoming the top dog. It was easy to see why businesses would jump on an idea like this. Third, the church was beginning to lose its influence. The church was losing its impact on people. It wasn't connecting to people. Basically, it wasn't real. People were searching for answers and the church failed to deliver. People were drawn to any idea that was out there. Evolution happened to be it at the time. Lastly, to a certain degree it seems to make sense. I mean, a person looks at a canyon, sees layer upon layer, of sediment. The idea that it takes time to make those layers makes sense. But it only makes sense initially. With more thinking and research on a person's part, the theory falls apart."

Carl was embarrased. He hated asking questions that first had many answers and then being so quickly answered.

Juan relaxed Carl by adding, "Don't be embarrased my friend. I am a professor. It is my job to have answers. Also, you are asking the questions. How many others don't ask questions? It is sad how many are accepting a lie by just accepting it at face value. So sad." Juan's laughter died as he spoke.

"Juan, if dinosaurs ruled the world according to evolutionists, then how did they die?" Carl was convinced that he had stumped Juan.

Juan leaned back and put his fingers together as he contemplated the question. "Let me answer the question by asking you some questions. Is that okay?"

Carl wasn't sure where Juan was going in the conversation but decided to go along. "That seems fine with me," uncertainty in his voice.

"Okay then, how did the dodo bird die out?"

"I'm not sure."

"Okay, how did the American bison almost die out?"

"From people hunting them."

"How did the passenger pigeon become extinct?"

Carl was seeing a trend but decided to continue the question and answer conversation.

"They were used in the army to send messages in World War One."

"How are most animals that are extinct end up that way?"

It was Carl's turn to contemplate the question. "Well, it seems that hunting is a major reason."

"Very good. Go on."

Carl tried to remember his high school biology class. He thought of animals being transported on ships to other places and having those animals create chaos to the newer environments.

"Another reason is change of environment I suppose."

"Correct again. From my first question, the dodo bird, there were three major reasons; the animal was captured and used for shows as a curiousity piece. Then, bigger animals were introduced on the Indian Ocean island of Mauritius, the home of the dodo. These new animals killed the dodo. Lastly, the nesting areas were being destroyed. Isn't that what almost happened to your American Bald Eagle?"

Carl was saddened at the thought. How could a country almost destroy it national symbol?

"Then let me ask you this, why couldn't these same things happen to the dinosaurs? Why couldn't man destroy the nesting places of dinosaurs? I mean, the eggs are on the ground, sometimes exposed. Then think about this, would you want to live in the same place with a dinosaur? I wouldn't. Remember St. Patrick of Ireland? The famous story is that he chased all the snakes out of Ireland making it a safer place. What are snakes but leftover dinosaurs."

Carl had a feeling that Juan was gearing up for the grand finale. "Now imagine you are a Native tribe. You see these enormous animals roaming around. That's a lot meat walking around! Then, a different type of man comes around and wants to hunt for the joy of hunting. Sound familiar?"

"American bison."

"Exactly. Why are the rules of extinction only applied to certain animals but not to dinosaurs? Because most scientist are hung up on the idea of millions of years. There is a different standard being applied to animals for the sake of reinforcing bad science."

Carl had never thought in those terms before. Magazines and TV shows depicted a cataclysmic event such as meteors, volcanoes, cool temperatures, or other animals evolved and wiped out the dinosaurs.

Carl stood up and looked over the campus. Here he was at a place of higher education. A place that promoted open thoughts and free thinking. Now Carl felt a betrayal in those whose job it was to introduce all theories and let curiousity takes its course among the students. Let the human mind do what it does best, explore.

Carl turned and guessed that his expression matched Juan's. "Makes you sick to your stomach doesn't it?"

Carl nodded in agreement.

A ringing distracted Carl's thoughts. Two rings later and a search of his pockets made him realize that it was cell phone. Looking at the number he realized it was Cathy's. Flipping it open he looked forward to the progress that Cathy was making.

"Hello Cathy. How are you?"

"I'm okay. How are you Carl?" There was concern in her voice.

"I'm fine. Have you heard from John yet?"

"No. Listen Carl. You haven't had anything weird happen around you have you?"

"No. What's going on Cathy?"

Cathy related what happened at the Gobi Desert. She mentioned how she is now in Anchorage and heard of an archeological site that may have some more answers to their questions.

"I will keep an eye open for anything strange. But tell me, did you find out anything new?" Cathy related her findings and what she learned. As she talked the concern and worry that was in her voice dissipated and was replaced with excitement.

When it was Carl's turn to share Cathy's excitement reached a whole new level.

"Maybe my father wasn't crazy. It seems that everything he has written down is true."

"If it wasn't why would someone try to hush it up?"

"That's what we thought. I'm going to try to get a hold of John. When do you want to get together again?"

Carl was thinking those thoughts on the boat ride back. The three of them need to get back together; to share the information, encourage each other, and celebrate. They are finding what they needed.

"Listen, my parents have a ranch in Arizona. It is secluded but easy to get to. There's plenty of room for all three of us. What do you say?"

"After being in Alaska during the winter I would love to be in Arizona."

Carl gave the directions and mentioned that his parents are used to guest coming and going. It was a way for them to serve the Lord and it helped Carl with some of his people when they needed time away for counseling.

"I will see you there Carl. And hey, be safe."

"You too. Enjoy the tundra."

Carl heard the click and hung up. It was good to hear her voice and know that she was safe. He couldn't imagine the ordeal that she went through.

Carl turned to Juan who overheard half of the conversation. "It seems that we have people not liking our searching and exploring," said Carl. He filled in the blank spots of Cathy's conversation with Juan.

"It seems that some people are desperate to hang onto a lie. I knew the cost were high. But murder." The words seemed to sting at Juan. "I am glad that your friend is alright now and safe."

Carl sat back down in his chair. "The big question is where or what do I do next? Do I go to Arizona and hole up and wait. Or…"

Juan jumped in, "There is one other place you need to see before you go. It will make you do cartwheels on what you'll discover there. It isn't far."

Carl looked up. Juan's surprise excursions were informative to his quest. He had trusted Juan up to this point might as well see it to the end. "Where are we headed?"

"How about the Andes Mountains to a place called Michu Pichu?"

SYDNEY, AUSTRALIA

The oceanside restaurant provided the needed distraction for Mike, David and John. After what happened in the office David and John rushed to the student bookstore and bought a Bible. John felt so energized, so alive with what happened. Containing his excitement was like a child waiting to get out of bed on Christmas morning.

David had promised that he would stick with John until it was deemed safe for him and that the other operatives would do the same. "Plus, you can help me understand this thing," as he held up his Bible. Already he had been reading and soaking up the words.

"I don't know how much help I will be. I am fairly new to this myself."

Mike laughed. He enjoyed new Christians the best. He loved the enthusiasm, the love, and passion that they demonstrated. They were what all Christians should be he thought. They didn't care about the color of the church carpet or the type of music being played on Sunday mornings. It was all about Jesus. It was all about sharing the Good News with others and embarassment be put to the side.

"Ok, I understand the ark thing. It had plenty of space for all the creatures. But, there are some other questions I don't understand that maybe you can help me out with Mike."

"Fire away. Just understand, I don't have all the answers. A lot of you questions though, I bet, have common sense answers if you just think about it."

John sat back. At first it rubbed him wrong to hear those words. It reminded him of his mom when he was growing up. The words 'What were you thinking?' kept popping into his mind.

Mike went on to clarify. "Let me help you out with this. Understand that first every scientist sees the same evidence. I see a fossil and an evolutionist sees a fossil. But our explanations are different. Why?"

"Well, it must come down to viewpoints."

"Exactly. A predetermined mindset is in place before a scientist even looks at a fossil."

David became engaged in the conversation, "Not very objective is it?"

"Not at all. An evolutionist looks at a fossil and says, 'See, proof that this was millions of years ago.' He is looking at proof to justify his position. A creationist looks at the fossil and says, 'See, proof of creation and the flood.' Then each side will back up their claims with other evidence."

John leaned forward, "Then where does one side fall apart more than the other?"

Mike leaned forward to meet John's gaze, "That is a great question. Creation doesn't fall apart. It fact, more and more evidence is popping up to reinforce the idea of creation." Mike collected his thoughts, "In Montana they found bones belonging to T-rex. Notice I said bones, they weren't fossilized yet. How can this be? Then recently there has been a plethora of findings of living fossils. Plants and animals thought to be extinct but are still living. Science has recently changed it view that fossils don't fossilize over a long period of time that fossilization requires a cataclysmic event which means a sudden burial. Think about this, why is every fossil that is found that shows a body intact, is shown in the midst movement? The animal didn't lie down and wait to die. It was running, fighting, eating, giving birth. The animal was living its life or saving its life."

"I never thought of that. I have dug up many fossils but have never connected the fact that the animals were in action. In fact, the more in action they were the bigger the find. It was a bragging point for paleotology."

With a cheeseburger in his mouth David asked, "Isn't that what happened with that one town and the volcano? What was the name of that town? I think it was in Italy."

"Pompeii. You are exactly right David. There is a different standard applied to dinosaurs than to other living creatures, including man. Those people were techinically fossilized in an instant. In seconds they became statues of movement; running, protecting their young, hiding, falling. They were in movement during a cataclysmic event."

David finished swallowing a bite of his burger, "And all of science believes in evolution."

"No. Not all of science. First let me clarify, science is not bad or evil. There are two types of science; historical or origins science and then there is operational science. The science that gives us cars, space exploration, better products, electricity is operational science. We like that kind of stuff. It improves our life with better medicine and technology. Operational science can have repeatable experiments, deals with how the world works like chemistry and physics. When you see shows on TV when they are doing experiments that is operational science. I mean , who doesn't like to blow things up?

But historical science is way different. It cannot have repeatable experiments and therefore it has to try to reconstruct the past with partial evidence. If a scientist has a certain viewpoint on the past, guess what the physical evidence is going to reinforce? Their viewpoints."

Mike and John looked at David. His insights so far have been enlightening for both of them. "So if I understand what you are saying, fossil finding is a split down the middle much like Democrats and Republicans. You are on one side or the other. People are going to stand by their side no matter what is presented to them for evidence."

"You would be correct in saying that. It is true that passions run high on this issue and not just among scientist. People in general have a position on this issue."

"How so," John asked.

"Well, if we all just evolved then we are nothing more than animals. If we are nothing more than animals then life means nothing to us. If life means nothing to us then we can justify actions like mercy killing, abortions, and torture. If we are nothing more than accidents of the cosmos, then who cares what we do to each other. It is survival of the fittest, I can justify eliminating others of my kind if it means my survival in the food chain. Others of my kind take my food and my resources.

Therefore, evolutionist need their theory because other items ride on it; abortion, assisted suicides, mercy killing, and the list goes on.

But a creationist believes that life is special and has purpose. We are not accidents but made in the image of God. All life, animal and man, has a purpose.

This idea of evolution and creation has far reaching tentacles. That is why people have such high passions about it. The consequences are great."

David soaked up what was said as his napkin soaked up the mustard and ketchup that was stuck on his chin. "I had idea. Well what now?"

As if on cue John's phone rang; it was Cathy.

"Hello Cathy how are you? I heard about what happened."

Cathy related the events. She mentioned that she was ok and was going to check on another site in Alaska. "How did you know about China?"

John mentioned David and that he had his friends helping in protecting them.

"Well I didn't have anybody protecting me. If it wasn't for….Yun?"

David looked up at John. "Wasn't Yun there to protect her?"

John waited for Cathy to come back on the phone.

"John, can I call you back?" Without waiting for a reply Cathy's phone went dead.

"I think that Cathy has some investigative work to do gentlemen."

ANCHORAGE, ALASKA

Cathy stared at the phone. The dots she was connecting in her at first seemed random but were becoming more clear with each connection.

Yun entered the room with ice from the machine down the hall. Cathy lifted her head and stared at the recent stranger in front of her.

"Who are you? Don't lie to me."

Yun's smile faded as he looked upon Cathy. He was hoping to not have to explain himself. He was finding he was having stronger feelings for Cathy. He enjoyed her sense of humor. He had never felt so comfortable around a woman, so at ease. He wanted to protect her not because it was his job, but because he truly cared for her.

"Everything I have told you is true. I worked and studied under your dad. I have studied paleotology and dabbled a bit in archeology. It is what I truly enjoy."

"But."

Yun's shoulders and head slumped giving a defeated look as if caught like a child with their hands in the cookie jar. "But, as a child I was taken from my family and raised by the military. I was tested like others and was found to have special talents. My agility was above the charts as well as my hand-eye coordination. This means that in hand to hand combat I am pretty good. So I was trained to be an assassin. I could sneak up on the enemy within close quarters and they wouldn't know what hit them."

Cathy took a step back as a look of disgust came over her. The man she cared for was a trained killer.

Yun hurried with his story, hoping to bring a positive ending to it. "As a cover each person was trained to operate in the 'real world.' I loved learning about the past so archeology and paleotology seemed like the perfect fit. I was sent to school in the States as part of my cover. It was over there I learned under dad and became a Christian."

Yun was hoping the last statement would be the only one Cathy would focus one. The tears and sobs spoke louder than words to Yun. Cathy was hurt. The trust was broken, and while Yun didn't have much experience with women, he did know that to regain trust with a woman would take time.

She was worth it.

"Cathy. Don't think that this changes how I feel for you. I would have protected you back in China because I care for you." Yun stepped forward with his hands reaching out to her.

She stepped back and tried to shrink away from his hands. His murderous hands.

"Cathy. I am one of the good guys. I protect people. That is what I do."

Cathy's face was sheening with tears. With her massacare running she had the look of a battered woman. Her body was wracked with sobs and hurt. "Just go away. Please go away."

Yun stopped approaching. He stood there and just stared at Cathy. He so badly wanted to hold her, comfort her, let her know that he would never hurt her or let anything hurt her. He understood that she could see no other threat except him. He saw her viewpoint. With reluctant acceptance he turned to leave the room. Before leaving the room he turned, "Cathy. I love you and would never hurt you. Please understand that, or at least try."

Then he left.

Cathy stayed in the infanct position next to the wall. The last forty-eight hours was a whirlwind of events.

The man she loved was trained to kill people. How does one handle news like that?

For the next four hours Cathy let all her burdens collapse within her; her father's death, her father's mystery, traveling the world, almost killed, and now, the man she was falling in love with. Wave after wave of nasea, tears, and sobs.

Confusion resided in her being. She wasn't sure what her life was about anymore. She was in her late twenties and had no boyfriend, no friends, no life. Her whole life revolved around books and research. Finding out about things that lived long ago and long dead.

Could she not relate to the living? Had personal contact eluded her? Who was she?

The sun was beginning to rise over the mountains. Cathy rose from her fetal positon. Cathy stared out across the city and watched the shadows beginning to ease from the buildings. The snow capped mountains glistened and glowed under the sun. A new day. New beginning.

A sun ray broke through the buildings and landed on the top of a church. Cathy stared at the white temple. A golden cross radiated. The light reflected on the buildings around it, touching everything near it.

Cathy turned around and headed for the shower. It had been a long night.

DALLAS, TEXAS

Troy was before the Trough residence once more. He mentioned to the Eleven what had happened the last time he was here. With encouragement and prayer Troy prepared for another day with Curtis.

Troy knew the real meaning of success in this situation would be the family. Would Curtis be able to build those relationships with his wife, son, and daughters? Troy knew that that would require a miracle and miracles require prayers.

Sharon opened the door this time, even before Troy knocked.

"Come in. I want to talk to you."

"Okay." Troy followed Sharon through the house and into her bedroom. For a child the room was the size of master bedroom twice over. On the walls were posters of pre-tween Hollywood stars. Troy could see the room transitioning from a pink and purple themed princess room to one of a teenager. Idolization was setting in for this child. Books were sitting on a shelf that ranged from classic to her idols' biographies, even though some of these idols were not much older than Sharon herself.

The room was complete with a TV with cable hook up, a computer with internet access, and next to that was Sharon's cell phone and MP3 player. A clarinet laid in its storage case next to the desk. Troy saw that there wasn't dust so he guessed that Sharon must actually enjoy the clarinet.

He was amazed at what Sharon had at her fingertips. She had access to the world but no supervision. She could connect to anyone, at anytime, for anything.

If Sharon had all this, he could only imagine the other two.

"Who are you?" Sharon cut right to the chase. She sat down in her chair by the desk and began the interrogation.

"I am Troy Reiner, a friend of your dad's."

Sharon studied the statement. "My dad has no friends."

Taken aback Troy gathered his senses. These kids were hardened. Troy could only imagine what Curtis must have done to them mentally and emotionally.

"I know it seems that right now your family has no friends or that nobody cares for you. But that isn't true. There are plenty of people who care."

"Then where are they?"

"Well, first there's me and I am right here." Troy gave a smile that he hoped would disarm the questioning attack of Sharon. It didn't work.

"Go on."

"Then there are my friends. Everyday we gather and pray for your dad and your family. We pray for each of you."

Sharon let out a laugh. To see such cynism in such a young age cut Troy to the heart. "Prayer? Prayer is a fancy word for talking to one's self. If there was a God, then why would he allow this to happen to my family? My dad traveled all around the world, talked to thousands, maybe millions of people, about family. Then mine falls apart and the world is watching. Our misery is splashed on the nightly news. I haven't been able to go outside this house in about a week. Guess how many times I have talked to someone in my family during that time? Guess!"

Troy not only saw the anger and resentment in Sharon but saw the hurt and heartache. How he so badly wanted to reach out and just hug her. Give her some human, loving contact.

"I don't know. I guess very little."

"That's a chicken answer. I have said hi to my mom when we pass each other in the kitchen. She can't even look at me. I haven't done anything wrong and my own mother can't even look at me. You want to know why? She is guilty about divorcing dad. She feels bad about bringing this circus to our front yard. So she deals with it by ignoring her own children. Great parent huh?"

How Troy's heart ached. He felt guilty sometimes for going and playing basketball with the guys once in awhile. He felt that that was too much time away from his kids as he knew that time is a precious commidity. Here in this house, each member was to fend for themselves.

"Then there's dad. Forget about getting father of the year award. Which ironically he won from some stupid organization who had no idea what dad was about." Sharon stood up and went to the window. She scanned the makeshift community of reporters and TV crews. "He used me. He used my brother and my sister. He used my mom. We were his pawns, part of the charade, the show." She continued to stare out the window. "Well, dad should be really happy right now. He doesn't have to travel to gain an audience; they have come to his front door." An icy steel tone spoke each word disgust.

Troy had no idea what the other family members were going through until now. The hurts ran deep, the emotions were high and tense, and the healing process has not even begun.

"Lord help me to help them. Guide me Lord." Troy began praying in his head.

"What are you doing?"

Without realizing it Troy looked up. A lifetime of bowing his head for prayer gained the attention of Sharon.

"I was praying for you." Troy met the hardened gaze of Sharon with a loving one. "I was praying that I would be able to help you. I was also praying that maybe, just maybe, you and I could be friends. I could always use a friend and it sounds like you need one to."

Sharon turned her body from Troy while keeping a dubious stare on him. This man has stopped by twice. She watched him being hassled by the reporters and yet he said nothing. She watched the news and saw him being banged and pushed around. He didn't say a thing. When he left the house last time he went through the process again.

"Why do you really come here? I mean, we have nothing, we are nothing. So why do you come?"

Troy lowered his head. Tears brimmed around his eyes. This girl with a hardened heart is going to see a grown man cry. How would that look he thought to himself. Be real. Be genuine. She needs to see that.

"I truly care for this family. I care about what is happening to it and where it is going. I believe that this family is worth saving."

Sharon turned around to face him. "You truly are crazy. This family doesn't even want to be saved. And even if we did, we wouldn't even know where to start. Some families are destined to fall apart. Ours is one of them. And you know what, that's okay. Families fall apart all the time. Hence step and ex." Sharon gave a cynical laugh, "But you probably don't believe in all that do you?"

"I believe in families. I believe that all families are meant to be together but it takes work. And yes, I do know where it starts." At this time Troy stood up and met Sharon's gaze. He would not back down from the truth.

Troy knew in his heart of hearts what God's plans were for families and he would fight for those plans. "This family, like mine and everyone else's, has a purpose. Each member of the family has a purpose. But a family needs guidance and structure. When a family has that…" Troy thought of his own family. He thought of how he cared so much for his own children that he would sacrifice his life for them. He thought of his wife, who two years ago was fighting cancer and he maintained nightly vigils to be by her side. He thought she was beautiful despite the loss of hair. Through good times and bad. Sickness and health. "When a family has that, it is one of the most special gifts that God has given to us."

"So you are going to defend my father."

"No. Your father made mistakes. As his friend, I have to hold him to those mistakes. In fact, I am also at fault here for not seeing what was happening and stepping in." Troy dropped to his knees and bowed his head. At this time he openly cried.

It was a strange scene to see. A grown man, a stranger, on his knees before a girl of twelve years of age. The girl was confused on what her role was in all of this and for the first time was speechless.

"Sharon, will you forgive me for not being a better friend to this family and to your dad? Will you forgive me for playing it safe and then not doing the right thing? I feel that I have hurt you and this family. I will pray that I will be a strong enough friend. But I ask for your forgiveness."

Troy bowed his head once more.

Sharon stood, frozen in place. Nobody admits for forgiveness. It's a sign of weakness. But this man braved reporters to come and talk to her family. That didn't seem weak. He shared nothing with the outside world on what was happening inside the house. Was he protecting them? Sharon didn't know what to do. She looked at the top of Troy's head. This man was either crazy as a loon or he meant what he said.

"I fogive you." She didn't know what else to say.

"Thank you. I will work harder to become a better friend, if you will allow me to."

"Um, yeah, that sounds okay."

"Sharon, I have a daughter your same age. Next time I come can I bring her?"

This man was truly crazy. He was going to bring his daughter through the reporters and to this house.

Troy looked at his watch. He couldn't believe how long he had been here. His purpose was to meet with Curtis but it was obvious that God had other plans. "Are you going to be okay Sharon?"

She nodded her head. "Yea. I'll be okay."

"Is there anything I can do for you?"

Sharon had to turn away. For the first time emotions were beginning to show on her face. "Will you continue to meet with my dad?"

Troy stood up. "I hope so. I will keep coming everyday."

"Then that's what I want. Help my dad. That's all."

Curtis sat outside the hallway or Sharon's room. He listened to the conversation of Troy and Sharon. He heard the prayers. He began to realize he had no clue who his children were. What were their likes and dislikes? Hobbies? Passions? What cut to the core was that his children had no friends.

Curtis saw himself for the first time as an abusive father. Not physically but emotionally and mentally. He agreed with Sharon's assessment; the children were pawns to help him sell books and tickets for his shows. They were props in his own personal play.

It dawned on Curtis that he had no concept of what family was really about. When Troy came back tomorrow he would have to ask him. If this man, Troy, could humble himself before his daughter and ask for forgiveness, then he could humble himself as well. What else do he have to lose?

As Troy and Sharon finished their conversation Curtis slipped away quietly and went downstairs to the kitchen. He wanted to catch Troy on his way out the door.

BEIJING, CHINA

Kim threw the glass across the room shattering it. He heard the news of the female escaping from Xi and made it to America. Xi had the woman but instead of going in and killing her Xi decided to play around. The result was failure.

Then there was the media coverage of the attack. Kim was going to have to tell Xi to hide out for awhile until things blew over. An international team of investigators were questioning the students and workers. Kim had no idea where the target went only that she left China in a hurry.

This mission was becoming a disaster before his eyes and for the first time since he was a child he felt hopeless. Road block after road block kept popping in his way. He had assigned Xi for Xi was the best. But Xi was unable to see things through.

Kim paced back and forth across the floor. Dinner sat on the desk getting cold which Kim thought ironic, it was matching his demeanor. Except for the street noise rising up it was silence in the room.

Kim needed a knock out punch and soon. His gut was telling him that the trio was getting close to figuring out something and releasing that information.

What were they after?

He went back to his desk and pulled out his atlas book. He loved this book. At least once a week he scanned through the book to be familiar with where countries were at, their capitals, and geography. Kim took the time to learn about as many countries leaders as possible as well as their enemies. Each country had its strengths and weaknesses. Kim wanted to know this so in case he needed to make military connections he would stay informed. Social sciences were his passion and his mistress.

Kim knew that one of the trio went to Australia. An informant mentioned a ride to an abandoned railcar yard. The other went to Peru and left on a boat ride. Destination unknown. There are many islands and islets. Then there was the girl who came to China and went to an archeological site in the Gobi Desert. A popular place for digging up dinosarus and fossils.

Kim knew that a group in America was backing the trio. "Maybe, just maybe, I have been going at this all wrong," thought Kim. "To destroy the snake you cut the head. To gain the information, you go right to the top."

A devilish smile replaced the scowl. Kim knew where to send Xi next.

"I hope he likes playing cowboy."

4000 YEARS AGO -

It was finished. Many years of backbreaking labor, ridicule from the locals, and going on absolute faith it was done.

Noah stared at the great structure before him. He could not believe it himself. His sons and him built this from scratch with only guidance from God.

There was not a lot of time for Noah to admire his achievement as noises from all around broke him from his thoughts. Noises of all kinds surrounded the landscape; grunts, squeals, roars, chirps, and squawks. Noah turned around to catch a glimpe of these creatures that were coming to him. Dust. There must be thousands of animals coming.

Noah went inside the ark and called for his sons; Shem, Ham, and Japheth. They went to the top of the ark to gain a better view.

It took their breath away.

They had all seen these creatures before. But to see them all coming together, as one large group, amazed even Noah. "Truly amazing my sons. Truly amazing."

The locals began to creep out of their homes to look as well. It was clear from their nakedness and drunkness that many were being wicked.

"The very reason why God had me build this," thought Noah as he gazed upon the people. Knowing that very soon they would be perishing.

The creatures that amazed Noah the most were the great lizards. Their sheer size and strength sent shivers up his spine. What amazed Noah even more is that they were going to fit on this ark along with all the other animals.

Noah had walked this land many times with his sons. They had to. They had to gather food and supplies for the time when the rains would come. They had to learn what each animal ate. God directed to take every kind of food that is to be eaten and store it away as food for them and for themselves.

Inside the ark were bushels upon bushels of leaves and grasses. Containers contained berries and fruits. Animals were hunted, skinned, packed, and preserved. There were containers of insects, worms, and bugs. Noah had Shem collect those as bugs gave him the heeby-jeebies.

Every animal was on this land. God wanted his people together, unified, and speaking the same language. Noah knew that all things were going to change after the flood.

Noah remembered taking a break from the building of the ark and was having something to drink. The container of water slipped from his hands and fell. The water rushed from the container and gurgled and splashed. The dirt changed from the rushing water. A dirt clomp was cut into two by the water. A mound was partially washed away. The softer dirt received a cut, like a miniature canyon.

All Noah could do at that point was pray. His world, literally, was about to change. The world before him was no longer going to exist. If water from a flask caused this little change within seconds; what was a major flood, that was going to cover the world, going to do? It was mind boggling to think about.

The animals came closer. Now, every local person had come out of their dwelling to gaze upon the site. To see all the animals moving as one was beyond description. Noah knew that the sight before them was an act of God. It could not be argued against. Yet he knew that the people below him will continue to deny God and his ways.

Noah and his sons went to the bottom of the ark to open the great door. It took all four of them, two on each side, to raise and lower the door. It's great size and weight was too much for one man to handle. The door also had to be strong enough to act as a ramp for getting the animals into the ark. As Noah gazed on the animals coming, he knew this better be one strong ramp.

Within four hours animals surrounded the ark. The locals came to take in the site. None of the animals were exotic or foreign. The animals roamed across the landscape, but to see them all at one place at one time.

Noah's family were already loading the animals. The great beasts were first. They would be on the lower deck where the larger compartments were at. Noah was praising God for his wisdom. It didn't take long to know that every pair were not true adults and not of mature size. The creatures obediantly entered the ark and allowed Noah and his family to direct and guide them to where they needed to be at.

Within a week all the animals were loaded. The grass and vegetation that surrounded the ark was either eaten or dead from the animals bedding down. "No matter," thought Noah, "it was going to soon die anyway."

Noah and his wife, along with their sons and their wives, entered the ark. The eight expected to hear animals noises but instead were met with silence. As they looked around many animals were already sleeping. Many of the animals curled up next the other for body heat and comfort.

Then the rains came.

The eight scrambled to their living quarters. The pounding on the ark from the rains deafened the pounding from the people begging to enter the ark. The ark swayed as a wave crashed into its side breaking the support beams and releasing the ark to the waters. Bobbing and swaying the ark finally found its balance. Shem looked pale and was turning green. He laid down with his eyes close and began to take long deep breaths.

Noah prayed for protection and patience. He knew that God was looking over them. He promised to.

The rains pounded on the boat like a million fists.

Waves crashed into the ark sending it swaying back and forth. Sometimes a wave would send the ark into a whole new direction, or turning it around altogether.

For forty days and nights the rains came. The eight got used to the thump thump thump on the ark. They busied themselves with the animals.

There was the feeding and watering of the animals. Each son took a deck to clean up the animal waste. The birds provided music and song for the eight. A bugle call would bellow from the middle deck and would drown out all other sounds.

Japheth's wife enjoyed playing with the dogs and cats. She groomed every animal on the top and middle deck. Noah admired her gift of caring for the animals.

It was hard to discern when the day began and when it ended. The rains blocked out the sun. Many of the animals hibernated so using them to tell time was pointless. When Noah needed rest he always went to the lower deck and admired the great creatures. They too hibernated throughout the trip. Noah couldn't imagine what it would have been like if they were awake and required movement.

After forty days and nights the rains stopped. For a few days it was hard to sleep as everyone adapted to the noise and rythmic tone. The sun bursted out of the clouds and shone upon the waters. Noah and his family looked out the windows and stared. There was nothing. Nothing but water. Even with the warning from God, the forty days and nights of rain, it was hard to fathom that amount of water.

There were no waves. The waters were calm and gave the appearance of glass. Ham's wife noticed how the clouds were reflected on the water's surface. Everyone stared into the waters to see how far down they could see. Murkiness, silt, and mud were active deeper in the waters.

Noah's wife said it reminded her of soup being stirred around. The top was calm but down deeper it was churning and mixing.

It was a total of hundred fifty days since the last rain. Noah went to the top of the ark along with a raven. The raven flew and flew. Noah had to squint for at times he lost site of the black bird, even against the blues of the sky and water. When the raven returned there was nothing.

The next day Noah went to the top of the ark again but he decided to take a dove. It too flew, searching and scouring the waters for land. Noah found it harder to track the white dove. The dove returned empty.

Noah was noticing the animals were beginning to wake from their hibernation. He knew that soon God was going to provide land and they would soon be off the ark. It was an interesting voyage. Each member of the family coped with the isolation in different ways. Each had their favorite animals to take care of. Work was the great distraction from what was happening outside and inside.

There were also times of play. Noah smiled as he recollected the day that Ham had to chase the pigs, dogs, and sheep for they all escaped from their pens. The sheep seemed to turn away from being grabbed at the last second every time that Ham reached for them. This caused Ham to keep tripping over his feet. On the third time he face planted himself against an ostrick. The ostrich didn't enjoy the sudden and unexpected way of waking up and it began to jump around and squawk. Shem jumped in to help Ham calm the ostrich down and then went after the sheep. By this time the dogs decided it was time to play. Shem and Ham went to chasing the sheep with dogs running all around their feet. Both boys were tripping over the dogs. It wasn't until Japeth's wife picked up a stick and threw it down the walkway that both dogs cleared away. By that time the sheep were put back into the pens.

It didn't take long to locate the pigs. Their squealing woke up the elk, wildabeast, and dodo birds. A chorus of bugles and screeches echoed throughout the ark. By this time every member of the family was chasing pigs and dogs; oftentimes running into each other.

When the animals were put back into their pens the family just stared at each other. When Ham let out a laugh the others joined in. It was good to laugh for the sake of laughing.

After seven days Noah sent out another dove. Each member of the family watched the dove and anticipated its return. The minutes turned into an hour. Then another hour. The dove did not return. A shout arose. There was land showing somewhere.

The ark glided over to a mountaintop. Shem was the first to see the land mass. It didn't take long to see that the ark and the mountain were on a collision course. The eight braced themselves for the landing. A grinding sound was heard underneath the ark. Noah's wife was bounced from her sitting position and ended up on top of Ham. The ark had a thud and all creatures on board were suddenly lifted up a few inches from the floor and landed hard on the surface. The chorus of animal sounds filled the cavernous area. Another bounce sent birds flying throughout the ark screeching and cawing.

Then it stopped.

The eight looked around them. For the first time in almost two hundred days the ark was not moving. The stillness under their feet seemed foreign. The weakness of muscle and retraining the legs for land took some moments for adjustments. It seemed the animals were feeling the same way.

Noah willed himself up to the windows and opened them. The birds at least could be free to fly out until the door was opened for all the others.

Noah looked out the window. It was apparent that Noah was on a new kind of terrain, one that did not exist before the flood. It sloped downward at a steep angle and was covered by something new as well. This new thing was white, cold, and melted on the touch.

In only a few days the water had dried up from the land and the surface was completely dry. The door was lowered and the women began to open the pens for the animals.

The first out were the great beasts from the lower decks. When they walked the ark moved and swayed. It was curious to Noah to see how the animals were adapting. Like man they squinted at the sun and waited for their eyes to adjust. They too were seeing the new terrain before them.

Within hours all the animals were released to the world except the ones for the sacrifice. Noah sacrificed some of the clean animals and clean birds and looked up. A sight in the sky made Noah drop to his knees. The voice of God spoke to Noah that never again would he destroy all living creatures despite that fact that every inclination of man is evil, even from childhood.

As Noah rose to his feet he gave a smile. In the distance, the great creature gave a mighty roar. The valley floor filled with the beast's call to its mate.

LIMA, PERU

Juan and Carl marched up the mountainside. It was their second day of hiking and while Carl's body fought against the additional excertion, it also craved the exercise and fresh air of the Andes. As part of Juan's regular M/O, Carl had no idea where they were going, only trusting the man ahead of him.

Carl's past fear of traveling overseas was welling up inside him. He had heard of reports of bandits in these mountains that kidnapped hikers and held them for ransom. They were particulary fond of Americans as they believed that all Americans were rich and able to pay for ransoms.

Still, the excitement of another discovery drowned out the fear and Carl pushed forward.

As the two near the ridgeline Carl took a moment to look about him. The view was breathtaking. Low hanging clouds clung to the mountainsides and gave a misty look. Lushness surrounded him as well as mystery. He knew he was in the heart of Inca territory, the great civilization that ruled this area. Mysteries surround the Inca like a Sherlock Holmes novel; was their a lost city of gold, did they posses knowledge of advanced medicine and astronomy, and is their a lost treasure of unheard of riches?

"If only these hills could talk. What do you think they would say Juan?"

Juan stopped for a moment and took a deep breath of fresh air. "These mountains hide the past too well. Many Peruvians look forward to the day when they will become powerful again like their ancestors. Funny thing is, most Peruvians descend from the Spanish. Still, they take it as a source of national pride. Me, I think that Peru has a better chance of achieving that goal if they looked to improving the future rather than wishing on the past."

The men continued their hike and crested over the ridge line. Below them lay Michu Pichu, the ancient city of the Incas. It lay in a valley surrounded by spiraling mountain towers. Rock formations outlined where the buildings and homes were and gave a baseball park comparison of how big the city was. The city seemed to slope downward with the terrain. Feeding off of the city were pathways that were the roadways.

The Incas were famous for having a well constructed road system to connect its cities and towns. It was how it was able to transports its armies and food supplies quickly through the rough terrain.

Hiking down the ravine towards Macchu Pichu was more difficult than hiking uphill. Carl caught himself a few times slipping and sliding. His legs ached from fighting the urge to just run down the hill. Carl sidestepped a good chunk of the hillside. Within minutes Juan and Carl were among the ruins.

A heavy past settled upon them as they imagined they were among the Incas. Today the street were abandoned and desolate. A few hundred years ago trade was happening, children played, and armies marched on these streets.

In the middle of the ruins Juan stopped. Carl ran right into Juan's back. If it was in a different setting the scene would have been comical.

"Sorry. Wasn't paying attention."

"It's okay my friend. We are in the middle of a civilization that was quite used to being around dinosaurs. It has been recorded that the Incas were familiar with at least the spinosaurus and the tyrannosaurs rex. It has also been documented that they were familiar with a thunder bird. This description is similar to the ones described by the Sioux and other native tribes in America."

"This is all written down?"

"Not only written but drawn out. If we go by ancient ways of documenting, we have pictures."

"So is there any of that evidence up here?"

"No my friend, that evidence is back at the university."

"You mean we hiked up here for nothing?" Carl was feeling anger rising in his body.

"Not for nothing. How many people can say they walked the way of the Incas, viewed the view of the Incas, and admired the beauty that surrounded a beautiful people? How many can claim that they have set foot in one of the most mysterious places on earth? My friend, I wanted you to experience a different world, a past civilization. It just goes to show that no matter how mighty a group of people get, they too will topple."

Carl looked over the sight again. "I'm sorry for not being grateful. You are right. This is amazing."

For the next hour Juan and Carl roamed around the ruins. "Hey Juan, come here."

Juan came hurried over to Carl. "What is it?"

Carl looked around sheepishly for any other people. Convinced that no one was around he moved some of the stones. Juan stared at the desecration that Carl was doing, convinced that Carl had gone mad. Between two stones was a parchment piece.

"I saw the corner of it when I walked by a couple of times. At first I thought it was nothing but I had to check it out." Carl placed the stones back into position, hoping to high heaven they were exactly as they were.

Carl handed the parchment over to Juan, "Your're the expert. Take a look."

Juan looked over the animal skin parchment. The feel of the parchment was suprisingly soft considering it has been exposed to the elements. Juan unrolled it and stared.

"What do you see Juan?"

"I'm not sure. I would have to authenticate the parchment to make sure it is not a forgery but at first site I believe we have our first documentation from the Incas." Juan studied it more. "Not only that; but more evidence of your dinosaur theory."

Carl looked around him. The mountains were beautiful and breath taking. He had hiked up here to see an ancient ruin. God delivered evidence.

"You know what to know something funny my friend? You know how many of the great archeological finds in history have been by amateurs and by accident. The Dead Sea Scrolls were by some farmers. The first dinosaur tooth was by an English doctor. And now you."

"Like you said, it needs to be confirmed. Let's head back and check it out."

Zing!

Juan and Carl stood there not knowing what the sound was. A moment later a crack of a weapon was heard.

"Bandits. We need to get out of here Carl. And fast."

SYDNEY, AUSTRALIA

John said good by to Mike at the airport. David decided to tag along with John for both protecting him and for learning more. John appreciated the company and enjoyed the passion that David had.

What John was not looking forward to was the flight to Los Angeles and then on to Phoenix. Twelve hours straight on a plane, over the ocean, fighting claustrophobia. John hoped that he had enough reading material to keep his mind busy. He also hoped that the company of David would be a nice distraction.

Within half a hour the two were on board and within minutes skyward.

"So tell me John, all my life I have been taught that we evolved. That everything we see around us has taken millions and millions of years. That we came from monkeys. That dinosaurs came from amphibians. But now you and I are supposed to believe in something else. What is that something else?"

"You got your Bible on you big guy?"

As if on cue David pulled out his Bible. John whipped out the fairly new but well marked Bible.

"Turn to the very beginning of your Bible. In Genesis, the first chapter God creates everything in six days."

"Six days? A little hard to believe."

John laughed. "I thought so too at first. But then I realized, I had a notion put in my head from science classes, magazines, books, and TV shows that things evolved. If I tried to eliminate those thoughts and look at this and take it literally, why couldn't God create everything in six days? Afterall, he is God."

"Good point. So God creates everything in six days."

"Not only that, but there is a progression. Each day brings a foundation for the next created thing. That next created thing is more complex until you get to man."

"Yea, we are kind of screw ups aren't we?"

"Actually, we are the crowing acheivement of God's creation. It says in verse twenty-seven, 'So God created man inhis own image, in the image of God he created him; male and female he created them.'"

"So we look like God? I have a hard time believing God has a big gut."

John was enjoying David's company. It certainly was making the trip faster and more lively.

"If I understand it right, God took his time with us. By image we are able to make choices, are able to think, but most importantly able to be with God. In a nutshell, we are to be in a relationship with God."

David let that thought settle in. God wants to be with us, more importantly with him. "What do you mean by relationship?"

"I thought that strange too but look at chapter two. God is with Adam as if you and I are right now. Talking, communicating, building a relationship. But look at chapter two a little more closely, God formed out of the ground all the beasts of the field and all the birds in the air. Down in verse twenty, 'So the man gave names to all the livestock, the birds of the air and all the beasts of the field.' Notice how livestock and beasts of the field are different categories."

"You are telling me that livestock and beasts of the field are different kinds of animals. For example, cows versus elephants."

"Yes sir. The beasts of the field are the non domesticated animals."

"That leaves it pretty wide open doesn't it. I mean. I have never heard of dinosaurs in the Bible."

"I didn't think so either."

"Either," interrrupted David, "You are telling me that the Bible mentions dinosaurs?"

John flipped through his tabs and sticky notes on pages. He came to the book of Job. "Job was dealt a series of hard knocks in his life. Toward the end of the book God is talking to Job. He mentions two creatures that fit the dinosaur description."

David flipped through his Bible. His mind trying to grasp the fact that there were dinosaurs in the Bible.

"Go to chapters forty and forty-one." David removed the pink sticky note that marked the two creatures. "In verse fifteen, read what it says."

David looked at the passage:

'Look at the behemoth, which I made along with you
And which feeds on grass like an ox.
What strength he has in his loins,
what power in the in the muscles of his belly?
His tail sways like a cedar; the sinews of his thighs are close-knit.
His bones are tubes of bronze, his limbs like rods of iron.
He ranks first among the works of God,
yet his Maker can approach him with his sword.
The hills bring him their produce, and all the wild animals play nearby.
Under the lotus plants he lies, hidden among the reeds in the marsh.

"David, can you tell me, by that description, what animal we are talking about?"

David scanned the passage searching for clues in the passage.

John put his finger on the first line, "Notice here, made along with you. God created us at the same time. Within the six days."

David continued to scan the passage. "Ok, first it is a herbivore. It feeds on the grass like an ox."

"Good, I saw that right away too. Keep going."

Like a detective on a high profile case David searched line by line. "Well, the next two lines are kind of vague, strength in loins and muscles in belly could be an elephant or a hippo. Those are the first two animals that come to mind."

John nodded approvingly. "You are thinking on the same lines as me. Keep going."

"But then the description gets weird. The tail sways like a cedar. If my mind serves me right an elephant and a hippo have short tails, more like fly swatters."

John let the laugh come out. "That's exactly right."

David scanned through the passage again, "Bones are tubes of bronze? Help me out John."

"The fossils of certain animals, in this case dinosarus, show bones as tubelike. The bones are also large as in the case of this description. What dinosaur is being described here? Take a guess."

David had to take himself back to when he was around eight to ten years old. He was fascinated by dinosaurs back then; bed coverings, curtains, lunch pail, birthday theme complete with cake. He knew every dinosaur by name and description. He missed many recesses for drawing dinosaurs in class rather than paying attention.

"According to the description and size, it sounds like a brachiosaurus."

John smiled. David had figured out a great mystery. "What if I told you there is more? Look at Job again, chapter forty-one."

David read through the chapter. "It's talking about a leviathan. A sea creature so fierce and so wild that no one can tame him." David continued to read, "Whoa, this can't be right. Look at the description:

His back has rows of shields tightly sealed together
Each is so close to the next that no air can pass between.
They are joined fast to one another;
they cling together and cannot be parted.
His snorting throws out flashes of light;
His eyes are like the rays of dawn.
Firebrands stream from his mouth;
Sparks of fire shoot out.
Smoke pours from his nostrils as from a boiling pot over a fire of reeds.
His breath set coals ablaze and flames dart from his mouth.
Strength resides in his neck; dismay goes before him.
The folds of his flesh are tightly joined; they are firm and immovable."

David stared at the passage. "This can't be right. It's impossible."
John looked at his friend. "What are you thinking?
"Well, um, if this passage is to be believed, the description matches that of a dragon. This creature can shoot out flames, has protective body armor, and it too is big. The earlier passages at first make it sound like the crocodile, but then the later passages talk of how the seas churn and the wake that is left behind." David turned to face John. "Is this true?"

John looked at the Bible in his hands. "If you would have asked me a week ago I would have said no way. But, that was a week ago. A week ago I wouldn't have believed that dinosaurs walked with man. But I have traveled to different locations and have seen evidence of it. A week ago I buried a friend who believed in the Bible and the evidence. That friend may have died because of what he knew was true. A week ago I didn't know God but now I do and everything changed. Let me put it this way.

Either the whole Bible is false or the whole thing is true. Based off of what I have learned, there is nothing out there that convinces me that the Bible is false. Archaeology, biology, history; they all point to proving the Bible true. So, I would have to believe that this is true also."

David leaned back in his cramped chair next to the window. He stared at the blue ocean below him, imagining a great beast so ferocious, so dangerous as to be described by God himself. He tried to imagine the existence of dragons and what life would have been like.

"One more question for you, those stories of dragons that we hear about, do you think that there is truth to them?"

John closed his eyes. "To every myth story there is an element of truth. It was how the people of the time explained things they didn't understand. There are obviously stories of knights slewing dragons. Those stories are mostly in England. But, it is recorded that Alexander the Great ran into a dragon-like creature in India in 330 B.C. A Sumerian story in 2000 BC tells of a hero named Gilgamesh who slew a dragon and cut off its head. More recently, in the 1500's, there was a scientific book called Historia Animalium, it would be considered a reliable reference book of the day, listed several animals we would consider as dinosaurs. But get this, on May 13, 1572 near Bolgna, Italy a peasant named Baptista encountered a dragon and killed it. The dragon fits the description of a Tanystropheus, a small dinosaur. Here's the kicker, a well-known naturalist named Ulysses Aldrovandus recorded the encounter. A scientist went to the sight and verified the evidence."

David couldn't believe what he was hearing.

"Then there is this, how is it that China is renowned for its dragon stories. Everywhere one looks in China you will see images of dragons. Petroglyphs of dragons have been found in many parts of the world. There are many peoples, cultures, and countries throughout the centuries that are familiar with dragons. Their descriptions are consistent with each other. How could this happen if it wasn't true? I can't take five people with me to a restaurant and have them agree on the type of pizza they want. But the descriptions, drawings, stories are consistent with each other despite language differences, geographical differences, and time differences in history."

David let it sink in. The hum of the plane droned in his head along with the information he had just listened to. He stared back out the window to the ocean.

Is it possible? Was it real?

John knew that David had to wrestle with these thoughts. The conversation helped John overcome the fear he had of sitting in close quarters on a plane. The claustrophobia was eased, at least for a little while.

He scanned the airplane and saw all the people sitting there, facing forward and staring at a wall. Did they realize the lies around them? The falsehoods the world was feeding them?

A feeling of pity swept over John.

To a person glancing over it looked like a man falling asleep.

John, without realizing it, was praying. He prayed that the truth would come out. That people's eyes would be opened. That people would come to know Jesus and the love he has for them.

The intercom from the captain, three hours later, interrupted the prayer warrior. John roused himself from his vigil. He looked over at David, still looking over the ocean and deep in thought.

It seemed that both men had things they had to wrestle with.

LIMA, PERU

Zing! Carl and Juan managed to escape into the trees. There was no doubt that they were being hunted now. There was optimism that maybe the first shot was hunters, but the cursing and yelling that echoed afterward let Carl and Juan know that they were now mere animals being hunted.

Carl checked to ensure the parchment was secure. Despite the dangers around him he kept in mind that this parchment had to get back to the university, somehow. Someway.

Through the trees the two hopped over tree trunks lying on the ground, avoided bushes, ducked under low hanging branches. Carl was reminded of his days in the football league. Each obstacle was a lineman. A sidestep here. A stutter step there. Car's instincts kicked into high gear and he was overjoyed to know that the body was wanting to maintain that.

Juan was running on absolute fear. He had heard of stories on television of the bandits and their doings. It became a regular feature on the nightly news. Juan knew nobody that would pay for his ransom. Beyond a shadow of a doubt if he was caught, he was dead. If he was caught, Juan hoped for a quick bullet to the head but knew that would be the best possible situation. He imagined the tortures, the cruelties that he would have to endure.

His adrenaline kicked into a higher gear.

Carl found himself struggling to keep up with Juan. Carl considered himself an athlete but Juan was flat out tearing up the mountainside. Carl wasn't sure if heading down a ravine was the smartest route. He wanted to stay high to avoid being trapped. Juan shot into the trees and just ran. As Carl followed he began to sense that something was going to happen.

Something bad.

Juan slipped ahead of Juan and fell onto his back. Within milliseconds

Carl scuttled up next to Juan. Juan was about to let loose a cry of pain when Carl covered up his mouth to keep him silent.

No one knew how close the bandits were.

Carl used hand signals to communicate with Juan. Juan, lowered Carl's hand and acknowledged that he understood that silence was necessary for survival. He pointed to his ankle.

Carl looked at Juan's ankle. Carl was no doctor but it didn't take one to recognize a break. Ankles don't bend right at ninety degree angles.

Taking a moment to listen and analyze the situation Carl thought out his options. He could tell by looking at Juan that Juan was in no state of thinking or acting clearly.

Carl had no idea where he was or where he needed to go. Darkness was going to start creeping over the mountains within a couple of hours.

"Couple of hours. I hope we make it that long," thought Carl.

Carl knew that time was critical but so also was Juan's condition. They needed a place to hide. A place where Carl can secure Juan's foot and get his bearings. A place where the bandits could not find them.

Carl turned to look behind him. A Peterbuilt truck may as well have been driven into the trees. Branches, twigs, and sticks were broken and bent. Carl was going to have to figure out a way to cover his tracks or find a way to confuse the bandits to buy him and Juan some time.

Carl grabbed a stick of wood and placed it in Juan's mouth and leaned towards his ear, "The next few minutes may be extremely painful. You have to trust me." With that Carl pick up Juan and carried him over his shoulder.

Carl could feel Juan's body shake with the pain of a bobbing broken ankle. Each step that Carl took bounced Juan's ankle. Carl felt sorry for Juan. He didn't know what was better. Having Juan's face in front of him to help give encouragement, or watching the bobbing broken ankle in front of him like a dangling carrot. He decided on the latter. He would have rather watched the ankle than see the pain in Juan.

Carl moved slower, that was anticipated. But he was careful about where he stepped. He wanted to start making their trail more difficult to follow.

Carl stopped. There was a new sound. Rushing water.

If he could get to the water there was a chance to he could erase their trail from the bandits.

He picked up the pace while concentrating on deliberate steps and pathways.

Zing!

A bullet chipped off some bark of a tree to Carl's right about ten feet. The bandits know which direction he was heading but the shot was awful. Either the man was a bad shot or it was a desperation shot to drive the two out.

Carl didn't bite. Focusing on reaching the water he methodically zig-zagged his way down the ravine. As often as possible he would step on rocks. Harder to track that a broken branch.

Carl had to fight for balance. With Juan draped over his left shoulder and zig-zagging down the ravine Carl felt his left leg weakening. Not now. Not now.

The sound of the water became distinct now. The river was just ahead, had to close.

Zing! Zing!

One bullet went to he left. Other to the right. The bandits must know that Carl was headed to the water and what that meant. Each party was picking up their pace.

The sound became a calling. Carl cast all caution to the wind and sprinted toward the water. Ahead of him was a clearing.

"That must be it. Please be it."

Carl excerted more determination. Survival was absolutely crucial.

A new fear hit Carl. The clearing was actually the edge of a cliff.

Carl didn't recogize it in time.

Carl and Juan found themselves falling.

ANCHORAGE, ALASKA

It was one of those days that people who lived in Alaska longed for. One could imagine photographers blanketing the countryside to get the photo that would be used in travel brochures, post cards, and billboards.

The sun beamed down on the city and people exited out of their workplaces and homes to bask in the light. An energy hit the town that caused people to extend more kindness, give encouraging smiles, and raised spirits.

Cathy watched the scenes on the streets while chewing on her bagel and sipping coffee in the hotel's restaurant.

Last night's events replayed in her head. At any moment she expected Yun to stop by and make amends. The protective armor of isolation and numbness were in place. Cathy couldn't handle being hurt anymore. She was tired of secrets and mindgames.

The coffee did little to wake up the senses. Still, the aroma and flavor was a necessary routine in the recent world of chaos. And while the body wasn't hungry the mind said it needed something in order to function. A bagel with grape jelly was going to have to suffice.

Cathy wasn't sure of what to do next. A part of her said to go back home. Bag the mission. Her dad was dead and so was his research. She had her own research to do; her own life to live. The other part of her said to continue. To honor her father and fulfill the mission, that the truth needed to be found.

Then there is the fact that her life was at stake and that she witnessed three murders and her neck was handled by the man's hands. Cathy couldn't help but feel her neck. Goosebumps emerged throughout her body at the recollection.

The final uncertaintity was John and Carl. She had no idea where they were and how they were doing. She left messages for Carl but no return calls. John said he already had protection but that was two days ago. Who knew where he was at now?

Deep in thought she stared at the bottom of her coffee cup.

"How are you doing?"

She looked up to see Yun. Despite the armor she wasn't prepared to meet him. His casualness of pulling out the chair and making himself comfortable before her further disarmed her.

"I want to say I'm sorry. I never meant to hurt you. I totally understand if you never want to speak to me again. But I need to clarify some things with you."

Cathy sat. Stared. No emotions were shown.

Yun wasn't sure how to read Cathy so he continued, "I want to be totally honest with you now. I did work for your father. I am a paleotologist. And I am a Christian. Going back to China, and being so young I had a hard time balancing my career with my faith. I was approached by some men who call themselves the Guardians. This group consists of former Green Berets, Seals, police officers, and experts in science and weaponery. Their mission is to protect God's workers in hostile environments. They have been in places like Sudan, Columbia, Iraq, Iran, Afghanistan, and China. It is where they recruited me. They trained me in arm to arm combat, small weapons and survival techniques. I have protected many missionaries from around the world in China. By escorting them into villages and towns where I know they can have great impact the Word of God is spreading at incredible speed in my country." Allowing the excitement to get under control Yun continued with a more somber air, "But, I have also escorted many out as their lives were at stake. Through underground channels and the generosity of people I have rescued people much like how I rescued you. I have at me beckon call helicopters, planes, cars, boats, and trains to get people to safety."

Cathy stared at him, "How do I fit in all this?"

Yun knew that Cathy was fragile at this moment. He cared for her but knew was not the time to lay that burden on her. "I was contacted by one of our support groups from the United States. They mentioned that there was a possibility of three of you coming to China to do some research that could change the mindset of the world. They asked if I could be a part of it. I couldn't help but agree seeing that as a scientist I wanted to be a part of the discovery. The group also mentioned that they had on good authority that someone was trying to stop the researchers from attaining their goals. To me it was a no brainer. I felt an obligation to help out. A duty which I was glad to do."

Cathy felt like crying but the tears had run out long ago. "So I was an obligation."

Yun could only imagine what the beautiful woman across from him was going through. She lost her dad, was traveling the world with strangers and by herself, and had her life almost taken. "Did you start out that way, yes. But, I have enjoyed the times we have been together. You are so much more to me than just a duty or fulfilling a job."

Yun felt as if a great weight was being taken off of his heart. "When I saw that mad man going after you, well, thoughts of not having you around terrified me. I am not a man that gets scared but living without you …" Yun hoped the right message was sent. He wasn't used to being under the spell of a woman. Something about this one told him to get out of his safety zone and take chances. It was going to be worth it.

Cathy wrapped both hands around the coffee cup. She knew if she raised her eyes she would forgive him. She wanted to accept what he was saying. For the first time in her life she found someone to connect with.

The anger gave her strength. She was too strong, too independent to give herself over to another person. She was hurt and a part of her wanted him to hurt too.

"I am going to need some time to think about this. Meanwhile, we both have a job to do. I believe that we are to go to certain site today and scope out some fossils and remains."

Yun noticed that Cathy never lifted her eyes. At least she was speaking, that was progress in the right direction. "Yea, I believe we are heading north. We probably need to get ready to go if we want to maximize the day. What's that saying from that cowboy John Wayne, 'We're burning daylight."

DALLAS, TEXAS

Xi knew that Kim was getting desperate. By sending him to Dallas Kim wanted the main supporters of the trio out of the picture. Kim was to send fear, even death to a couple of them, to remind them that this was no game.

Xi enjoyed being in the United States. As much as he liked China it was nothing to what America had to offer. Every indulgence could be fulfilled at a moment's notice. If one wanted a woman, she was a phone call away and she would come to you. It was like ordering pizza, another luxury of being in America. Stores and restaurants stayed open twenty-fours a day. On the radio was every kind of entertainment that one wanted; news, sports, music, and talk.

Every need was catered to. From what was available in automobiles to homes to work. He chuckled when he heard of Americans complain of working conditions. They had no idea of poor working conditions. He thought of the people back in China. Twelve to sixteen hours a day in warehouses without ventilation, no breaks, and poor pay. He knew of children that had lost fingers and hands due to poor equipment. If someone complained, they were fired and replaced by one of hundreds who were willing to work under the conditions.

Xi knew of areas in China were the smog was so thick that children were unable to describe what a cloud looked like. They didn't even know what a star was or tell a person the correct color of the sun.

Xi thought of these things as he drove through the traffic. People were driving in state of the art vehicles while talking on their cell phones. Children were watching movies in the backseat with their headphones. Motorhomes and RV trailers were destined for pristine camping spots or parks near tourist attractions. SUV's occupied prime interstate real estate as they seemed twice as big as a car. Xi got a kick out the pick up trucks.

Anything and everything was hauled in these machines; four wheelers, furniture, lumber, trash.

"Americans have no idea how good they have it," thought Xi.

He guided the car through the six lanes of traffic and manuevered to the right side so he could prepare to exit. Two lanes shifted off and sent Xi skimming over the interstate and circling back towards another interstate. "The infrastructure is amazing here." Sticking to the right hand lanes Xi found the exit he needed to get off the arterial and onto city streets.

Down at ground level Xi was inaundated with fast food restaurants, themed restaurants, a pleathora of businesses offering the same materials, goods, and services. There were at least three tire shops within two blocks, four check cashing stores, and five bars. A Starbucks dotted the corner of one intersection along with three gas stations.

Xi loved America.

All one had to do was go somewhere else and then they would appreciate America.

Xi pushed these ideas out of his head. He began to focus his thoughts on his targets. He would soon be within site of the campus. He wanted to first scour the campus and get a feel for it before checking into his hotel that was just off campus grounds.

Once that was done, he would go through his plans tonight of gathering information on each man searching for weaknesses and pinpoints that would make them crumble under pressure.

Xi smiled as he began to think of ways to exert terror and fear. He knew that children were going to be involved, as well as women.

This was going to be fun.

DALLAS, TEXAS

Laughter and smiles were shared. News had reached the Eleven that Cathy was safe and that the other two were alerted. John was heading back to the states and word was that he was going to Arizona. A sense of jubilation filled the air.

Troy enjoyed the commaradie. It was joy to be around other Christian men and share in their stories of triumphs. He was hoping that soon he would have one to share.

Curtis and his family had hit a dead end. For the last week the five of them were imprisoned in their home, rarely did they talk to each other. The distance between them was growing. Curtis remembered the talk he had with Sharon. He didn't see or hear another member of the family during this talk.

A clink of glasses garnered his attention.

"Gentlemen, we are here because our trio are making progress despite the enemy's attempts. We must still exercise caution as the enemy will not stop for there is much to lose. Prayer is our number one offense. God is in control. He will protect them. He has demonstrated already that he will for his will be done."

Amens followed from the group of men.

Troy had lost interest in the trio since the downfall of Curtis. They seemed so far away, so distant. He was concerned for their safety but he could see the hurt on Curtis' and Sharon's face. He could see the family falling apart. There was a purpose in his life to help this family, to come alongside them and nurture and guide.

While the other members of the Eleven saw the significance of the trio's mission, he saw his as saving a family. Troy remembered reading in Galations, 'Brothers, if someone is caught in a sin, you who are spiritual should restore him gently. But watch yourself, or you also may be tempted.

Carry each other's burdens, and in this way you will fufill the law of Christ.'

Curtis was Troy's friend, through good times and bad. While the trio's discovery may change the way the world thinks it won't bring this family together. Prayer, time, commitment, and being real with each member will be the only way to help the family.

"Now gentlemen, we made a commitment to helping out a brother, brother Curtis. Troy, do you have anything you want to say?"

Nervously, Troy stood up and stared at his coffee mug. He didn't want to share but he knew that he needed the prayer's of these men for strength and guidance.

"I have talked to Curtis on two different occassions and also with the youngest daughter Sharon. Gentlemen, that family is broken. But it is a family worth saving. I see a desperation in their faces, a longing for something. Each member is lost and confused. Most of all, they are alone. They have isolated themselves from the world and from each other."

"Troy, are they getting their needs met? I mean, the oldest girl is pregnant right? Is she getting the right medical attention? Is the son able to go to counseling? I have seen the reporters and vans in front of their house, are they able to get groceries and supplies?"

"I don't know." Troy felt like he was failing the group. These were questions he didn't even consider. He remembered what Curtis looked like the last time he saw him, gaunt and worn out. Troy remembered thinking that it looked as though Curtis hadn't eaten but it was chalked up to stress and nerves.

"Troy, if we gathered up some of these things…"

"I would be more than happy to deliver them."

"Troy, how are you doing?"

Troy could always count on Dr. Livingston. Dr. Livingston was the oldest of the group. He had been involved in church plants and watched churches fall apart. He had been a part of several miracles; families reconciling, a paralyzed man was able to walk, and numerous births of babies that shouldn't have happened according to the modern medicine experts. His sense of seeing past the façade to the real person was his gift.

"I am doing well thank you."

"And your family?"

Troy noticed the room had gone quiet. Faces stared at him, not with curious eyes looking to gain some tantalizing bits of information, but with looks of concern and love. It was then that Troy knew he too had a warrior prayer group.

"They are doing fine. My wife wants to join men in going over to Curtis' house. She wants to come alongside Kathleen. We both know that in order for the family to come together the marriage has to be strong. It is the foundation."

"But"

"But, it's like I said, it is broken. It has to be rebuilt."

Troy thought of Curtis' eyes at their first meeting. It was a man who had lost everything. Everything around him was destroyed; his children, reputation, job, finances.

"Troy, one last thing, is there anything else we can do? Do you need one of us to go with you?"

"I thought of that. Right now crowds of any sort would be a roadblock. Even though the house has the feel of a cave, the atmosphere of crowds of people surround that place. You can hear the thumping of helicopters throughout the house. Every window has a view of vans and reporters. In that house there is no santuary. I think it would be best to keep visitors to a minimum for their sake."

"That is wise counsel. For now we will gather up groceries and other supplies. I'm sure our wives will help with female things. I look around this room and I don't see a single soul who understands a woman. They are far too precious and complex to be understood." Dr. Livington looked upon Troy as a father looks upon his son when he realizes that his son is no longer a boy but a man. "Be careful. We will continue to pray for you and guide you. But, you are in God's hands."

"Thank you. Everyone of you have been instrumental. Trust me when I say, when I need help I will ask for it."

Chuckels rounded the room. Pats on the back and the shaking of hands came to Troy. He knew that if he wasn't careful he would let the popularity get to his head.

"God, your will be done. Use me as you see fit."

PERU-

Carl searched frantically for Juan. The current kept pulling him under. Carl was having to use his energies on keeping afloat, twisting his body to scan the waters, and fighting for control.

The current felt like an iron hand was around Carl's legs. He kicked and fought the urge to go under. Then as if Carl was nothing more than a rag doll he was pulled under. Around him white water swirled. His arms stretched for the surface. Then like a corkscrew he would pop up and gain sweet oxygen.

Carl spotted Juan floating along the bank ahead of him. A calm pool was coming up. If Carl could reach Juan at that pool area and get to shore they may just survive this ordeal.

The thoughts of the bandits were no longer lingering. A new danger of drowning and hypothermia replaced being shot at. Carl began to freestyle stroke over to Juan. In all of his years of conditioning for football he never remembered being so exhausted as fighting these waters. Muscles were burning, aching. The lack of substantial food was beginning to take its toll on Carl.

Carl was within ten feet of Juan and the waters slowed. Like a crocodile Carl closed the gap quickly. Wrapping his left arm around Juan Carl aimed for shore. To him it made no difference which shore was better. All he knew was that land was better than water at this point. Carl knew in the back of his mind to expect the worse about Juan. There was the broken ankle and the bruising ordeal of the waters. It would not be a surprise to see Juan's body in shock.

Pumping. Striving. Kicking. Carl worked for the shoreline. Then like manna from above the ground rushed to his feet. Carl wrapped both arms around Juan and carried him to shore. Carl checked for breath. Faint. But there. Juan's lips weren't turning blue. Carl tenderly moved body parts to put Juan into a more comfortable position. Carl knew he had to check the ankle. He prepared his mind for a mangled mess of bone and flesh. The falling off of the cliff, the waters churning the ankle around and around, the possibility of the ankle banging on rocks as Juan came down the river were rushing through Carl's mind.

He lifted up the pants leg as a parent would lift a blanket on a sleeping child.

The sight was worse than expected.

A bone protruded from skin. The foot was hanging on by skin and tendons, but even these were ripped and sheared. Blood flowed into Juan's shoe and up his pant leg.

Carl looked around. The forest was preparing for the oncoming night. The sun was sinking over the mountain ridge and the cooler temperatures were setting in.

For a brief moment Carl was overwhelmed with a sense of hopelessness. What can I do? He didn't know how to help Juan. His skills for being in the outdoors were limited. He had no food. No shelter. There was no possible way to communicate to the outside world. Then the fear that the bandits may still be looking for them crept into his mind.

For the first time in his life Carl felt like crying.

Pressure appeared on his left arm. Carl thought at first that an insect had just bitten him. "That would be the topper to today's events. Survive all this just to die by an insect bite" he thought.

He looked down. It was Juan's hand. "It's ok my friend. I will be ok. We need fire. Build a fire."

Carl was dumbfounded. First there the relief that Juan was awake, talking. Second, that Juan had the presence of mind of what needed to be done. Carl placed his hand on Juan's. "We will get through this."

Carl scavenged the area for dry twigs and branches. He had no idea how to start the fire but the activity gave him hope and a purpose. Much like his Christian faith. He could sit there and hope for a fire, but the activity, the motion of doing something about it was encouraging. Bring back an armful of kindling Carl dumped the load above Juan's head.

Finding a bigger stick Carl went about the task of digging out a pit for the fire. Carl remembered seeing on a survival show of how to start fires in damp, tropical places. He then sorted through the kindling for the smallest and driest pieces. Arranging them in the pit he began to think of ways of how to start this fire. "Should I soak it with water and ask God to start it for me," he said aloud. He didn't doubt that God could do it. But he was liking the fact that his mind was occupied on this activity rather than the million other things that could distract and discourage him.

Satisfied with the pile before him he began to think of how to start the fire. The sun was setting so direct sunlight was not going to work. His and Juan's clothes were soaked so the idea of using paper or other starting material was out of the question as well. The only idea that came to Carl was to rub two sticks together.

Running out of ideas and sunlight Carl grabbed two sticks and began to saw them against each other. Within minutes smoke wafted up. Heat was felt on the sticks and soon a fire was warming in the pit. Carl collected bigger pieces of wood. He wanted the fire to go all night if possible.

He even managed to move Juan closer to the fire and farther from the water's edge.

Feeling satisfied with the fire Carl knew that shelter was next. By now the sun was setting and building anything was going to be impossible. For now he had to be content with the fire and the fact that Juan was alive and alert.

Gazing across the fire he saw Juan sleeping. He couldn't imagine the pain that he must be going through. Carl then directed his eyes into the dancing flames. As is common around campfires one begins to gather deep thoughts.

Carl began to think of his wife and children. He hadn't spoken to them for over a week. He could imagine his wife Latasha being worried sick, trying to occupy her thoughts with busy work. Carl knew he was missing his oldest son's basketball games. Matthew was the point guard for his seventh grade team. Carl could see leadership qualities in him and a love for the Lord. He imagined Matthew being a pastor someday, although Matthew had his sights on the NBA. Then there was Halory. His little princess. Carl was missing the tea parties and having his hair done by a seven year old.

The thoughts turned on why he was here in the first place. Was he on a wild goose chase? Was the evidence he sought worth losing one's life over? He quickly dismissed the thoughts. God put him here for a purpose. Carl already had overcome his fear of traveling overseas. Even being shot at by bandits didn't freeze Carl in his tracks. A part of him was enjoying sitting next to the fire in the Andes Mountains and surviving the old fashion way. He took great pride in knowing how to start a fire without a lighter or a match.

Then, like a smack on the back of the head, he remembered the parchment. It couldn't possibly survived the water. He reached into his pocket and felt around. He expected a clump. Instead the parchment was whole and not damaged. Carl tenderly unfolded it and held it up.

Not only was the parchment not damaged but it seemed to improve with the water. The markings were more distinct, easier to read. Back at Machu Piccu Carl had to strain to make out the markings; squinting his eyes and moving his head back and forth. In comparison this was like reading a billboard on a clear day.

With the fire providing light from behind Carl stared. He wanted to wake Juan and share the good news with him but dismissed the idea quickly. Juan needed to rest his body. Who knew what tomorrow was going to bring? Carl instead set about the task of memorizing the markings. Should anything happen to the parchment Carl didn't want the journey to be a waste.

Throughout the night a lonely voice was heard, speaking the same things over and over again.

PHOENIX, ARIZONA

"Spring time in the desert is amazing," said David. "I never knew it could be so beautiful."

The Dodge Caravan glided over the Interstate 40. Cactus flowers were blooming and grasses stretched from the ground. All around there were assortment of flowers popping up. The colors ranged among pinks, yellows, reds, and even blues. David was surprised to see so much green. Not just from the famous cactus the dotted the landscape but from the other vegetation.

As the morning sun rose its light bounced off of the rocky terrain of formations. Spires looked liked fingers pointing to the sky. Mesas reflected back the light giving a heavenly glow.

David had his own ideas of what a desert should be. The rolling hills and active vegetation changed his perspective on beauty. Throw in the mild temperatures of being in the seventies in April and it was no wonder the American Southwest was growing in population.

John had visited Arizona many times. It was a treasure trove of fossils and ancient findings. Scientist and even non-scientist couldn't help but use the Grand Canyon as an example of explaining evolution. There, in layer upon layer, were different colors of sediments. For over two hundred and twenty-seven miles a gorge was carved by the Colorado River. A perfect representation of the ancient world from its beginning.

John was beginning to understand the canyon for the first time.

The more he read about Noah's flood, the more convinced he became it was real. He looked up a fairly recent, cataclysmic event that happened in Washington state. In May of 1980 Mount Saint Helens erupted. Ash was blown as far east as Wyoming. The power behind this singular event was beyond human understanding. Trees were ripped from the ground like toothpicks. Cars, trucks, semis, were rolled and tossed like toys.

Buildings were leveled in mere milliseconds. In an instant an entire geographical area was changed.

A lake was completely wiped out. According to scientist it would have taken millions of years to have this lake come about but in an instant, it no longers exists. Canyons were formed in seconds from the force of the blast. Rivers were rerouted. Hillsides were leveled while new ones were created.

In one day the geography was changed within one hundred miles of Mount Saint Helens.

Within five years new growth was already springing up through the ash. It seemed as if nature adapted quickly to its new look.

John wondered about other events that have happened that have changed geographical areas. In the early 1990's Hurricane Andrew roared into Florida. He remembered an aunt and uncle lived across the street from the ocean. From their front window one could see an island. Before the hurricane the island was one, after, the island was cut down the middle and became two separate islands.

Hurricane Katrina left a lasting imprint on the Mississippi Delta. The force of the hurricane was so strong it sent the Mississippi River flowing back upstream. The tornadoes and storms that accompany hurricanes created chaos across the American south.

John thought of the tsunami that hit India and parts of the Far East. Entire beaches were erased, millions of trees were ripped from the ground and thousands of people were dragged out to sea. John read that islands were reformed or were destroyed. The wave washed into certain areas by up to two miles.

All these events happened in mere moments and without warning.

John shared his thoughts with David. "David, if these events happened to change the landscape around them, and they were small in comparison to a world wide flood, could you imagine the changes that would happen in a world wide flood?"

"I've thought about that too. I kind of imagine a large kettle of soup. You throw all kinds of stuff into it. You stir it around, but then you dump it out on your floor. You would have onions next to potatoes next to pieces of meat next to celery and so on. From what you told me, we will find fossils of fish here in the desert. The only way that is possible is if there was water of a large scale here."

John and David took in the scope of that statement. For the last four hours they had driven across California and Arizona. Desert as far as the eye can see. It was hard to fathom that this endless landscape of rocky cliffs, sand, and sparse vegetation under a blanket of water. Fish, whales, sharks swam around this barren terrain.

"Ok, if dinosaurs lived at the same time as humans why the denial? I mean, a scientist could really make a name for himself, gain some fame, earn a lot of money by letting people know of this. Why be so secretive?"

"That is the big question of the day. First, you have to remember that most scientist work in universities and colleges. They get their money through grants and endowments. In essence, they are at the mercy of whoever gives them money. You heard the term 'Don't bite the hand that feeds you?' There you go. So a scientist researches and comes up with theories based on the perogative of whoever gave them the money."

"You mean that the idea of open minded scientist…"

John shook his head as he stared down the interstate. "It doesn't really exist. Also, professors are under contract with their universities and colleges to publish on a regular basis. If something comes up that brings a bad light on the institution, well, that professor may not have a job much longer. Then the chances of getting a job are even harder."

"So, a scientist plays it safe by reinforcing an idea that is out there already?"

"Exactly. In this way he gains a good reputation, earns a paycheck, and secures himself among his peers and superiors. It also gives him a better chance of receiving more grants. Let's face it, follow the money trail. Science is no different than any other institution. Are scientist greedy? Are they above earning extra cash? Are there some that are scrupulous and dishonest? Absolutely. The idea of survival of the fittest fits best in the academia world. The weak or different are pushed out of the way. To survive is to conform. Reinforce current ideas no matter how ridiculous they are."

David thought of his own department. There were people willing to sell out their partners for a chance at promotion. It seemed that everywhere people were willing to hurt, lie, and undercut others for a chance at more money and more recognition. It was a nasty world to live in.

"Do scientists know they are promoting a lie? I mean, are they aware of what they are doing? I have a hard time accepting the fact that all those people are willing accomplices to something so outright wrong."

"You are on to something. Over a week ago I was an accomplice to this lie and I didn't know it. I mean, think about it, thousands of intelligent people say that this theory is fact. They have degrees upon degrees from prestigious institutions. They can't possibly be wrong. So you go along with the theory. If your mindset is already believing it, then anything you do will reinforce it."

"But doesn't that contradict scientific belief? I thought that science was to be open minded and search out new things, ideas?"

"It should be that way." John thought back to his college days and early in his career. He remembered thinking that he was going to change the world. He would be the next great explorer. He would come across the next find that would change the world. At that time he had in his mind something like the Pyramids of Egypt. That would have been the safe way of doing it. Not traveling the world, reinforcing an idea that will cause him to possibly lose his job, contracts with publishers, and teaching anything above junior high science classes. "But it's not. Like most things, there are strings attached to the money. The biggest string is politics. People have agendas."

A road sign indicated that Phoenix was a hundred eight miles away. John calculated that they would be getting there in less than a hour and half. Just in time for lunch. Just the thought began to make his stomach rumble.

"I had no idea it was so complicated."

"Actually, it is quite the opposite. It is so easy that it is scary. What complicates the process is if someone deviates from the theory norm; in this case, evolution is a fact.Yet there is no evidence, none, that supports this theory."

"Wait a second. There is no evidence of evolution. All I hear about…"

"Are lies. Do real research. When you see Time magazine come out with a front page article on the missing link, look further. A few months down the road they had a disclaimer that the missing link was not the missing link. Each find for an evolutionist scientist, brings a hope that it will be the evidence required for proving evolution. Not a single shred of evidence has been found. For every bit of evidence they find, there are numerous examples of things that contradict that evidence. Do you know what that means?"

David had to think it through. "It seems as if someone, or something, purposely throws curve balls into the evolution theory."

John had to laugh, "That is exactly right. Scientist believed that certain trees and plants were extinct. Bam! They find those trees and plants existing. We call them living fossils. Evolutionist cannot explain certain animals because those animals contradict evolutionary thinking; for example, giraffes, woodpeckers, the gecko, beavers, and the bombadier beetle. It makes no sense why the animals do what they do. According to evolution, these animals should be extinct based off of how they operate and do things."

"What do you mean? I thought the giraffe evolved with the long neck so it could reach the top of trees to eat?"

"Then explain this, how does it keep from passing out when it gets a drink of water? The heart has to beat the blood up that long neck and back down again. The heart has to defy gravity. When the giraffe gets a drink of water it is no longer defying gravity but working with it. How come the blood doesn't rush into the brain and cause death? Then answer this, when it raises its head from drinking, how come no lightheadness? It is able to run from danger at the old drinking hole immediantly from raising its head. How is that possible?"

David had never thought the giraffe was so complicated. It ate, drank, ran away from danger. What was the big deal?

"According to evolution the animal would have died and thought to itself, I need a new way of getting blood to my brain and back with out it exploding. Of course it can't do this and evolve because it would keep dying. Technically speaking, the giraffe should not be here with us today. It is not considered among the fittest and therefore should not be surviving."

"Yet it is."

John nodded. "Yes it is. I always thought God had a great sense of humor. Look at the hippo, giraffe, and elephant. Then for good measure to confuse us humans, he throws in the platypus. There are animal that defies all evolution theories. A mammal that lays eggs, has fur like a beaver and a bill like a duck. Then it searches out its food not with smell or by its eyes but by electronic impulses. According to evolution, the platypus should have figured out some way to use its eyes underwater like other creatures such as the beaver or otter.

David grinned at the thought of the animals. He always thought of himself as a man's man, but few people knew that he went to school to become a veterinarian. He loved caring for animals.

"So tell me, are there any scientist standing up for the truth? As a person who looks to scientist for improving my life through science and medicine, as well as providing facts to understand the world around, I find it frightening to know most scientist don't stand up for the truth."

"There are some. And they pay a heavy price. I am afraid that I too will pay that price when this expedition is over. The scientific community does not want to face the reality that God is the creator or that God even exists."

"Why not? It seems so logical, it makes more sense."

"What happened when you came face to face with God?"

David was taken aback.

"Tell me, what happened to you when you came face to face with God?"

"I, well, I had to deal with it."

"That's right. No matter what it changed you didn't it? You cannot come face to face with God and not be changed. To recognize God, to acknowledge him, means you deal with everything that comes with God; his way of playing the game, his way of dealing with people, his way of living. People want to be in control of their lives. They want to control their destiny. Then when things go bad, they blame God. You see, people want to be their own god. They want to live a life with no boundaries, no safety nets, no consequences."

David thought of that life. He couldn't imagine a life like that again. He remembered feeling lost, pointless, and confused. There was no purpose in his life, no meaning. Now, the feeling is indescribable. He felt alive from the inside. He knew what the meaning of life was, knew that his life had a purpose.

"It is hard to get people to change, isn't it?"

"Harder than getting this person in front of me to change lanes, that's for sure."

David laughed and read the sign. Phoenix – 13. Almost there.

North Slope near the Coleville River, Alaska

"Heat. I would do just about anything right now for heat," thought Cathy. The Sno-cat sped across the snow covered terrain. Cathy was amazed at the speed and agility of these machines. Already the sno-cat plowed over drifts, rumbled through streams, manuevered through thick trees with little damage, and in the open shot across with remarkable smoothness.

The plane ride north was a paradox in and of itself. A little Cessna, bit enough for four people and some luggage took off from Anchorage. While the bucket of bolts seemed unable to hold itself together, it managed to show some breathtaking scenery. Rugged mountains, with a combination of rock, snow, and trees, shot up through the clouds. Lush forest spanning as far as the eye could see. River and creeks criss-crossed the landscape giving a contorted view of a mosaic. All things below and around her were succint. The mountains, trees, and rivers were clear and defined yet blended together to form a beautiful scene.

Cathy could see why Alaska was an outdoor paradise. She imagined the lakes and rivers teeming with trout. Bear, elk, moose, and deer wandered the state, adding to the beauty.

Then in a moment everything went white. Snow reached to the horizon as the trees and lushness fell behind the plane. Cathy knew why they were coming here. Like the other sites she was still grappling with the facts.

Yun mentioned that in the early eighties a discovery happened up here that changed the rules on dinosaurs. Paleotologists still visit the site today to see if the stories are true but are given direct instruction to not talk about it. Not until all the information is gathered and verified.

To Cathy this was like telling her not to stick her hands in the cookie jar and then walking away. Better believe that those hands are going into that cookie jar.

Up ahead was an outcrop of buildings and vehicles.

"That's the place," yelled Yun. The sno-cat's engine droned loud enough to drown out all other noises. Each person wore ear-guards for protection.

Cathy stared at the buildings. Trickles of smoke rose into the blue sky then dissipated into nothing. The blinding white of the snow made it difficult to focus too long. Cathy found her eyes constantly darting around.

When the sno-cat stopped and the doors opened Cathy soon realized how warm she was in the vehicle. The confined space along with the body heat had kept her quite warm compared to being outside in the open. There was no wind, "thank goodness," thought Cathy. Still, the arctic cold hung in the air and stabbed at the skin.

Cathy and Yun made their way to the largest of the buildings assuming it was the headquarters of the outfit. Once inside their instincts proved to be correct. Cathy took a moment to let the heat soak into her. She felt the cold slipping away from her and the tingling sensations to her fingers, ears, and toes let her mind know that the body was appreciating getting feeling back.

"Can I help you," asked a gentleman.

Cathy saw before her a man of incredible size. If he had been wearing a brown jacket Cathy would have sworn she had just encountered a talking bear. His hand reached out, "I am Ronald Debois. I'm the head paleotologist and in charge of this rag-tag outfit. You must be Yun and Cathy, am I right?"

Yun eagerly took Ronald's hand. Cathy noticed that Yun's hand was swallowed by the size of Ronald's. "You are correct sir."

"Stop with the sir thing. I am glad to have you here. We don't get many visitors up here. Once a month we get a supply plane. About twice a year we get visitors, mostly college students who need some field experience, but not usually people who purposely want to come here. From what I heard we have been considered off limits by most organizations in the scientific community."

Cathy reached her hand out. Despite the sheer size there was a gentleness to Ronald's hand. "I am Cathy Jurkovich. Glad to meet you."

"Sorry to hear about your dad. He was a great scientist and even better friend. That man was was as tough as they come."

Cathy had never heard of her father being tough. Especially from the mountain of a man before her. She had seen her father give lectures, write books, and study. To her, her father was more of a man who felt more comfortable in settings with books than arctic cold.

"Come, I have some coffee ready. I'm sure you will want to warm up and have some questions. Let me tell you something first, your dad was onto something Ms. Jurkovich, something big. And, this place was important to his findings. I think you will be excited."

Cathy looked over to Yun who raised his eyebrows. He seemed comfortable in the presence of Ronald. Most men get intimidated by larger men. "But," Cathy thought, "Yun is trained as a killer and could probably take out Ronald in a split second." Cathy turned away from Yun. She was here strictly on business. Her father's business.

Cathy and Yun followed Ronald down a hallway that was lined with photos of people working. There were group photos of students who had visited the site as well as distinguished professors who had come to visit. A constant figure was Ronald who was hard to miss as he towered in every picture.

The office seemed unable to contain the desk, shelves, and Ronald. Ronald poured three cups of coffee and set them on the desk. He then pulled off a contortionist act to get his body behind the desk and into the chair. Suddenly Cathy felt sympathy for the chair.

The coffee felt good as it drained down the throat and warmed the pit of her stomach. She closed her eyes to enjoy the sudden warmness in her. Another sip strenghthened the warmth.

"I know why you are here. Let me tell you though. I am able to continue working here because of donations. The scientific community and organizations don't want me to continue. So, true scientific organizations, ones who believe in finding the truth, are supporting as well as faith based organizations."

"You mean, churches?" Cathy was stunned. She couldn't imagine churches supporting scientific work.

"Not specifically churches. There are faith based scientific think tanks that are able to gather funds from organized faith communities. The think tanks sponsor people like me and the job we are doing. They believe, like I do, that science supports the Bible. Every bit of evidene out there proves it. I believe my job is to gather as much evidence as possible."

"And you believe you have found some of this evidence," asked Cathy.

"Some? My little lady I have found a plethora of evidence. Enough to convince a skeptic a thousand times over. Believe it or not, here in northern Alaska, we have proof to back up the Bible."

Ronald leaned back and placed his hands on the chair rails. It amazed her that the chair didn't crumble under the strength of the man.

"How is that possible?"

"Come with me." The contortionist act began again as Yun and Cathy moved through the doorway with their cups of coffee, each holding on as if the liquid was vital to living.

Ronald squeezed through the doorway and Yun and Cathy. Heading down the hallway to another part of the building they followed a maze of hallways. Finally Ronald opened a door to a room so different from the others. The room was lined with x-ray photographs with the light shining from behind. Deep drawers lined one wall and reached the ceiling. A table sat in the middle with a glass top.

"Go ahead. Open one of the drawers."

Cathy walked around the table to a drawer. She felt like a game show contestant, wondering what was on the other side. Her hand shook, even as she held the coffee cup. She turned around and placed the cup on the glass table. If it left a mark she figured it was easier to ask for forgiveness rather than permission. Turning back to the drawers she closed her eyes and reached for one.

Pulling on the brass handle she was surprised on how easily the drawer slid out. She noticed that Yun was beside her now, also eager to see what was inside. She was beginning to believe what Yun said back in Anchorage. He too was a scientist.

The drawer was deep and she soon realized she needed an extra pair of hands to hold onto the drawer. Cathy and Yun went to each side of the drawer and grabbed the long ends. They finished pulling the drawer out.

"Go ahead and place it on the table. This is going to be cool."

Cathy stared at the drawer in her hands. She couldn't see in as it was covered in black. Yun and her scuttled their feet in order to place the drawer on the table. Cathy was surprised on how the drawer fit perfectly on the table, as a counter top.

Ronald took a step forward. "What you are about to see, well, very few people have seen." Reaching a switch the table came alive with light.

Before Cathy were bones. She knew her mouth was open, which she knew from her upbringing was considered rude, but she didn't care. "Is this a duckbill dinosaur?"

"It is." Ronald's grin matched his size. "Get this, these are bones, not fossils. In 1981 the bones were thought to have been bison bones. Made sense. They were fresh, up in Alaska, fit the terrain. But, we have found several bones of not just duckbill dinosaurs but also of horned dinosaurs and small carnivorous ones. None of them fossilized."

"And they are…"

"Right behind ya little lady."

Cathy felt as if her legs were giving away on her. Unfossilized bones in northern Alaska. Dinosaurs were supposed to be in tropical areas. Bones were supposed to be fossilized.

"Don't think that this is the only place in the world for unfossilized bones. A t-rex was found in Montana. Its bones still contained blood cells and hemoglobin. Those bones were found in 1990."

"How is this possible? It doesn't make sense?"

"Actually it makes perfect sense. At first it was thought the cold would have frozen the bones. But that contradicts the idea that dinosaurs could only live in tropical areas and the new belief that fossilization has to happen with a cataclymic event. It has to be quick as well. There is new evidence that DNA breaks down in less than 10,000 years."

"Whoa. Wait a second. If these are unfossilized bones, which means they are bones. And bones contain DNA, then…"

"Here is proof that dinosaurs lived on the earth less than 10,000 years ago."

"Then how did the bones get here?"

Yun knew the answer. "It is the same answer as the fighting dinosaurs."

Cathy looked into Yun's eyes. Her hands were clenched white on the table to keep from falling over. "The flood."

"The flood."

"So man and dinosaur lived together." Cathy sighed out loud.

"The way I look at it is this; what you are looking at is like looking at a photograph only better. You look at the picture and say 'yep that is a dog'. But with techonology these days people can manipulate photos. You can't manipulate bones. There is no mistaking what these bones are and where they were found. Science, by it own practices and laws, have confirmed that dinosaurs were around pretty recently."

Cathy felt her legs give way. She let herself fall to a sitting position with her arms between her legs.

Yun and Ronald rushed to her side. "Are you alright?"

"I can't believe it. My father proved his theory."

Ronald lifted Cathy up as if she was nothing more than a loaf of bread. His eyes met hers, "He did prove it and he was tying all the pieces together. His hope was not to convince the public of this fact. His hope was to convince the scientific circles. He knew if he could convince them, then the public would follow suit. That is why he ended paying with his life."

His strong hands wrapped around the tiny shoulders of Cathy. "It is the only part of your dad's intentions I disagreed with. I told him to take it to the public and let them force the scientific community to deal with the pressure. He was ever the professional and still believed in protocols. He didn't want to believe that those protocols were dead."

"I have to finish his work."

"You can only finish his work if you believe in what your father believed," Yun said. "Without his faith, you too will not be able to grasp the evidence before you. Eventually you will come up with reasons to discount what your very eyes see."

"I have to believe in God to believe what is before me?"

"Exactly. How many others have seen the evidence only to discount it on the basis of lack of faith?"

"He's right. I had to come to that conclusion twenty years ago when I first started here. Your father helped me realize that."

Cathy was sitting here with two men that her father had a profound impact on. Their lives were forever changed because of him.

"What do I need to do? To know?"

"Well, first...."

BEIJING, CHINA

Kim waited nervously outside of Chin Lang's office. Chin hated meetings, enjoyed his privacy, and interruptions were always met with consequences. Routine was the sacred rule.

The waiting room was adorned with pictures of China's past. Kim expected to see pictures that showed glorious victories and grand military leaders. There were some of those up on the wall such as Ghengis Khan.. But there were pictures that showed China's more dismall days and defeats. A photograph showed a city just after it was bombed by Japan in World War Two.

The secretary at the desk ignored Kim. She knew when people were called into see Chin it was not good so better to ignore the person. Don't give sympathy or a warm smile. For all she knew this man in the office was heading for prison or some unknown outpost. So she continued to pretend to type away while keeping an eye on the man wandering the office.

The voice from the speaker phone made both people in the office jump a little as the silence up to that point was heavy like a wet blanket. "Please send in Commander Kim."

With that a door was opened. The secretary never said a word to Kim. She merely touched a button that automaticall opened the door. Kim felt like he was walking into a predator's mouth. As he crossed through the doorway the doors automatically shut behind him.

He was now in the belly of the beast. But the belly had good taste. Lining the walls were swords of every type. Kim recognized the swords from his studies in military history. If some of these were originals they would fetch millions in auctions and from museums. Maps of the world hung from a unit that allowed the maps to roll and unroll from the ceiling.

Kim focused on keeping himself collected. Behind the oak desk sat

Chin. The man may look small in stature but his presence was looming. The military since Chin came into leadership, became more disciplined, focused, and had grown. Basic training requirements were raised to prepare a better army. Skills and techniques once taught only to special forces were now taught in basic training. Chin believed in having the best military in the world with no ands, ifs, or buts.

"Commander Kim. It has come to my attention that you have met with Ambassador Bortho. Why?"

Kim didn't know whether to keep standing or take a seat. Since the seat wasn't offered he decided to stand. He knew that Chin was going to use techniques of mind games and power plays to get information. Kim used them himself. Kim just didn't know who was going to be better at the game.

"We happened to be a dinner gathering together and by chance we met each other and talked."

"About what?"

Kim knew he was going to have to make a choice. Lie and take his chances he won't get caught. Tell the truth and hope the conseqences aren't so bad. He decided to bend a little of both.

"I believe that we have some enemies coming into China from America. These enemies can be dealt with if we had America's help."

Kim was hoping the idea of diplomacy would go over with Chin.

"Who are these enemies and why wasn't I informed of them before?"

The man was relentless. No cordial talk to ease the atmosphere. No drink offered. Kim knew that Chin had some information, but not knowing specifics but Kim on the defensive and that was a bad position to be in. Each question made Kim make the hard choice, lie or truth. It took split seconds to weigh the consequences and think of outcomes.

"I'm not sure at this point. Until I was sure of the enemies I was going to inform you. Without having specifics I felt that I would be wasting your time. I wanted to give to you as complete a picture as possible."

Kim could see Chin dwellling on each word that was spoken. Kim relied on his strengths when dealing with difficult people. Speak in short but specific sentences. Cater to their ego. Leave the door open for future options. It seemed, judging from the lack of questions, that Chin was weighing the statement.

"You are aware of protocol are you not Commander Kim?"

"I am."

"Then why would you break protocol to meet with a foreign dignitary without permission? On two different occassions?"

Kim was feeling the noose a little. Chin was using the technique of explanding the situation a little at a time. Kim knew that Chin could possibly accept the dinner as accidental, pure chance. But the flight to Hong Kong was purposeful. Kim was running through answers in his mind.

"I thought it would be rude, and unbecoming of us, as representatives of China, to not follow through on promises spoken. At the dinner the Ambassador wanted to meet with me again. As a sign of good faith I agreed to meeting him in Hong Kong."

Kim studied Chin's face. The man was stone. If there was emotion at all it was buried deep inside the man.

"Let me see if I understand what you are saying."

"Oh boy," thought Kim. "Here is where he gets me."

"You met the Ambassador by chance at a dinner party. I know for certain that you hate dinner parties. Then you happen to talk. The conversation lasted more that normal for a casual chance meeting. Then the ambassador wants to meet with you again, away from Beijing, in Hong Kong, to discuss more of what was discussed at the dinner. During this whole time, I am not aware of these conversations nor privy to the information. I am to wait until you decide that I am ready to hear the information. It is your discretion that I am to wait, all the while protocol is being broken. Am I understanding this correctly?"

Kim felt fear grasping at his heart. Chin was holding back something. That something was going to be the final squeeze. Kim had to answer.

"Yes sir. I apologize if it seems that I was undermining you."

"Undermining me? You haven't answered any of my questions. You have given no specifics. Who are these enemies? What is the plan? I believe that you are planning something I wouldn't approve of. So you go behind my back. You are working on something that may benefit you personally and further undermine me. That is what I believe. How do you answer to that?"

Kim felt the noose. The gamble on the lie and truth was coming around. If he backtracked now the hole he was in would become deeper. The consequences would be more severe. Kim now knew what a no win situation felt like. He knew that no matter what he said those words would be used against him.

"I don't have an answer."

"Don't have an answer? How could you not have an answer? You will tell me what you said and discussed with the Ambassodor. You will relate to me your plan and its specifics. You will tell me everything. Do you understand?"

Kim felt like the boy in the village all over again. Defeated. Hopeless. All around him were things going on that were outside of his control. Events were happening that seemed out of control. Chaotic. The repercussions of when he was a little boy were life changing. He felt the same would happen now. Life altering events were happening.

Kim began to prepare his heart, body, and mind for the consequences. The plans he had set in place were in full motion. They cannot be changed; they were outside of even Chin's power. By the time Chin caught up to Xi people more people would be killed. The plan to eradicate Christian missionaries was already in motion. He had Su Lee send out the necessary information to begin the process. Like dominoes falling, the events were going according to plan.

Kim let a smile show. "I understand perfectly."

PERU

Carl memorized the entire parchment. While keeping watch over the camp and checking on Juan, Carl didn't want this excursion going to waste. The sun was already above the mountains and the heat and humidity was rising.

Today was not going to be an easy day.

Carl packed away the parchment and looked over at Juan. The breathing was consistent but labored. Juan was losing the flesh color in the cheeks and a paleness was settling in. Carl knew that between nature, beasts, clansmen, and an injured man that the odds of coming out alive were against him. Carl had read stories of human survival, of overcoming the odds, and beating the impossible. Would this be his survival story? Would this episode of his life inspire others like the stories have done for him?

There was only one way to find out. Carl bowed his head and prayed. He prayed for the journey ahead. He prayed for Juan and a recovery. He prayed for John and Cathy that they would be protected and successful. Finally he prayed for those hunting him and wanting to kill him. That they would be unsuccessful and see the wrong that they are doing.

With that Carl put Juan into a piggy-back position. Carl's mind flashed to NFL camps of carrying teammates up and down the football field. Only the field was level and mowed. Carl had to avoid holes, trees, branches, and creeks. Every so often Carl would have to adjust Juan to a different position; from piggy back to fireman's carry to over the shoulder. Every thirty minutes Carl needed to rest. His lower back screamed in pain and his legs were numb. He would rest for ten minutes and began the hike again.

Carl lost track of time as his body became like a robot. The brain no longer commanded the legs to move. The moved because it was the only thing to do. If the brain was in control the body would have shut down.

Nothing was making sense. The survival instinct would have kicked in in the deepest, primal areas of the brain. The part that said to abandon Juan, survival of the fittest, conserve your enery. The part of the brain the spewed logic would have yelled that moving on was futile.

But the heart said otherwise.

The heart was determined to survive. It was determined to save Juan. The heart told Carl that his wife and children were worth the effort and the pain and the agony.

After five hours of hiking Carl's body decided enough was enough. The basic needs had to be cared for; food, water, rest. Carl found a stream and good coverage of overhanging branches and leaves. A log stretched between two boulders and provided a nice shelter from three directions. Overgrowth and moss covered the space making a natural cave. Carl scooped out dirt to level a place for Juan to lay down. The breathing was consistent but the color was fading. Juan was hurting. Carl's frustration was not knowing where or how to help.

The stream was about twenty feet across and looked to have fish in it. A glance around the area showed animal tracks of rabbit and squirrel. Carl had a few hours until nighttime and it so there was time to do some hunting.

Using tree limbs and rocks Carl devised traps and weapons. Holes were dug to trap animals, pointed branches were fashioned, rocks were tied together by grasses to make crude slings. Carl had never been in the wild before and surely was ignorant on hunting animals. But he did watch survival shows and enough movies that he hoped some of that would transfer to the situation he was in.

Withing three hours Carl managed to catch two rabbits. Using the sharpened sticks he managed to remove the skin. The meat was mangeled but there was enough to eat. Carl knew that he would have to make a fire and the fire would produce smoke. He hoped that enough distance and time had passed that the mountain pirates would have given up. He decided to take his chances. Besides, Juan needed nourishment if he was going to survive another hike like today.

Within a hour Carl was savoring his first rabbit. The protein felt good to the body. He managed to get some bite size pieces for Juan and hoped the vitamins and nutrients would do the trick. He cooked the second rabbit and would carry the meat for tomorrow. He knew resources may not always be available and he was not sure how far he had gone, or to where he needed to be. It finally dawned on Carl he wasn't sure on where he was heading. He was just running.

Carl noticed the stream flow. Unless something happens tonight he thought, better to follow the stream flow. Once the second rabbit cooked Carl extinguished the fire. Take no unnecessary chances. Carl scrounged around the area looking for fallen tree limbs and branches. He wanted to cover up the natural opening and hopefully keep the body heat of Juan and himself contained. Plus, there was always the thought of being discovered and killed.

As the sun was setting Carl felt the coolness moving in. His thoughts remained on his wife and kids. He wondered about John and Cathy. There was also a calmness. Words from Paul spoke from his heart. While Paul was in chains he remained content in all things.

Carl decided that today was a good day. Tomorrow remained unknown to all but one.

Let God decide tomorrow for God is good thought Carl. God is good.

ANCHORAGE, ALASKA

Cathy continued tossing the ideas in her head. The airplane flight from northern Alaska back to Anchorage gave little opportunity to sift out the ideas and theories that Ronald and Yun presented. Yun continued the barrage of information on the puddle jumper. Along with the constant hum of the plane Cathy could do little else but listen.

Now in the silence of the hotel room she began sorting out the ideas. A mosaic of lined paper with notes blanketed the floor. Over on the cheap round table were the notes about the unfossilized bones of the Montana T-rex. Cathy searched the web and made phone calls to her collegues. The "fossils" contained blood cells, flexible blood vessels, and soft, pliable tissue. These characteristics are completely contradictory to fossilization processes.

Scattered across the adjacent bed were the notes on the China fighting dinosaurs. Fossilization states that time is a key ingredient. Yet two, active dinosaurs are fossilized. Common sense states that when impending doom comes that survival instinct would take over. Both dinosaurs would have left the fight and sought some sort of safety. Instead a velociraptor and protoceratops are locked in battle. The protceratops holding onto the raptor's right arm in its jaws. The raptor's hands clinching onto the head shield of the protoceratops. Even the claw, sickle in shape, seems lodged into the body cavity of the protoceratops. Only a cataclysmic event such as a flood could cause this event to happen.

Among the notes were other specimens preserved in the much the same way; lizards, crocodiles, and small mammals. The bodies were buried quickly.

Cathy sat there stunned that two pieces of evidence were destroying an entire establishment. And still there were notes.

On the desk, under the lamp were the notes on the polar fossils in northern Alaska. Near the Coleville River were bones that included gorgosaurs, toodon, and the dromaessaurus. Plant eaters included the edmontonsaurus, pachyrhinosaurus, pachycephalosaurus and the thescelosaurus. The timeline of the dinosaurs' deaths didn't match up with the ice age timeline many scientists proposed. "Could dinosaurs survive arctic conditions," said Cathy out loud. As impossible as it seemed, Cathy was beginning to believe that the impossible was possible and what was considered possible was in fact a lie.

Another spattering of notes on the floor stated how humans would have escaped a flood by retreating to higher ground. This is verified by the recent discoveries of mummies in mountainous areas such as Peru. Mummy remains such as Lucy are not considered missing links but instead are evidence of fleeing humans. The countless articles stated why dinosaur bones and human bones are not found together.

On top of the television was a pile of how the dinosaurs became extinct. The flood would have wiped out many dinosaurs, much like the other animals. Article after article state human activity to be a huge reason. Human activity was the reason that the dodo bird, passenger pigeon, and the great elephantbird became extinct. Hunting wiped out entire species. In recent history game hunting almost wiped out the American bison. Pesticides almost destroyed the American bald eagle and the Andean and California condor.

Pages and pages showed the thousands of animals that were extinct. More pages showed hundreds more that are endangered.

"How far-fetched is it to consider that maybe man could have wiped out the dinosaur as well?" Thoughts of survival came to Cathy's mind. Would man really want to live with dinosaurs? The answer would be no and therefore the easiest answer to the problem would be elimination. Cathy couldn't agree with the outcome but could understand the reasoning.

Ireland prided itself on the idea that St. Patrick banished snakes from the island. If an entire country could believe that then how come man as a whole couldn't wipe out giant lizards for hunting, creating tools, and generally survive?

Cathy scanned the hotel room. Evidence upon evidence contradicted popular scientific theory. The evidence pointed, like a laser, to one outcome.

Fossils happened by a cataclysmic event. That event must be sudden and unexpected. And that event happened all over the world at the same moment.

Cathy went to one more pile. This pile sent chills up her spine and created angst that sat in the pit of her stomach. It was articles of scientist of knew of this evidence but chose to accept it. Men and women who knew the truth but decided that the public didn't need to know. There were copies of letters from universities and businesses stating that any thing other than Darwin and evolution was not aligned with best practices. That millions of dollars would be lost if there were other theories. The amount of time and resources to print new books, to verify the information, to provide multiple sides was not cost effective.

Government papers showed a trend of grants and other monies given to scientific organizations that were evolutionist in nature. Not a single intelligent design group has received any money for their research.

Cathy was seeing the pit that her father was in. The danger he faced was brought to life in her, not only in China but also in the solitude of the room.

There was something not aligned in the scientific circles. She had heard of blackballing of scientists in universities and colleges across the United States. Now, her father, may have died for this very reason.

A knock on the door summoned her out of her thoughts. It didn't dawn on Cathy that it was two in the morning. The information before her weighed her down. Any distraction at this point was a good one.

The knock came again and annoyance crept over Cathy.

Through the peephole Cathy could see Yun. He looked ready to knock again but she noticed that he was scanning both sides of the hallways. Over his shoulder was his carry bag.

Cathy unbolted the door and turned the knob. Yun rushed into the room and quickly closed the door and bolted it back up.

"Hey! What's going on?"

"Cathy, you need to pack and now. We need to go." Yun stared out across the room at the piles. "What's this?"

"My homework if you really need to know. What's the matter?"

"I just received a call. Ronald was murdered about two hours ago. I believe his murderer in on his way here."

Thoughts of China and the killings that happened there flashed through Cathy's mind. She remembered the screams and the iron grip that was strangling her.

"I need all this. Plus my clothes."

Together the two managed to pack everything in a matter of minutes. Deciding against using the elevator and risk being seen by hotel employees Yun and Cathy descended down the stairways. When they reached the bottom the lobby was empty. Not even a desk clerk was present. They hurried through the lobby and out into the frigid night air of Alaska.

The desk clerk heard the door open and reluctantly left the employee work room. On the television was the Seahawks game that a friend recorded for him. He scanned the lobby area and didn't see anyone. He knew someone had left from the coldness that swept through the room. He scanned again and wondered who would leave at two in the morning on a Wednesday.

Oh well, at least I get to see the rest of the game he thought.

PHOENIX, ARIZONA

John and David enjoyed the meals before them. John put his napkin on his plate. Evidence of chicken chimichangas, salsa, and guacamole were splattered on the napkin. David was finishing up his beef enchilidas and sipping on his Mountain Dew.

John was revitalized by the talk they had in the car. He was amazed by how much he could relate his testimony to David being a new believer.

After lunch they headed towards Arizona State University. The university had a great reputation for its studies of ancient tribes of North America. John was hoping to run into an old friend his. Dr. Blaine Bradford was an expert in indigenous tribes, particulary of the southwest. There was no one better at knowing the hunting, eating, and daily living patterns of the Navaho, Anaszi, Hopi, Sioux, and others. Throughout his adult life Dr. Bradford lived the ancient life of certain tribes. During one summer he decided to becomd nomadic and dressed in the ancient garb, carried the ancient tools, and ate only what nature provided. The experience nearly killed him but gained him honary status as a member of the Navaho tribe. From then on his reputation earned him into the inner circles of many tribes allowing him to learn ancient languages, customs, and secrets.

It was John's hope that Blaine would be willing to divulge some of these secrets. John knew it would take a convincing argument to part these secrets from Blaine but he was hoping that the evidence that he had gathered in the last few days would be enough.

John knew that Blaine was the biggest skeptic. An inner motive was that if John could convince Blaine, then Blaine's enforsement would resonate across the scientific community.

All this was hope.

David guided the car around the campus. Like most campuses it was well manicured, orderly, and spacious. It was strange to John and David to see students strolling around in shorts and t-shirts in February. Only days ago was John in Wyoming battling snow and wind. Here, the sun shone in a cloudless sky with a radiant blue.

John gave directions to David as they found the anthropology department. John called Blaine when they landed and he was eager to see his old friend.

David and John entered the building and were greeted by artifacts of several native tribes. Black and white pictures showed native people in traditional garb. In the background of each picture were grass huts, fire pits, and horses. Mountains would border the background of some of the pictures. Others showed white people interacting with families.

Every picture showed weathered faces of forlorn looking eyes; as if a piece of history, a way of life will be gone forever.

David followed John as they went up the spiral staircase to the second floor. Halfway down the massive hallway was Dr. Blaine Bradford. John was amazed by the appearance of Blaine. The man looked like a Ken doll; blond surfy hair, tall and lean, and tan from the constant Arizona sun with pearl white teeth. There were no worry lines or crow's feet to be found on his face.

Life can be so unfair.

"Good afternoon John. I see that you made it here alright. Must be a nice change from snow and wind, am I right?" A smile spread across the perfect face.

"It is refreshing to be here. It is even better to see you old friend." John and Blaine had a long history together with the centerpiece of those adventures being Mike. "Forgive me, this is David. He is here to help me out with our, well, mystery if you will."

"Glade to meet you David. A friend of John's is a friend of mine. But, be forwarned, this friend will give you adventures that will make your hair curl."

"So I've heard. It is good to meet y ou as well."

"John, your call sounded urgent. Before I forget, sorry I didn't make it to Mike's funeral. It was so unexpected and things were…"

"I know. I almost didn't make it as well. We can talk about that later. I need some information about the tribes who lived in this area, say about five to six thousand years ago. Earlier if possible. Specifically I need to know what animals they hunted, what animals were around, and how did they use the animals."

Blaine settled into his chair behind hs large oak desk. Trapped on the perfect face was a thoughtful expression, one covering racing thoughts behind wondering eyes.

"If it helps I really curious on only one type of animal."

Blaine leaned forward and gave a quizzical look. "Would this animal be reptile in nature?"

John had to chuckle. "Yes. The big ones in particular."

Blaine sat back in his chair. "There are many pictographs around the Southwest of large animals that no longer exist. You told me you were at Arches and found several petroglyphs of dinosaur like drawings. That was just one example. You see, there is a reason this city is called Phoenix. The Sioux people hunted what they called the Thunder Bird. Their drawings match perfectly to the pterosaur pterandon. In the San Rafael Swell there are examples of rock art of this same type of bird. Both are consistent with a large flying reptile. There are pictures of not just our flying friend. In Havasupai Canyon, here in Arizona, there is a petroglyph of a creature that has an upright stance and a balancing tail; common too many of the dinosaurs, not like what we see today."

David had to throw in his question, "So what? What makes petroglphs so important? Anyone could draw them? Frankly, it looks like a kid drew those types of drawings anyway." He didn't mean to be sarcastic but he was curious to know the importance.

"You bring up a good point David. Petroglyphs were our ancestors way of taking pictures. Think of it this way; when you plan a big family event what do you bring? I am willing to bet that one item is a camera. What does every hunter and fisherman do when they snag the big one? They take a picture. Mostly because who would believe a fisherman's story anyway? Well, man has not changed in over ten thousand years. I man still likes to brag about his trophy catch and the story of how he caught the trophy. What is the only way ancient man had of telling his hunting story…"

"through pictures." John said finishing Blaine's thoughts.

"Through pictures," repeated David.

"Answer me this," went on Blaine. His eyes now looking out towards the distant mountains to the north. "Why is it man is willing to accept the dodo bird existed? Have you seen it? I haven't. Yet I know it existed. How do I know that?"

David felt like a first grade student all over again. Confidently he felt like he knew the answer but didn't have the courage to answer. Sheepishly he answered, " Through pictures?"

"Absolutely! There were drawings that depicted what the dodo looked like but I don't see anybody saying that the dodo didn't exist. Why is that?"

Now it was John's turn to act the sheepish student. "Because people don't want to?"

Blaine spread a grin of pure delight. His excitement, barely contained as it was, was now seeping out. "Not just because people don't want to, but because people are easily convinced. People would rather live in a fantasy world and dinosaurs have become a fantasy world. To make them real, well, it is unfathomable to most people. They cannot, I don't mean would not, I mean they cannot wrap their minds around the fact of dinosaurs living with people."

"But if it is true, what is so hard about people believing in the truth?"

Blaine lost his grin and a deep sadness settled in his eyes. "Look how long it took to build the lie. Look at how long it took to convince the world that evolution was the answer. Look at how many fought and were punished for their belief in evolution and later would become martyrs. Don't you see, the lie is so entrenched in the world's fabric that comprehending anything else is, well, almost impossible."

David was dumbfounded. "How could scientist be so readily accepting of this?"

In his chair John had listened and was able to relate to what Blaine was stating. A sorrow beyond words weighed upon his heart. "If we are willing to replace God with science, then guess what, science becomes our god. Human nature states that we must serve a god. Even accepting the fact that there is no god is a god-like belief. Scientist have become the priests of science, the labs are the temples, theories are the new doctrines, and acceptance is a lifetime goal." John gave a sorrowful look over at Blaine. "It is no longer about seeking truth or making new discoveries is it?"

Blaine reciprocated the look, "Not anymore. It is about establishing the new world belief in every way possible."

David switched his focus between the two men. "What does this all mean?"

"That is the scary question David. We don't know? More importantly, do the people, however noble in their causes involved in this, are they thinking the same thing? Do they know where this path leads to?"

"I hope to God they figure it out."

DALLAS, TEXAS

Xi had scouted out the Twelve for several days. Well eleven of them anyway. He went by each of their homes and saw their children and wives. Each man had a nice home in the perfect location of town. Green grass wrapped around each home, sidewalks connected streets to neighborhoods.

Each many had many things to lose.

Xi learned long ago that to kill an organization you cut off the head. And that was what Xi was doing now. Figuring out which of the eleven men was the actual leader. If that man was weakened, humiliated, and then broken, the rest would scatter and the support for the three travelers would end.

The only snag was figuring out who the leader was. It seemed that the men took their turns in leading and in serving the others of the group. While the group was well organized and disciplined it was also loosely formed in hierarchy. Much like the rebels back in China.

"Maybe I don't need to worry about a leader. Maybe I just need to eliminate one and send a clear message to the others." The idea rattled around Xi's head until it became a plan.

Sitting on a bench along a walkway, soaking in the sunshine from the Texas sun, Xi studied the biographies before him. Eleven men. Every person has a breaking point. Each organization also has a breaking point.

Xi found the point.

PERU

Carl was surprised that he awoke. Considering that he laid upon dirt and rock. Roving mountain pirates scouring the hillsides for him. A hunger gnawing within his gut. Despite all the obstacles Carl found himself refreshed.

Juan on the other hand didn't look as refreshed. In fact, he looked worse. Carl crawled over to examine Juan. The breathing was labored, irregular and despite the coolness of the cave a layer of sweat covered Juan and drenched his clothes. A new color replaced the paleness of yesterday. A gray tone settling in. Carl checked on the broken leg.

It didn't take a doctor to know that if Juan didn't receive medical attention soo there would be dire consequences.

Carl checked the food supply. The rabbit from yesterday was safe from rodents and bugs. Knowing that he needed energy for the long day ahead Carl took a few bites. He offered some to Juan but to no avail.

"Please Lord. Protect us today. Guide us to someone or somewhere where Juan can receive help. I submit everything to you. Your plan, your will be done."

Carl checked to make sure the parchment was still one piece and protected. The rabbit was also secured. Carl realized that there would be no way to make Juan totally comfortable so he decided to carry him in fireman style.

The groans were weak from Juan when Carl picked him up and slung him over his left shoulder. Not a good sign. As Carl exited the cave he stayed with his gut feeling of last night. Follow the stream.

The morning coolness gave way to noonday heat. Time had no meaning as Carl weaved around trees, stumps, and rocks. At times he had to stop and rest the legs and shoulders. A numbing sensation would take over his arms. If it wasn't for the weight of Juan bearing down on him, Carl wouldn't feel him at all.

The minutes turned into hours as Carl continued to follow the stream. Strange noises would awaken Carl from the zombie-like state and make him alart again. Hanging in the air was the presence of pirates.

The stream provided the one welcoming respite. During the breaks, and they became more frequent throughout the day, Carl was able to quench his thirst and clean himself. It also allowed him to check on Juan. So far, by God's grace, Juan's conditions haven't changed. Carl changed the deranged wrapping on the leg on every rest. He didn't want some animal to track them by a blood scent. So far the plan was working. To keep the bandits from tracking them Carl would wrap the old wrappings in leaves and bury them in the ground. The heat was torching the skin as Carl ripped of more of his shirt to create more wrappings. Confuse the animals. Avoid the bandits. The rest breaks were short and Carl would heave Juan back upon his shoulders and continue to move forward.

By nightfall Carl wasn't sure how many miles were covered but he was thankful for the setting of the sun. He prayed for safety throughout the night and Juan's recovery. He also prayed for an end to this madness. He wasn't convinced if he could make it through another day like today.

YUKON

The snow hypnotized Yun as he drove the winding mountainous roads. It was difficult to pull one's eyes away from the funnel of snow in front and concentrate on the road. There was a focal point, seemed to be about fify feet ahead, that garned attention. It was exhausting.

Punishing the car was S curves, whipping wind, and black ice. It was as if an offensive line of some NFL team was practicing blocking skills on the vehicle. The ice was unseen and treacherous.

Still, it was the second time that Cathy escaped death. She wasn't sure where she was going but her trust in Yun had become a blind faith ambition. Twice she was attacked. Twice she had been rescued by Yun.

A knight in shining armor.

"Cathy, your father was trying to prove this theory of dinosaurs living with man. Is that true?"

Grateful for lifting the weight of silence Cathy was craving conversation. The days and nights of silence were now behind her. She had learned that they accomplished little except pity parties.

"Yes. For the last three years it seems that he had traveled the world and sought out evidence to prove this theory. It also seems that this theory had cost him his life."

"You don't seem so sad about this fact."

"I'm sorry to say I don't. Not anymore. I did about a week ago. But a week ago I had the luxury of ignorance. Now...well, now I have information and nothing is worse than having information."

Yun had to laugh. "What could you possible mean?"

Cathy had to let out a slight laugh as well. "I have learned that when you learn something, you are accountable to it. It changes you. . You have to make a choice on each thing that you learn. It starts as early as childhood. When a child learns his or her letters then it is expected that they will be able to spell their names. For the rest of their lives their name is on every single document they produce."

"That is kind of stretching it isn't it? I mean, what about tidbit trivia. Isn't that leraning?"

"For some I guess it is. But how many people change a behavior, a thought process, or perception based off of tidbit trivia?"

"So, okay, you have learned all this information in the last week, how has it changed you?"

Cathy was struggling with that very question for the last week. "Here is what I know; there is strong evidence that dinosaurs lived with man. So much so that they theory is ready to go from hypothical to being tested and then to fact. In that is the case then it proves that evolution is and always was a farce. The alternative is to investigate option B, creationism."

"God?"

The word seemed to echo throughout the Subaru.

"I guess that would ultimately be the answer to creationism."

So if God is the answer, what is your question or questions?"

Cathy just realized that she had been outdone. Yun had a "got you" smile. "I just have a hard time accepting a god. I mean, how many problems, wars, evils have been done in the name of religion. And if a god did create all this then why didn't he do a better job? Why all the pain? Death? Hurts? Sorrow? Take me right here. Right now. I am scared. Scared for Carl. For John. For myself. I'm scared of how my father died and that the same will happen to me. I'm afraid that the truth will not get out there and that people died in vain. Why would a god allow this? You and I are trying to do what is right and we are being hunted like animals. If we are being hunted like animals then we must be animals. Nothing more than beasts just trying to survive."

Cathy looked over and saw Yun. Tears were running down his face. Here was a man who was trained to kill and had saved her life twice and he showed an unexpected softness. "Do you honestly think that God wanted this for the world he created? If you created something would you introduce bad things into it? No you wouldn't. But if you created something wouldn't you want it to love you back? Would you create that thing with free will? Wouldn't you want that thing to have a choice to love you or not? Isn't that one way a person shows love towards another? By giving them a choice to love. Is forced love truly love?"

Yun took a breath and continued, " Man was different than all the other animals in that he was created in the image of God. That doesn't means we look like God. I see my uncle and let's hope that God doesn't look like him. In his image means that we have God's characteristics in us. That we love, think, forgive, grant mercy and grace and can choose. God wanted to have a relationship with us but he gave us a choice to be in that relationship. A true relationship means that both parties choose to be involved."

"Like a man proposing to his girlfriend. He is making a choice to be in a relationship with that person. The girlfriend also has to make the choice to be in that relationship. Is that right?"

"That's the right idea. We as man had that relationship but we chose to break it off by sinning. We thought we were better than God. Think about it, how many times do you and I still think we can do better than God?"

"Okay, so God creates this relationship with us, we break it off, now what? I mean the world is still evil and bad things are still happening."

"That's true, but we now have the opportunity to have that relationship with God. You and I can have peace in this world, despite everything that is happening. God still desires to have us love him. He still loves us and he has proven it."

"He has?"

"A little over two thousand years ago he sent his only son to die for us. He died a cruel and terrible death. God sacrificed his only son because he loves us so much. Think about it, would you sacrifice your child for a total stranger? I didn't think so, but God did. This sacrifice had to be paid for all the sins of the world. It allowed us, you and me and all people, to have that relationship with God. All you and I have to do is accept that sacrifice and believe."

"Accept what?"

"Jesus. Accept Jesus."

DALLAS, TEXAS

For the first time Troy was looking forward to visiting the Trough residence. Deep within him he felt a burning passion for the family. He was not naïve enough to know that all the problems were close to being taken care of, but he and the Eleven had prayed and Troy's faith in God was not wavering.

He felt a breakthrough of some sort was going to happen today.

The city of vans and cameras remained outside the house, keeping a watchful eye on every movement being made. "Just like America to focus on the negatives and non-essentials in our society. If we put as much energy into building people up…." Troy let his thoughts wander on the topic. "Better to have the pipe-dream than no dream at all."

As Troy prepared for the onslaught of cameras and questions he noticed that Emily was looking out of her bedroom window. For a brief second Troy thought he glanced a smile. Just as quickly the shades were drawn back for a protective barrier and she was gone.

Breakthrough.

Troy numbed his body and mouth as he paraded through the media crowd. As he prepared to knock on the door it opened. Silently and unexpectedly , like some B-rated horror film it welcomed him in with no face or person on the other side. As he entered he saw Sharon hiding behind the door with the slyest smile. She closed the door. "Good morning Mr. Reiner."

"Good morning to you Ms. Trough. How are you today?" Always a dangerous question but it was better to be real and honest with the family.

"Better. Last night, I was able to sleep all the way through with no nightmares."

"I am glad to hear that Sharon." Troy expected that sleep was a luxury in the home but to hear it and then hear it being overcome was a praiseworthy event. Troy was sensing that something was different in the home. "Is your dad around?" Troy knew that Curtis as but good manners are a great security blanket in times like these.

"I think he is in his study. Do you want me to show you where it is?"

"No, I know, but thank you. I hope to see you again soon Sharon."

"You will, I promise."

With that Sharon left the entryway and bounded up the stairs. Troy was glad to see energy in the house again. For such a long time a depression rooted itself into the house. He understood why but it was good to see a ray of sunshine amongst the clouds.

Troy moved to the hallway on his left and saw the dark, wooden oak door that led into Curtis' study. This room is where Curtis wrote his books, prepared his speeches on family, and counseled many young men into the preaching profession. Himself included.

The three knocks echoed down the hallway and no answer from the other side. Troy knocked again and put his ear to the door. Still no answer. He reached for the knob and turned it.

A sudden moment of clarity hit Troy. "Something is not right here," he thought to himself. There was Emily smiling from her window. Sharon in a totally different mood. But the silence coming from the study was unnatural.

Pushing open the door Troy saw a low light emanating from the lamp on Curtis' desk. Opening the door more Troy glanced about the room. Everything seemed to be in its place. He looked over at the desk and noticed the black leather chair had its back facing Troy.

Something was definitely wrong.

"Curtis? Are you here?"

Troy walked carefully, fearfully, up to the desk fearing and yet hoping that Curtis was asleep. Troy knew how much he hated to be woke up unexpectedly and be scared silly. "Curtis?"

Troy was at the desk now and tried to look over the chair without being too conspicuous. The urge of curiosity was too strong and Troy inched himself around the desk.

Curtis was in his chair but his lower face was missing. Blood covered the entire front side of Curtis. Bound to the arms of the chair was Curtis' arms. Cut marks zig-zagged up each arm from wrist to shoulder. The strangest part of this spectacle were the hands and feet. Each hand was facing upward with spikes driven into each palm. The feet were bound together with an electrical cord and a spike was also driven through both feet. Stuffed into the mouth was wadded up paper, pages from the Bible, and held into the mouth with Curtis' tie. What was disturbing the most were the eyes. Open and bulging with fear. Frozen upon his leftover face.

"Was Curtis alive during all this?" Troy felt the gag reflex coming. The eyes were just staring.

Troy looked down and noticed that he was standing in a puddle of blood. A new fear overcame him as thoughts of being a suspect. A selfish thought overcome hime. Thoughts of his reputation. His family flashed through his mind. He scanned the room and saw the phone. He knew he needed to call the police.

"God, put your hand on this situation. Whatever this situation is?"

Xi knew that Curtis Trough was the best target. His fame and fall were public knowledge. Picking him would fan the media circus already in place. In fact, the hardest part was getting in and out of the home without being noticed by the media. By acting as one of them he was able to get close to the house. The, when the coast seemed clear, he darted for the cellar door. He noticed earlier that it was unlocked and partially open. That was his ticket into the house. Xi took the time to study his surroundings and noticed that when the man would come by the reporters would divert their attention to him.

So yesterday he waited until the man left the house and be bombarded by questions and flashing bulbs. The opportunity was there and Xi took advantage. Ducking behind the bushes Xi crouched and moved quickly to the cellar door. Within less than ten seconds Xi was in the house, undetected, and not missed.

The stairs would lead Xi into the hallway where to his right was the kitchen and to the left was Curtis' study. Taking the time to survey his surroundings he heard someone walking to him. The man of the house. The target. Xi watched as the man entered the study and left his door open.

Too easy.

Taking inventory of his surroundings again to ensure not being caught Xi made his way to the study. Taking quick peeks inside he noticed that the man was already in his chair and drinking some scotch. The back of the chair was facing to the door so getting close to the man would not be a problem.

Xi stayed low and he made his way around the desk. When the man turned to his left to put the glass down Xi made his move. He knocked the man uncounscious so as to prepare him.

When the man awoke he knew he couldn't speak or move. Staring at him was a man with a smile on his face. A smile that put fear into any man.

"So you are a man of God. I have studied your religion and it seems quite strange to me. It states that you are to be like God. Isn't that what you strive for? Yet you strived after other things such as power and fame. Your family resents you. You have lost favor with your friends. Oh, and you have no credibility. But I am here to help you. You see, I will help you become like God and draw closer to him."

Curtis' eyes opened wide at the butcher knife before him. He recognized from his kitchen.

"I believe that your God received forty lashes. Isn't that correct?"

Xi grabbed ahold of Curtis' left arm and began slicing. After counting off twenty cuts Xi switched to the other arm. Curtis tried to scream but couldn't. Something was blocking the sound. Tears of pain and fear streamed down Curtis' face. "Is this really happening?"

Xi stopped and looked upon the man before him. A satisfying but also hungry smile was upon him. "I also believe that your God wore a crown of thorns. I apologize, I do not have a crown of thorns but I can improvise." Standing back up Xi took the knife and began poking the top of Curtis' head. Poke. Poke. Poke. Blood was washing down along with tears. When Xi was done Curtis' head resembled a bloody, hamburger patty.

"But I saved the best for last." Xi help up three spikes and a hammer. Curtis realized what was next. "Oh dear God no." Curtis recognized the spikes and hammer as gifts he received from a parishioner a few years ago. The man was a welder and had come to accept Christ. As a token of thanks the man custom made the spikes and hammer to remind Curtis of the ultimate sacrifice.

Now these gifts were to become death tools.

"I believe one in each hand and one in both feet. Yes?"

Xi delivered the first spike into the right hand. Curtis' head shot back in pain, an electric pain shooting from his hand to his entire body. A cry erupted from the deepest parts of his being but nobody could hear. He had never felt such pain in his life.

Xi delivered the second spike into the other hand. A new level of pain erupted. Curtis squeezed his eyes trying to force himself through the indescribable pain. Wave after wave pulsated throughout his body. Shakes overtaking his body. Black spots popping in front of his eyes.

"Last but not least."

Curtis felt his bones breaking and nerves being destroyed as his feet were nailed to the floor. He felt his body shaking uncontrollably as it fought against the intense invasion.

"If the story is correct, I now wait. You will not die from hanging on the cross but from blood loss. For forty minutes Curtis felt his life slipping away. Each time that his eyes would come shut the man in front of him would punch or slap him awake. As his body reacted to the punches it caused his hands and feet to move sending lightening flashes of pain throughout the body.

When Curtis was about to give up the fight Xi revealed his pistol equipped with silencer. "I do not have time to watch you die but is has been fun to watch you suffer. I will help you by putting you out of your misery." A pop whispered in the office.

Xi looked outside and saw that it was dark. The media people would be on low alert and the rest of the family were already camping out in their respective rooms. It was good to do homework and scout out the family beforehand.

Xi went back down the the hallway and out again through the cellar door. When the lights from the news helicopter moved from the back of the yard to the front Xi hurried across the yard and into the neighbor's bushes. After hopping through and around five yards Xi felt comfortable enough to walk in the open. It wasn't long before he was back in the rental car and speeding towards his hotel.

"That should send a strong message."

PERU

Carl opened his eyes. Waking up was a miracle in itself. The dew drops clung tightly to branches and leaves before falling to the earth. The cool mountain air was brisk and refreshing and roused in Carl a new eagerness.

Granted, his body ached and was sore for not having slept well in three nights and then caring for Juan.

Juan.

Carl rolled over to see to Juan. A sense of terror came over Carl that Juan didn't make it through the night. A movement, slight, in the chest and a whisper of a breath granted a small relief. Juan was dying and Carl knew it. He had to get Juan to a doctor. Carl crawled on his hands and knees to the entrance to the cave. It was easier to stretch out than standing straight up. A sight in the distance gave Carl a reason to jump to his feet.

A reflection, more like a glow, was seen. Carl searched the area, squinted his eyes, prayed that he was not seeing an illusion. The glow was light from a village and it looked to be about five miles away.

"Thank you God. Thank you. Thank you." Carl couldn't hold back the tears and sobs. Relief. Hope. Overwhelming feelings were released and came in wave after wave. Carl didn't even fight back. "You are an awesome God."

Carl took the time to scan the way to the village looking for landmarks, pathways, anything that would help hasten the trip and ensure he wouldn't get disoriented. It seemed the stream led right to the village. Makes sense, a water supply. Carl couldn't guess the size of the village but hoped it was big enough to have a doctor.

Carl went back to Juan. "Juan, stay with me. I found a village. It looks close but I need you to stay strong. We are almost there. Stay with me."

Carl lifted Juan. Sheer determination raced through Carl's veins. Five miles would be nothing compared to the last two days. Saving Juan's life gave new energy to the determination. Tenderly he picked up Juan. It was like picking up fine China. Carl felt as if the slightest movement would break Juan's fragile, bony frame. There was no choice.

Step after step Carl fought through every stumble, trip, and awkward footing. Grit built up inside. Nothing was going to stop the now immovable force called Carl. Carl remembered back when he was a child; there was a villain named the Juggernaut that was able to plow through walls, buildings and was unstoppable. Carl was Juggernaut. He stepped through tree branches, over and between rocks, and around trees. Obstacles were nothing to the sheer determination of Carl. Juan will make it home again.

The stream gave a constant temptation of stopping and being refreshed. Juan couldn't afford such luxuries. He needed help. Carl plowed on.

The steps became yards. Yards became miles. As the distance grew so did time as minutes became hours.

"How long does it take to cover five miles?" Carl rembered back in training camp in his pro football days of running five miles a day. It was no big deal to cover five miles in as little as forty-five minutes. Then again, he wasn't dehydrated, trouncing through hills and woods, carrying a wounded man, and starving. "Soon."

Carl began to hear sounds. There were creaking sounds. Clopping sounds of horses. Civilization. A new surge of energy built within Carl. Carl scanned Juan. He was so pale. And not just pale but gray.

"Juan, please stay strong. We are close. Hang in there."

Carl quickened his speed. The sounds became more distinct.

"Please, God grant me strength."

With a break in the trees Carl could see the village. Carl expected huts but there buildings, roads, and lights. Confusion replaced excitement as Carl had to decided what to do next. He gazed upon the people staring back at him. He could only imagine what he must have looked like. Four days of traveling through the mountains. He was covered in dried blood with tattered clothes. Juan laying in his arms, unmoving. Silence hung in the square as people stopped and stared.

"Senor?"

Carl looked in the direction of the voice. A woman wearing an emerald dress, a girl on her left hand and a boy on her right, was approaching.

Having not seen another human in three days sent a shiver of fear through Carl.

"Senor? Can I help you?"

She speaks English? Confusion clouded reason.

"Your friend. He hurt bad? I can show doctor. Come."

In a robotic trance Carl followed the woman. It was less than two blocks when a Red Cross symbol stared back at Carl. The weight of Juan was not noticeable as Carl continued on in the trance. The woman held the door open as Carl moved into the doorway.

The open area showed beds and people in white coats moving all around. The hustle and activity of other human beings added to Carl's confusion. Human activity was foreign. For four days he was isolated and alone; the only real comfortable he had was feeling the weight of Juan and enduring the pain and hunger.

"Senor. Can I help you?"

In a haze Carl answered. "My friend. He's hurt. We traveled from the forest. Hunted. No food and little water."

Hands grabbed at Juan. Carl fought back. Juan was his comfort object, the only human touch and contact for three days. Carl felt that it was being taken away from him. There people were fighting back.

The confusion was heightened by the hunger and dehydration. In the midst of the battle Juan was gone from Carl. Carl felt a darkness over him.

Soon, all was silent and black.

COUER D ALENE, IDAHO

The sun was setting on the west end of the lake. In the last thirty hours Yun and Cathy had traveled from Alaska and across the Yukon and British Columbia then into the United States. In recent months security was tighter with restrictions on who can come and go through the northern borders. Cathy took only two hours for a background check to verify she was an American citizen. Yun on the other hand was almost deported back to China. Not that he would mind going back home but he wanted to make sure Cathy remained safe until they reached Dallas.

Coeur d Alene was nestled among a lake and mountains to the east and prairie to the west. It was a hub for the logging industry and then in the 1980's recreation and tourism took root. People relocated from across the United States for the cheaper cost of living, the scenery, and opportunity. Overnight it seemed the city grew and became one of the best places to live.

As Cathy and Yun relaxed on the boardwalk drinking coffee and enjoying the serene evening Cathy couldn't help but come to the realization that for the first time in days she was calm. She felt no fear, no stress, no angst. She stared at the majesty before her. The lake was surrounded by the rolling hills covered with tamaracks, pine and elm. She could hear ducks and the occasional boat sound from a far distance echoing.

Calm. Quiet.

Cathy was frightened by the change of pace. Her emotion filled, roller-coaster adrenaline schedule was full speed and no looking back. There were a few moments of reflection and those moments were exhausting because of the emotional toll and still no fulfillment or contentment.

It didn't take long to realize that it wasn't only the scene around her that gave her a sense of security; it was also the man beside her. Yun had not only saved her life but was also willing to bear through her emotional berating of him. Despite it all, Yun stuck around.

"I'm sorry."

It came out. Cathy couldn't look up to tell Yun face to face. The guilt was overpowering. "I'm sorry for not thanking you for saving my life and for the way I treated you. I wasn't myself and I shouldn't have taken it out on you." Even that was half true. Cathy knew she was being herself. It was with Yun she realized she didn't like who she was; she wanted to be better. Not for herself but for Yun. For the first time, in a long time, Cathy knew she wasn't being selfish. She felt, deep inside her heart, a feeling of contentment she had not felt before.

Cathy felt hands on her shoulders and being turned. With a hand coming under her chin her eyes were lifted up. She saw a smile and felt her heart melt. A little more lifting and she was staring into his eyes. She now understood what it meant to be lost in someone else. The world around her disappeared. The last few days erased. All that existed was this moment of two people feeling safe, secure, and also exciting.

"Cathy. I will always be here for you. I need you. I love you."

That was all she needed to hear. She stood up on her tip-toes to kiss Yun. The kiss. It was daring but smooth. Soft and hard at the same time. Secure and exilerating.

Suddenly it broke off. Vulnerable and scared Cathy asked, "What's wrong?"

Yun began laughing. A robust stomach filled laugh. She realized it wasn't her. Well, it was. She felt the wet warmness of his coffee on her shirt. In the moment and suddenness of the kiss Yun did not have time to move his coffee cup from between them.

The laugh felt like an old friend to Cathy. It came naturally and was welcomed. It had been a long time since Cathy had a good laugh. With her studies in school, her father's passing, and this crazy expedition, there was not much to laugh about. Without caring about the mess she threw herself, coffee mess and all, into his arms.

Being lost in time she realized she was cold. She didn't know how they ended up at the boardwalk but the breeze off the water reminded her where she was. With continued laughs, talking and sharing Yun and Cathy climbed back onto the walkway. Cathy felt alive again. She was being silly and childish. The part of her that was stored away and hoping to come back was rising. She didn't care about other people and their finger pointing. She cared about life. She cared about living. She cared about the man holding her hand.

This was a freedom she didn't know existed and she loved it. How could someone be attached to another and feel such liberty at the same time? "If this is love, I am looking forward to it," she thought to herself.

Her every thought for the rest of the night was Yun. As they walked back to their hotel, up the elevator. When he dropped her off at her room and even while she was cleaning herself up it was Yun. Later as they met over more coffee and dessert Cathy was intoxicated with Yun. Even when the night was finished and she was getting ready for bed, difficult when one was filled with so much youthful energy, she couldn't stop thinking of Yun.

She wanted to jump between the two beds like she did when she was six. She wanted to call him up just to hear his voice and talk to him. Even though he just dropped her off at her room for the second time that night. Cathy could not wait until morning to see Yun again.

This expedition was becoming exciting indeed.

DALLAS, TEXAS

News reports on Curtis' death spread through every network like a highly contagious virus. Truth became distorted as each network tried to exaggerate every morsel that was dropped.

It did not take long for the family members to become suspects. Soon cameras caught the Trough family outside their home for the first time in weeks. All the cameras caught were the back of hands and hair trying to cover faces. Police pushed the crowd back with the stoic, tough faces.

"What happened in there?"

"Which one of you did it?"

"Any comment you want to share?"

Each member was pushed into different police vehicles. The lead car plowed an opening through the crowd. Lights circled while the siren screamed out the warning.

The Eleven watched the events unfold on the television. How could this have happened? Each thought progress was happening. Troy called the Eleven after he called the police to pray for guidance and he related what he saw. Troy had enough sense to send photos via his cell phone to the Eleven.

"Something is not right here and I don't mean just the death. I don't think any of the family did this. This was done by a professional." Troy spoke with confidence to the group.

"How are you sure?"

"I believe that our stalker, mysterious phone caller, is the same one that is after Cathy, Carl and John. Only now he is in Dallas. It is the only idea that makes sense at this moment.." Troy took a breath. "Pray. Pray for protection and guidance and I mean that for us." Troy hung up.

Dr. Simpsone clicked the phone off and looked to the Eleven. It was then that Dr. Brown turned on the television and watched more of the events. Reporter after reporter took the serious tone and gave the worry concerned look when speaking.

"Sometime this afternoon Curtis Trough, the well-known preacher on family values, was found dead this morning inside his house. At this time the details are sketchy but Channel Six was the first to learn that each family member was escorted out of the house and into police vehicles. EMT's are currently inside the house. Recently Mr. Trough was in the national news for his son and daughter. His son was recently released from jail for drug possession and his sixteen year daughter was confirmed pregnant. Curtis Trough and his family have secluded themselves in their home and have only opened their doors to select visitors. Channel Six is working with local law enforcement tolearn of these visitors as they are persons of interest."

On the screen flashed Troy's picture and an Asian looking man.

"Police are encouraging that if you see either of these two people to please contact the number below." A phone number, blinked over and over.

"This is Mike Ballwood reporting from North Dallas."

"Mike, is there any knowledge of how Mr. Trough died?"

"Not yet Phil. Authorities are still searching the house and again there is the search for the people of interest."

"Thanks Mike. Channel Six will continue to follow this story as it develops. Next, we have coverage of the Community Fathers Parade that happened in downtown."

Dr. Brown turned off the television. His heart and the others weighed too much. They knew that Troy had talked to the police already. Dr. Simpson scanned the group. Dr. Farre crossed the room, bent and hunched over as if carrying more burdens than one could handle. Could a heavy heart affect one's stature? Dr. Simpson now believed. As he scanned the group there was not a dry eye.

Xi cursed. His picture was staring back at him on the screen. The plan was perfect and went without any problems. The visitor was to take the blame. He was not careless. Quite the opposite. Care was taken and all tracks and traces covered. Xi was a shadow that nobody saw.

But apparently someone did. It could have been a neighbor? A reporter? Camerman? The list was now endless on who would have seen Xi. It was a loose end that would forever be hanging out in the wind.

Curses continued to spew.

He knew that Commander Kim would not be happy and that there would be consequences. Severe consequences.

"There are only consequences if one gets caught," thought Xi. "Only if one gets caught."

PERU

The soft candelight made opening the eyes easier. Carl wasn't sure how long he was out; minutes, hours, days? Rolling over to his side he grasped meaning out of his surroundings. He remembered waking up on Monday mornings from a game on Sunday. Being pummeled by linebackers and lineman meant waking up feeling battered.

This was a whole different level of pain.

Muscles throbbed out of defiance of having to move and react. Carl noticed that he was sucking in heavy, labored breaths. Not good. Poring every bit of energy into turning his head Carl wanted to take in his surroundings. There were two standing lamps facing each other from either side of the room. His bed sat next to a wall, paint peeling showing layers of paint-overs. There was another bed underneath the opposite lamp. A table sized rug was thrown in the middle of the room. A crude attempt to bringing a home-feeling to a ruditamentary setting. Flanking the walls were cabinets straight out of the seventies. A door was next to Carl's bed.

At this moment it was too early to tell if the environment was hostile or friendly.

Carl could hear the sounds of the town. People mingled just outside of his window. Children were playing and a dog barked in the distance. Somewhere in the building a fire crackled.

Carl heard a new sound. A groan. Turning his head back to the opposite bed he could see that it was occupied.

"Juan? Is that you?" Carl didn't expect a response nor did he get one. He prayed that it was Juan. The groan would have been music from heaven. It meant that Juan was still alive.

Prayer. Carl relaxed his neck muscles and stared at the ceiling. His fears of traveling overseas seems so childish now. Despite the pain, the conditions, and the experiences, he felt content. His wife and children must be in a panic by now. He prayed for their comfort. The Twelve must be worried and feeling immense guilt. He prayed for their guidance and wisdom. John and Cathy and a prayer of protection. Throughout the day Carl found himself praying. One person led to a need. A need led to a circumstance. A circumstance led itself to another person. On and on the circle went. Friends. Family. Carl found himself crying at times and laughing at others.

Voices were heard outside the door and a streak of light flooded the room. The light blinded Carl forcing a new pain in his head and body as he turned to avoid the sunlight.

"Buenos dias senor. Como estas?"

Carl's weak grasp of the language was just enough to understand the speaker.

"Bueno…asi asi."

The laugh from the speaker brought small relief and comfort to the situation. Carl's eyes adapted to the light and he made out three forms standing over his bed. "Do you speak English?"

"Yes. A little. You seemed to be the one who saved your friend over there."

So the mysterious bedmate was Juan.

"Is he okay?"

"He will be fine."

"What happened? Where am I?"

"My friend, you are about two hundred kilometers from Lima. I could say the name but it would mean nothing to you. I doubt most Americans know anything much about Peru except Lima and Micchu Pichu. As soon as you and your friend can travel we have arrangements set up to get you back to Lima."

"How is this possible?"

A finger came straight at Carl. A fear washed over him until he realized that the man was pointing to his necklace. Dangling on the end was a cross. Carl looked back up to the man.

"You are a brother. Brothers take care of each other. Now is the time for rest. Sleep."

With that the three men left.

Carl laid in bed stunned. All of his prayers were for others yet God answered an unasked prayer. Now, with renewed vigor Carl focused on Juan.

"Lord, if it be your will, lay your healing hand upon Juan. Strenthen him…."

ARIZONA

Stretching far into the horizon were Joshua trees and sequoia cacti. Mesas broke up the endless rolling hills and flatlands. A lizard would scamper off the road but only after a vehicle would pass by. John was surprised to see white on some of the mesas and jugged peaks. It was relaxing to let Blaine do the driving and he could enjoy the landscape. Behind him sat David. David was more interested in reading his Bible. John envied the man. Reading while in a moving car made him naseous and quizzy.

They left the metropolis of Phoenix to head to the largest reservation in America, the Navaho Indian Reservation. The reservation was a forsaken land of dirt and little else. In the late 1800's when the west wars were winding down the American government decided to be generous to the native tribes. The tribes were allocated tracts of land to retain language, customs, and heritage. Some tribes ended up better than others. Some tribes had reservations with rolling hills blanketed with trees and resources and streams and lakes. The land was rich in natural resources. Other tribes ended up with some bad deals. The Navaho tribe was one.

The Navaho tribe is synomonous with America lore. In the west wars for land and resources, there were villains and heroes on both sides of the battle.

John wasn't thinking of the history of the Navaho tribe. His thoughts were on Cathy and Carl. It had been over a week since he had heard from either of them. He heard of the attack on Cathy and was relieved to know that she was safe. David informed him that she was on her way to Arizona and they would rendevous in a day or two. Carl was a different story. Nobody has heard a word from him. David tried contacting his peer, the bodyguard for Carl, and no response. The cloud of doubt and worry hung over John's thoughts. He hoped that no harm or danger had come to Carl but he was aware of Carl's fears of traveling overseas. He prayed that those fears were not being realized.

"The Navaho religion is much like other native religions. It is based on the surroundings and geography around them. The gods tend to be animalistic in nature. Again, like other tribes certain animals tend to be heroes while others are tricksters or deceivers. Very few have villains or monsters. But, some tribes do have this aspect. The southwest tribes have a commonality among them; great beast or monsters that fly through the air and move across the ground. The pictographs, from all over the southwest, show these animals or beasts. Across the tribes the pictures are consistent."

"So remind me again why we are going to the Navaho reservation?" David asked without taking his eyes from his reading.

"There is an elder, a good friend of mine, who hangs onto the secrets of the tribe. I have worked with him before as I continue to learn about the tribes. He is quite a character once he warms up to you. I am hoping he will divulge some information to help you with your mystery."

John still had to remind himself of the last few days. Never in his lifetime would he imagine an adventure quite like this. Even though it started with the death of a friend Mike left a gift of knowledge, adventure, and truth in his wake and Mike bequeathed it to his daughter, himself, and to Carl. Family. Friend. Stranger. What a lasting impact upon the world. John had to respect the plan that Mike had laid out.

The highway sign indicated that they had just entered the reservation and the only change were the presence of firework shops, cigarette stores, and a gas station. Without slowing down Blaine kept pushing the Explorer forward. John continued to stare at the desolation around him, trying to comprehend how a people could survive on such scarcity. Among the landscape now was single wide trailers, permanment RV's for living in, and broken down vehicles.

Blaine said that there would be answers here and John certainly hoped so.

In half an hour the Explorer pulled up to a hole that was cut out of a rock wall. As John exited the vehicle he looked up and estimated that the wall stretched at least four stories high. At ground level was a cave entrance with smoke escaping from it. Outside the entrance was a pile of wood, chopped and split.

"Where does he get the wood," David asked with a hint of sarcasm.

"I was thinking the same thing."

"There are hidden pockets of wood. Gochi is a respected elder so he gets treated with more respect from the tribe and therefore gets first crack on resources. In essence, he is considered royalty."

"This is royalty? No offense but living in a cave is not my idea of living large."

"It is when the elder chooses to shed off modern ways and live like the ancestors' customs not meant for today's world. Let me do the talking when we get in there. If you have questions give them to me and I will ask. Like I said before, he trusts me. He does not know you and he does not trust outsiders. Capeche?"

"No problem."

"David?"

"My mouth is shut."

Okay gents, let us go and meet Gochi."

With that Blaine led the way into the cave. John wasn't sure what to expect but he sure didn't plan on seeing this. Once away from the sunlight and letting his eyes adjust he saw a great cavern. The inside was as big around as two houses. While the outside wall was four stories high the inside cavern stretched to two stories. A staircase, cut from the rock, curved along the wall to the pinnacle. Stone blocks were laid in a circular formation around the base. In the middle of the base ws a pit with two stone blocks facing each other. Along the walls were pictographs showing hunts, village life, and the cycles of life. John noticed a family celebrating the birth of a new child. Another scene showed a funeral. All aspects of life were pictured around the wall.

While John was amazed on the pictographs he searched out particular ones. The ones showing animals, particulary any showing great beasts. This infatuation of Mike's was becoming his as well.

Sitting in the middle of the pit, between the two blocks was a man. At least it looked like a man. John did not believe in skeletons until now. The figure stood to face his visitors. John could count the man's ribs. The cheeks sunk and clung to the bone. To guess the man's age was difficult as was guessing the height. The man walked with a slight limp and hunch in the back. John did not mistake the man's vibrancy on looks alone for he could tell in the man's eyes there was an intensity and energy.

"Good morning Gochi. It is good to see you again. I have brought friends. John and David." Blaine had to tell John and David what he said as he spoke in the Navaho language.

"Welcome back. You must have questions and expect me to have answers. You must think I am one smart man." John didn't understand what was being said but for the first time he saw Gochi smile.

"I do. My friends are on a quest for knowledge. Their quest has taken them around the world and now to you. The seek answers from the past."

Gochi turned and walked back to the pit and two stone blocks. John thought that the conversation was over, that something wrong was said, or worse he or David crossed some sacred line. Instead Gochi waved for them to follow him into the pit.

As they settled Gochi was studying David and John. It was unnerving to have him search and scan as eyes locked on each other. He was seeing past the exterior and diving into the person. John was used to being analyzed by college students on the first day of class. He even considered it humorous as they sized him up, looking for an angle, and shopping the class out. This was uncomfortable. Something about how Gochi was staring and probing with his eyes created an eery feeling within John's gut.

"My friend, what is it you seek?"

Blaine lowered his eyes from Gochi. John remembered that among many tribes, looking into eyes was a social taboo. Maybe that was what made John so uncomfortable. Here was a native leader doing the very thing that was considered unacceptable.

"Gochi, these men are learned men. They seek understanding on the animals, beasts of the past. The great beasts."

Gochi lifted his head and stared around the great cavern. John followed Gochi's stare. John was gazing again at the same pictures as he did when he entered the cave. The hunts, the daily life of skinning animals. Drawings of people drying skins on racks and there were caravans of animals crossing the desert landscape.

Gochi lowered his head and spoke with such sadness that John's heart felt heavy, as if it would fall out of his chest.

"The beasts of old roamed over the land and flew through the air. They provided meat, and bones for tools that our people would use. The ancestors stated that the beasts would lay on rocks, heating themselves in the sun. There would be enough vegetation in certain areas to support the plant eaters. Despite the theories of today the animals could go days without eating. Much like our tribes to the north with the bison, we would use every part of the animal. Care was taken to not waste and we appreciate the animals. But then the cloud came."

John was taken aback. "A cloud?"

"From the south a great cloud crawled across the sky. For many days our people observed the cloud. A wind came before the cloud. A hot, intense, burning wind. The wind drove the flying beasts from the area first. Within hours vegetation dried out. Leaves on trees turned from green to brown. Hours afterward the trees themselves withered. It was two moons of wind and black dust. Our people suffered greatly. There was choking and sickness. They looked to the sky for answers but there was no sky. The old and wise began to die. Many in the tribe began to head north to try to escape the black cloud. Others sought shelter in cave much like this one. Any living thing with legs began leaving.

Then the cloud came.

Darkness blacked out the sun. It was a darkness beyond description. It was said that families tied themselves together to keep from losing one. Also, it was the only way to account for each other. As people traveled north many became insane from the heavy blackness, the heated wind, and the dust handing in the air. Many people died along the way. Carcasses of animals and people were strewn across the landscape. Even the flying creatures laid upon the ground. After two days, the wise men guess, the wind died away but the darkness remained. More and more carcasses were tripped over as our people continued to head north. Finally, in the land of the bison, the darkness thinned but half of our people had died.

The story of the great migration was told to the next generation and the one after. On the third generation the wise men decided it was time to head back to our homeland. The elders clung to the story of the beasts, hoping that they too survived the black cloud. But, it was not meant to be. The beasts died out. With them a piece of our way of life also died. The cloud, even after two generations, hung in the air but was dissipating. The farter south our people went the more the landscape changed. The vegetation spots of old were goen. A desert had grown in its place. But our people believed in the land, believed it to be sacred and so they commited themselves to returning. Unfortunately, we were alone on returning. The only remants of the beasts are snakes, lizards, and tortoises. The ones that could hide underground, away from the cloud and heat and dust did."

The last sentence hit John like a wrecking ball. For years scientists have often wondered why only the smallest reptiles survived and not the mighty ones. Current reptiles could bury themselves in the ground or water. Alligators and turtles could bury themselves in mud for protection. They can stay underwater for long periods of time. Snakes and lizards hid underground for protection.

John focused back on Gochi while retaining the information in his head.

"So our people came back. They had to adapt to a new environment. New customs were born and so a new way of living." Gochi finished with tears in his eyes.

Even David sat stoic in Gochi's story. Silence hung so heavy it caused all four heads to hang low.

John broke the silence. "Blaine, ask him why outsiders don't know about the beasts?"

Blaine repeated the question in Navaho and Gochi raised his head. "Outsiders did know about the beasts. But, over time, they chose to not want to know. They have forsaken their own stories and chose to live in a fantasy world. So, I do not know why they don't know about the great animals."

Blaine looked at John with a look of questioning. John knew it was his cue to stop asking more questions. Besides, what he had just learned was more than he bargained for already. David seemed as if his head ached with understanding.

Blaine thanked Gochi for his time and promised that next time his visit would be social and soon. Gochi gave a slight nod, not looking up. Tears still streamed off of the old man's face.

The three exited the cave and the sunlight blinded, much like exiting a movie theater during mid day. There was no complaining. Blue sky greeted along with a scurrying lizard. As the three piled back into the Explorer John scanned the landscape. He tried to wrap his mind around the story he had just heard and layering with the landscape before him. No wonder it was easy to believe in the fantasy; he couldn't fathom a black cloud and intense winds that could change an entire geographical area. He was also trying to still wrap his head around the idea of dinosaurs and man living together.

An electronic melody interrupted his thoughts. "David here." John was impressed that David's cell phone had coverage in the middle of nowhere. He reminded himself that David was a special agent and probably didn't have a normal cell phone. "I understand. I am on my way. I will be there tonight."

Putting his cell phone back into his holster David got into the vehicle, "Gentlemen. We need to hurry back to Phoenix and head straight to the airport. The sooner the better."

ANCIENT YUCATAN PENNISULA

Sosy looked to the sky each morning. For the last four mornings the bright circle in the sky grew bigger and bigger. This morning was no different. She held up her thumb and closed her left eye as a way of measuring the new object in the sky. It was getting bigger.

Many of the people in the village were wondering about the new fire in the sky. Was it a sign from the gods? Is it their wrath? A blessing? Without knowing there was no way to prepare. Sosy knew that many animals in the village were disappearing because of the sacrifices necessary to appease the gods.

There was even talk of human sacrifices.

This was a new fear for Sosy since she was at the age of going from child to adult. She was considered pure and her father was held in high regard. She would make a perfect sacrifice. Sosy knew that in her heart she would do what she needed to in order to protect her people. Fear was not to be considered at the time of the sacrifice but, now, fear did consume her.

It wasn't just that the village animals were disappearing. Among the hunters there was talk that the jaguars and other beasts of the jungle were gone. They were not just hiding, they were gone. Messengers to other villages reported the same thing. Leaders of each village gathered to discuss this new phenomenon. Instead of filling the people with hope it created a strange uneasiness.

The only time the village leaders gathered was to discuss war or marriages to prevent war. Sosy and the others in the village knew that war was not the issue. The animals disappearing and the object in the sky were related but nobody knew why.

Today, Sosy noticed that the hairs on her arms and the back of her neck were standing up. There was a strange energy in the air, and while she hugged her mother earlier there was a shocking sensation between them. Looking around the village she noticed that peoples' hair were sticking up and separating. If there wasn't such fear hanging in the air it would be considered humorous. Sosy noticed that her father's hair stood straight out from his head, like he had been running fast and his hair just stayed in that position.

Sosy looked up at the object. It was getting bigger. Which meant closer. Whatever it was it was coming here.

Sosy decided to escape the village and the rumors and the fears. Being up in the mountains and jungle eased her mind and was relaxing. Sosy began hiking up to the point of her favorite mountain. From there she could see across her village's valley as well as to the next neighboring villages. She could even see the big water to the east. Someday she wanted to go to the big water but as curious as she was about the big water fear kep her in place. The jungle was her home. She was used to trees and valleys. The vastness of the water overwhelmed her senses.

When she reached the peak she became revitalized by the exercise. The view was refreshing. Sosy looked about the sky. Things were not right. She was unable to see the sky from the hike because of the canopy of the jungle, but now the sky looked like it had a burning scar. The burning ball was no longer a faraway object to be admired and wondered at. It was an object bowling towards her.

A burning wind suddenly picked Sosy up and dropped her on the ground. In an instant the temperature rose to agonizing intensity. Sosy felt like she was bread baking in her mother's oven. She turned her head to look up at the sky scar. A streak of fire cut across the sky then burned above her and headed east toward the big water.

Sosy couldn't' tell which was worse; not being able to breathe or the noise. Sosy felt the air being sucked out of her as she cupped her hands over her ears. The air became harder to breathe. She was gasping. When her father would catch fish and pulled them from the water she watched with fascination as they would slowly die. The fish would gasp and strain for breath. She felt that way now.

But there was the noise. When the streak went over it left behind a deafening noise. A thousand waterfalls couldn't match the rumble filling the air. Sosy remembered a few years ago of running into a tree while playing with friends. As she crumbled to the ground she felt her front side throb with pain, crying for some relief. This was worse many times over. Her ears wanted to explode to escape the noise.

Sosy dared to lift her head to gaze east. Imprinted on her mind was a sight that only the gods themselves could produce. A plume of dirt, water, fire, and smoke rose from the big water. The plume shot for the clouds in a blink of an eye. At the same moment water tumbled over the hillsides and dirt shot the mountainsides like ramps. Instantly her clothes began to catch on fire. Her hair began to dry out. Sosy looked desperately around for shelter; the tears in her eyes made it difficult to see. But, coming in her direction, in mere seconds, was devastation. She saw a hole in the ground and scrambled after it. Just as she was entering the hole the wall of devastation came roaring towards her.

She entered the hole and fell. The hole happened to be a soft spot in the earth that opened into a cave. Sosy fell fifteen feet. Dazed and out of breath her curiosity overwhelmed pain and she glanced back up at the hole opening. Racing across hole was fire.

Sosy had been in many caves before. The caves were great on those summer days when the temperatures were warm outside because the caves always stayed the same temperature. Not today. The racing fire above was intense enough to begin warming up the cave. Sosy began to feel a new panic. Was she really like the bread in her mother's oven? Was she going to be baked alive? The fire was also ripping the oxygen from the cave and Sosy fought for air.

Sosy crawled to the edge of the cave while using the hole as a guide. She knew people became lost in caves and died because of confusion and disorientation. There had to be a place to hide and gain better shelter.

Outside the howling of the wind continued. Sosy imagined trees being ripped apart, burned, torn from the ground. Mama! Papa! Would her family escape the fire wind? She glanced up and tried to conceive how it would have been possible to outrun this devastation. Sosy began to accept the fate of her family. Her village. Everything was gone and she was alone.

A new sound emerged from the hole. Sosy looked up. The fire wind disappeared. In its place a sucking sound grew. The sound grew to a roar as if the fire was grasping for more fuel, oxygen, life.

Then silence.

Sosy glanced up and ash and tree limbs fell through the hole. Darkness replaced the fire wind. An eery silence replaced the roars. In the darkness, for many days, Sosy sat. She didn't know when one day ended and the other began for blackness blanketed . Then, a ray of sunshine, a stream of light, beamed into the hole and lit up the cave.

With a mixture of curiousity and fear, and a hunger that overwhelmed all other senses, Sosy began contemplating her options. She wanted to see outside but was afraid of what of what she would see. She began to prepare her mind for the outside. Sosy remembered seeing a rough staircase that led to the hole. Searching she saw it in the light's shadows. Within minutes she was near the top. Each step Sosy prepared herself for the outside. She was used to seeing firepits. Once, she saw a home on fire and remembered the ash and burnt timbers, the blackness of the wood and the smell. As she got closer to the top the smell of the world hit her like a punch to the face. It smelled as if the whole world was burnt. Before popping out of the hole she took another breath and collected her thoughts. Already it was hard to breathe and ash continued to fall through the hole.

Popping out of the hole Sosy saw nothing but ash. It rained down on her. She began to choke on the burning smells. Her eyes burned and she couldn't fight the gag reflex any longer. Bent over she emptied her stomach.

Around her was a whole new world.

The lush jungle was gone. Every tree was stripped from the ground. Through the raining ash and burnt air Sosy turned in circles. Every living thing was gone. Every plant disappeared.

She had no idea where to go or who to see. Sosy was alone in a new world. Deep within her a voice spoke. A desire to survive and to overcome grew. Sosy knew that she needed to move in order to survive. The big water was east. A cloud of steam was in that direction covering all of the water.

Sosy decided to head north, as far away from the devastation as possible. The ground was warm underneath her feet. She couldn't remember if it was daylight or night. It didn't matter. Devastation surrounded her. Time meant nothing.

Sosy walked. Hoping for a better world. A new beginning.

LIMA, PERU

Gratefulness was an understatement. Juan ended up losing his foot but he was alive. On the the way to Lima he sat stunned and felt awkward as Carl related his tale of how they were able to survive. Juan felt a pang of guilt of having to put Carl through all that pain and misery.

Another part of him knew that he would have done the same if the roles were reserved. Juan knew that Carl did what he did because of the strength in his faith and the friendship that was formed. Juan respected Carl's perserverance and dedication.

Juan knew that having only lost a foot was a small price to pay. He got to live; it was another day to speak boldly. Sure, life was going to be awkward for awhile, for sure the rest of his life. He stared at the rounded nub at the end of his leg and still expected to see a foot, an ankle. His mind even played the trick of wiggling the toes. The mind thought it, the nerves carried the message, muscles flexed up and down the leg. Everything worked like it was supposed to except there were no toes to wiggle or foot swaying back and forth.

Still, a gratefulness filled his heart. A man was willing to sacrifice his life for him. Not just his life in terms of surviving but Carl had a family. A wife depended upon Carl and his love. Children needed to be raised by their father. A friendship was built.

Juan knew enough about Carl that the sacrifice; the life of living, would have been the hardest to give up.

Juan leaned back in the helicopter seat and stared out upon the mountains giving way to a city. To the west was the ocean. In front of him sat Carl. Juan felt an eternal debt to this man.

Juan struggled with Carl's willingness. He felt so small yet so big, so important. He felt indebted and even guilty.

"Is this what I was supposed to be feeling towards Jesus?" Being a believer Juan knew to be thankful for Jesus' willingness to go to the cross and die; he had always been aware of the implications. Now, having been on the verge of death and have someone else pay the price mentally, physically, and emotionally; Juan felt a new sensation towards the cross.

A new fear crept into Juan. Would Carl ever know how thankful he was? Could he thank Carl enough and mean it? What could he do to show his thankfulness? Juan didn't want to come across as ungrateful.

More guilt came rolling into the heart.

Juan continued to stare across the city and knew that they were heading to the hospital. He made up his mind to have a talk with Carl and express the fact that he was truly thankful.

MISSOULA, MONTANA

In the distance the Rockies barricaded the horizon. The rolling plain stretched out and as time and miles stretched on, the plains became flatter and flatter.

Cathy enjoyed the scenery of Missoula. A quaint college town set in the middle of the Rockies. All around were tree towering peaks. Just entering a pure college town energized Cathy. The tranquil setting of youth and learning; about setting out to seek your dreams and not being scared. Being fearless.

She felt that way now. She knew that someone or something was looking out for her. Deep in the recesses of her mind and deep in her heart she had always felt something missing. Even being around Yun didn't feel the whole need.

But having your life threatened, twice, sure makes a good wake-up call.

As Yun continued to drive I-90 Cathy felt contentment she had never felt before. She had lost her father, threatened, her life's purpose had taken a topsy-turvy turn, and she had never felt happier. She accepted Jesus as her Lord and Savior. It seemed that things that were confusing were not confusing anymore. And the world, while a messed up place, she now understood why. People did not know better.

Cathy knew from her research that Montana was the place for dinosaurs. Many big discoveries had happened here and she wanted to check some of the sites. She knew Yun was not too happy because of safety. Finally, he relented. It seems that this love power thing works both ways, thought Cathy.

Bozeman came into view and it the home of Montana State Univesity. The closest institution to many of the big finds and Cathy wanted to go there first. She had to see credentials to see somebody with no prior appointment. If need be, she would use her father's name to gain access to somebody.

What Missoula was Bozeman was not. Instead of towering peaks high plains. Replacing trees were sagebrush. Deep pit mining copper was king. The youthful energy replaced by blue, collar, hard working miners. Cathy respected what the town offered but knew it was not for her.

Yun followed the signs that directed to Montana State University. It wasn't hard to spot the dorms rising above all other buildings. Even without the signs Yun navigated around the campus easily. The hard part would be finding someone once there.

After the long drive it was good to get out and stretch the legs. Cathy suggested just walking around campus, getting a feel for where things are. Yun, always to the point, suggested a visit to the visitor's center and save time.

Cathy decided to use the love power again and won.

Walking around campus, hand in hand with Yun, Cathy thought back to her undergraduate days. So wrapped up in herself that she didn't make time or felt the need to have personal relationships. Often, Cathy thought of those couples she saw walking around campus and a small amount of jealousy would rise in her. Selfish ambitions would kick in and that feeling quickly extinguished. Now, she felt like one of those couples. Sure she was older, not a student at this campus, and lived a life a little more, but she felt like one of those that others now felt jealousy for.

After touring around campus and grabbing tuna fish sandwiches from the campus commons area they both decided to get down to business. The lanky-twenty something boy, young man Yun corrected Cathy, pointed them to the natural history department. Yun sighed when he figured out that it was on the other side of campus. Cathy giggled as they were there just fifteen minutes ago. She wanted more walking.

After leaving the commons and trekking back across campus Cathy thought a little of her future. She heard Yun's voice as he talked but it was more of background noise in her head. She wasn't being rude. It was just that major questions had risen in her head that needed to be answered. Would Yun stay with her after this crazy adventure ended? Would she go to China? Would he be willing to move? She didn't want these times with Yun to go away but she realized the realist in her was coming out.

Covered with ivy and a rich past stood the building of natural history. Entering it Cathy knew that they had entered the right place. In glass cases were bones, fossils, stuffed animals from around the western United States and parts of Canada. Hanging from the ceiling a pterodactyl. Pictures of students and faculty doing digs hung on the walls. Newspaper articles were framed that spoke of the more famous finds.

Cathy read below each picture and the newspaper articles. The same name seemed to appear over and over.

Dr. Blake Hunter.

Cathy's gut told her this was the guy they needed to see. Next to the elevator were the department listings. On the third floor was Dr. Hunter's office. Room 313. In mere moments Yun and Cathy were outside of Dr. Hunter's office and a feeling of butterflies came over Cathy. She heard voices inside, one male and one female. The context of the conversation couldn't be heard but it was easy to discern that it was heated. Cathy heard a crash, stomping, the the door flew open and a woman passed by without even glancing at Cathy and Yun.

Cathy and Yun exchanged the what do we do now glance. Cathy took the lead and knocked on the already open door.

"Now what," Cathy heard from inside the office.

"Dr. Hunter. I am so sorry to disturb you and without an appointment. It's just that my companion and I have traveled so far and have so many questions."

"Well, you have caught me at a very bad time. A bad time indeed. I am not really in the mood."

Cathy decided to play her trump card. "My name is Cathy Jurkovich, Mike Jurkovich's daughter. I just have some questions."

Dr. Hunter stood. "Mike's daughter? My dear, come in, come in. I am so sorry. It has been just an awful day. No more awful that the passing of your father. God rest his soul. That was my wife, well, soon to be ex-wife. It seems that despite my mild wealth, youth will win among certain ladies."

Cathy looked to Yun who gave a don't give me that kind of look look.

"Well, what can I do for you two?"

Cathy explained their adventures and their finds. She wasn't sure on where Dr. Blake Hunter stood on faith and spiritual matters so she gave just the facts. Cathy, desperate to hear some answers wanted some clarification.

"Dr. Hunter, as I mentioned before, we have seen evidence of dinosaurs that don't fit the model of being millions of years old. I know you are familiar with the T-rex find here in Montana where the blood did not fossilize. Can you help me understand better what all this means?"

Dr. Hunter got up and paced about his office. Yun and Cathy sat, anxious and waiting. "You have stumbled upon the great problem of science and I am willing to bet with most organizations. That is communication and training. But let me explain the find for you.

What the paleontologist found was a femur of a teenage T-rex. Of course they jumped to the conclusion that the femur's age stood at 70 million years old. Here is what is amazing."

Cathy noticed that Dr. Hunter sounded like a child on Christmas morning. Eager and anticipating.

"The femur contained tissues. Soft, flexible, and stretchy tissue. That is not supposed to happen. Fossilization states a loss of liquids and a chemical change. Here they found a bone and tissue. From 70 million years ago? I don't think so. Common sense has to step in sooner or later.

Second, and this is most disturbing. To keep the idea going of evolution, scientists have said that the proteins extracted from the T-rex tissue were mostly similar to modern-day chickens. They did a comparative analysis to firm up this discovery. Do you see what they are doing; creating bridges to evolution. Even if there is clear, substantial evidence that breaks the rules of evolution, they will make up these bridges. Sad really. My personal joke is that truly, everything is like chicken."

Cathy leaned back to hide her surprise. "Dr. Hunter, you mentioned the great problem of the science world. Could you explain that? I too am a scientist and your statement intrigued me."

Dr. Hunter gave a paternal look to Cathy. Cathy recognized an aspect of her father in those eyes; the look of caring and hoping for the best for the next generation. It was also a look of sorry to burst your bubble of the world but you need to know what is going on look. "You see. To indoctrinate someone you must train them. For science that teaching, or indoctrination, happens when people are young. That is why there is such passion and division over textbooks in schools. People realize, probably indirectly, that what is taught at a young age stays with a person up into adulthood. Tell enough children, over enough time, and you have successfully indoctrinated a society. The problem is that this method can backfire."

Cathy didn't fight her surprise this time. "Backfire?"

"Absolutely. Let me think of a good example here." Dr. Hunter searched his thoughts for the right example of science gone wrong and backfiring. "Global warming."

Yun and Cathy lifted eyebrows. "Global warming? I thought global warming is real? I mean governments, corporations, and businesses are going green. This involves billions of dollars. Global warming?"

Dr. Hunter shared the look of, here comes the roller coaster ride that will rock your world. "In the early seventies this idea of global warming took root. It seemed to make sense. Hot summer days. Maybe a shortened winter or spring. Soon, organizations jumped on this idea to promote their cause. Animal rights groups used it to protect arctic animals. To protect jungle animals and so on. These groups eventually got backing and financial support. Soon the idea, the cause, became a theory. Now this theory creeped into classrooms and to the young. Within a generation the theory became an accepted fact. Politicians wanted to be elected so they promised to take care of the environment. I mean, who doesn't want to take care of the environment and the animals. You would have to be sadistic to say no.

So now companies are fined elaborate fees for dirtying the environment. Car engines have had to evolve; sorry for the pun. Building codes have changed. Our shopping has changed. And for what?"

Staring at Dr. Hunter were two blank faces.

"A lie. Recently it has been found that scientists have made up documentation to promote this idea. They were under pressure from government agencies. It seems that global warming is nothing more than a myth. Yet, with so much and money invested in it, people are not just going to roll over and admit defeat."

Cathy remembered on the news a scandal about global warming. It just so happened at the time that world leaders were meeting about the world's climate and how to clean up the environment.

"You see, science, like any other organization, is political. Once something has taken hold and money is involved, it is difficult to change. So, the easiest thing to do, which I call lazy science, is to build these bridges of fantasy. Even if these bridges contradict one's own laws and processes."

A moment of clarity swept over Cathy. Her father connected these ideas. He built bridges but in the other direction. She imagined that he realized that the current bridges being built made no sense; they were contrary to science protocol. It must have been painful for her father to realize his peers, his friends have bought into this lie. More painful, she imagined, for these same people to ridicule him and demean. Ultimately, these new bridges led to his death.

"Dr. Hunter? Who would have the means to stop an idea? My father believed that evolution did not exist. I believe he was killed for this idea. His name and reputation would have carried weight for a contrary theory. Who could have done something like that?"

Lowering his head, Dr. Hunter searched his shoes for an answer. "My dear, that list is endless. Scientist, throughout history, have been persecuted. The persecutors have come from various backgrounds and organizations. It used to be religious institutions, and to some degree that holds true today. It has been leaders such as kings and queens. It has been from business. If a business or corporation is producing something and science has found a better product, a product that can fail a business, you will face persecution."

"So we may never know who killed my father?"

When Dr. Hunter looked up tears were running down his face. "I believe you may be right."

DALLAS, TEXAS

Kelsey was in the middle of his prayer when the phone rang. He hated interruptions during prayer time. Four-thirty every morning he would wake up to study his Bible and do his prayers. Not many people get up in the early morning and even less conduct business. So when the phone rang it was either a wrong number or an emergency. Kelsey was guessing emergency.

"Kelsey? Sorry if I woke you up."

Kelsey recognized the deep Southern drawl of his friend and mentor Julius. "No, I was up already."

"I figured you were my old friend. I apologize for interrupting your Bible study."

"There may be a break in the murder case. Remember the phone call we received a few days ago. The FBI traced the call. It seems that the caller and the murder may be connected."

The group had been praying earnestly for the safety of Carl, John, and Cathy. Wide awake now he still had more questions. "Julius, does the FBI know who this man is?"

"Yes. Remember the shooting in Ankor Wat. One of the men assigned to protect the three saw the shooter but lost him during the mayhem of bullets. He was the one assigned to protect John. He is being called away from Arizona to intensify the search and get this guy."

Kelsey, at the wee hours of the morning felt adrenaline pumping. Could this really be happening? An answer to prayer this fast. This was truly a miracle.

"I was going to wait to tell you until later, but, I knew you would be up praying and studying. Figured this was a good thing to pray about."

Kelsey had to chuckle under his breath. His friend did know him well. "Your timing couldn't be more perfect. By God's grace let us pray this is resolved quickly and that true justice be done."

"Amen to that. I will see you in a couple of hours."

"Yes. In a couple of hour. Bye Julius."

"Bye Kelsey."

In the glow of the table lamp and aroma of the coffee Kelsey prayed. The adrenaline still pumping as events were beginning to unfold. God is definetly controlling things here thought Kelsey. Kelsey knew his gift was prayer. He enjoyed being a prayer warrior. There were times when people would ask him to pray for more money from their jobs, or that so-and-so would leave so there would be peace at work. But this, this was God's plan! Human activity could not plan a more perfect set of circumstances to bring about his grace, mercy, and justice.

So Kelsey kept praying.

When his wife entered the kitchen, ninety minutes later, he knew that time had flown and he was running late to meet with the Eleven.

DALLAS, TEXAS

Panic. Xi had exerted this feeling upon others many times. It brought pleasure to him. Now, he felt trapped. Hiding in the hotel room was wrong and he knew it. The room did bring solitude which allowed him to think, plan.

Xi ran through scenarios over and over in his head. Where to go? To whom should he go to? How long would that person allow him to hideout? Who would risk being seen with him? All those connections he made to exort people came hauntily back to him. Across the United States he had connections to weapons, false ID's, vehicles. With his face splashed on TV and the internet those connections disappeared. He knew that people would rat him out in order to collect the money and plus, the big plus, was to get rid of Xi forever.

The power he had over people, the fear, evaporated.

Xi felt hopeless.

He also knew that to stay in the hotel room was a trap. Very soon he could anticipate a knock and find agents of various law enforcement branches waiting on the other side of the door.

If he ran he would manage to hide for awhile, wait for the dust to settle. Where to hide?

Connections?

The hopeless scenarious ran round and round in his head.

He could kidnap and hold a child hostage, a child to one of the connections. For the child's safety he would only ask for a place to hide. Too risky Xi thought. Most people are horrible actors and could not tell convincing lies.

More and more ideas came only to be shot down by a little logistical issue.

Xi felt the invisible noose tightening. He even felt trouble breathing.

Sitting and waiting was a bad plan. He finally decided to at least have action. Leaving the hotel room and taking the stairs to the main floor Xi decided to take to the streets.

The crowds would at least hide him for the time being.

Down the stairwell cameras on each floor landing caught glimpses of a man hurrying down. Once outside the pedestrian warning's camera caught a picture of the group waiting to cross the road. While crossing a portrait picture was taken revealing Xi's left scar beginning under the ear and wrapping to the beginning of his chin. Once across, another camera caught the pedestrians safely at their destination.

Screen 42 recorded the eight people crossing the street. A red background alerted the young Peter Roach that someone in the group fulfilled a high profile suspect.

Two years ago Dallas police implemented a complex camera system. Pictures were taken at traffic lights, entrances to parks, and government buildings. These pictures then were processed in milliseconds for identifying people. Ninety-nine percent of the time the people were innocent, regular folks. Once in awhile the drug dealer or unregisterd sex offender would pop up alerting agencies of the the suspects whereabouts. This time a wanted fugitive was highlighted. The Asian man in the blue sports coat with hands stuffed into the side pockets. He did not fit in with the rest of the morning crowd. Everyone else had ties, dress clothes, and fine dress shoes. The Asian wore jeans, sportcoat, and not talking on a cell phone. The man stood out.

Peter ran a background on the picture. Peter recognized the news broadcast playing from earlier this morning while finishing the Denver omelete that his wife made him.

Peter notified the dispatcher of coordinates and directions.

This guy didn't have a chance. Not a chance thought Peter.

YUCATAN PENISULA

After much discussion, much of it with Juan being on pain medications, deciding that Carl could tour the Aztec sites and Juan can journey ahead to Phoenix. John was notified of Juan's arrival. Carl promised John he would be there within two to three days.

Heartened by John's voice, Carl felt relief and a sense of release to hear of what John had learned. He couldn't wait to meet up with his friend to share each other's stories.

When John asked him why the pit stop, Carl answered that a burden laid on his heart to do so.

The Yucatan, much like the Galapogos Islands, was the epicenter of many scientific theories as well as myths. Here many scientists believe a large meteorite crashed into earth. The end result a worldwide devastation with the impact like a thousand volcanoes erupting at once.

When Mt. Saint Helens erupted, Carl, could remember travel restrictions on airplanes and road vehicles. The ash and dust clogged engines and eliminated visibility.

In 2010 a volcano erupted in Iceland suspended travel throughout Europe. Presidents, kings, and dignitaries from around the world could not travel in for the funeral of the Poland president who had died from an airplane crash. The dust would have clogged plane engines resulting in more crashes and deaths.

Both volcanoes, Carl remembered, had ash clouds go around the world. People reported around the world of suffering breathing difficulties. In some places, the sun could't be seen for up to a month or longer.

So a meteorite crashing to earth, equaling a thousand volcanoes intrigued Carl. It was also a defining argument on the extinction of the dinosaurs.

Carl left Mexico City on a tour bus bound for the Aztec ruins. So far, the ancient peoples of the world; from Cambodia to Peru, from Australia to the United States, had answers that today's modern world did not have.

People were crammed like logs on the bus. The luckiest sat in an aisle seat. Carl was not so lucky. With every seat occupied, the bodies and noon day heat baked the inside of the bus.

Carl usually had a strong stomach, until this bus trip. The body odor, city smells of animals and foods cooking sent his stomach rolling. Thankfully windows were down but that only limited the smells. The windows did allow a minimal of fresh air. Carl could not imagine a July day bus trip. Make a mental note in case I ever bring the wife and kids here for a vacation he thought.

Within two hours of leaving Mexico City Carl stepped out and took in the great Aztec ruins. Towering above all others was a stepped pyramid. Unlike its brethren in Egypt, the Aztecs purposely built the pyramids to have a step-like look. Carl assumed it meant something significant. He didn't care about that.

Like other tourists Carl walked the grounds. There were carvings and drawings of many different types of animals; jaguars, eagles, dogs, and a variety of birds. None stood out like dinosaurs. Carl was disappointed but not discouraged. What he really wanted was something that showed a destructive force.

The sun baked over the ancient grounds and for two hours Carl searched and searched. Relenting his pride he decided to ask a guide. He knew his wife would be chuckling at this moment and even Carl let a smile come to his face. A man asking for directions.

A sad tranquility filled Carl. Here was a civilization, advanced and aware of its surroundings but misguided. Their temples and carvings demonstrated that the Aztecs were deeply religious. They honored every aspect of nature; from the animals to the sun.

Then, in a moment, disaster happened. Not a chance for repentance or to turn to God. Carl remembered Paul's words that evidence is all around of God's existence, that none are without excuse. As Carl searched for a guide he gazed at the jungle around him, the sun beating down, and surrounding him were mountains. No excuse but misplaced faith thought Carl.

Carl, after some time, found the familiar dress of the local guides. In white khaki pants with matching shirts Carl bee-lined towards the guide. As he strode across the ceremonial grounds he thought out how to frame his words into a question that would make sense. How does one ask about the famous meteor that destroyed the world? Carl decided that upfront would prove to be the best tactic.

The guide turned out to be a woman. Her features were striking as her brown complexion was glowing with a tan from being in the sun daily. Her black hair hung loose down her back. Carl was caught off guard from her sheer beauty. "Excuse me. My name is Carl. Do you speak English?"

The guide laughed. "Yes. I speak English quite well. You Americans are our number one visitors. It, um, does us well to speak English. What can I do for your sir?"

"I am doing some research. In this general area," Carl swept his arm around the plaza, "a meteor crashed. It caused great devastation. Is there any evidence of the impact of this meteor?"

"You must be talking about the one that destroyed the dinosaurs. We get many scientists and researchers who ask about this meteor. I have actually checked into this meteor for I have been curious myself."

Carl noticed a look of disappointment.

"I hope you did not come all the way out here to seek the evidence. There is none."

Carl felt the weight of disappointment, wondering if this little excursion a waste of time and energy? There was something else here; he could feel it.

Still, Carl knew deep in his heart that he wouldn't find anything. Mike's notes didn't mention anything about the Yucatan and nothing about a meteor or the destruction of the dinosaurs.

Maybe that was the point. Maybe there was no destruction of the dinosaurs. Carl hoped that there would be answers amongst the ancient grounds and temples. Did these people walk among the dinosaurs?

Carl looked around again. The jungle wrapped around the grounds like a blanket. Unlike a blanket, Carl felt no security, no sense of finality. Carl placed his feelings and thoughts into prayer. This moment allowed Carl to surrender the unknown to the Known. Accepting the fact that some questions may never receive answers is an act of obedience and faith. Some things were better left to God and his word.

BEIJING, CHINA

Kim knew about the tortures inflicted upon political prisoners. He also knew the means and ways of extracting information from captured soldiers. The screams excited him and brought great joy.

Now it was his screams echoing throughout the chamber.

The Commander learned that Kim kept secrets and telling lies. Kim diverted resources and running underground missions using the intel and weapons of the military.

Further, Kim had killed Chinese citizens. Some of whom had served in the military and were decorated soldiers. Entire villages were razed, burned to the ground, destroyed. All for Kim's purposes.

Two days ago the Commander called Kim into his office. What Kim did not know was that at the same time his secretary, Sun Lee, allowed the Commander's hackers onto Kim's computer. File after file showed the targets of Kim's rampage. The evidence condemning.

A phone call was placed into the Commander's office. Picking up the phone his face showed no emotion. While still on the phone, his left hand pushed a button underneath the desk, signaling for soldiers to enter the office and place Kim under arrest.

Kim oblivious to all the actions around him.

In mere seconds four armed soldiers entered the Commander's office. Guns were aimed at Kim's head as he was pushed to the ground. His arms were chicken-winged behind him as his wrists were secured. He tried to kick his legs but found his ankles were also being tied together. A gag shoved into his mouth and a blindfold wrapped around his head. The last thing he saw was the Commander's look of hatred and anger.

Now, Kim felt hot needles being put into his skin. The needles were being pulled out of a fire by a device similar to pliers. Then, the needles, white hot and glowing, were put into his skin. The pain undescribable.

The piercing itself was torturous. Each needle felt like a knife stab. Kim lost count of how many needles were in him at this point.

There the heat. As the needle entered his body a burning raced along the nerves sending agony throughout his muscles. Spasms raked his body. Once the needles were in the heat burned the flesh around the needle infusing the needle to the body.

Many times Kim felt as though he was going to pass out. After so many needles questions were asked of Kim and he answered. He didn't care. He automatically answering without thinking of the questions. Part of his brain knew that the more he answered the more the pain would come. He overflowed with information. He also knew if he didn't answer the pain would increase.

The no win situation.

Xi compromised. The meeting with Ambassador Burtha was spilled. His hatred for Christians were known. His motives. Childhood. Everything.

"See, that wasn't so bad now was it? You should appreciate the irony."

Kim, in a moment of calmness felt a new fear. He knew what was coming. The pain he had been feeling was nothing to what was coming next.

"This was your technique was it not?" Sarcasm dripped from the man's lips.

"No. No. I beg of you. Please no."

The man leaned down so his nose no more that two inches above Kim's. "Did you provide mercy to those you had killed? Did you not enjoy their suffering and their deaths? What about the children you brainwashed, only to go out and kill their family and friends? Did you provide them mercy?"

Kim had thousands of images of faces flashing through his mind. Faces of contorted pain. Screams now raged in his head. The screams that he took pride in now haunted.

"Please no. "I'm sorry. I'm sorry. I'm sorry." Tears came down his face.

'Don't humor me with tears. You are only sorry because you were caught. You are not remorseful."

Kim knew what was next. Tilting his head up slightly he saw a string going through every needle's eye. He saw above him the metal hook. Once the needles were strung the string strapped to the hook.

"The mighty Commander Kim. You had it all. Power. Position. Influence. But you got greedy. It's a shame really. Are you ready?"

Kim wasn't. Never would be. It didn't matter. The pain was coming. The undescribable pain.

"Kim, this will be quick."

Kim saw the strings tighten as the hook lifted up.

"In three seconds this will be over."

Kim closed his eyes and waited. Anticipation being the worse feeling.

The hook jerked up, pulling every needle from Kim's body. Flesh, having been burned to each needle, was ripped upward. A scream, unlike anything that had escaped from Kim's lips, erupted.

Dangling above his body were hundreds of hooks and pieces of flesh.

DALLAS, TEXAS

Nervousness was not in Xi's DNA. Understanding fear was. He had not heard from Kim in days. All forms of contact were gone. Cell phone. Satellite phone. Email. All gone. Plus, he was holed up in a second-hand hotel on the outskirts of Dallas hoping by all luck that he could get into Mexico.

Every TV station plastered his face. Hours ago he was a shadow but now, a celebrity of the infamous kind. The man who killed a pastor in cold blood. Driving to Mexico seemed out of the question. Checkpoints were set up on every roadway. The airport also useless as security would be tighter.

Once, already he had come close to getting caught. He knew better that to go into the Ready-Go Mart. He hoped that by playing a low profile and sheer luck the cameras wouldn't get a good enough picture and people wouldn't recognize him.

Fat chance.

It there was one thing Americans love is for their fifteen minutes of fame. Every person in Dallas seemed aware of his picture. Within moments of entering the store he was recognized by a teenage girl. Soon, the old lady by the milk began pointing. The man in the beer section turned to look at the commotion. The girl continued saying, "That's him. That's him. I swear it's him."

It Xi didn't need food so bad he could have forgot the food and hurried out the store. Instead he tried to ignore the finger pointing and murmuring behind his back. He paid in cash. Low profile. Stay off the grid for as long as possible.

Soon the crowd inched itself closer to him. The noose was closing. He paid; grabbed the bag and left. Not bothering to get the change. Stupid. That would have aroused suspicion he thought to himself.

After leaving the store he quickly hid in the alleyways and shadows.

Xi could not believe the last twenty-four hours. Just yesterday he intimidated others using fear. Now, a teenage age girl intimidated him.

Still, the greatest fear was the lack of communication from Kim. It was not like him to go this long without contacting Xi.

Xi meandered the alleyways to his car which located five blocks away. Even so, as sirens went by Xi found himself freezing in his tracks and holding his breath. The sound would fade away and Xi continued on. Once at his car he would drive five more miles to the hotel.

While the comforts were subpar it was just the place that the locals wouldn't call the cops. One cop couldn't handle the drug pushers, dealers, prostitutes, and abusers who resided in Starlit Hotel. It was a sort of sanctuary.

Walking up the stairs Xi could make out the smells of marijuana and cigarette smoke. A variety of alcoholic drinks swam into the nostrils. The entire place reeked of other various aromas that fell into three categories; drugs, alcohol, or something related to the body.

As Xi entered his room he stuck to his traditional habits of checking the room and ensuring that no intruders had entered. Clean.

Xi rechecked the door for security. Good. For a brief moment the world was calm. Xi closed his eyes and visualized the dog barking outside. He heard the children playing in the parking lot. Cars rushed by on the three lane road providing a constant hum.

The calmness interrupted by the last sound he wanted to hear.

Sirens.

Were they after him? Not knowing for sure sent Xi into action. He had a plan for just this type of situation. Xi knew in the back of his mind that the cops would sooner or later catch up to him. One thing about American cops, relentless.

Xi stood next to the window and pulled a bit of the curtain to the side.. There were two vehicles and it sounded like more on the way. Three cops were standing next to their vehicles while one came out of the manager's office. Sweat beaded on Xi's face.

He dreaded the scene playing out in the parking lot. If the one came out of the manager's office pointed up towards Xi then it was over. The cop pulled his shirt lapel over to speak into it. Not good.

Xi continued to watch the scene A dread overcame Xi as the cop pointed up. The point may as well been a laser. A new sense of desperation welled up inside Xi. Quickly he pulled back the curtain. It was only a matter of seconds until the banging on the door happens. The door crashing in. The the flurry of lights, guns, and voices directed at him. Two or three cops will have him pinned on the ground forcing handcuffs on him. Sure he may get in a punch or a kick but in the end it a losing battle.

Xi went next to the bed and found his black bag. Inside was his 9mm.

"I have always controlled my destiny."

PHOENIX, ARIZONA

Excitement was building. John had heard from Cathy and Carl that they were traveling to Phoenix. Earlier he stopped by St. Luke's to visit Juan. The story of survival was amazing and talking to Juan was like meeting with an old friend, even though this was the first time the two had met. Their faith and bond in Carl was enough to establish a friendship.

John tried to fight the nervous anticipation. The nerves were firing, much like the Green Beret missions of long ago. Carl's parchment excited and brought great concern to John and couldn't wait to see and study it.

There will still questions lingering. John knew as a scientist that answers only led to more questions. In the science world it was called job security. Even some answers were ignored to groups and people would continue to receive grants and donations; the more liberal faction of science famously did this collecting of millions for outdated research. Push for an agenda that seems good and put the right names and credentials behind it and all of a sudden it becomes legitimate.

But real research came up with answers. It may be an answer a person does not like, but it is still an answer. To find more answers John knew that more places that needed to be visited. A place of great mystery. It held answers to man's beginnings; what man ate, how man hunted, how man lived. Many believed Africa was the place of the earliest civilization. Located on its continent were unique species and the climate is conducive to reptile creatures. Many tribes on the continent have not changed their ways in over two thousand years. It was why Africa remained one of the most popular spots for mission groups.

John decided to go once Cathy and Carl arrived. He would make the necessary arrangements.

"Africa?" John muttered to himself. "I am going to Africa."

DALLAS, TEXAS

"Africa? Why Africa?" Dr. Simpson gazed around the circle. "What is to be gained by going to Africa? Do we not have all the evidence that is needed for going public?"

Murmurs rippled around the circle.

"Let's face it. No matter the size of evidence, will it have the impact on the the world that is needed? Unless one finds a dinosaur, most minds will not change."

"That may be true. But like you said, most minds will not change but some will. And isn't that worth fighting for? Tony Reiner known to bring clarity to the group, "Besides, Carl, Cathy, and John have risked their lives while we sat here. At least let them capstone their research by going."

More murmurs.

"Is there anybody we can trust in Africa? We are sending in three Americans to fact find Christianity. The Muslim population in Africa can be dangerous to Christians."

The Eleven remembered the mission group that went to Sudan. Fourteen young Christians left from the United States to Sudan to establish a church. For two weeks the group worked in the village with the people. A well was dug and medicine was brought in for the children. The locals enjoyed the young, enthusiastic Americans. Every day the missionaries and children played soccer and by the end of the two weeks baptisms were happening.

Then came trouble. Word reached to other towns of what was happening and Muslim teenagers organized themselves. Provoked with centuries of rage and religious zeal the teenagers came into the village. Each Christian missionary tortured. The women were traped one by one while the others were forced to watch. The men were humiliated and painfully tortured. Toes were cut off one by one. A slice of an ear. Broken bones. Finally, in relief each member had lost their lives. None of the missionaries had turned on their faith.

Word came from that village, months and years after how the village still grew in the Christian faith. The groups' dedication and own religious fervor inspired the villagers. The leaks included secret Bible meetings, Bibles secretly being distributed to surrounding villages and stealth baptisms.

"There are some we can trust. Where the three would be going is not known to have hostilities. They would be heading to South Africa, not north."

"I believe that Tony may be right. It would only be fair for us to allow them to finish their mission."

With heads nodding the Eleven agreed.

PHOENIX, ARIZONA

The 737 screeched down the runway. John still had the childlike curiousity of watching the massive machines taking off and landing. It amazed him that hundreds of tons of weight could rise into the air and move at such incredible speeds.

But it wasn't the planes that brought him to Phoenix International, Carl had arrived.

Yesterday he had heard from Carl would be in from Mexico City. John knew that Carl had changed on his trip; who wouldn't after being chased by bandits, surviving in the wilds of the Andes Mountains, soak up the culture of village life, all the while saving another man's life.

John couldn't wait to hear Carl's story firsthand. The wait for him to make it to baggage claim seemed longer than fifteen minutes. Then the smile shown among the faces. Carl had dropped his carry-on and embraced John in a bear hug that literally took John's breath away.

"John, you look wonderful. How are you?"

"Fine, fine. You look great considering your adventures." John noticed a look of aw-shucks on Carl's face.

"God is good. That is all that needs to be said. I would not have made it, nor Juan, if it wasn't for him."

"Amen to that. Do you need help with anything?"

The two chatted as they meandered among the crowds towards the baggage claim. Each shared a story or two of what they had learned.

"Is Cathy coming?" Carl searched the faces hoping to see Cathy's.

"In a couple of days. She is driving down from Montana as we speak. She wanted to check on a couple of things so she chose to drive." John noticed the worried look on Carl's face. "Don't worry my friend; she is safe now. She just wanted to check out a couple of areas that her dad mentioned."

Carl seemed to relax a little from the news. Still, he wouldn't be completely relieved until he saw Cathy.

"I hope you are ready for good ol January warmth of Phoenix. I tell you what, I am starting to understand the snowbird idea."

As Carl exited the airport and followed John the instant warmth of sun and heat comforted like a blanket. It was the warmth that made a person want to relax and soak in the refreshing air. And, after being overseas for so many days, it was good to be back home in America. The sights and sounds were comforting; from the cars in traffic, business logos that stood out on street corners and that lined boulevards, to even the air. It all felt like home.

Carl had heard that when military people came home from deployment they take a moment to soak in the air and gather in the sights around them. There was something to returning back to America. Carl felt the same now.

John looked at Carl. "I know that look. Mike and I had that same look when we were both in the Green Berets. I never tired of getting off the plane and coming home. It was an instant pick-me-up from where we were. Reminded us of what we were fighting for."

After throwing the baggage into the trunk and settling into the flow of Phoenix traffic Carl asked, "Are you fully convinced of what we are doing and finding out?"

John let out a deep sigh. "I am. Everything we are finding and learning points to the same conclusion. Even the peripheral items like the flood and ark. Those answers fill in the blanks. But what really convinced me was the evidence from the southwestern and western tribes of the United States. The drawings and oral history clearly state that the dinosaurs lived among men. They were hunted and revered much like the buffalo of the plain tribes.

"I see your point. What conviced me was the dedication that Juan had to his theory. He lost his job, which led to his losing his family, but he never wavered. Then, like you stated, all the physical evidence. I am eager to hear Cathy's story but I believe that she will say the same thing."

John chuckled, "No doubt, the evidence she came across, probably the most convincing."

Carl suddenly went sullen. "Not necessarily, while at Machu Pichu, Juan and I stumbled across a papyrus roll." Reaching into his briefcase Carl pulled out the darkened roll. "I am hoping that you can help out with this."

COLORADO

Dinosaur National Monument was an archeological Disneyland. Visitors could look through glass windows and watch scientists, college students, and volunteers dig through layers of sediment to find fossils. The site had a plethora of digging sites and each one yielded the promise of the next great find.

Cathy knew this place well. It was here that she first took spade to dirt and where she came into contact with her fossil find. Her dad brought her here to encourage the family business. He wanted her to gain confidence and to touch something tangible and receive immediate satisfaction of her hard work. Over the years the finds had been more difficult and most times the sites have yielded nothing; still, the awe and feeling of the first find and dig never left her.

Ironic that she would find herself here, now, under the present circumstances. On that first dig she was twelve years old. She listened as the guide described the millions of years it took to create the fossils. Dinosaurs ruled for millions of years on the earth. Between the dynasty of dinosaurs and the dawn of man walking on the earth, another million years have passed. Cathy now realized that the millions of years were becoming something ridiculous. Now she viewed this site differently.

The excitement of the digs were still exciting but through a whole new mindset. Instead of seeing the millions of years of layers she now saw a major cataclysmic event that swept the world. She now understood, for the first time, what this place really meant. This gathering place of dinosaurs became a mass grave.

The guide continued to ramble on about the fossilization process but Cathy had long ago ignored the droning and concentrated instead of finding her father's long lost friend. Zach Albans was like family to Cathy as she grew up. Zach, second to John, was the closest family friend. Now,

Zach was the overseer of Dinosaur National Monument and still kept close contact with Cathy and Mike.

Much like a college student returning home from their first year and enjoying the comforts of home, Cathy found a peace of walking the hallways and being in the rooms of the museum. Cathy had to constantly remind herself that she was her on a mission, with a purpose, and to not let things like nostalgia distract her. Still, she felt a comforting peace.

Zach Albans had the appearance of Albert Einstein and Kareem Abdul-Jabbar. Dr. Albans stood well over six-five and the tangled mess on his head called hair gave a madman look. Dr. Albans enjoyed the looks he received from people on meeting him for the first time. He would reach out his extensively long fingers and wrap his hand around theirs. To lessen the intimidating appearance he radiated, he would bow down on introducing himself. Within seconds, his quirky sense of humor and mountain man ways of storytelling disarmed any awkward feelings one would have. Within minutes Zach made a new lifelong friend.

Cathy anxiously awaited to see Yun's face upon meeting Zach. As if on cue the eyebrows raised and head popped back when Zach opened his office door and then wrapped the serpent like arms around Cathy in a hug. Yun could only stand there and work on regaining his composure.

"My goodness, my little Cat has become a woman. I was afraid that someday you would grow up into a woman. It seems that day has arrived."

Cathy, through a blushed embarrassed face, "Zach, this is my friend Yun. I told you about him on the phone."

"Ah, Cat's savior and friend. Who is a boy? A boyfriend?"

Yun blushed with embarrasement. The man's smooth drawl made a person feel at ease and welcoming.

"Zach, recently I have learned some, well, interesting things. Some about my father, some about paleotology, and some about life itself. Do you have some time to talk?"

"Of course. I just made some hazelnut coffee. Come in and have a seat." Zach turned around and went into his office.

Lining one of the walls were pictures of paleotologists standing in various places of the world; Egypt, Peru, Montana, Mexico, China, and Russia. On the opposite wall were books and magazine holders full of professional journals on archeology and ancient civilizations. The L-shaped desk was tucked towards the corner of the room with the sharp edge pointed towards the middle of the room. It allowed Zach to see the room, the door, and still be able to stare out the windows to the landscape. Despite Zach's position and years of experience, he was still a dirt digger at heart.

After filling up three mugs full of coffee and letting the aroma of fresh brew fill the room, Zach sat in a chair not behind his desk. It was clear he wanted the personal and not the executive approach to the conversation.

"My dear, I am truly sorry about your father. He was the dearest of friends."

Cathy took Zach's hands, "You were a true friend and a blessing to my father and me. If people were allowed to pick family, you would have asked to join."

Zach looked into Cathy's eyes and Cathy could see tears welling. Cathy gripped is hands tighter, knowing the bond that her father had with this man. They were like brothers and she knew that he was hurting from Mike's loss.

"Zach, my father was researching something the last three years. It was something big. I have followed his research and, well, it has been life changing. But I need your help clarifying some things."

Zach lowered his mug from his lips, "Of course, what can I do."

Cathy explained the discoveries from Utah to Cambodia to China and Alaska. She went on tell of how she was attacked on two different occasions. "I believe in what my father was researching. The problem is, I don't have the sway, the reputation to bring my father's finding public. I was hoping you would help in that."

Zach raised the mug to lips and lowered his eyes. When he looked back up again there was a new look, strange and menacing look that sent a chill up Cathy's spine.

"I respected your father with my entire being. In the last three years he went around the world to conduct this research and it destroyed his reputation. It was foolishness! All scientific data that is worthy has demonstrated that your father wrong. And Cathy, you are wrong too. I'm sorry but I cannot defend such nonsense."

Cathy felt her stomach tightening and a feeling of shock was shooting through her body. The most trusted man for most of her life was destroying her father and his findings.

"What do you mean nonsense? Didn't you just hear what I had to say?"

Zach shook his head back and forth. "A person will believe anything put before them if that person comes with a frame of mind that is not open and is already set on something else. Then of course they can explain, or give explanation to what they see. Your father believed that dinosaurs lived with man. Don't worry, he was contacting me over the last three years. Your father went around the world to defend this idea. He found pictures in the desert and unique finds in China and Montana. He put his spin on these items and tried to come up with an explanation. He took evidence and warped it into his way of thinking. He manipulated evidence to back up his personal beliefs. Your father was wrong in doing that."

Cathy felt her temper rising. This man, friend, was destroying her father's most important work. This man, someone so dear and so close, was saying the most destructive things.

"Zach, what are you saying?"

Zach gave a sympathetic look, as a grandfather would look upon his granddaughter. Cathy hated that look from her childhood. She thought of it as demeaning, as if never smart enough or old enough to understand.

For Zach that was the idea.

"My dear, your dad was an intelligent man and respected scientist. But over the last three years he squandered it on some fairy tale. Every bit of evidence points to what scientist are saying today, man and dinosaurs aer from separate times. Ruled in different eras. Evolved throughout millions of years. Why would we as scientist make something up like this? It is our job to find these things out, to verify all the information. It is our job to seek out the truth to our existence."

Cathy shuddered at the last statement. It was true then, man used science to become their own gods. "I cannot accept that."

"Mr Alban, do you really believe we went from goo, to zoo, to you?" Yun felt desire to protect and defend Cathy.

"Oh no, not you too? Yun. Yun. Weren't you one of Mike's pupils?"

"Yes sir. And he taught me a lot. Taught me more that just history and ancient civilizations. He saved my life."

Zach switched his stare between Cathy and Yun. "I am sorry Cathy. I cannot in good conscience endorse your father's theory."

"Have you looked at the evidence? Read his findings?"

Zach sighed, "I don't need to. Every bit of reliable science verifies that your father's hypothesis is not valid."

Stunned, Cathy couldn't think of a response. Zach, a dear friend, did not even give her father's research a chance. She imagined the research being sent from her father to Zach only to have it thrown away to the unknown depths of some waste pile.

"Mr. Albans, I believe it is time for us to go. We thank you for your time."

As if in a fog-like trance Yun escorted Cathy back to their car. Cathy tried to assemble the shattered thoughts and feelings that now exploded within her. The air felt like a professional boxer had smacked her in the gut. She felt a betrayal unlike any she had felt in her life. A close collegue and friend had given up on her father. Anger welled up inside and she quickly pushed it away. It wasn't in her to be angry and bitter. Not anymore.

Instead, Cathy chose to announce to the world her father's research. "I will not fail you father. I choose, like you, to seek after the truth." Putting these thoughts into her head, she quickly began putting the negative thoughts and feelings away and focused on what she could control.

"Yun, are we alone in our idea about all this? I mean, the world all over believes that we evolved. How do we know that our ideas, our faith, is the right one?"

Yun leaned back and put his head briefly on the headrest and quickly shot back to driving position. "I think of the scientist in the past who defied society's rules and presuppositons. That defiance changed the world's thinking. Galileo went against the church to prove his theory that the earth is not the center of the universe. He had to recant to save his life but he put that idea out there and proved it. Remember, back then the church was the rule of thumb for society. Don't you see, these people, people like Zach, are scared. They have built up a lifetime of prestige and awards. They have worked on proving and re-proving a theory. If that theory or idea crashed, they can lose everything and look like liars. In their mindset, they feel they have no choice."

Cathy stared at the floormat in the car. It looked like she felt and how her life has been. Well worn, thin in some places, and dirty. Deep stains were located in various areas and ragged around the edges. "But Zach was a friend."

Sighing, "Zach is also about self-preservation. Maybe it would be different if your father was alive and could convince him face to face. But with Mike gone, in Zach's mind, why take the risk. Life is safe again."

As the car moved down the highway, Cathy stared off into the horizon. Swirling thoughts swam in her head. "I guess my father was braver than I thought. He went against everyone to seek the truth, even his best friends."

GRAND CANYON NATIONAL PARK, ARIZONA

Staring across the canyon David felt that he had Xi trapped. For the last three days he had tracked Xi from Dallas to here, the Grand Canyon. Along the way he learned much about the assassin. The man was pure evil. During the last few days Xi had left plenty of markers in which to track him; first there was the businessman from Dallas. Xi had pulled the man out from the vehicle and sliced the throat and left him in the middle of the road. Then there was the young family in Truth and Consequences, New Mexico. David has seen some terrible, carnal horrors done to people while on special assignments around the world. What Xi did was unconscionable. Every member killed, hacked to death and left contorted in the living room. The third marker wsa in Flagstaff where Xi single-handedly torched a city block taking ten people's lives and injuring numerous others.

Through it all Xi made mistakes.

These mistakes showed David that Xi was stoppable and desperate. Each event was worse that the one before. David knew that Xi was trying to distract the hunters. Trying to buy time. Yet Xi made simple, stupid mistakes along the way.

Xi was leaving fingerprints. The amount of crimes now associated with Xi was growing day by day from the FBI database. This information was being sent out to every law enforcement agency in America.

Xi was also being caught on cameras. Every marker that gave Xi away was because he needed gas to keep moving. Cameras captured his every move; from getting out of the vehicle, picking up the gas nozzle, pushing for unleaded regular, and then waiting unpatiently for the tank to fill. Xi was easy to pinpoint as he was caught doing the ancy dance in all three places. His head swiveled back and forth keeping a look out for anyone following him.

It wasn't until Xi had left Flagstaff that he finally knew he was actually being followed.

That was David's mistake.

A wild car chase took place on Arizona's highways as Xi tried to lose David. A well timed call brought in a helicopter and more vehicles. After two hours Xi made for the north rim of the Grand Canyon where he stole a motorcycle from a garage. The man was crazy enough to take it into the canyon. The motor echoed off of the walls creating some confusion on which direction he was going. Then, no more than a couple of minutes, the helicopter would sound off Xi's location. After an hour the bike was found with no rider.

As David and the rest of the agents arrived they now knew why Xi ditched the bike. Both sides of the canyons were lined with holes, caves, and openings.

The perfect place to hide and wait patiently, to set up traps.

David knew, from studying Xi, that Xi was anticipating that the agents would split up and begin searching the walls. David wasn't going to take the bait. Xi was a hunter at heart. There was no way David would sit by and let his men die off one by one. Instead, David decided to box Xi in.

David was banking on the fact that Xi had no food. The adrenaline rush would eventually wear off for Xi and the normal bodily reaction is to eat to replenish the body. David also wanted to tighten the box. At different times David informed his men to downsize the perimeter and contain Xi.

David wanted Xi to become desperate.

A hunter hates being hunted. They understand the fear they put into others but when that fear is reciprocated back onto the hunter, a new level of paranoia sets in. It was this paranoia that David was banking on.

All he needed was for Xi to do something stupid.

After three grueling hours of tightening the box, Xi finally broke.

PHOENIX, ARIZONA

"Good morning Carl. How good it is to see you again. Are you doing well?"

Carl had to smile back at the scree. Here was his mentor and friend in Dallas using Skype to communicate with him. In the background he could see the others of the Eleven, leaning forward and all smiling.

"I'm doing well thank you. Juan sends his blessings as well. He should be out of the hospital in a couple of days."

"What an answer to prayer."

Carl was thrilled that the Eleven were offering Juan a job as a history professor. Considering all that Juan had gone through, it was good to see him being awarded.

"It truly is an answer to prayer. Cathy should be here tomorrow. She called us right before you did and mentioned that she had no more delays or obligations and was eager to meet up with us."

"Splendid. I take it that John is also joining us?"

On cue John sat next to Carl. From the Dallas perspective it was humorous to see the two on the screen. The screen, despite its size, could barely contain the two faces.

"I am here. Good morning."

Laughs were heard in the background.

"Good morning. On behalf of our group I want to say we are all proud of you and for the work that you have done."

On the screen Carl and John gave blushing looks.

"You two, and Cathy, are to be commended for seeking the truth despite terrifying obstacles. So we understand if you don't want to contine with our next request."

John and Carl went from embarrassing to instant surprise. There was more to do?

"It seems that in Africa Mike left one last clue. The, well, the capstone to his research. Here, take a look."

Popping up on the screen in Arizona was a letter from Mike.

> Dear Twelve;
>
> Should you deem necessary, if my daughter and John are successful in their endeavours and are convinced beyond a shadow of doubt in my hypothesis, then I would like them to continue on to Africa. To be more precise, I would like them to examine a particular area in the Congo area of Africa.
>
> It is here, that I believe they will find the most convincing evidence of all of when dinosaurs existed.
>
> I wanted you to be the discretionary agents. Many will mistake my intentions or my work. Please, for the love of God above, don't let this happen. I want the truth to be know without any worldly distractions.
>
> I thank you for your service and belief in me. May God bless you and protect you. Pray for my friend and daughter as I love them very much.
>
> Sincerely,
Mike Jurkovich

As John and Carl leaned back a piece of paper was held up to the screen The letter sent to the Twelve was flipped over and before them was a hand written response from Mike.

> John, I found it! I have found a living, breathing dinosaur and it is here in Africa. Mention Mitumbo to the tribes along the Nile while in the Congo area. Mitumbo means great beast. This will serve you well. He will lead you. They are anticipating you. May God bless you my friend.

"Amazing," John whispered amazed.

GRAND CANYON NATIONAL PARK, ARIZONA

Xi knew that he was trapped. He guessed that the men outside would have him boxed in. He was hoping for a cave or crevice where he could slink away and hide for awhile. The plan backfired.

Like the traditional game of hide-and-seek, a person goes to hide and plans on staying hidden. That person will go someplace usually dark and small and then tuck themselves away and wait. Eventually, the person either gets found or becomes impatient and comes out. Either way, the person is found and caught.

Xi was playing the life and death version of hide-and-seek.

It was only a matter of time before the men were right outside the cave opening. While Xi had a pistol, there were only four shells. Xi doubted that there were only four men outside. He was guessing closer to ten to twelve.

It had been three hours since he had come into the cave and human instincts were kicking in. Xi knew these fears would come. Many times he inflicted them onto others. It was a domino effect. First the trapped feeling. The victim would be cornered and the fight or flight instinct would surface. When the victim realizes that flight is not an option desperation sets in. Many people succumb to this desperation feeling and it ends up costing them their lives. Xi was disappointed by how quickly people become weak-minded. If a person could overcome the desperation stage, then the survival stage would come.

The victim would become an animal in this stage. Xi found this stage to be the most fun. A person would attack savagely, without any thought to context of the situation. Adrenaline and fear drove the person. Mind and reason checked out.

Now, Xi was in desperation stage. He had gone without food for many hours. The adrenaline rush had long ago vanished. The body was craving some sort of nourishment and Xi could not provide.

Xi felt the survival stage settling in and it scared him. Xi was a tactical assassin. Able to think out the plan before implementing it. Able to control every situation and the people in it. Now, he was being controlled and manipulated. No wonder so many of his victims fought wildly against him. Being controlled by fear and having no freedom to think and act weighed upon a person.

He thought about early in his life when he would hunt Christians back in China. When these people faced death there was a glimmer in their eyes. A contentment that would settle in. It was as if they welcomed death and felt freedom.

Xi found this fascinating. He had heard that the Christians believed in an afterlife unlike other religious beliefs. He had never followed up on what they believed but he could tell by their actions and words they believed in this afterlife.

All other people clung to their life as a baby clings to a rattle. Take the rattle away and the baby cries. People were the same. Threaten them with their life, watch the true colors come out.

Xi waited and waited. Soon his true colors would come out. He was scared on what those colors would be. He always believed that a person's character is defined not by the life thy led but by how they approach death.

His character was about to be transparent.

COLORADO SPRINGS, COLORADO

Sunrise crawled out of the east and Cathy and Yun welcomed its morning warmth. The Rockies glimmered in gold from the morning rays. Snow blanketed the streets of Colorado Springs and the traffic was just waking, bringing with the buzz of hustle and bustle.

Both were looking forward to being in Arizona and its desert warmth. For now, they were just enjoying the warmth of each other's company. Cathy needed time to to get over the hostility she was now feeling towards Zach Albans. Zach was someone that Cathy thought she could trust; he was a family friend for as long as she could remember. His words were so cold; his reaction was not what she expected. She needed someone she could trust and that could promote her father's research. "Funny," she thought, "about a month ago I would have claimed this as my own." She needed someone that understood the scientific community and its politics and that had weight with the governing bodies.

That was now gone.

Cathy was hoping that John would have that prestige and that he would be willing to fill that role.

Sitting on the hotel couch and lazily glancing through the paper Cathy finished her bagel and coffee. She tried as much as possible to dismiss the last thirty some hours and replace the thoughts with the next couple of days.

As Cathy sipped on her coffee she found herself staring at Yun who was at the counter. In the last week they had been through more than most married couples. Through it all he had been caring and strong, open and masculine, soft-hearted and confident. She knew and recognized the fact that she was in the early stages of puppy love romance. Part of her knew that Yun was not perfect but all she could see was the shining image at the counter.

Cathy dropped her eyes as Yun returned. He looked childishly handsome as he juggled his grande coffee, a Danish pastry, and two bagels in a white pocket sleeve that was dangling precariously from his mouth.

"What are you thinking?" Yun asked as he sorted the contents on the table before sitting down.

"I'm not sure." There was no way she was going to proclaim what she was really thinking. She decided to move the conversation into the professional realm. Being the control freak she wanted to control her surroundings and conversation. "I'm trying to piece together what Zach said and what my dad found out. I didn't realize how controversial this subject was."

"Yea, it does get people fired up doesn't it? I know that many things in science are politicized, or are skewed dur to which group wants credit for the finding and which group wants to discredit the same findings. Archeology is famous for this."

Cathy knew he was right. Biblical archeology was notorious for mixed messages. She remembered an ossuary that created tidal waves of controversy. "I know what you mean. A few years ago an ossuary was found and it raised some eyebrows. Even made newscasts."

"Ossuary?"

"Sorry. Back in biblical Israel the Jews would bury their dead in marked spots in the ground. On the one year anniversary of the person's death the relatives would dig up the body, which of course would be bones, and then place those bones into a box. The box is called an ossuary. The box would be made from a variety of materials; it depended on the wealth of the family, resources of where they lived and types of materials in the area. Anyway, on the sides of the ossuary would be the name of the deceased and the family name. Once in awhile a third name would be on there. That third name would be there if the deceased was related to someone famous. This controversial ossuary that was found had inscribed on the side ' James, sons of Joseph, brother of Jesus'."

"Say what!" Bagel crumbs sprayed out across the table.

"You can imagine the uproar. Many groups declared the ossuaryafake. Others said more research so they can buy time to come up with more substantial arguments. Still, others claimed definitive proof of what the Bible states."

"What did they decide? Is it real or is it fake?"

"Well, the fight is still raging. Enough people have stepped forward that now, every bit of evidence has been scrutinized and questioned. Is is the ultimate case of walking on eggshells. Every move is watched by a team of observers waiting for an opportunity to discredit or take credit for the discovery." Shaking her head Cathy continued on, compassion creeping into her words. "It's a great shame. A reall embarrassment. A great find that could lead to other great finds and it is held up in politics and pride." Thoughts of Zach popped into her mind. Cathy fought again to turn them away.

"Think of the silver lining; when the truth comes out, and it will, think of the ripple effect it will have."

"I have thought of that. But, I have also seen that depending on how long it takes to get to the truth, even when the truth comes out, it is piled under so much other garbage that nobody believes it anyway. The scrutinization has clouded the truth and therefore the evidence before a person may not be trusted."

Sipping on his coffee yun lifted his eyes towards Cathy. "You believe that this will happen with your father's work? The truth will go forth and it will be attacked and scrutinized, and discredited for possibly years to come. When the dust settles, it may not make a difference and the time and effort your father, and you, have put into the research will be wasted. You believe this?"

Sighing and cupping both hands around the coffee mug for false security, "That is exactly what I am fearing."

PHOENIX, ARIZONA

A lighthearted excitement filled the room. Carl and John knew that it was only minutes until Cathy arrived. Like little children anticipating the arrival of grandparents, both men were fidgeting and anxious. Carl paced back and forth across the main entrance of the administration building. John sat and tried to work out a crossword puzzle. In the half hour of waiting he only figured out two words. Thoughts kept straying to Cathy and her arrival.

Every car that passed by caused a glance and a whip of the heads. John's cell phone rang and excitement fill his voice.

"Yes we are both here. Waiting for you. Where are you?"

As Carl watched John talk he saw a glazed look come over John's eyes. Then, slowly, he watched John turn his head to the left. Mirroring John's actions Carl turned in the same direction. Sitting on a chair with her feet propped up on a glass table was Cathy, holding a cellphone.

John flipped is phone shut and crossed over the short span of space. Carl followed right behind. Cathy lazily took her legs off the table and stood up. In an instant she was swallowed up in hugs. At this moment she considered herself the luckiest person on earth. She had a man who lover her and for the first time in her life, real friends.

"How long have you been waiting here?" John didn't know whether to be happy or upset.

"I just got here. But I saw how you two were all nervous and, well, I thought to surprise you."

"You certainly did that. I thought John was going to have a heart attack when you called."

"So, we are here and altogether. I am starved and I believe you haven't met Yun." Cathy introduced Yun. Yun was nervous meeting the John and Carl but after the handshakes and hugs he felt he was among family.

The four chattered as they walked across Arizona State University campus searching for a restaurant. As if sensing privacy was needed, the four were led to a booth at the back of the restaurant and away from the handful of other customers. John and Carl sat next to each other and Cathy and Yun sat across. After receiving their waters John took control of the conversation.

"Judging by what we all found out, Mike was onto something. Let me ask this first, do we all agree what what Mike discovered, that man and dinosaurs existed together and thus proving the Bible to be correct?"

There was a moment of silence before voices were raised. Each sounded off a yes, of course, with conviction and surety. Around this table, at this moment, there was no doubt.

"Okay, then the next step if to finish what Mike started. There are two steps left but they are the toughest. Cathy. Yun. We received from the Twelve a letter stating that in Africa there may be living, breathing, dinosaurs. Second, we must decide, as a group, whether to publish and stand by what Mike discovered and what we learned."

Cathy couldn't decide what would be harder to do; to see a dinosaur or to face the attacks of the world. She remembered the backlash from Zach, a close friend and colleague. How would the world react?

Carl didn't hesitate. "I know we all faced great difficulties in learned this information. Cathy and I almost paid the same price as Mike. Having gone through all that, I would like to finish this out. I believe that God put us together on this for a reason. Not sure why. Not sure I will ever understand. But here we are, in Arizona, after splitting up and seeing different parts of the world. We are on a mission for the truth. Plus, not to put unnecessary pressure on anybody, who would want to live out their lives with the regret of not having finished the job?"

Smiles crossed across the faces as everybody knew that they were in this together. The bond of friendship and loyalty was too strong now. Brought together by Christ, united in toil, dedicated to the truth, and loved by each other, there was no other choice but to move on.

The waitress arrived to take orders. When she left Carl reached into his jacket and pulled out the papyrus roll from Peru. After clearing off some space on the table he unrolled it out.

A gasp escaped Cathy. "This is Incan. Well, a form of Incan language. It may even be evolving Incan."

"Evolving Incan?"

"Languagesevolve and change over time. They are much like

civilizations and groups of people. For example, the English language is a combination of several other languages, noticeably French based."

Carl was completely confused. "How is this possible?"

Cathy enjoyed the opportunity to strut her knowledge. "When groups of people 'bump' into each other they share things. It could be technology, language, foods, and many other things. During the Crusades soldiers returned to England bringing with them new weapons, new foods, and a new knowledge of the world. When the Normans were invaded by the French, the two groups merged together their languages into the English language. We see this even today in our society."

Cathy noticed the wrinkles building in Carl's forehead.

"Okay, in this part of the country, we have people coming from Central America and South America and Mexico. Millions of people have come into this part of our country for many decades. They bring with them their language, customs, foods, and backgrounds. This mergence of cultures brings forth a new culture. I have heard the term Spanglish. We have fast food chains for Mexican food but not for Italian, German, or Russian. Why is that?"

Carl relaxed and was intrigued. "What about the great immigration that happened in America?"

A smug smile came over Cathy's face. "American immigration is a perfect example. The Russians, Irish, French, Germans, most of Europe, brought with them their language, customs, values, and beliefs. All these things changed America. It changed our language in a big way. They integrated words into our current speak. It is why our English is different than say, Australia or British for example."

Carl leaned back in the booth. "How does this relate to our research again?"

Cathy pointed back to the roll. "This language pre-dates what we know about Incan language. I would have to have someone, an expert in Incan language to verify it for us." With that, Cathy whipped out her cell phone and snapped off a picture of the scroll. Then in a blaze of thumbs and fingers she sent the picture. Looking up she met three pairs of glazed eyes.

"What? I just sent it to a friend of mine at the Universidad de Mexico. Dr. Miguel Hernandez is one of the leading experts in anything Incan. Now then what is next on the agenda?"

Yun turned to John hoping for an answer but knew he wasn't going to get an answer. John was looking to Yun hoping for the same thing.

Carl finally took the lead. "Well, there seems to be evidence in Africa. Your father, Mike, mentions in his notes some interesting things." Carl took out some of the notes from a binder. "Here it is. It seems that Africa has been home to some interesting archeological digs lately. Human bones have been found that seem to be older that the ones previously found. Your father found it interesting. He writes, 'How could each find be older than the ones before?' Then he did some amazing questioning. He listed down the questions he wanted answers to."

Carl placed the list of questions in the middle of the table. Yun, Cathy, and John leaned forward as if seeing something mystical in front of them. Carl sounded off the questions.

"How could the T-rex findings in Montana not be fossilized or destroyed given that his animal would have existed millions of years ago. How could several groups of people from around the world, at different time periods in our history, describe similar animals with detailed accuracy? How could the human bones in Africa be in the same shape as the T-rex findings in Montana and nobody see a direct correlation? How is it that science has changed its stance on what it takes for bones to be fossilized? And, why more changes to its stance in more recent years?" Carl paused.

"How is it possible that we as mankind can accept that many animals have become extinct due to man, climate change, or a cut off of food supply but we don't apply these same conditions to dinosaurs?"

Carl pointed to the list. The questions went on and on. "It seems that your dad demanded some answers."

"Here you are. Who ordered the chicken chimichanga?" Carl raised his hand. "Here you are. Four bean burrito?" Yun lifted his hand. "Here you go. Okay, I have a fifty-fifty chance on this one. Enchiladas? Here you are ma'am and for you sir taco soup. Anything else?" Seeing the heads going back and forth the waitress took her cue. "Okay, let me know if there is anything else I can do for you." With that she strode down the aisle and back to the kitchen.

An uneasy silence settled over the booth as the meals were eaten. John broke the silence, "Judging from the silence we are all questioning things now. It seems that we have no choice but to go to Africa and see this through. Mike didn't get his chance to go but we can finish what he started. Besides, the real challenge will come when we are ready to go public with the information."

"Then, let's get ready to go," voiced Cathy.

GRAND CANYON, ARIZONA

Xi could almost feel their breath upon his back. There was only one advantage that Xi had, the coverage of the cave. If he could possibly take advantage of the cave he believed that he had a chance of surviving.

The chance was slim.

He didn't focus on the disadvantages, although there were many. Men. Guns. Highground. "Didn't dwell on them. Focus on me. I will control this situation." Xi harnessed this determination into every fiber of his body. Dying was not an option.

Xi knew that the men would come in tactical formation. As they came deeper into the cave the formation would naturally be broken by the funnel formation. At this funnel only one man can enter at a time.

Xi knew he could make his stand here.

Knowing that most people don't look up when scanning an area Xi perched himself upon a rock shelf above the entrance. In his mind he played out the series of events that would gain him more breathing room and possibly freedom.

In no less than minutes he could hear footsteps and see waving lights stream from flashlights. Xi played what the scene must look like in his head. The men would scan every inch of the cave before moving forward. Each man would stay in tactical formation and trust his comrades. Xi was counting on this trust and discipline. He would use it against them.

The streams of light became more constant in the small opening below Xi's perch. They were close. Adrenaline pulsed throughout the body as Xi anticipated his attack. He didn't hear voices. "They must have helmets and radio transmitters," Xi was hoping they would talk so as to gain an estimate on number as well as hear their plan.

A minor setback.

Then the lights became steady in the opening. One would flicker attempting to scan the area beyond the funnel. Xi knew that the only way to inspect the area was to enter. One at a time. Weapons down.

A shadow was cast as one prepared to enter the opening. The light from the remaining flashlights cast a solid wall of light. At first the man attempted to enter with his gun raised. But the step he had to go over and the wetness of the walls demanded the use of two hands and sure footing.

Like a cat ready to pounce, Xi prepared for his attack. The man would be blind coming in. His shadow blocked out the security of the light. He was his own eclipse.

Xi saw the man's hands come through the entry. Then a foot. Xi knew that next would be the head to scan the area. As if on cue the man's head popped in. Xi studied the gear the man was wearing. Helmet. Face protection.

"Good," thought Xi. I may have a chance at this after all.

Inch by inch the man came into the cave. Xi noticed a knife by the man's chest. "This will work," Xi thought.

The soldier was fully in the cavern now. Xi knew he was describing the area to his comrades. Holding out his flashlight the soldier began the routine of scanning the area.

"When the drops drops, just a little."

As the soldier circled back to the opening in which he came, the gun dropped just a couple of inches. A sign that the perimeter was safe and all is well. This lack of judgement was what Xi needed.

Pouncing from his perch Xi jumped onto the man. Xi was used to working in dark spaces. He reached for the knife case and flicked open the latching. Pulling the grip up Xi knew what kind of knife he now possessed. A traditional, government issued survival knife. A compass was on the handle, that can be screwed off the handle. Inside the handle was a kit for survival; string, needles, ointment, and matches.

Xi wrapped his body to the soldier's belly and searched for the exposed neck. With the helmet and face guard Xi assumed that the neck would have protection as well. A cloth draped from the helmet. The cloth was the same material as a bullet proof vest. Weaving his hand around the cloth Xi found skin. In a blink Xi clasped his fingers on the arteries like a vice. Xi manipulated the knife around the neck. By hitting certain areas in precise ways the victim would die more quickly and leave little blood trace.

Hollywood always showed throat slices as bloody messes. A true assassin would leave as little evidence as possible. In this cas, Xi wanted no evidence.

Xi removed the helmet and placed it upon his own head. He heard voices spewing forth question after question.

'What's going on in there?"

"Jack? Are you alright?"

"What happened?"

"Get ready to move in."

Xi had mere moments.

To buy more time he faced the gun toward the opening and shot off a few rounds. The helmet voices went off again.

"Jack! You okay?"

"If he is shooting he is still alive. We go in on his cue."

"Excellent," thought Xi.

Xi had learned and practiced the art of camoflauge. To change one's appearance in mere seconds. Xi was familiar with the soldiers outfit and removed all the man's clothes. Every so often a spat of gunfire would buy more time. Xi removed his own clothes and placed them on the dead man. Soon, Xi was Jack.

"Jack. Is it safe to come in?"

Going into heavy breathing to help disguise his voice Xi responded, "Wait. Wait. I think I have him." A dramatic pause to sell the ruse. Xi then let loose gunfire all over Jack's face and body. Happy that the man was now undistinguishable, Xi was ready for the next bold step. Facing the larger group of soldiers.

"What was that? Jack! Okay, we are heading in."

Lights flickered around the cavern. Xi placed the knife, now clean as he wiped the blood off on Jack. Xi noticed that there were more clips around his waist. "Excellent," he thought.

"Come in. Come in. The area is secure." Xi continued in his heavy breathing voice.

Then like ants marching towards a hill the soldiers entered. Beams of light shot into all directions. One hit Xi right in the face. The tinted shield and gear hid him perfectly.

"Holy cow Jack! The poor sap didn't' have a chance."

The men gathered around the corpse to admire Xi's handiwork.

"Went a little crazy did we?" The statement was followed by a chuckle. "What happened?"

"He came from nowhere. Tackled me to the ground…" Xi continued with the made up story. What Xi was doing was sizing up the group. There were six in all. He wasn't sure how many more were back in the main area, back through the opening. For now he had to play it safe. He knew that once they were outside the gear would come off and he would be exposed. Between now and then he had to escape or kill off the soldiers.

Either way it didn't matter to him.

After finishing his story and receiving back slaps for a job well done the soldier in charge suggested they leave the cavern and get back outside. Judging from the hand movements Xi distinguished who the leader was. Cut off the head and the body dies.

As the group left the cavern and went through the space Xi scanned ahead to see if there were others on the other side. To his amazement, there was nobody. Another thought entered his mind.

"What about the outside of the cave?"

Xi decided that the true soldiers were here with him. They would be the most protected with gear and weapons. Anyone outside would be without protection. Plus, with these six dead, he would have more weapons.

Once all six came through the crack Xi thought out his plan. These men were trained and yet right now, at this moment, all their mental and physical defenses were down.

Xi eyed the leader. He was a big man, around six-five and wide as a barn. "A great human shield," thought Xi.

Inching his way to the leader he saw the soldiers begin taking their helmets off. Xi could feel the confidence in the air. This confidence would be their death.

Standing beside the leader, Xi watched as he took off his helmet. He was the last to do so. The man had a block head with scars criss-crossing his face. Evidence of previous battles. Xi had to admire the toughness of the man.

A soldier made a joke about hamburger and wondering where to get some. As he pointed back through the opening the others laughed.

Now was the time.

Xi raised his weapon. Pulled out his knife. The left hand shot off bullets to soldiers' heads. At the same moment the knife was plunged into the leader's head. Leaving the knife in place Xi finished off the last soldier.

Four of the six hit the ground eyes open. The shock and surprise was clearly unanticipated. This wasn't usually Xi's style but a man must survive.

It wouldn't be long before outside reinforcements would be coming in or scaling the exit. Xi had to act fast.

Feeling disappointed in not being able to relish his work he gathered some weapons and moved toward the exit. Xi was still unidentifiable with all the gear on. Take advantage of every opportunity.

Stepping closer to the opening Xi was taken aback by the sunlight.

He was in there longer than he thought.

Tasting freedom he moved closer and with caution.

PHOENIX, ARIZONA

The next four days were a blur of hustle, packing, and preparation. Cathy was in charge of everything that had to deal with flight arrangements and customs. She assigned Carl on working up contacts so the three could have help and have guidance. Cathy was jealous of John as he gathered up information on the continent and the history of archeological digs and finds. But, the experience of John in the field finally won out and Cathy conceded. Yun worked on providing security for them given recent events.

Newscasts splashed across screens of the recent murders at the Grand Canyon. Yun's gut told him that somehow the murders were related to the attempts on Cathy's life. One body was beyond recognition. Six others were killed. Five by head shots and one with a knife stab to the head. The killer was surrounded and boxed in. It had to be a professional. Based on nothing more than pure instinct, Yun was guessing the killer would come and finish the job with Cathy.

Yun tried to get in contact with David but feared the worse as he knew that David was at the Grand Canyon.

Cathy was amazed at the efficiency of each member; working diligently on their tasks. Carl contacted the Twelve to update them on their progress. He also shared Yun's concerns. The conversation ended in prayer. Prayer for accomplishment and for safety. Cathy noticed that one face was missing from the group.

That night the four went out for a meal. The last one they would have in the states. Since most of their traveling would be over water it was decided that seafood made an appropriate theme.

Afterwards, Carl decided it was time to visit a friend. With John driving they made their way to Desert Memorial Hospital. Riding the elevator to the third floor the four greeted Juan.

Juan was overjoyed to see Carl and Carl was heartened by Juan. Juan had his original color in his face, was sitting up, and back to his animated self. For the next three hours the five discussed their adventures and knowledge. Laughter and tears were shed. Juan wished his friends well and ended in prayer.

As the four traveled back to their hotel a surreal silence filled the vehicle. Each was lost in what the next few days would hold. Would questions have answers? Would knowledge and truth prevail? Will they remain strong til the end?

Good nights were said as each departed the elevator and made their way to their rooms. To an outsider it looked like four strangers leaving an elevator and going their separate ways. But each was unified in purpose.

Seek the truth.

ACKNOWLEDGEMENTS

I have never understood how hard it is to write a book until now. For the last three years I have balanced work, family, and writing. It has been a labor of love. Through the process I have learned how wonderful God is. There are so many to thank but for my first book I want to thank those dearest to my heart and who have supported me through the process of writing.

There are so many people to thank but more important to be grateful for. I would like to thank my mom and dad. Their love and devotion is beyond awesome! In life we make mistakes and we have celebrations, through it all they have been there for me and I am so thankful for having such extraordinary parents.

I would also like to thank my three children; Blaine, Blake, and Kailey. It is one thing to teach our children to go after their dreams, it is another to live it out. They have been my inspiration to reach for my dreams and write this book. It has been a challenge, has involved a great amount of time, and many sacrifices. All the ingredients of achieving one's dream. I hope that my children will seek out their own dreams.

I would also like to thank my lovely wife. She is truly a gift from God to me. I am so thankful to have someone who believes in me, loves me, and is also my friend. Kimberly, thank you for putting up with me all these years andI look forward to many, many more.

Finally, I thank God. I have learned that everything one does in life should bring God glory and show his love for all humanity. I pray and hope that this book does that. I hope this book show God's almighty glory and power. My hope is that this book helps to educate and also entertain my readers.

ABOUT THE AUTHOR

Matthew Coleman enjoys being with his wife and three children. He enjoys researching Biblical history, coaching youth sports, and being with family and friends. He holds two masters degrees and has been a teacher and school administrator for fifteen years. He currently lives in north Idaho.